Murder in Our Midst

Murder in Our Midst

INCLUDING

THE BODY IN THE LIBRARY

THE MURDER AT THE VICARAGE

THE MOVING FINGER

By Agatha Christie

DODD, MEAD & COMPANY

New York

Library of Congress Catalog Card Number: 67–18228
Printed in the United States of America

Contents

The characters, places, incidents, and situations in this book are imaginary and have no relation to any person, place, or actual happening

The Body in the Library

I

Mrs. Bantry was dreaming. Her sweet peas had just taken a First at the flower show. The vicar, dressed in cassock and surplice, was giving out the prizes in church. His wife wandered past, dressed in a bathing suit, but, as is the blessed habit of dreams, this fact did not arouse the disapproval of the parish in the way it would assuredly have done in real life.

Mrs. Bantry was enjoying her dream a good deal. She usually did enjoy those early-morning dreams that were terminated by the arrival of tea. Somewhere in her inner consciousness was an awareness of the usual noises of the household. The rattle of the curtain rings on the stairs as the housemaid drew them, the noises of the second housemaid's dustpan and brush in the passage outside. In the distance the heavy noise of the front-door bolt being drawn back.

Another day was beginning. In the meantime she must extract as much pleasure as possible from the flower show, for already its dreamlike quality was becoming apparent.

Below her was the noise of the big wooden shutters in the drawing room being opened. She heard it, yet did not hear it. For quite half an hour longer the usual household noises would go on, discreet, subdued, not disturbing because they were so familiar. They would culminate in a swift, controlled sound of footsteps along the passage, the rustle of a print dress, the subdued chink of tea things as the tray was deposited on the table outside, then the soft knock and the entry of Mary to draw the curtains.

In her sleep Mrs. Bantry frowned. Something disturbing was penetrating through the dream state, something out of its time. Footsteps along the passage, footsteps that were too hurried and too soon. Her ears listened unconsciously for the chink of china, but there was no chink of china.

The knock came at the door. Automatically, from the depths of her dream, Mrs. Bantry said, "Come in." The door opened; now there would be the chink of curtain rings as the curtains were drawn back.

But there was no chink of curtain rings. Out of the dim green light Mary's voice came, breathless, hysterical. "Oh, ma'am, oh, ma'am, there's a body in the library!"

And then, with a hysterical burst of sobs, she rushed out of the room again.

Mrs. Bantry sat up in bed.

Either her dream had taken a very odd turn or else—or else Mary had really rushed into the room and had said—incredibly fantastic!—that there was a body in the library.

"Impossible," said Mrs. Bantry to herself. "I must have been dreaming."

But even as she said it, she felt more and more certain that she had not been dreaming; that Mary, her superior self-controlled Mary, had actually uttered those fantastic words.

Mrs. Bantry reflected a minute and then applied an urgent conjugal elbow to her sleeping spouse. "Arthur, Arthur, wake up."

Colonel Bantry grunted, muttered and rolled over on his side.

"Wake up, Arthur. Did you hear what she said?"

"Very likely," said Colonel Bantry indistinctly. "I quite agree with you, Dolly," and promptly went to sleep again.

Mrs. Bantry shook him. "You've got to listen. Mary came in and said that there was a body in the library."

"Eh, what?"

"A body in the library."

"Who said so?"

"Mary."

Colonel Bantry collected his scattered faculties and proceeded to deal with the situation. He said, "Nonsense, old girl! You've been dreaming."

"No, I haven't. I thought so, too, at first. But I haven't. She really came in and said so."

"Mary came in and said there was a body in the library?"

"Yes."

"But there couldn't be," said Colonel Bantry.

"No—no, I suppose not," said Mrs. Bantry doubtfully. Rallying, she went on, "But then why did Mary say there was?"

"She can't have."

"She did."

"You must have imagined it."

"I didn't imagine it."

Colonel Bantry was by now thoroughly awake and prepared to deal with the situation on its merits. He said kindly, "You've been dreaming, Dolly. It's that detective story you were reading—*The Clue of the Broken Match*. You know, Lord Edgbaston finds a beautiful blonde dead on the library hearthrug. Bodies are always being found in libraries in books. I've never known a case in real life."

"Perhaps you will now," said Mrs. Bantry. "Anyway, Arthur, you've got to get up and see."

"But really, Dolly, it must have been a dream. Dreams often do seem wonderfully vivid when you first wake up. You feel quite sure they're true."

"I was having quite a different sort of dream—about a flower show and the vicar's wife in a bathing dress—something like that." Mrs. Bantry jumped out of bed and pulled back the curtains. The light of a fine autumn day flooded the room.

"I did not dream it," said Mrs. Bantry firmly. "Get up at once, Arthur, and go downstairs and see about it."

"You want me to go downstairs and ask if there's a body in the library? I shall look a fool."

"You needn't ask anything," said Mrs. Bantry. "If there is a body—and of course it's just possible that Mary's gone mad and thinks she sees things that aren't there—well, somebody will tell you soon enough. You won't have to say a word."

Grumbling, Colonel Bantry wrapped himself in his dressing gown and left the room. He went along the passage and down the staircase. At the foot of it was a little knot of huddled servants; some of them were sobbing.

The butler stepped forward impressively. "I'm glad you have come, sir. I have directed that nothing should be done until you came. Will it be in order for me to ring up the police, sir?"

"Ring 'em up about what?"

The butler cast a reproachful glance over his shoulder at the tall young woman who was weeping hysterically on the cook's shoulder. "I understood, sir, that Mary had already informed you. She said she had done so."

Mary gasped out, "I was so upset, I don't know what I said! It all came over me again and my legs gave way and my insides turned over! Finding it like that— Oh, oh, oh!"

She subsided again onto Mrs. Eccles, who said, "There, there, my dear," with some relish.

"Mary is naturally somewhat upset, sir, having been the one to make the gruesome discovery," explained the butler. "She went into the library, as usual, to draw the curtains, and—and almost stumbled over the body."

"Do you mean to tell me," demanded Colonel Bantry, "that there's a dead body in my library—my library?"

The butler coughed. "Perhaps, sir, you would like to see for yourself."

"Hullo, 'ullo, 'ullo. Police station here. Yes, who's speaking?"

Police Constable Palk was buttoning up his tunic with one hand while the other held the telephone receiver.

"Yes, yes, Gossington Hall. Yes? . . . Oh, good morning, sir." Police Constable Palk's tone underwent a slight modification. It became less impatiently official, recognizing the generous patron of the police sports and the principal magistrate of the district. "Yes, sir? What can I do for you? . . . I'm sorry, sir, I didn't quite catch– A body, did you say? . . . Yes? . . . Yes, if you please, sir. . . . That's right, sir. . . . Young woman not known to you, you say? . . . Quite, sir. . . . Yes, you can leave it all to me."

Police Constable Palk replaced the receiver, uttered a long-drawn whistle and proceeded to dial his superior officer's number.

Mrs. Palk looked in from the kitchen, whence proceeded an appetizing smell of frying bacon.

"What is it?"

"Rummest thing you ever heard of," replied her husband. "Body of a young woman found up at the Hall. In the colonel's library."

"Murdered?"

"Strangled, so he says."

"Who was she?"

"The colonel says he doesn't know her from Adam."

"Then what was she doing in 'is library?"

Police Constable Palk silenced her with a reproachful glance and spoke officially into the telephone. "Inspector Slack? Police Constable Palk here. A report has just come in that the body of a young woman was discovered this morning at seven-fifteen–"

Miss Marple's telephone rang when she was dressing. The sound of it flurried her a little. It was an unusual hour for her telephone to ring. So well ordered was her prim spinster's life that unforeseen telephone calls were a source of vivid conjecture.

"Dear me," said Miss Marple, surveying the ringing instrument with perplexity. "I wonder who that can be?"

Nine o'clock to nine-thirty was the recognized time for the village to make friendly calls to neighbors. Plans for the day, invitations, and so on, were always issued then. The butcher had been known to ring up just before nine if some crisis in the meat trade had occurred. At intervals during the day spasmodic calls might occur, though it was considered bad form to ring up after nine-thirty at night.

It was true that Miss Marple's nephew, a writer, and therefore erratic, had been known to ring up at the most peculiar times; once as late as ten minutes to midnight. But whatever Raymond West's eccentricities, early rising was not one of them. Neither he nor anyone of Miss Marple's acquaintance would be likely to ring up before eight in the morning. Actually a quarter to eight.

Too early even for a telegram, since the post office did not open until eight.

"It must be," Miss Marple decided, "a wrong number."

Having decided this, she advanced to the impatient instrument and quelled its clamor by picking up the receiver.

"Yes?" she said.

"Is that you, Jane?"

Miss Marple was much surprised. "Yes, it's Jane. You're up very early, Dolly."

Mrs. Bantry's voice came, breathless and agitated, over the wire. "The most awful thing has happened."

"Oh, my dear!"

"We've just found a body in the library."

For a moment Miss Marple thought her friend had gone mad. "You've found a what?"

"I know. One doesn't believe it, does one? I mean I thought they only happened in books. I had to argue for hours with Arthur this morning before he'd even go down and see."

Miss Marple tried to collect herself. She demanded breathlessly, "But whose body is it?"

"It's a blonde."

"A what?"

"A blonde. A beautiful blonde—like books again. None of us have ever seen her before. She's just lying there in the library, dead. That's why you've got to come up at once."

"You want me to come up?"

"Yes, I'm sending the car down for you."

Miss Marple said doubtfully, "Of course, dear, if you think I can be of any comfort to you—"

"Oh, I don't want comfort. But you're so good at bodies."

"Oh, no, indeed. My little successes have been mostly theoretical."

"But you're very good at murders. She's been murdered, you see; strangled. What I feel is that if one has got to have a murder actually happening in one's house, one might as well enjoy it, if you know what I mean. That's why I want you to come and help me find out who did it and unravel the mystery, and all that. It really is rather thrilling, isn't it?"

"Well, of course, my dear, if I can be of any help."

"Splendid! Arthur's being rather difficult. He seems to think I shouldn't enjoy myself about it at all. Of course, I do know it's very sad and all that, but then I don't know the girl—and when you've seen her you'll understand what I mean when I say she doesn't look real at all."

A little breathless, Miss Marple alighted from the Bantrys' car, the door of which was held open for her by the chauffeur.

Colonel Bantry came out on the steps and looked a little surprised. "Miss Marple? Er—very pleased to see you."

"Your wife telephoned to me," explained Miss Marple.

"Capital, capital. She ought to have someone with her. She'll crack up otherwise. She's putting a good face on things at the moment, but you know what it is—"

At this moment Mrs. Bantry appeared and exclaimed, "Do go back and eat your breakfast, Arthur. Your bacon will get cold."

"I thought it might be the inspector arriving," explained Colonel Bantry.

"He'll be here soon enough," said Mrs. Bantry. "That's why it's important to get your breakfast first. You need it."

"So do you. Much better come and eat something, Dolly."

"I'll come in a minute," said Mrs. Bantry. "Go on, Arthur."

Colonel Bantry was shooed back into the dining room rather like a recalcitrant hen.

"Now!" said Mrs. Bantry with an intonation of triumph. "Come on."

She led the way rapidly along the long corridor to the east of the house. Outside the library door Constable Palk stood on guard. He intercepted Mrs. Bantry with a show of authority.

"I'm afraid nobody is allowed in, madam. Inspector's orders."

"Nonsense, Palk," said Mrs. Bantry. "You know Miss Marple perfectly well."

Constable Palk admitted to knowing Miss Marple.

"It's very important that she should see the body," said Mrs. Bantry. "Don't be stupid, Palk. After all, it's my library, isn't it?"

Constable Palk gave way. His habit of giving in to the gentry was lifelong. The inspector, he reflected, need never know about it.

"Nothing must be touched or handled in any way," he warned the ladies.

"Of course not," said Mrs. Bantry impatiently. "We know that. You can come in and watch, if you like."

Constable Palk availed himself of this permission. It had been his intention anyway.

Mrs. Bantry bore her friend triumphantly across the library to the big old-fashioned fireplace. She said, with a dramatic sense of climax, "There!"

Miss Marple understood then just what her friend had meant when she said the dead girl wasn't real. The library was a room very typical of its owners. It was large and shabby and untidy. It had big, sagging armchairs, and pipes and books and estate papers laid out on the big table. There were one or two good old family portraits on the walls, and some bad Victorian water colors, and some would-be-funny hunting scenes. There was a big vase of flowers in the corner. The whole room was dim and mellow and casual. It spoke of long occupation and familiar use and of links with tradition.

And across the old bearskin hearthrug there was sprawled something new and crude and melodramatic. The flamboyant figure of a girl. A girl with unnaturally fair hair caught up off her face in elaborate curls and rings. Her thin body was dressed in a backless evening dress of white spangled satin; the face was heavily made up, the powder standing out grotesquely on its blue, swollen surface, the mascara of the lashes lying thickly on the distorted cheeks, the scarlet of the lips looking like a gash. The fingernails were enameled a deep blood red, and so were the toenails in their cheap silver sandal shoes. It was a cheap, tawdry, flamboyant figure, most incongruous in the solid, old-fashioned comfort of Colonel Bantry's library.

Mrs. Bantry said in a low voice, "You see what I mean? It just isn't true?"

The old lady by her side nodded her head. She looked down long and thoughtfully at the huddled figure.

She said at last in a gentle voice, "She's very young."

"Yes; yes, I suppose she is." Mrs. Bantry seemed almost surprised, like one making a discovery.

There was the sound of a car scrunching on the gravel outside.

Constable Palk said with urgency, "That'll be the inspector."

True to his ingrained belief that the gentry didn't let you down, Mrs. Bantry immediately moved to the door. Miss Marple followed her.

Mrs. Bantry said, "That'll be all right, Palk."

Constable Palk was immensely relieved.

Hastily downing the last fragments of toast and marmalade with a drink of coffee, Colonel Bantry hurried out into the hall and was relieved to see Colonel Melchett, the chief constable of the county, descending from a car, with Inspector Slack in attendance. Melchett was a friend of the colonel's; Slack he had never very much taken to—an energetic man who belied his name and who accompanied his bustling manner with a good deal of disregard for the feelings of anyone he did not consider important.

"Morning, Bantry," said the chief constable. "Thought I'd better come along myself. This seems an extraordinary business."

"It's—it's"—Colonel Bantry struggled to express himself—"it's incredible—fantastic!"

"No idea who the woman is?"

"Not in the slightest. Never set eyes on her in my life."

"Butler know anything?" asked Inspector Slack.

"Lorrimer is just as taken aback as I am."

"Ah," said Inspector Slack. "I wonder."

Colonel Bantry said, "There's breakfast in the dining room, Melchett, if you'd like anything."

"No, no, better get on with the job. Haydock ought to be here any minute now. . . . Ah, here he is."

Another car drew up and big, broad-shouldered Doctor Haydock, who was also the police surgeon, got out. A second police car had disgorged two plainclothes men, one with a camera.

"All set, eh?" said the chief constable. "Right. We'll go along. In the library, Slack tells me."

Colonel Bantry groaned. "It's incredible! You know, when my wife insisted this morning that the housemaid had come in and said there was a body in the library, I just wouldn't believe her."

"No, no, I can quite understand that. Hope your missus isn't too badly upset by it all."

"She's been wonderful—really wonderful. She's got Miss Marple up here with her—from the village, you know."

"Miss Marple?" The chief constable stiffened. "Why did she send for her?"

"Oh, a woman wants another woman—don't you think so?"

Colonel Melchett said with a slight chuckle, "If you ask me, your wife's going to try her hand at a little amateur detecting. Miss Marple's quite the local sleuth. Put it over us properly once, didn't she, Slack?"

Inspector Slack said, "That was different."

"Different from what?"

"That was a local case, that was, sir. The old lady knows everything that goes on in the village, that's true enough. But she'll be out of her depth here."

Melchett said dryly, "You don't know very much about it yourself yet, Slack."

"Ah, you wait, sir. It won't take me long to get down to it."

In the dining room Mrs. Bantry and Miss Marple, in their turn, were partaking of breakfast.

After waiting on her guest, Mrs. Bantry said urgently, "Well, Jane?"

Miss Marple looked up at her, slightly bewildered.

Mrs. Bantry said hopefully, "Doesn't it remind you of anything?"

For Miss Marple had attained fame by her ability to link up trivial village happenings with graver problems in such a way as to throw light upon the latter.

"No," said Miss Marple thoughtfully. "I can't say that it does—not at the moment. I was reminded a little of Mrs. Chetty's youngest—Edie, you know—but I think that was just because this poor girl bit her nails and her front teeth stuck out a little. Nothing more than that. And, of course," went on Miss Marple, pursuing the parallel further, "Edie was fond of what I call cheap finery, too."

"You mean her dress?" said Mrs. Bantry.

"Yes, a very tawdry satin, poor quality."

Mrs. Bantry said, "I know. One of those nasty little shops where everything is a guinea." She went on hopefully, "Let me see. What happened to Mrs. Chetty's Edie?"

"She's just gone into her second place, and doing very well, I believe," said Miss Marple.

Mrs. Bantry felt slightly disappointed. The village parallel didn't seem to be exactly hopeful.

"What I can't make out," said Mrs. Bantry, "is what she could possibly be doing in Arthur's study. The window was forced, Palk tells me. She might have come down here with a burglar, and then they quarreled—But that seems such nonsense, doesn't it?"

"She was hardly dressed for burglary," said Miss Marple thoughtfully.

"No, she was dressed for dancing or a party of some kind. But there's nothing of that kind down here or anywhere near."

"N-no," said Miss Marple doubtfully.

Mrs. Bantry pounced. "Something's in your mind, Jane."

"Well, I was just wondering—"

"Yes?"

"Basil Blake."

Mrs. Bantry cried impulsively, "Oh, no!" and added as though in explanation, "I know his mother."

The two women looked at each other.

Miss Marple sighed and shook her head. "I quite understand how you feel about it."

"Selina Blake is the nicest woman imaginable. Her herbaceous borders are simply marvelous; they make me green with envy. And she's frightfully generous with cuttings."

Miss Marple, passing over these claims to consideration on the part of Mrs. Blake, said, "All the same, you know, there has been a lot of talk."

"Oh, I know, I know. And of course Arthur goes simply livid when he hears him mentioned. He was really very rude to Arthur, and since then Arthur won't hear a good word for him. He's got that silly slighting way of talking that these boys have nowadays—sneering at people sticking up for their school or the Empire or that sort of thing. And then, of course, the clothes he wears! People say," continued Mrs. Bantry, "that it doesn't matter what you wear in the country. I never heard such nonsense. It's just in the country that everyone notices." She paused and added wistfully, "He was an adorable baby in his bath."

"There was a lovely picture of the Cheviot murderer as a baby in the paper last Sunday," said Miss Marple.

"Oh, but, Jane, you don't think he—"

"No, no, dear, I didn't mean that at all. That would indeed be jumping to conclusions. I was just trying to account for the young woman's presence down here. St. Mary Mead is such an unlikely place. And then it seemed to me that the only possible explanation was Basil Blake. He does have parties. People come down from London and from the studios—you remember last July? Shouting and singing—the most terrible noise—everyone very drunk, I'm afraid—and the mess and the broken glass next morning simply unbelievable—so old Mrs. Berry told me—and a young woman asleep in the bath with practically nothing on!"

Mrs. Bantry said indulgently, "I suppose they were film people."

"Very likely. And then—what I expect you've heard—several week ends lately he's brought down a young woman with him—a platinum blonde."

Mrs. Bantry exclaimed, "You don't think it's this one?"

"Well, I wondered. Of course, I've never seen her close to—only just getting in and out of the car, and once in the cottage garden when she was sun-bathing with just some shorts and a brassière. I never really saw her face. And all these girls, with their make-up and their hair and their nails, look so alike."

"Yes. Still, it might be. It's an idea, Jane."

II

It was an idea that was being at that moment discussed by Colonel Melchett and Colonel Bantry. The chief constable, after viewing the body and seeing his subordinates set to work on their routine tasks, had adjourned with the master of the house to the study in the other wing.

Colonel Melchett was an irascible-looking man with a habit of tugging at his short red mustache. He did so now, shooting a perplexed sideways glance at the other man.

Finally he rapped out, "Look here, Bantry; got to get this off my chest. Is it a fact that you don't know from Adam who this woman is?"

The other's answer was explosive, but the chief constable interrupted him, "Yes, yes, old man, but look at it like this: Might be deuced awkward for you. Married man—fond of your missus and all that. But just between ourselves, if you were tied up with this girl in any way, better say so now. Quite natural to want to suppress the fact; should feel the same myself. But it won't do. Murder case. Facts bound to come out. Dash it all, I'm not suggesting you strangled the girl—not the sort of thing you'd do. I know that! But, after all, she came here—to this house. Put it, she broke in and was waiting to see you, and some bloke or other followed her down and did her in. Possible, you know. See what I mean?"

"I've never set eyes on that girl in my life! I'm not that sort of man!"

"That's all right then. Shouldn't blame you, you know. Man of the world. Still, if you say so— Question is, what was she doing down here? She doesn't come from these parts, that's quite certain."

"The whole thing's a nightmare," fumed the angry master of the house.

"The point is, old man, what was she doing in your library?"

"How should I know? I didn't ask her here."

"No, no. But she came here all the same. Looks as though she wanted to see you. You haven't had any odd letters or anything?"

"No, I haven't."

Colonel Melchett inquired delicately, "What were you doing yourself last night?"

"I went to the meeting of the Conservative Association. Nine o'clock, at Much Benham."

"And you got home when?"

"I left Much Benham just after ten. Had a bit of trouble on the way home, had to change a wheel. I got back at a quarter to twelve."

"You didn't go into the library?"

"No."

"Pity."

"I was tired. I went straight up to bed."

"Anyone waiting up for you?"

"No. I always take the latchkey. Lorrimer goes to bed at eleven, unless I give orders to the contrary."

"Who shuts up the library?"

"Lorrimer. Usually about seven-thirty this time of year."

"Would he go in there again during the evening?"

"Not with my being out. He left the tray with whisky and glasses in the hall."

"I see. What about your wife?"

"She was in bed when I got home, and fast asleep. She may have sat in the library yesterday evening, or in the drawing room. I didn't ask her."

"Oh, well, we shall soon know all the details. Of course it's possible one of the servants may be concerned, eh?"

Colonel Bantry shook his head. "I don't believe it. They're all a most respectable lot. We've had 'em for years."

Melchett agreed. "Yes, it doesn't seem likely that they're mixed up in it. Looks more as though the girl came down from town—perhaps with some young fellow. Though why they wanted to break into this house—"

Bantry interrupted. "London. That's more like it. We don't have goings on down here—at least—"

"Well, what is it?"

"Upon my word!" exploded Colonel Bantry. "Basil Blake!"

"Who's he?"

"Young fellow connected with the film industry. Poisonous young brute. My wife sticks up for him because she was at school with his mother, but of all the decadent useless young jackanapes— Wants his behind kicked. He's taken that cottage on the Lansham Road—you know, ghastly modern bit of building. He has parties there—shrieking, noisy crowds—and he has girls down for the week end."

"Girls?"

"Yes, there was one last week—one of these platinum blondes." The colonel's jaw dropped.

"A platinum blonde, eh?" said Melchett reflectively.

"Yes. I say, Melchett, you don't think—"

The chief constable said briskly, "It's a possibility. It accounts for a girl of this type being in St. Mary Mead. I think I'll run along and have a word with this young fellow Braid—Blake—what did you say his name was?"

"Blake. Basil Blake."

"Will he be at home, do you know?" asked Melchett.

"Let me see, what's today? Saturday? Usually gets here sometime Saturday morning."

Melchett said grimly, "We'll see if we can find him."

Basil Blake's cottage, which consisted of all modern conveniences enclosed in a hideous shell of half timbering and sham Tudor, was known to the postal authorities and to William Booker, Builder, as "Chatsworth"; to Basil and his friends as "The Period Piece"; and to the village of St. Mary Mead at large as "Mr. Booker's new house."

It was little more than a quarter of a mile from the village proper, being situated on a new building estate that had been bought by the enterprising Mr. Booker just beyond the Blue Boar, with frontage on what had been a particularly unspoiled country lane. Gossington Hall was about a mile farther on along the same road.

Lively interest had been aroused in St. Mary Mead when news went round that "Mr. Booker's new house" had been bought by a film star. Eager watch was kept for the first appearance of the legendary creature in the village, and it may be said that as far as appearances went Basil Blake was all that could be asked for. Little by little, however, the real facts leaked out. Basil Blake was not a film star, not even a film actor. He was a very junior person, rejoicing in the position of about fifteenth in the list of those responsible for set decorations at Lenville Studios, headquarters of British New Era Films. The village maidens lost interest and the ruling class of censorious spinsters took exception to Basil Blake's way of life. Only the landlord of the Blue Boar continued to be enthusiastic about Basil and Basil's friends. The revenues of the Blue Boar had increased since the young man's arrival in the place.

The police car stopped outside the distorted rustic gate of Mr. Booker's fancy, and Colonel Melchett, with a glance of distaste at the excessive half timbering of Chatsworth, strode up to the front door and attacked it briskly with the knocker.

It was opened much more promptly than he had expected. A young man with straight, somewhat long black hair, wearing orange corduroy trousers and a royal-blue shirt, snapped out, "Well, what do you want?"

"Are you Mr. Basil Blake?"

"Of course I am."

"I should be glad to have a few words with you if I may, Mr. Blake."

"Who are you?"

"I am Colonel Melchett, the chief constable of the county."

Mr. Blake said insolently, "You don't say so. How amusing."

And Colonel Melchett, following the other in, understood precisely what Colonel Bantry's reactions had been. The toe of his own boot itched.

Containing himself, however, he said, with an attempt to speak pleasantly, "You're an early riser, Mr. Blake."

"Not at all. I haven't been to bed yet."

"Indeed?"

"But I don't suppose you've come here to inquire into my hours of bed-going, or if you have it's rather a waste of the county's time and money. What is it you want to speak to me about?"

Colonel Melchett cleared his throat.

"I understand, Mr. Blake, that last week end you had a visitor—a—er—fair-haired young lady."

Basil Blake stared, threw back his head and roared with laughter. "Have the old cats been on to you from the village? About my morals? Damn it all, morals aren't a police matter. You know that."

"As you say," said Melchett dryly, "your morals are no concern of mine. I have come to you because the body of a fair-haired young woman of slightly—er—exotic appearance has been found—murdered."

" 'Struth!" Blake stared at him. "Where?"

"In the library at Gossington Hall."

"At Gossington? At old Bantry's? I say, that's pretty rich—old Bantry! The dirty old man!"

Colonel Melchett went very red in the face. He said sharply through the renewed mirth of the young man opposite him, "Kindly control your tongue, sir. I came to ask you if you can throw any light on this business."

"You've come round to ask me if I've missed a blonde? Is that it? Why should— Hullo, 'ullo, 'ullo! What's this?"

A car had drawn up outside with a scream of brakes. Out of it tumbled a young woman dressed in flapping black-and-white pajamas. She had scarlet lips, blackened eyelashes and a platinum-blond head.

She strode up to the door, flung it open, and exclaimed angrily, "Why did you run out on me?"

Basil Blake had risen. "So there you are. Why shouldn't I leave you? I told you to clear out, and you wouldn't."

"Why should I because you told me to? I was enjoying myself."

"Yes, with that filthy brute, Rosenberg. You know what he's like."

"You were jealous, that's all."

"Don't flatter yourself. I hate to see a girl I like who can't hold her drink and lets a disgusting Central European paw her about."

"That's a lie. You were drinking pretty hard yourself and going on with the black-haired Spanish girl."

"If I take you to a party, I expect you to be able to behave yourself."

"And I refuse to be dictated to, and that's that. You said we'd go to the party and come on down here afterwards. I'm not going to leave a party before I'm ready to leave it."

"No, and that's why I left you flat. I was ready to come down here and I came. I don't hang round waiting for any fool of a woman."

"Sweet, polite person you are."

"You seem to have followed me down, all right."

"I wanted to tell you what I thought of you."

"If you think you can boss me, my girl, you're wrong."

"And if you think you can order me about, you can think again."

They glared at each other.

It was at this moment that Colonel Melchett seized his opportunity and cleared his throat loudly.

Basil Blake swung round on him. "Hullo, I forgot you were here. About time you took yourself off, isn't it? Let me introduce you—Dinah Lee—Colonel Blimp, of the county police. . . . And now, colonel, that you've seen that my blonde is alive and in good condition, perhaps you'll get on with the good work concerning old Bantry's little bit of fluff. Good morning!"

Colonel Melchett said, "I advise you to keep a civil tongue in your head, young man, or you'll let yourself in for trouble," and stumped out, his face red and wrathful.

III

In his office at Much Benham, Colonel Melchett received and scrutinized the reports of his subordinates.

". . . so it all seems clear enough, sir," Inspector Slack was concluding. "Mrs. Bantry sat in the library after dinner and went to bed just before ten. She turned out the lights when she left the room, and presumably no one entered the room afterwards. The servants went to bed at half past ten, and Lorrimer, after putting the drinks in the hall, went to bed at a quarter to eleven. Nobody heard anything out of the usual, except the third housemaid, and she heard too much! Groans and a bloodcurdling yell and sinister footsteps and I don't know what. The second housemaid, who shares a room with her, says the other girl slept all night through without a sound. It's those ones that make up things that cause us all the trouble."

"What about the forced window?"

"Amateur job, Simmons says, done with a common chisel, ordinary pattern; wouldn't have made much noise. Ought to be a chisel about the house, but nobody can find it. Still, that's common enough where tools are concerned."

"Think any of the servants know anything?"

Rather unwillingly Inspector Slack replied, "No, sir, I don't think they do. They all seemed very shocked and upset. I had my suspicions of Lorrimer—reticent, he was, if you know what I mean—but I don't think there's anything in it."

Melchett nodded. He attached no importance to Lorrimer's reticence. The energetic Inspector Slack often produced that effect on the people he interrogated.

The door opened and Doctor Haydock came in. "Thought I'd look in and give you the rough gist of things."

"Yes, yes, glad to see you. Well?"

"Nothing much. Just what you'd think. Death was due to strangulation. Satin waistband of her own dress, which was passed round the neck and crossed at the back. Quite easy and simple to do. Wouldn't have needed great strength—that is, if the girl was taken by surprise. There are no signs of a struggle."

"What about time of death?"

"Say between ten o'clock and midnight."

"You can't get nearer than that?"

Haydock shook his head with a slight grin. "I won't risk my professional reputation. Not earlier than ten and not later than midnight."

"And your own fancy inclines to which time?"

"Depends. There was a fire in the grate, the room was warm—all that would delay rigor and cadaveric stiffening."

"Anything more you can say about her?"

"Nothing much. She was young—about seventeen or eighteen, I should say. Rather immature in some ways but well developed muscularly. Quite a healthy specimen. She was *virgo intacta,* by the way."

And with a nod of his head the doctor left the room.

Melchett said to the inspector, "You're quite sure she'd never been seen before at Gossington?"

"The servants are positive of that. Quite indignant about it. They'd have remembered if they'd ever seen her about in the neighborhood, they say."

"I expect they would," said Melchett. "Anyone of that type sticks out a mile round here. Look at that young woman of Blake's."

"Pity it wasn't her," said Slack. "Then we should be able to get on a bit."

"It seems to me this girl must have come down from London," said the chief constable thoughtfully. "Don't believe there will be any local leads. In that case, I suppose, we should do well to call in the Yard. It's a case for them, not for us."

"Something must have brought her down here, though," said Slack. He added tentatively, "Seems to me, Colonel and Mrs. Bantry must know something. Of course I know they're friends of yours, sir—"

Colonel Melchett treated him to a cold stare.

He said stiffly, "You may rest assured that I'm taking every possibility into account. Every possibility." He went on, "You've looked through the list of persons reported missing, I suppose?"

Slack nodded. He produced a typed sheet.

"Got 'em here. Mrs. Saunders, reported missing a week ago, dark-haired, blue-eyed, thirty-six. 'Tisn't her. And anyway, everyone knows, except her husband, that she's gone off with a fellow from Leeds—commercial. Mrs. Barnard—she's sixty-five. Pamela Reeves, sixteen, missing from her home last night, had attended Girl Guide rally, dark brown hair in pigtails, five feet five—"

Melchett said irritably, "Don't go on reading idiotic details, Slack. This wasn't a schoolgirl. In my opinion—"

He broke off as the telephone rang. "Hullo. . . . Yes, yes, Much Benham police headquarters. . . . What? . . . Just a minute."

He listened and wrote rapidly. Then he spoke again, a new tone in his voice. "Ruby Keene, eighteen, occupation, professional dancer, five feet four inches, slender, platinum-blond hair, blue eyes, retroussé nose, believed to be wearing white diamanté evening dress, silver sandal shoes. Is that right? . . . What? . . . Yes, not a doubt of it, I should say. I'll send Slack over at once." He rang off and looked at his subordinate with rising excitement. "We've got it, I think. That was the Glenshire police." Glenshire was the adjoining county. "Girl reported missing from the Majestic Hotel, Danemouth."

"Danemouth," said Inspector Slack. "That's more like it."

Danemouth was a large and fashionable watering place on the coast not far away.

"It's only a matter of eighteen miles or so from here," said the chief constable. "The girl was a dance hostess or something at the Majestic. Didn't come on to do her turn last night and the management was very fed up about it. When she was still missing this morning, one of the other girls got the wind up about her, or someone else did. It sounds a bit obscure. You'd better go over to Danemouth at once, Slack. Report there to Superintendent Harper and co-operate with him."

IV

Activity was always to Inspector Slack's taste. To rush off in a car, to silence rudely those people who were anxious to tell him things, to cut short conversations on the plea of urgent necessity—all this was the breath of life to Inspector Slack.

In an incredibly short time, therefore, he had arrived at Danemouth, reported at police headquarters, had a brief interview with a distracted and apprehensive hotel manager, and, leaving the latter with the doubtful comfort of "Got to make sure it is the girl first, before we start raising the wind," was driving back to Much Benham in company with Ruby Keene's nearest relative.

He had put through a short call to Much Benham before leaving Danemouth, so the chief constable was prepared for his arrival, though not perhaps for the brief introduction of "This is Josie, sir."

Colonel Melchett stared at his subordinate coldly. His feeling was that Slack had taken leave of his senses.

The young woman who had just got out of the car came to the rescue. "That's what I'm known as professionally," she explained with a momentary flash of large, handsome white teeth. "Raymond and Josie, my partner and I call ourselves, and of course all the hotel know me as Josie. Josephine Turner's my real name."

Colonel Melchett adjusted himself to the situation and invited Miss Turner to sit down, meanwhile casting a swift professional glance over her.

She was a good-looking young woman of perhaps nearer thirty than twenty; her looks depending more on skillful grooming than actual features. She looked competent and good-tempered, with plenty of common sense. She was not the type that would ever be described as glamorous, but she had, nevertheless, plenty of attraction. She was discreetly made up and wore a dark tailor-made suit. She looked anxious and upset, but not, the colonel decided, particularly grief-stricken.

As she sat down she said, "It seems too awful to be true. Do you really think it's Ruby?"

"That, I'm afraid, is what we've got to ask you to tell us. I'm afraid it may be rather unpleasant for you."

Miss Turner said apprehensively, "Does she—does she look very terrible?"

"Well, I'm afraid it may be rather a shock to you."

"Do—do you want me to look at her right away?"

"It would be best, I think, Miss Turner. You see, it's not much good asking you questions until we're sure. Best get it over, don't you think?"

"All right."

They drove down to the mortuary.

When Josie came out after a brief visit she looked rather sick. "It's Ruby, all right," she said shakily. "Poor kid! Goodness, I do feel queer! There isn't"—she looked round wistfully—"any gin?"

Gin was not available, but brandy was and, after gulping a little down, Miss Turner regained her composure. She said frankly, "It gives you a turn, doesn't it, seeing anything like that? Poor little Ruby! What swine men are, aren't they?"

"You believe it was a man?"

Josie looked slightly taken aback. "Wasn't it? Well, I mean—I naturally thought—"

"Any special man you were thinking of?"

She shook her head vigorously. "No, not me. I haven't the least idea. Naturally, Ruby wouldn't have let on to me if—"

"If what?"

Josie hesitated. "Well, if she'd been—going about with anyone."

Melchett shot her a keen glance. He said no more until they were back at his office. Then he began, "Now, Miss Turner, I want all the information you can give me."

"Yes, of course. Where shall I begin?"

"I'd like the girl's full name and address, her relationship to you and all that you know about her."

Josephine Turner nodded. Melchett was confirmed in his opinion that she felt no particular grief. She was shocked and distressed, but no more. She spoke readily enough. "Her name was Ruby Keene—her professional name, that is. Her real name was Rosy Legge. Her mother was my mother's cousin. I've known her all my life, but not particularly well, if you know what I mean. I've got a lot of cousins; some in business, some on the stage. Ruby was more or less training for a dancer. She had some good engagements last year in panto and that sort of thing. Not really classy, but good provincial companies. Since then she's been engaged as one of the dancing partners at the Palais de Danse in Brixwell, South London. It's a nice, respectable place and they look after the girls well, but there isn't a great deal of money in it." She paused.

Colonel Melchett nodded.

"Now this is where I come in. I've been dance and bridge hostess at the Majestic in Danemouth for three years. It's a good job, well paid and pleasant to do. You look after people when they arrive. Size them up, of course—some like to be left alone and others are lonely and want to get into the swing of things. You try and get the right people together for bridge and all that, and get the young people dancing with one another. It needs a bit of tact and experience."

Again Melchett nodded. He thought that this girl would be good at her job. She had a pleasant, friendly way with her and was, he thought, shrewd without being in the least intellectual.

"Besides that," continued Josie, "I do a couple of exhibition dances every evening with Raymond. Raymond Starr—he's the tennis and dancing pro. Well, as it happens, this summer I slipped on the rocks bathing one day and gave my ankle a nasty turn."

Melchett had noticed that she walked with a slight limp.

"Naturally, that put the stop to dancing for a bit and it was rather awkward. I didn't want the hotel to get someone else in my place. There's always a danger"—for a minute her good-natured blue eyes were hard and sharp; she was the female fighting for existence—"that they may queer your pitch, you see. So I thought of Ruby and suggested to the manager that I should get her down. I'd carry on with the hostess business and the bridge and all that. Ruby would just take on the dancing. Keep it in the family, if you see what I mean."

Melchett said he saw.

"Well, they agreed, and I wired to Ruby and she came down. Rather a chance for her. Much better class than anything she'd ever done before. That was about a month ago."

Colonel Melchett said, "I understand. And she was a success?"

"Oh, yes," Josie said carelessly. "She went down quite well. She doesn't dance as well as I do, but Raymond's clever and carried her through, and she was quite nice-looking, you know—slim and fair and baby-looking. Overdid the make-up a bit—I was always at her about that. But you know what girls are. She was only eighteen, and at that age they always go and overdo it. It doesn't do for a good-class place like the Majestic. I was always ticking her off about it and getting her to tone it down."

Melchett asked, "People liked her?"

"Oh, yes. Mind you, Ruby hadn't got much comeback. She was a bit dumb. She went down better with the older men than with the young ones."

"Had she got any special friend?"

The girl's eyes met his with complete understanding.

"Not in the way you mean. Or, at any rate, not that I knew about. But then, you see, she wouldn't tell me."

Just for a moment Melchett wondered why not. Josie did not give the impression of being a strict disciplinarian. But he only said, "Will you describe to me now when you last saw your cousin."

"Last night. She and Raymond do two exhibition dances. One at ten-thirty and the other at midnight. They finished the first one. After it, I noticed Ruby dancing with one of the young men staying at the hotel. I was playing bridge with some people in the lounge. There's a glass panel between the lounge and the ballroom. That's the last time I saw her. Just after midnight Raymond came up in a terrible taking; said where was Ruby; she hadn't turned up and it was time to begin. I was vexed, I can tell you! That's the sort of silly things girls do and get the management's back up, and then they get the sack! I went up with him to her room, but she wasn't there. I noticed that she'd changed; the dress she'd been dancing in—a sort of pink, foamy thing with full skirts—was lying over a chair. Usually she kept the same dress on, unless it was the special dance night—Wednesdays, that is.

"I'd no idea where she'd got to. We got the band to play one more fox trot. Still no Ruby, so I said to Raymond I'd do the exhibition dance with him. We chose one that was easy on my ankle and made it short, but it played up my ankle pretty badly all the same. It's all swollen this morning. Still Ruby didn't show up. We sat about waiting up for her until two o'clock. Furious with her, I was."

Her voice vibrated slightly. Melchett caught the note of real anger in it. Just for a moment, he wondered. He had a feeling of something deliberately left unsaid.

He said, "And this morning, when Ruby Keene had not returned and her bed had not been slept in, you went to the police?"

He knew, from Slack's brief telephone message from Danemouth, that that was not the case. But he wanted to hear what Josephine Turner would say.

She did not hesitate. She said, "No, I didn't."

"Why not, Miss Turner?"

Her eyes met his frankly. She said, "You wouldn't—in my place!"

"You think not?"

Josie said, "I've got my job to think about! The one thing a hotel doesn't want is scandal—especially anything that brings in the police. I didn't think anything had happened to Ruby. Not for a minute! I thought she'd just made a fool of herself about some young man. I thought she'd turn up all right, and I was going to give her a good dressing down when she did! Girls of eighteen are such fools."

Melchett pretended to glance through his notes. "Ah, yes, I see it was a Mr. Jefferson who went to the police. One of the guests staying at the hotel?"

Josephine Turner said shortly, "Yes."

Colonel Melchett asked, "What made this Mr. Jefferson do that?"

Josie was stroking the cuff of her jacket. There was a constraint in her manner. Again Colonel Melchett had a feeling that something was being withheld.

She said rather sullenly, "He's an invalid. He—he gets all het up rather easily. Being an invalid, I mean."

Melchett passed from that. He asked, "Who was the young man with whom you last saw your cousin dancing?"

"His name's Bartlett. He's been there about ten days."

"Were they on very friendly terms?"

"Not specially, I should say. Not that I knew, anyway." Again a curious note of anger in her voice.

"What does he have to say?"

"Said that after their dance Ruby went upstairs to powder her nose."

"That was when she changed her dress?"

"I suppose so."

"And that is the last thing you know? After that, she just—"

"Vanished," said Josie. "That's right."

"Did Miss Keene know anybody in St. Mary Mead? Or in this neighborhood?"

"I don't know. She may have. You see, quite a lot of young men come in to Danemouth to the Majestic, from all round about. I wouldn't know where they lived unless they happened to mention it."

"Did you ever hear your cousin mention Gossington?"

"Gossington?" Josie looked patently puzzled.

"Gossington Hall."

She shook her head. "Never heard of it." Her tone carried conviction. There was curiosity in it too.

"Gossington Hall," explained Colonel Melchett, "is where her body was found."

"Gossington Hall?" She stared. "How extraordinary!"

Melchett thought to himself, Extraordinary's the word.

Aloud he said, "Do you know a Colonel or Mrs. Bantry?"

Again Josie shook her head.

"Or a Mr. Basil Blake?"

She frowned slightly. "I think I've heard that name. Yes, I'm sure I have, but I don't remember anything about him."

The diligent Inspector Slack slid across to his superior officer a page torn from his notebook. On it was penciled: "Col. Bantry dined at Majestic last week."

Melchett looked up and met the inspector's eye. The chief constable flushed. Slack was an industrious and zealous officer and Melchett disliked him a good deal, but he could not disregard the challenge. The inspector was tacitly accusing him of favoring his own class—of shielding an "old school tie."

He turned to Josie. "Miss Turner, I should like you, if you do not mind, to accompany me to Gossington Hall."

Coldly, defiantly, almost ignoring Josie's murmur of assent, Melchett's eyes met Slack's.

V

St. Mary Mead was having the most exciting morning it had known for a long time.

Miss Wetherby, a long-nosed, acidulated spinster, was the first to spread the intoxicating information. She dropped in upon her friend and neighbor, Miss Hartnell.

"Forgive me coming so early, dear, but I thought perhaps you mightn't have heard the news."

"What news?" demanded Miss Hartnell. She had a deep bass voice and visited the poor indefatigably, however hard they tried to avoid her ministrations.

"About the body of a young woman that was found this morning in Colonel Bantry's library."

"In Colonel Bantry's library?"

"Yes. Isn't it terrible?"

"His poor wife!" Miss Hartnell tried to disguise her deep and ardent pleasure.

"Yes, indeed. I don't suppose she had any idea."

Miss Hartnell observed censoriously, "She thought too much about her garden and not enough about her husband. You've got to keep an eye on a man all the time—all the time," repeated Miss Hartnell fiercely.

"I know. I know. It's really too dreadful."

"I wonder what Jane Marple will say? Do you think she knew anything about it? She's so sharp about these things."

"Jane Marple has gone up to Gossington."

"What? This morning?"

"Very early. Before breakfast."

"But really! I do think—well, I mean, I think that is carrying things too far. We all know Jane likes to poke her nose into things, but I call this indecent!"

"Oh, but Mrs. Bantry sent for her."

"Mrs. Bantry sent for her?"

"Well, the car came. With Muswell driving it."

"Dear me. How very peculiar."

They were silent a minute or two, digesting the news.

"Whose body?" demanded Miss Hartnell.

"You know that dreadful woman who comes down with Basil Blake?"

"That terrible peroxide blonde?" Miss Hartnell was slightly behind the times. She had not yet advanced from peroxide to platinum. "The one who lies about in the garden with practically nothing on?"

"Yes, my dear. There she was on the hearthrug, strangled!"

"But what do you mean—at Gossington?"

Miss Wetherby nodded with infinite meaning.

"Then Colonel Bantry too—"

Again Miss Wetherby nodded.

"Oh!"

There was a pause as the ladies savored this new addition to village scandal.

"What a wicked woman!" trumpeted Miss Hartnell with righteous wrath.

"Quite, quite abandoned, I'm afraid!"

"And Colonel Bantry—such a nice quiet man—"

Miss Wetherby said zestfully, "Those quiet ones are often the worst. Jane Marple always says so."

Mrs. Price Ridley was among the last to hear the news. A rich and dictatorial widow, she lived in a large house next door to the vicarage. Her informant was her little maid, Clara.

"A woman, you say, Clara? Found dead on Colonel Bantry's hearthrug."

"Yes, mum. And they say, mum, as she hadn't anything on at all, mum—not a stitch!"

"That will do, Clara. It is not necessary to go into details."

"No, mum, and they say, mum, that at first they thought it was Mr. Blake's young lady what comes down for the week ends with 'im to Mr. Booker's new 'ouse. But now they say it's quite a different young lady. And the fishmonger's young man, he says he'd never have believed it of

Colonel Bantry—not with him handing round the plate on Sundays and all."

"There is a lot of wickedness in the world, Clara," said Mrs. Price Ridley. "Let this be a warning to you."

"Yes, mum. Mother, she never will let me take a place where there's a gentleman in the 'ouse."

"That will do, Clara," said Mrs. Price Ridley.

It was only a step from Mrs. Price Ridley's house to the vicarage. Mrs. Price Ridley was fortunate enough to find the vicar in his study. The vicar, a gentle, middle-aged man, was always the last to hear anything.

"Such a terrible thing," said Mrs. Price Ridley, panting a little because she had come rather fast. "I felt I must have your advice, your counsel about it, dear vicar."

Mr. Clement looked mildly alarmed. He said, "Has anything happened?"

"Has anything happened!" Mrs. Price Ridley repeated the question dramatically. "The most terrible scandal! None of us had any idea of it. An abandoned woman, completely unclothed, strangled on Colonel Bantry's hearthrug."

The vicar stared. He said, "You—you are feeling quite well?"

"No wonder you can't believe it! I couldn't at first! The hypocrisy of the man! All these years!"

"Please tell me exactly what all this is about."

Mrs. Price Ridley plunged into a full-swing narrative.

When she had finished, the Reverend Mr. Clement said mildly, "But there is nothing, is there, to point to Colonel Bantry's being involved in this?"

"Oh, dear vicar, you are so unworldly! But I must tell you a little story. Last Thursday—or was it the Thursday before—well, it doesn't matter—I was going up to London by the cheap day train. Colonel Bantry was in the same carriage. He looked, I thought, very abstracted. And nearly the whole way he buried himself behind *The Times*. As though, you know, he didn't want to talk."

The vicar nodded his head with complete comprehension and possible sympathy.

"At Paddington I said good-by. He had offered to get me a taxi, but I was taking the bus down to Oxford Street; but he got into one, and I distinctly heard him tell the driver to go to— Where do you think?"

Mr. Clement looked inquiring.

"An address in St. John's Wood!" Mrs. Price Ridley paused triumphantly.

The vicar remained completely unenlightened.

"That, I consider, proves it," said Mrs. Price Ridley.

At Gossington, Mrs. Bantry and Miss Marple were sitting in the drawing room.

"You know," said Mrs. Bantry, "I can't help feeling glad they've taken the body away. It's not nice to have a body in one's house."

Miss Marple nodded. "I know, dear. I know just how you feel."

"You can't," said Mrs. Bantry. "Not until you've had one. I know you had one next door once, but that's not the same thing. I only hope," she went on, "that Arthur won't take a dislike to the library. We sit there so much. What are you doing, Jane?" For Miss Marple, with a glance at her watch, was rising to her feet.

"Well, I was thinking I'd go home, if there's nothing more I can do for you."

"Don't go yet," said Mrs. Bantry. "The fingerprint men and the photographers and most of the police have gone, I know, but I still feel something might happen. You don't want to miss anything."

The telephone rang and she went off to answer. She returned with a beaming face.

"I told you more things would happen. That was Colonel Melchett. He's bringing the poor girl's cousin along."

"I wonder why?" said Miss Marple.

"Oh, I suppose to see where it happened, and all that."

"More than that, I expect," said Miss Marple.

"What do you mean, Jane?"

"Well, I think, perhaps, he might want her to meet Colonel Bantry."

Mrs. Bantry said sharply, "To see if she recognizes him? I suppose—oh, yes, I suppose they're bound to suspect Arthur."

"I'm afraid so."

"As though Arthur could have anything to do with it!"

Miss Marple was silent. Mrs. Bantry turned on her accusingly. "And don't tell me about some frightful old man who kept his housemaid. Arthur isn't like that."

"No, no, of course not."

"No, but he really isn't. He's just, sometimes, a little bit silly about pretty girls who come to tennis. You know, rather fatuous and avuncular. There's no harm in it. And why shouldn't he? After all," finished Mrs. Bantry rather obscurely, "I've got the garden."

Miss Marple smiled. "You must not worry, Dolly," she said.

"No. I don't mean to. But all the same I do, a little. So does Arthur. It's upset him. All these policemen looking about. He's gone down to the farm. Looking at pigs and things always soothes him if he's been upset. . . . Hullo, here they are."

The chief constable's car drew up outside. Colonel Melchett came in, accompanied by a smartly dressed young woman.

"This is Miss Turner, Mrs. Bantry. The cousin of the—er—victim."

"How do you do," said Mrs. Bantry, advancing with outstretched hand. "All this must be rather awful for you."

Josephine Turner said frankly, "Oh, it is. None of it seems real, somehow. It's like a bad dream."

Mrs. Bantry introduced Miss Marple.

Melchett said casually, "Your good man about?"

"He had to go down to one of the farms. He'll be back soon."

"Oh." Melchett seemed rather at a loss.

Mrs. Bantry said to Josie, "Would you like to see where—where it happened? Or would you rather not?"

Josephine said, after a moment's pause, "I think I'd like to see."

Mrs. Bantry led her to the library, with Miss Marple and Melchett following behind.

"She was there," said Mrs. Bantry, pointing dramatically. "On the hearthrug."

"Oh!" Josie shuddered. But she also looked perplexed. She said, her brow creased, "I just can't understand it! I can't!"

"Well, we certainly can't," said Mrs. Bantry.

Josie said slowly, "It isn't the sort of place—" and broke off.

Miss Marple nodded her head gently in agreement with the unfinished sentiment. "That," she murmured, "is what makes it so very interesting."

"Come now, Miss Marple," said Colonel Melchett good-humoredly, "haven't you got an explanation?"

"Oh, yes, I've got an explanation," said Miss Marple. "Quite a feasible one. But of course it's only my own idea. Tommy Bond," she continued, "and Mrs. Martin, our new schoolmistress. She went to wind up the clock and a frog jumped out."

Josephine Turner looked puzzled. As they all went out of the room she murmured to Mrs. Bantry, "Is the old lady a bit funny in the head?"

"Not at all," said Mrs. Bantry indignantly.

Josie said, "Sorry. I thought perhaps she thought she was a frog or something."

Colonel Bantry was just coming in through the side door. Melchett hailed him and watched Josephine Turner as he introduced them. But there was no sign of interest or recognition in her face. Melchett breathed a sigh of relief. Curse Slack and his insinuations.

In answer to Mrs. Bantry's questions, Josie was pouring out the story of Ruby Keene's disappearance.

"Frightfully worrying for you, my dear," said Mrs. Bantry.

"I was more angry than worried," said Josie. "You see, I didn't know then."

"And yet," said Miss Marple, "you went to the police. Wasn't that—excuse me—rather premature?"

Josie said eagerly, "Oh, but I didn't. That was Mr. Jefferson."

Mrs. Bantry said, "Jefferson?"

"Yes, he's an invalid."

"Not Conway Jefferson? But I know him well. He's an old friend of ours. . . . Arthur, listen. Conway Jefferson, he's staying at the Majestic, and it was he who notified the police! Isn't that a coincidence?"

Josephine Turner said, "Mr. Jefferson was there last summer too."

"Fancy! And we never knew. I haven't seen him for a long time." She turned to Josie. "How—how is he nowadays?"

Josie considered. "I think he's wonderful, really—quite wonderful. Considering, I mean. He's always cheerful—always got a joke."

"Are the family there with him?"

"Mr. Gaskell, you mean? And young Mrs. Jefferson? And Peter? Oh, yes."

There was something inhibiting in Josephine Turner's rather attractive frankness of manner. When she spoke of the Jeffersons there was something not quite natural in her voice.

Mrs. Bantry said, "They're both very nice, aren't they? The young ones, I mean."

Josie said rather uncertainly, "Oh, yes; yes, they are. I—we—yes, they are really."

"And what," demanded Mrs. Bantry as she looked through the window at the retreating car of the chief constable, "did she mean by that? 'They are really.' Don't you think, Jane, that there's something—"

Miss Marple fell upon the words eagerly. "Oh, I do; indeed I do. It's quite unmistakable! Her manner changed at once when the Jeffersons were mentioned. She had seemed quite natural up to then."

"But what do you think it is, Jane?"

"Well, my dear, you know them. All I feel is that there is something, as you say, about them which is worrying that young woman. Another thing. Did you notice that when you asked her if she wasn't anxious about the girl being missing, she said that she was angry? And she looked angry—really angry! That strikes me as interesting, you know. I have a feeling—perhaps I'm wrong—that that's her main reaction to the fact of the girl's death. She didn't care for her, I'm sure. She's not grieving in any way. But I do think, very definitely, that the thought of that girl, Ruby Keene, makes her angry. And the interesting point is: Why?"

"We'll find out!" said Mrs. Bantry. "We'll go over to Danemouth and stay at the Majestic—yes, Jane, you too. I need a change for my nerves after what has happened here. A few days at the Majestic—that's what we need. And you'll meet Conway Jefferson. He's a dear—a perfect dear. It's the saddest story imaginable. He had a son and a daughter, both of whom he loved dearly. They were both married, but they still spent a lot of time at home. His wife, too, was the sweetest woman, and he was devoted to her. They were flying home one year from France and there was an accident. They were all killed. The pilot, Mrs. Jefferson, Rosamund and Frank. Conway had both legs so badly injured they had to be amputated. And he's been wonderful—his courage, his pluck. He was a very active man, and now he's a helpless cripple, but he never complains. His daughter-in-law lives with him; she was a widow when Frank Jefferson married her, and she had a son by her first marriage—Peter Carmody. They both live with Conway. And Mark Gaskell, Rosamund's husband, is there, too, most of the time. The whole thing was the most awful tragedy."

"And now," said Miss Marple, "there's another tragedy."

Mrs. Bantry said, "Oh, yes, yes, but it's nothing to do with the Jeffersons."

"Isn't it?" said Miss Marple. "It was Mr. Jefferson who reported to the police."

"So he did. You know, Jane, that is curious."

VI

Colonel Melchett was facing a much annoyed hotel manager. With him was Superintendent Harper, of the Glenshire police, and the inevitable Inspector Slack—the latter rather disgruntled at the chief constable's willful usurpation of the case.

Superintendent Harper was inclined to be soothing with the almost tearful Mr. Prestcott; Colonel Melchett tended toward a blunt brutality.

"No good crying over spilt milk," he said sharply. "The girl's dead—strangled. You're lucky that she wasn't strangled in your hotel. This puts the inquiry in a different county and lets your establishment down extremely lightly. But certain inquiries have got to be made, and the sooner we get on with it the better. You can trust us to be discreet and tactful. So I suggest you cut the cackle and come to the horses. Just what, exactly, do you know about the girl?"

"I knew nothing of her—nothing at all. Josie brought her here."

"Josie's been here some time?"

"Two years—no, three."

"And you like her?"

"Yes, Josie's a good girl—a nice girl. Competent. She gets on with people and smooths over differences. Bridge, you know, is a touchy sort of game." Colonel Melchett nodded feelingly. His wife was a keen but an extremely bad bridge player. Mr. Prestcott went on, "Josie was very good at calming down unpleasantness. She could handle people well—sort of bright and firm, if you know what I mean."

Again Melchett nodded. He knew now what it was that Miss Josephine Turner had reminded him of. In spite of the make-up and the smart turnout, there was a distinct touch of the nursery governess about her.

"I depend upon her," went on Mr. Prestcott. His manner became aggrieved. "What does she want to go playing about on slippery rocks in that damn-fool way for? We've got a nice beach here. Why couldn't she bathe from that? Slipping and falling and breaking her ankle! It wasn't fair on me! I pay her to dance and play bridge and keep people happy and amused, not to go bathing off rocks and breaking her ankle. Dancers ought to be careful of their ankles, not take risks. I was very annoyed about it. It wasn't fair to the hotel."

Melchett cut the recital short, "And then she suggested that this girl—her cousin—come down?"

Prestcott assented grudgingly. "That's right. It sounded quite a good idea. Mind you, I wasn't going to pay anything extra. The girl could have her keep, but as for salary, that would have to be fixed up between her and Josie. That's the way it was arranged. I didn't know anything about the girl."

"But she turned out all right?"

"Oh, yes, there wasn't anything wrong with her—not to look at, anyway. She was very young, of course; rather cheap in style, perhaps, for a place of this kind, but nice manners—quiet and well-behaved. Danced well. People liked her."

"Pretty?"

It had been a question hard to answer from a view of the blue, swollen face.

Mr. Prestcott considered. "Fair to middling. Bit weaselly, if you know what I mean. Wouldn't have been much without make-up. As it was, she managed to look quite attractive."

"Many young men hanging about after her?"

"I know what you're trying to get at, sir." Mr. Prestcott became excited. "I never saw anything! Nothing special. One or two of the boys hung around a bit, but all in the day's work, so to speak. Nothing in the strangling line, I'd say. She got on well with the older people, too; had a kind of prattling way with her. Seemed quite a kid, if you know what I mean. It amused them."

Superintendent Harper said in a deep, melancholy voice, "Mr. Jefferson, for instance?"

The manager agreed. "Yes, Mr. Jefferson was the one I had in mind. She used to sit with him and his family a lot. He used to take her out for drives sometimes. Mr. Jefferson's very fond of young people and very good to them. I don't want to have any misunderstanding. Mr. Jefferson's a cripple. He can't get about much—only where his wheel chair will take him. But he's always keen on seeing young people enjoy themselves; watches the tennis and the bathing, and all that, and gives parties for young people here. He likes youth, and there's nothing bitter about him, as there well might be. A very popular gentleman and, I'd say, a very fine character."

Melchett asked, "And he took an interest in Ruby Keene?"

"Her talk amused him, I think."

"Did his family share his liking for her?"

"They were always very pleasant to her."

Harper said, "And it was he who reported the fact of her being missing to the police?"

He contrived to put into the words a significance and a reproach to which the manager instantly responded, "Put yourself in my place, Mr. Harper. I didn't dream for a minute anything was wrong. Mr. Jefferson came along to my office, storming and all worked up. The girl hadn't slept in her room. She hadn't appeared in her dance last night. She must have gone for a drive and had an accident, perhaps. The police must be informed at once. Inquiries made. In a state, he was, and quite high-handed. He rang up the police station then and there."

"Without consulting Miss Turner?"

"Josie didn't like it much. I could see that. She was very annoyed about the whole thing—annoyed with Ruby, I mean. But what could she say?"

"I think," said Melchett, "we'd better see Mr. Jefferson. . . . Eh, Harper?"

Superintendent Harper agreed.

Mr. Prestcott went up with them to Conway Jefferson's suite. It was on the first floor, overlooking the sea.

Melchett said carelessly, "Does himself pretty well, eh? Rich man?"

"Very well off indeed, I believe. Nothing's ever stinted when he comes here. Best rooms reserved, food usually à la carte, expensive wines—best of everything."

Melchett nodded.

Mr. Prestcott tapped on the outer door and a woman's voice said, "Come in."

The manager entered, the others behind him.

Mr. Prestcott's manner was apologetic as he spoke to the woman who turned her head, at their entrance, from her seat by the window. "I am so sorry to disturb you, Mrs. Jefferson, but these gentlemen are from the police. They are very anxious to have a word with Mr. Jefferson. Er—Colonel Melchett, Superintendent Harper, Inspector—er—Slack, Mrs. Jefferson."

Mrs. Jefferson acknowledged the introduction by bending her head.

A plain woman, was Melchett's first impression. Then, as a slight smile came to her lips and she spoke, he changed his opinion. She had a singularly charming and sympathetic voice, and her eyes—clear hazel eyes—

were beautiful. She was quietly but not unbecomingly dressed and was, he judged, about thirty-five years of age.

She said, "My father-in-law is asleep. He is not strong at all, and this affair has been a terrible shock to him. We had to have the doctor, and the doctor gave him a sedative. As soon as he wakes he will, I know, want to see you. In the meantime, perhaps I can help you? Won't you sit down?"

Mr. Prestcott, anxious to escape, said to Colonel Melchett, "Well—er—if that's all I can do for you—" and thankfully received permission to depart.

With his closing of the door behind him, the atmosphere took on a mellow and more social quality. Adelaide Jefferson had the power of creating a restful atmosphere. She was a woman who never seemed to say anything remarkable, but who succeeded in stimulating other people to talk and in setting them at their ease.

She struck, now, the right note when she said, "This business has shocked us all very much. We saw quite a lot of the poor girl, you know. It seems quite unbelievable. My father-in-law is terribly upset. He was very fond of Ruby."

Colonel Melchett said, "It was Mr. Jefferson, I understand, who reported her disappearance to the police."

He wanted to see exactly how she would react to that. There was a flicker—just a flicker—of—annoyance?—concern?—he could not say what exactly, but there was something, and it seemed to him that she had definitely to brace herself, as though to an unpleasant task, before going on.

She said, "Yes, that is so. Being an invalid, he gets easily upset and worried. We tried to persuade him that it was all right, that there was some natural explanation, and that the girl herself would not like the police being notified. He insisted. Well"—she made a slight gesture—"he was right and we were wrong!"

Melchett asked, "Exactly how well did you know Ruby Keene, Mrs. Jefferson?"

She considered. "It's difficult to say. My father-in-law is very fond of young people and likes to have them round him. Ruby was a new type to him; he was amused and interested by her chatter. She sat with us a good deal in the hotel and my father-in-law took her out for drives in the car."

Her voice was quite noncommittal. Melchett thought: She could say more if she chose.

He said, "Will you tell me what you can of the course of events last night?"

"Certainly, but there is very little that will be useful, I'm afraid. After dinner Ruby came and sat with us in the lounge. She remained even after the dancing had started. We had arranged to play bridge later, but we were waiting for Mark—that is, Mark Gaskell, my brother-in-law—he married Mr. Jefferson's daughter, you know—who had some important letters to write, and also for Josie. She was going to make a fourth with us."

"Did that often happen?"

"Quite frequently. She's a first-class player, of course, and very nice. My father-in-law is a keen bridge player and, whenever possible, liked to get hold of Josie to make the fourth, instead of an outsider. Naturally, as she has to arrange the fours, she can't always play with us, but she does whenever she can, and as"—her eyes smiled a little—"my father-in-law spends a lot of money in the hotel, the management is quite pleased for Josie to favor us."

Melchett asked, "You like Josie?"

"Yes, I do. She's always good-humored and cheerful, works hard and seems to enjoy her job. She's shrewd without being at all intellectual and —well, never pretends about anything. She's natural and unaffected."

"Please go on, Mrs. Jefferson."

"As I say, Josie had to get her bridge fours arranged and Mark was writing, so Ruby sat and talked with us a little longer than usual. Then Josie came along, and Ruby went off to do her first solo dance with Raymond—he's the dance and tennis professional. She came back to us afterward, just as Mark joined us. Then she went off to dance with a young man and we four started our bridge."

She stopped and made a slight, significant gesture of helplessness.

"And that's all I know! I just caught a glimpse of her once, dancing, but bridge is an absorbing game and I hardly glanced through the glass partition at the ballroom. Then, at midnight, Raymond came along to Josie very upset and asked where Ruby was. Josie, naturally, tried to shut him up, but—"

Superintendent Harper interrupted. He said in his quiet voice, "Why 'naturally,' Mrs. Jefferson?"

"Well—" She hesitated; looked, Melchett thought, a little put out. "Josie didn't want the girl's absence made too much of. She considered herself responsible for her in a way. She said Ruby was probably up in her bedroom, said the girl had talked about having a headache earlier. I don't think that was true, by the way; Josie said it by way of excuse. Raymond went off and telephoned up to Ruby's room, but apparently there was no answer, and he came back in rather a state—temperamental, you know. Josie went off with him and tried to soothe him down, and in the end she danced with him instead of Ruby. Rather plucky of her, because you could see afterward it had hurt her ankle. She came back to us when the dance was over and tried to calm down Mr. Jefferson. He had got worked up by then. We persuaded him, in the end, to go to bed; told him Ruby had probably gone for a spin in a car and that they'd had a puncture. He went to bed worried and this morning he began to agitate at once." She paused. "The rest you know."

"Thank you, Mrs. Jefferson. Now I'm going to ask you if you've any idea who could have done this thing?"

She said immediately, "No idea whatever. I'm afraid I can't help you in the slightest."

He pressed her, "The girl never said anything? Nothing about jealousy? About some man she was afraid of? Or intimate with?"

Adelaide Jefferson shook her head to each query. There seemed nothing more that she could tell them.

The superintendent suggested that they should interview young George Bartlett and return to see Mr. Jefferson later. Colonel Melchett agreed and the three men went out, Mrs. Jefferson promising to send word as soon as Mr. Jefferson was awake.

"Nice woman," said the colonel, as they closed the door behind them.

"A very nice lady indeed," said Superintendent Harper.

VII

George Bartlett was a thin, lanky youth with a prominent Adam's apple and an immense difficulty in saying what he meant. He was in such a state of dither that it was hard to get a calm statement from him.

"I say, it is awful, isn't it? Sort of thing one reads about in the Sunday papers, but one doesn't feel it really happens, don't you know?"

"Unfortunately there is no doubt about it, Mr. Bartlett," said the superintendent.

"No, no, of course not. But it seems so rum somehow. And miles from here and everything—in some country house, wasn't it? Awfully county and all that. Created a bit of a stir in the neighborhood, what?"

Colonel Melchett took charge. "How well did you know the dead girl, Mr. Bartlett?"

George Bartlett looked alarmed. "Oh, n-n-not well at all, s-s-sir. No, hardly, if you know what I mean. Danced with her once or twice, passed the time of day, bit of tennis—you know!"

"You were, I think, the last person to see her alive last night?"

"I suppose I was. Doesn't it sound awful? I mean she was perfectly all right when I saw her—absolutely."

"What time was that, Mr. Bartlett?"

"Well, you know, I never know about time. Wasn't very late, if you know what I mean."

"You danced with her?"

"Yes, as a matter of fact—well, yes, I did. Early on in the evening, though. Tell you what. It was just after her exhibition dance with the pro fellow. Must have been ten, half past, eleven—I don't know."

"Never mind the time. We can fix that. Please tell us exactly what happened."

"Well, we danced, don't you know. Not that I'm much of a dancer."

"How you dance is not really relevant, Mr. Bartlett."

George Bartlett cast an alarmed eye on the colonel and stammered, "No—er—n-n-no, I suppose it isn't. Well, as I say, we danced round and round, and I talked, but Ruby didn't say very much, and she yawned a bit. As I say, I don't dance awfully well, and so girls—well, inclined to give it a miss, if you know what I mean too. I know where I get off, so I said 'righty ho,' and that was that."

"What was the last you saw of her?"

"She went off upstairs."

"She said nothing about meeting anyone? Or going for a drive? Or—or having a date?" The colonel used the colloquial expression with a slight effort.

Bartlett shook his head. "Not to me." He looked rather mournful. "Just gave me the push."

"What was her manner? Did she seem anxious, abstracted, anything on her mind?"

George Bartlett considered. Then he shook his head. "Seemed a bit bored. Yawned, as I said. Nothing more."

Colonel Melchett said, "And what did you do, Mr. Bartlett?"

"Eh?"

"What did you do when Ruby Keene left you?"

George Bartlett gaped at him. "Let's see now. What did I do?"

"We're waiting for you to tell us."

"Yes, yes, of course. Jolly difficult, remembering things, what? Let me see. Shouldn't be surprised if I went into the bar and had a drink."

"Did you go into the bar and have a drink?"

"That's just it. I did have a drink. Don't think it was just then. Have an idea I wandered out, don't you know. Bit of air. Rather stuffy for September. Very nice outside. Yes, that's it. I strolled around a bit, then I came in and had a drink, and then I strolled back to the ballroom. Wasn't much doing. Noticed what's-er-name—Josie—was dancing again. With the tennis fellow. She'd been on the sick list—twisted ankle or something."

"That fixes the time of your return at midnight. Do you intend us to understand that you spent over an hour walking about outside?"

"Well, I had a drink, you know. I was—well, I was thinking of things."

This statement received more incredulity than any other. Colonel Melchett said sharply, "What were you thinking about?"

"Oh, I don't know. Things," said Mr. Bartlett vaguely.

"You have a car, Mr. Bartlett?"

"Oh, yes, I've got a car."

"Where was it—in the hotel garage?"

"No, it was in the courtyard, as a matter of fact. Thought I might go for a spin, you see."

"Perhaps you did go for a spin?"

"No, no, I didn't. Swear I didn't."

"You didn't, for instance, take Miss Keene for a spin?"

"Oh, I say, look here. What are you getting at? I didn't, I swear I didn't. Really, now."

"Thank you, Mr. Bartlett. I don't think there is anything more at present. At present," repeated Colonel Melchett, with a good deal of emphasis on the words.

They left Mr. Bartlett looking after them with a ludicrous expression of alarm on his unintellectual face.

"Brainless young ass," said Colonel Melchett. "Or isn't he?"

Superintendent Harper shook his head. "We've got a long way to go," he said.

VIII

Neither the night porter nor the barman proved helpful. The night porter remembered ringing up Miss Keene's room just after midnight and getting no reply. He had not noticed Mr. Bartlett leaving or entering the hotel. A lot of gentlemen and ladies were strolling in and out, the night being fine. And there were side doors off the corridor as well as the one in the main hall. He was fairly certain Miss Keene had not gone out by the main door, but if she had come down from her room, which was on the first floor, there was a staircase next to it and a door out at the end of the corridor leading onto the side terrace. She could have gone out of that, unseen, easily enough. It was not locked until the dancing was over at two o'clock.

The barman remembered Mr. Bartlett being in the bar the preceding evening, but could not say when. Somewhere about the middle of the evening, he thought. Mr. Bartlett had sat against the wall and was looking rather melancholy. He did not know how long he was in there. There were a lot of outside guests coming and going in the bar. He had noticed Mr. Bartlett, but he couldn't fix the time in any way.

As they left the bar they were accosted by a small boy about nine years old. He burst immediately into excited speech.

"I say, are you the detectives? I'm Peter Carmody. It was my grandfather, Mr. Jefferson, who rang up the police about Ruby. Are you from Scotland Yard? You don't mind my speaking to you, do you?"

Colonel Melchett looked as though he were about to return a short answer, but Superintendent Harper intervened. He spoke benignly and heartily.

"That's all right, my son. Naturally interests you, I expect?"

"You bet it does. Do you like detective stories? I do. I read them all and I've got autographs from Dorothy Sayers and Agatha Christie and Dickson Carr and H. C. Bailey. Will the murder be in the papers?"

"It'll be in the papers all right," said Superintendent Harper grimly.

"You see, I'm going back to school next week and I shall tell them all that I knew her—really knew her well."

"What did you think of her, eh?"

Peter considered. "Well, I didn't like her much. I think she was rather a stupid sort of girl. Mum and Uncle Mark didn't like her much, either. Only grandfather. Grandfather wants to see you, by the way. Edwards is looking for you."

Superintendent Harper murmured encouragingly, "So your mother and your Uncle Mark didn't like Ruby Keene much? Why was that?"

"Oh, I don't know. She was always butting in. And they didn't like grandfather making such a fuss of her. I expect," said Peter cheerfully, "that they're glad she's dead."

Superintendent Harper looked at him thoughtfully. He said, "Did you hear them—er—say so?"

"Well, not exactly. Uncle Mark said, 'Well, it's one way out anyway,' and mum said, 'Yes, but such a horrible one,' and Uncle Mark said it was no good being hypocritical."

The men exchanged glances. At that moment a clean-shaven man neatly dressed in blue serge came up to them. "Excuse me, gentlemen. I am Mr. Jefferson's valet. He is awake now and sent me to find you, as he is very anxious to see you."

Once more they went up to Conway Jefferson's suite. In the sitting room Adelaide Jefferson was talking to a tall, restless man who was prowling nervously about the room. He swung round sharply to view the newcomers.

"Oh, yes. Glad you've come. My father-in-law's been asking for you. He's awake now. Keep him as calm as you can, won't you? His health's not too good. It's a wonder, really, that this shock didn't do for him."

Harper said, "I'd no idea his health was as bad as that."

"He doesn't know it himself," said Mark Gaskell. "It's his heart, you see. The doctor warned Addie that he mustn't be overexcited or startled. He more or less hinted that the end might come any time, didn't he, Addie?"

Mrs. Jefferson nodded. She said, "It's incredible that he's rallied the way he has."

Melchett said dryly, "Murder isn't exactly a soothing incident. We'll be as careful as we can."

He was sizing up Mark Gaskell as he spoke. He didn't much care for the fellow. A bold, unscrupulous, hawklike face. One of those men who usually get their own way and whom women frequently admire. But not the sort of fellow I'd trust, the colonel thought to himself. Unscrupulous—that was the word for him. The sort of fellow who wouldn't stick at anything.

In the big bedroom overlooking the sea, Conway Jefferson was sitting in his wheeled chair by the window.

No sooner were you in the room with him than you felt the power and magnetism of the man. It was as though the injuries which had left him a cripple had resulted in concentrating the vitality of his shattered body into a narrower and more intense focus.

He had a fine head, the red of the hair slightly grizzled. The face was rugged and powerful, deeply sun-tanned, and the eyes were a startling blue. There was no sign of illness or feebleness about him. The deep lines on his face were the lines of suffering, not the lines of weakness. Here was a man who would never rail against fate, but accept it and pass on to victory.

He said, "I'm glad you've come." His quick eyes took them in. He said to Melchett, "You're the chief constable of Radfordshire? Right. And you're Superintendent Harper? Sit down. Cigarettes on the table beside you."

They thanked him and sat down.

Melchett said, "I understand, Mr. Jefferson, that you were interested in the dead girl?"

A quick, twisted smile flashed across the lined face. "Yes, they'll all have told you that! Well, it's no secret. How much has my family said to you?" He looked quickly from one to the other as he asked the question.

It was Melchett who answered. "Mrs. Jefferson told us very little beyond the fact that the girl's chatter amused you and that she was by way of being a protégée. We have only exchanged half a dozen words with Mr. Gaskell."

Conway Jefferson smiled. "Addie's a discreet creature, bless her. Mark would probably have been more outspoken. I think, Melchett, that I'd better tell you some facts rather fully. It's necessary, in order that you should understand my attitude. And, to begin with, it's necessary that I go back to the big tragedy of my life. Eight years ago I lost my wife, my son and my daughter in an aeroplane accident. Since then I've been like a man who's lost half himself—and I'm not speaking of my physical plight! I was a family man. My daughter-in-law and my son-in-law have been very good to me. They've done all they can to take the place of my flesh and blood. But I've realized—especially of late—that they have, after all, their own lives to live.

"So you must understand that, essentially, I'm a lonely man. I like young people. I enjoy them. Once or twice I've played with the idea of adopting some girl or boy. During this last month I got very friendly with the child who's been killed. She was absolutely natural—completely naïve. She chattered on about her life and her experiences—in pantomime, with touring companies, with mum and dad as a child in cheap lodgings. Such a different life from any I've known! Never complaining, never seeing it as sordid. Just a natural, uncomplaining, hard-working child, unspoilt and charming. Not a lady, perhaps, but thank God neither vulgar nor—abominable word—ladylike.

"I got more and more fond of Ruby. I decided, gentlemen, to adopt her legally. She would become, by law, my daughter. That, I hope, explains my concern for her and the steps I took when I heard of her unaccountable disappearance."

There was a pause. Then Superintendent Harper, his unemotional voice robbing the question of any offense, asked, "May I ask what your son-in-law and daughter-in-law said to that?"

Jefferson's answer came back quickly. "What could they say? They didn't, perhaps, like it very much. It's the sort of thing that arouses prejudice. But they behaved very well—yes, very well. It's not as though, you see, they were dependent on me. When my son Frank married, I turned over half my worldly goods to him then and there. I believe in that. Don't let your children wait until you're dead. They want the money when they're young, not when they're middle-aged. In the same way, when my daughter Rosamund insisted on marrying a poor man, I settled a big sum of money on her. That sum passed to him at her death. So, you see, that simplified the matter from the financial angle."

"I see, Mr. Jefferson," said Superintendent Harper.

But there was a certain reserve in his tone. Conway Jefferson pounced upon it, "But you don't agree, eh?"

"It's not for me to say, sir, but families, in my experience, don't always act reasonable."

"I dare say you're right, superintendent, but you must remember that Mr. Gaskell and Mrs. Jefferson aren't, strictly speaking, my family. They're not blood relations."

"That, of course, makes a difference," admitted the superintendent.

For a moment Conway Jefferson's eyes twinkled. He said, "That's not to say that they didn't think me an old fool! That would be the average person's reaction. But I wasn't being a fool! I know character. With education and polishing, Ruby Keene could have taken her place anywhere."

Melchett said, "I'm afraid we're being rather impertinent and inquisitive, but it's important that we should get at all the facts. You proposed to make full provision for the girl—that is, settle money upon her—but you hadn't already done so?"

Jefferson said, "I understand what you're driving at—the possibility of someone's benefiting by the girl's death. But nobody could. The necessary formalities for legal adoption were under way, but they hadn't yet been completed."

Melchett said slowly, "Then, if anything happened to you?" He left the sentence unfinished, as a query.

Conway Jefferson was quick to respond, "Nothing's likely to happen to me! I'm a cripple, but I'm not an invalid. Although doctors do like to pull long faces and give advice about not overdoing things. Not overdoing things! I'm as strong as a horse! Still, I'm quite aware of the fatalities of life. I've good reason to be! Sudden death comes to the strongest man—especially in these days of road casualties. But I'd provided for that. I made a new will about ten days ago."

"Yes?" Superintendent Harper leaned forward.

"I left the sum of fifty thousand pounds to be held in trust for Ruby Keene until she was twenty-five, when she would come into the principal."

Superintendent Harper's eyes opened. So did Colonel Melchett's.

Harper said in an almost awed voice, "That's a very large sum of money, Mr. Jefferson."

"In these days, yes, it is."

"And you were leaving it to a girl you had only known a few weeks?"

Anger flashed into the vivid blue eyes. "Must I go on repeating the same thing over and over again? I've no flesh and blood of my own—no nieces or nephews or distant cousins, even! I might have left it to charity. I prefer to leave it to an individual." He laughed. "Cinderella turned into a princess overnight! A fairy godfather instead of a fairy godmother. Why not? It's my money. I made it."

Colonel Melchett asked, "Any other bequests?"

"A small legacy to Edwards, my valet, and the remainder to Mark and Addie in equal shares."

"Would—excuse me—the residue amount to a large sum?"

"Probably not. It's difficult to say exactly; investments fluctuate all the time. The sum involved, after death duties and expenses had been paid, would probably have come to something between five and ten thousand pounds net."

"I see."

"And you needn't think I was treating them shabbily. As I said, I divided up my estate at the time my children married. I left myself, actually, a very small sum. But after—after the tragedy I wanted something to occupy my mind. I flung myself into business. At my house in London I had a private line put in, connecting my bedroom with my office. I worked hard; it helped me not to think, and it made me feel that my—my mutilation had not vanquished me. I threw myself into work"—his voice took on a deeper note; he spoke more to himself than to his audience—"and by some subtle irony, everything I did prospered! My wildest speculations succeeded. If I gambled, I won. Everything I touched turned to gold. Fate's ironic way of righting the balance, I suppose."

The lines of suffering stood out on his face again. Recollecting himself, he smiled wryly at them.

"So, you see, the sum of money I left Ruby was indisputably mine, to do with as my fancy dictated."

Melchett said quickly, "Undoubtedly, my dear fellow. We are not questioning that for a moment."

Conway Jefferson said, "Good. Now I want to ask some questions in my turn, if I may. I want to hear more about this terrible business. All I know is that she—that little Ruby was found strangled in a house some twenty miles from here."

"That is correct. At Gossington Hall."

Jefferson frowned.

"Gossington? But that's—"

"Colonel Bantry's house."

"Bantry! Arthur Bantry? But I know him. Know him and his wife! Met them abroad some years ago. I didn't realize they lived in this part of the world. Why, it's—" He broke off.

Superintendent Harper slipped in smoothly, "Colonel Bantry was dining in the hotel here Tuesday of last week. You didn't see him?"

"Tuesday? Tuesday? No, we were back late. Went over to Harden Head and had dinner on the way back."

Melchett said, "Ruby Keene never mentioned the Bantrys to you?"

Jefferson shook his head. "Never. Don't believe she knew them. Sure she didn't. She didn't know anybody but theatrical folk and that sort of thing." He paused, and then asked abruptly, "What's Bantry got to say about it?"

"He can't account for it in the least. He was out at a Conservative meeting last night. The body was discovered this morning. He says he's never seen the girl in his life."

Jefferson nodded. He said, "It certainly seems fantastic."

Superintendent Harper cleared his throat. He said, "Have you any idea at all, sir, who can have done this?"

"Good God, I wish I had!" The veins stood out on his forehead. "It's incredible, unimaginable! I'd say it couldn't have happened, if it hadn't happened!"

"There's no friend of hers from her past life, no man hanging about or threatening her?"

"I'm sure there isn't. She'd have told me if so. She's never had a regular boy friend. She told me so herself."

Superintendent Harper thought, Yes, I dare say that's what she told you. But that's as may be.

Conway Jefferson went on, "Josie would know better than anyone if there had been some man hanging about Ruby or pestering her. Can't she help?"

"She says not."

Jefferson said, frowning, "I can't help feeling it must be the work of some maniac—the brutality of the method, breaking into a country house, the whole thing so unconnected and senseless. There are men of that type, men outwardly sane, but who decoy girls, sometimes children, away and kill them."

Harper said, "Oh, yes, there are such cases, but we've no knowledge of anyone of that kind operating in this neighborhood."

Jefferson went on, "I've thought over all the various men I've seen with Ruby. Guests here and outsiders—men she'd danced with. They all seem harmless enough—the usual type. She had no special friend of any kind."

Superintendent Harper's face remained quite impassive, but, unseen by Conway Jefferson, there was still a speculative glint in his eye. It was quite possible, he thought, that Ruby Keene might have had a special friend, even though Conway Jefferson did not know about it. He said nothing, however.

The chief constable gave him a glance of inquiry and then rose to his feet. He said, "Thank you, Mr. Jefferson. That's all we need for the present."

Jefferson said, "You'll keep me informed of your progress?"

"Yes, yes, we'll keep in touch with you."

The two men went out.

Conway Jefferson leaned back in his chair. His eyelids came down and veiled the fierce blue of his eyes. He looked, suddenly, a very tired man. Then, after a minute or two, the lids flickered. He called, "Edwards?"

From the next room the valet appeared promptly. Edwards knew his master as no one else did. Others, even his nearest, knew only his strength; Edwards knew his weakness. He had seen Conway Jefferson tired, discouraged, weary of life, momentarily defeated by infirmity and loneliness.

"Yes, sir?"

Jefferson said, "Get on to Sir Henry Clithering. He's at Melborne Abbas. Ask him, from me, to get here today if he can, instead of tomorrow. Tell him it's very urgent."

IX

WHEN THEY WERE outside Jefferson's door, Superintendent Harper said, "Well, for what it's worth, we've got a motive, sir."

"H'm," said Melchett. "Fifty thousand pounds, eh?"

"Yes, sir. Murder's been done for a good deal less than that."

"Yes, but—"

Colonel Melchett left the sentence unfinished. Harper, however, understood him. "You don't think it's likely in this case? Well, I don't, either, as far as that goes. But it's got to be gone into, all the same."

"Oh, of course."

Harper went on, "If, as Mr. Jefferson says, Mr. Gaskell and Mrs. Jefferson are already well provided for and in receipt of a comfortable income, well, it's not likely they'd set out to do a brutal murder."

"Quite so. Their financial standing will have to be investigated, of course. Can't say I like the appearance of Gaskell much—looks a sharp, unscrupulous sort of fellow—but that's a long way from making him out a murderer."

"Oh, yes, sir, as I say, I don't think it's likely to be either of them, and from what Josie said I don't see how it would have been humanly possible. They were both playing bridge from twenty minutes to eleven until midnight. No, to my mind, there's another possibility much more likely."

Melchett said, "Boy friend of Ruby Keene's?"

"That's it, sir. Some disgruntled young fellow; not too strong in the head perhaps. Someone, I'd say, she knew before she came here. This adoption scheme, if he got wise to it, may just have put the lid on things. He saw himself losing her, saw her being removed to a different sphere of life altogether, and he went mad and blind with rage. He got her to come out and meet him last night, had a row with her over it, lost his head completely and did her in."

"And how did she come to be in Bantry's library?"

"I think that's feasible. They were out, say, in his car at the time. He came to himself, realized what he'd done, and his first thought was how to get rid of the body. Say they were near the gates of a big house at the time. The idea comes to him that if she's found there the hue and cry will center in the house and its occupants and will leave him comfortably out of it. She's a little bit of a thing. He could easily carry her. He's got a chisel in the car. He forces a window and plops her down on the hearth-rug. Being a strangling case, there's no blood or mess to give him away in the car. See what I mean, sir?"

"Oh, yes, Harper, it's all perfectly possible. But there's still one thing to be done. *Cherchez l'homme.*"

"What? Oh, very good, sir."

Superintendent Harper tactfully applauded Melchett's joke, although, owing to the excellence of the colonel's French accent, he almost missed the sense of the words.

"Oh—er—I say—er—c-c-could I speak to you a minute?" It was George Bartlett who thus waylaid the two men.

Colonel Melchett, who was not attracted to Mr. Bartlett, and who was eager to see how Slack had got on with the investigation of the girl's room and the questioning of the chambermaids, barked sharply, "Well, what is it—what is it?"

Young Mr. Bartlett retreated a step or two, opening and shutting his mouth and giving an unconscious imitation of a fish in a tank.

"Well—er—probably isn't important, don't you know. Thought I ought to tell you. Matter of fact, can't find my car."

"What do you mean, can't find your car?"

Stammering a good deal, Mr. Bartlett explained that what he meant was that he couldn't find his car.

Superintendent Harper said, "Do you mean it's been stolen?"

George Bartlett turned gratefully to the more placid voice. "Well, that's just it, you know. I mean, one can't tell, can one? I mean someone may just have buzzed off in it, not meaning any harm, if you know what I mean."

"When did you last see it, Mr. Bartlett?"

"Well, I was tryin' to remember. Funny how difficult it is to remember anything, isn't it?"

Colonel Melchett said coldly, "Not, I should think, to a normal intelligence. I understood you to say that it was in the courtyard of the hotel last night."

Mr. Bartlett was bold enough to interrupt. He said, "That's just it—was it?"

"What do you mean by 'was it'? You said it was."

"Well, I mean I thought it was. I mean—well, I didn't go out and look, don't you see?"

Colonel Melchett sighed. He summoned all his patience. He said, "Let's get this quite clear. When was the last time you saw—actually saw—your car? What make is it, by the way?"

"Minoan Fourteen."

"And you last saw it when?"

George Bartlett's Adam's apple jerked convulsively up and down. "Been trying to think. Had it before lunch yesterday. Was going for a spin in the afternoon. But somehow—you know how it is—went to sleep instead. Then, after tea, had a game of squash and all that, and a swim afterward."

"And the car was then in the courtyard of the hotel?"

"Suppose so. I mean, that's where I'd put it. Thought, you see, I'd take someone for a spin. After dinner, I mean. But it wasn't my lucky evening. Nothing doing. Never took the old bus out after all."

Harper said, "But as far as you knew, the car was still in the courtyard?"

"Well, naturally. I mean, I'd put it there, what?"

"Would you have noticed if it had not been there?"

Mr. Bartlett shook his head. "Don't think so, you know. Lot of cars going and coming and all that. Plenty of Minoans."

Superintendent Harper nodded. He had just cast a casual glance out of the window. There were at that moment no fewer than eight Minoan 14's in the courtyard—it was the popular cheap car of the year.

"Aren't you in the habit of putting your car away at night?" asked Colonel Melchett.

"Don't usually bother," said Mr. Bartlett. "Fine weather and all that, you know. Such a fag putting a car away in a garage."

Glancing at Colonel Melchett, Superintendent Harper said, "I'll join you upstairs, sir. I'll just get hold of Sergeant Higgins and he can take down particulars from Mr. Bartlett."

"Right, Harper."

Mr. Bartlett murmured wistfully, "Thought I ought to let you know, you know. Might be important, what?"

Mr. Prestcott had supplied his additional dancer with board and lodging. Whatever the board, the lodging was the poorest the hotel possessed.

Josephine Turner and Ruby Keene had occupied rooms at the extreme end of a mean and dingy little corridor. The rooms were small, faced north onto a portion of the cliff that backed the hotel, and were furnished with the odds and ends of suites that had once represented luxury and magnificence in the best suites. Now, when the hotel had been modernized and the bedrooms supplied with built-in receptacles for clothes, these large Victorian oak and mahogany wardrobes were relegated to those rooms occupied by the hotel's resident staff, or given to guests in the height of the season when all the rest of the hotel was full.

As Melchett and Harper saw at once, the position of Ruby Keene's room was ideal for the purpose of leaving the hotel without being observed, and was particularly unfortunate from the point of view of throwing light on the circumstances of that departure.

At the end of the corridor was a small staircase which led down to an equally obscure corridor on the ground floor. Here there was a glass door which led out on the side terrace of the hotel, an unfrequented terrace with no view. You could go from it to the main terrace in front, or you could go down a winding path and come out in a lane that eventually rejoined the cliff road. Its surface being bad, it was seldom used.

Inspector Slack had been busy harrying chambermaids and examining Ruby's room for clues. They had been lucky enough to find the room exactly as it had been left the night before.

Ruby Keene had not been in the habit of rising early. Her usual procedure, Slack discovered, was to sleep until about ten or half past and then ring for breakfast. Consequently, since Conway Jefferson had begun his representations to the manager very early, the police had taken charge of things before the chambermaids had touched the room. They had actually not been down that corridor at all. The other rooms there, at this season of the year, were opened and dusted only once a week.

"That's all to the good, as far as it goes," Slack explained. "It means that if there were anything to find, we'd find it, but there isn't anything."

The Glenshire police had already been over the room for fingerprints, but there were none unaccounted for. Ruby's own, Josie's, and the two chambermaids'—one on the morning and one on the evening shift. There were also a couple of prints made by Raymond Starr, but these were accounted for by his story that he had come up with Josie to look for Ruby when she did not appear for the midnight exhibition dance.

There had been a heap of letters and general rubbish in the pigeon-holes of the massive mahogany desk in the corner. Slack had just been carefully sorting through them, but he had found nothing of a suggestive nature. Bills, receipts, theater programs, cinema stubs, newspaper cuttings, beauty hints torn from magazines. Of the letters, there were some from Lil, apparently a friend from the Palais de Danse, recounting various affairs and gossip, saying they "missed Rube a lot. Mr. Findeison asked after you ever so often! Quite put out, he is! Young Reg has taken up with May now you've gone. Barney asks after you now and then. Things going much as usual. Old Grouser still as mean as ever with us girls. He ticked off Ada for going about with a fellow."

Slack had carefully noted all the names mentioned. Inquiries would be made, and it was possible some useful information might come to light. Otherwise the room had little to yield in the way of information.

Across a chair in the middle of the room was the foamy pink dance frock Ruby had worn early in the evening, with a pair of satin high-heeled shoes kicked off carelessly on the floor. Two sheer silk stockings were rolled into a ball and flung down. One had a ladder in it. Melchett recalled that the dead girl had had bare legs. This, Slack learned, was her custom. She used make-up on her legs instead of stockings, and only sometimes wore stockings for dancing; by this means saving expense. The wardrobe door was open and showed a variety of rather flashy evening dresses and a row of shoes below. There was some soiled underwear in the clothes basket; some nail parings, soiled face-cleaning tissue and bits of cotton wool stained with rouge and nail polish in the wastepaper basket—in fact, nothing out of the ordinary. The facts seemed plain to read. Ruby had hurried upstairs, changed her clothes and hurried off again—where?

Josephine Turner, who might be supposed to know most about Ruby's life and friends, had proved unable to help. But this, as Inspector Slack pointed out, might be natural.

"If what you tell me is true, sir—about this adoption business, I mean—well, Josie would be all for Ruby breaking with any old friends she might have, and who might queer the pitch, so to speak. As I see it, this invalid gentleman gets all worked up about Ruby Keene being such a sweet, innocent, childish little piece of goods. Now, supposing Ruby's got a tough boy friend—that won't go down so well with the old boy. So it's Ruby's business to keep that dark. Josie doesn't know much about the girl, anyway—not about her friends and all that. But one thing she wouldn't stand for—Ruby's messing up things by carrying on with some undesirable fellow. So it stands to reason that Ruby—who, as I see it, was a sly little piece!—would keep very dark about seeing any old friend. She wouldn't let on to Josie anything about it; otherwise Josie would say, 'No, you don't, my girl.' But you know what girls are—especially young ones—always ready to make a fool of themselves over a tough guy. Ruby wants to see him. He comes down here, cuts up rough about the whole business and wrings her neck."

"I expect you're right, Slack," said Colonel Melchett, disguising his usual repugnance for the unpleasant way Slack had of putting things. "If so, we ought to be able to discover this tough friend's identity fairly easily."

"You leave it to me, sir," said Slack with his usual confidence. "I'll get hold of this Lil girl at that Palais de Danse place and turn her right inside out. We'll soon get at the truth."

Colonel Melchett wondered if they would. Slack's energy and activity always made him feel tired.

"There's one other person you might be able to get a tip from, sir," went on Slack. "And that's the dance-and-tennis-pro fellow. He must have seen a lot of her, and he'd know more than Josie would. Likely enough she'd loosen her tongue a bit to him."

"I have already discussed that point with Superintendent Harper."

"Good, sir. I've done the chambermaids pretty thoroughly. They don't know a thing. Looked down on these two, as far as I can make out. Scamped the service as much as they dared. Chambermaid was in here last at seven o'clock last night, when she turned down the bed and drew the curtains and cleared up a bit. There's a bathroom next door, if you'd like to see it."

The bathroom was situated between Ruby's room and the slightly larger room occupied by Josie. It was unilluminating. Colonel Melchett silently marveled at the amount of aids to beauty that women could use. Rows of jars of face cream, cleansing cream, vanishing cream, skin-feeding cream. Boxes of different shades of powder. An untidy heap of every variety of lipstick. Hair lotions and brightening applications. Eyelash black, mascara, blue stain for under the eyes, at least twelve different shades of nail varnish, face tissues, bits of cotton wool, dirty powder puffs. Bottles of lotions—astringent, tonic, soothing, and so on.

"Do you mean to say," he murmured feebly, "that women use all these things?"

Inspector Slack, who always knew everything, kindly enlightened him.

"In private life, sir, so to speak, a lady keeps to one or two distinct shades—one for evening, one for day. They know what suits them and they keep to it. But these professional girls, they have to ring a change, so to speak. They do exhibition dances, and one night it's a tango, and the next a crinoline Victorian dance, and then a kind of Apache dance, and then just ordinary ballroom, and of course the make-up varies a good bit."

"Good Lord," said the colonel. "No wonder the people who turn out these creams and messes make a fortune."

"Easy money, that's what it is," said Slack. "Easy money. Got to spend a bit in advertisement, of course."

Colonel Melchett jerked his mind away from the fascinating and age-long problem of woman's adornments. He said, "There's still this dancing fellow. Your pigeon, superintendent."

"I suppose so, sir."

As they went downstairs Harper asked, "What did you think of Mr. Bartlett's story, sir?"

"About his car? I think, Harper, that that young man wants watching. It's a fishy story. Supposing that he did take Ruby Keene out in that car last night, after all?"

X

Superintendent Harper's manner was slow and pleasant and absolutely noncommittal. These cases where the police of two counties had to collaborate were always difficult. He liked Colonel Melchett and considered him an able chief constable, but he was nevertheless glad to be tackling the present interview by himself. Never do too much at once, was Superintendent Harper's rule. Bare routine inquiry for the first time. That left the persons you were interviewing relieved, and predisposed them to be more unguarded in the next interview you had with them.

Harper already knew Raymond Starr by sight. A fine-looking specimen, tall, lithe and good-looking, with very white teeth in a deeply bronzed face. He was dark and graceful. He had a pleasant, friendly manner and was very popular in the hotel.

"I'm afraid I can't help you much, superintendent. I knew Ruby quite well, of course. She'd been here over a month and we had practiced our dances together, and all that. But there's really very little to say. She was quite a pleasant and rather stupid girl."

"It's her friendships we're particularly anxious to know about. Her friendships with men."

"So I suppose. Well, I don't know anything. She'd got a few young men in tow in the hotel, but nothing special. You see, she was nearly always monopolized by the Jefferson family."

"Yes, the Jefferson family." Harper paused meditatively. He shot a shrewd glance at the young man. "What did you think of that business, Mr. Starr?"

Raymond Starr said coolly, "What business?"

Harper said, "Did you know that Mr. Jefferson was proposing to adopt Ruby Keene legally?"

This appeared to be news to Starr. He pursed up his lips and whistled. He said, "The clever little devil! Oh, well, there's no fool like an old fool."

"That's how it strikes you, is it?"

"Well, what else can one say? If the old boy wanted to adopt someone, why didn't he pick upon a girl of his own class?"

"Ruby never mentioned the matter to you?"

"No, she didn't. I knew she was elated about something, but I didn't know what it was."

"And Josie?"

"Oh, I think Josie must have known what was in the wind. Probably she was the one who planned the whole thing. Josie's no fool. She's got a head on her, that girl."

Harper nodded. It was Josie who had sent for Ruby Keene. Josie, no doubt, who had encouraged the intimacy. No wonder she had been upset when Ruby had failed to show up for her dance that night and Conway Jefferson had begun to panic. She was envisaging her plans going awry.

He asked, "Could Ruby keep a secret, do you think?"

"As well as most. She didn't talk about her own affairs much."

"Did she ever say anything—anything at all—about some friend of hers—someone from her former life—who was coming to see her here or whom she had had difficulty with? You know the sort of thing I mean, no doubt."

"I know perfectly. Well, as far as I'm aware, there was no one of the kind. Not by anything she ever said."

"Thank you. Now will you just tell me in your own words exactly what happened last night?"

"Certainly. Ruby and I did our ten-thirty dance together."

"No signs of anything unusual about her then?"

Raymond considered. "I don't think so. I didn't notice what happened afterward. I had my own partners to look after. I do remember noticing she was not in the ballroom. At midnight she hadn't turned up. I was very annoyed and went to Josie about it. Josie was playing bridge with the Jeffersons. She hadn't any idea where Ruby was, and I think she got a bit of a jolt. I noticed her shoot a quick, anxious glance at Mr. Jefferson. I persuaded the band to play another dance and I went to the office and got them to ring up Ruby's room. There wasn't any answer. I went back to Josie. She suggested that Ruby was perhaps asleep in her room. Idiotic suggestion really, but it was meant for the Jeffersons, of course! She came away with me and said we'd go up together."

"Yes, Mr. Starr. And what did she say when she was alone with you?"

"As far as I can remember, she looked very angry and said, 'Damned little fool. She can't do this sort of thing. It will ruin all her chances. Who's she with? Do you know?'

"I said that I hadn't the least idea. The last I'd seen of her was dancing with young Bartlett. Josie said, 'She wouldn't be with him. What can she be up to? She isn't with that film man, is she?' "

Harper said sharply, "Film man? Who was he?"

Raymond said, "I don't know his name. He's never stayed here. Rather an unusual-looking chap—black hair and theatrical-looking. He has something to do with the film industry, I believe—or so he told Ruby. He came over to dine here once or twice and danced with Ruby afterward, but I don't think she knew him at all well. That's why I was surprised when Josie mentioned him. I said I didn't think he'd been here tonight. Josie said, 'Well, she must be out with someone. What on earth am I going to say to the Jeffersons?' I said what did it matter to the Jeffersons? And Josie said it did matter. And she said, too, that she'd never forgive Ruby if she went and messed things up.

"We'd got to Ruby's room by then. She wasn't there, of course, but she'd been there, because the dress she had been wearing was lying across a chair. Josie looked in the wardrobe and said she thought she'd put on her old white dress. Normally she'd have changed into a black velvet dress for our Spanish dance. I was pretty angry by this time at the way Ruby had let me down. Josie did her best to soothe me and said she'd dance herself, so that old Prestcott shouldn't get after us all. She went away and changed her dress, and we went down and did a tango—exaggerated style and quite showy, but not really too exhausting upon the ankles. Josie was very plucky about it, for it hurt her, I could see. After that, she asked me to help her soothe the Jeffersons down. She said it was important. So, of course, I did what I could."

Superintendent Harper nodded. He said, "Thank you, Mr. Starr."

To himself he thought, It was important, all right. Fifty thousand pounds.

He watched Raymond Starr as the latter moved gracefully away. He went down the steps of the terrace, picking up a bag of tennis balls and a racket on the way. Mrs. Jefferson, also carrying a racket, joined him, and they went toward the tennis courts.

"Excuse me, sir." Sergeant Higgins, rather breathless, was standing at Superintendent Harper's side.

The superintendent, jerked from the train of thought he was following, looked startled.

"Message just come through for you from headquarters, sir. Laborer reported this morning saw glare as of fire. Half an hour ago they found a burnt-out car near a quarry—Venn's Quarry—about two miles from here. Traces of a charred body inside."

A flush came over Harper's heavy features. He said, "What's come to Glenshire? An epidemic of violence?" He asked, "Could they get the number of the car?"

"No, sir. But we'll be able to identify it, of course, by the engine number. A Minoan Fourteen, they think it is."

XI

Sir Henry Clithering, as he passed through the lounge of the Majestic, hardly glanced at its occupants. His mind was preoccupied. Nevertheless, as is the way of life, something registered in his subconscious. It waited its time patiently.

Sir Henry was wondering, as he went upstairs, just what had induced the sudden urgency of his friend's message. Conway Jefferson was not the type of man who sent urgent summonses to anyone. Something quite out of the usual must have occurred, decided Sir Henry.

Jefferson wasted no time in beating about the bush. He said, "Glad you've come. . . . Edwards, get Sir Henry a drink. . . . Sit down, man. You've not heard anything, I suppose? Nothing in the papers yet?"

Sir Henry shook his head, his curiosity aroused. "What's the matter?"

"Murder's the matter. I'm concerned in it, and so are your friends, the Bantrys."

"Arthur and Dolly Bantry?" Clithering sounded incredulous.

"Yes; you see, the body was found in their house."

Clearly and succinctly, Conway Jefferson ran through the facts. Sir Henry listened without interrupting. Both men were accustomed to grasping the gist of a matter. Sir Henry, during his term as commissioner of the Metropolitan Police, had been renowned for his quick grip on essentials.

"It's an extraordinary business," he commented when the other had finished. "How do the Bantrys come into it, do you think?"

"That's what worries me. You see, Henry, it looks to me as though possibly the fact that I know them might have a bearing on the case. That's the only connection I can find. Neither of them, I gather, ever saw the girl before. That's what they say, and there's no reason to disbelieve them. It's most unlikely they should know her. Then isn't it possible that she was decoyed away and her body deliberately left in the house of friends of mine?"

Clithering said, "I think that's far-fetched."

"It's possible, though," persisted the other.

"Yes, but unlikely. What do you want me to do?"

Conway Jefferson said bitterly, "I'm an invalid. I disguise the fact—refuse to face it—but now it comes home to me. I can't go about as I'd like to, asking questions, looking into things. I've got to stay here meekly grateful for such scraps of information as the police are kind enough to dole out to me. Do you happen to know Melchett, by the way, the chief constable of Radfordshire?"

"Yes, I've met him."

Something stirred in Sir Henry's brain. A face and figure noted unseeingly as he passed through the lounge. A straight-backed lady whose face was familiar. It linked up with the last time he had seen Melchett.

He said, "Do you mean you want me to be a kind of amateur sleuth? That's not my line."

Jefferson said, "You're not an amateur, that's just it."

"I'm not a professional any more. I'm on the retired list now."

Jefferson said, "That simplifies matters."

"You mean that if I were still at Scotland Yard I couldn't butt in? That's perfectly true."

"As it is," said Jefferson, "your experience qualifies you to take an interest in the case, and any co-operation you offer will be welcomed."

Clithering said slowly, "Etiquette permits, I agree. But what do you really want, Conway? To find out who killed this girl?"

"Just that."

"You've no idea yourself?"

"None whatever."

Sir Henry said slowly, "You probably won't believe me, but you've got an expert at solving mysteries sitting downstairs in the lounge at this minute. Someone who's better than I am at it, and who, in all probability, may have some local dope."

"What are you talking about?"

"Downstairs in the lounge, by the third pillar from the left, there sits an old lady with a sweet, placid, spinsterish face and a mind that has plumbed the depths of human iniquity and taken it as all in the day's work. Her name's Miss Marple. She comes from the village of St. Mary Mead, which is a mile and a half from Gossington; she's a friend of the Bantrys and, where crime is concerned, she's the goods, Conway."

Jefferson stared at him with thick puckered brows. He said heavily, "You're joking."

"No, I'm not. You spoke of Melchett just now. The last time I saw Melchett there was a village tragedy. Girl supposed to have drowned herself. Police, quite rightly, suspected that it wasn't suicide but murder. They thought they knew who did it. Along to me comes old Miss Marple, fluttering and dithering. She's afraid, she says, they'll hang the wrong person. She's got no evidence, but she knows who did do it. Hands me a piece of paper with a name written on it. And, Jefferson, she was right!"

Conway Jefferson's brows came down lower than ever. He grunted disbelievingly.

"Woman's intuition, I suppose," he said skeptically.

"No, she doesn't call it that. Specialized knowledge is her claim."

"And what does that mean?"

"Well, you know, Jefferson, we use it in police work. We get a burglary and we usually know pretty well who did it—of the regular crowd, that is. We know the sort of burglar who acts in a particular sort of way. Miss Marple has an interesting, though occasionally trivial, series of parallels from village life."

Jefferson said skeptically, "What is she likely to know about a girl who's been brought up in a theatrical milieu and probably never been in a village in her life?"

"I think," said Sir Henry Clithering firmly, "that she might have ideas."

Miss Marple flushed with pleasure as Sir Henry bore down upon her. "Oh, Sir Henry, this is indeed a great piece of luck, meeting you here."

Sir Henry was gallant. He said, "To me, it is a great pleasure."

Miss Marple murmured, flushing, "So kind of you."

"Are you staying here?"

"Well, as a matter of fact we are."

"We?"

"Mrs. Bantry's here too." She looked at him sharply. "Have you heard yet– Yes, I can see you have. It is terrible, is it not?"

"What's Dolly Bantry doing here? Is her husband here, too?"

"No. Naturally, they both reacted quite differently. Colonel Bantry, poor man, just shuts himself up in his study or goes down to one of the farms when anything like this happens. Like tortoises, you know; they draw their heads in and hope nobody will notice them. Dolly, of course, is quite different."

"Dolly, in fact," said Sir Henry, who knew his old friend fairly well, "is almost enjoying herself, eh?"

"Well–er–yes. Poor dear."

"And she's brought you along to produce the rabbits out of the hat for her?"

Miss Marple said composedly, "Dolly thought that a change of scene would be a good thing and she didn't want to come alone." She met his eye and her own gently twinkled. "But of course your way of describing it is quite true. It's rather embarrassing for me, because, of course, I am no use at all."

"No ideas? No village parallels?"

"I don't know much about it all yet."

"I can remedy that, I think. I'm going to call you into consultation, Miss Marple."

He gave a brief recital of the course of events. Miss Marple listened with keen interest.

"Poor Mr. Jefferson," she said. "What a very sad story. These terrible accidents. To leave him alive, crippled, seems more cruel than if he had been killed, too."

"Yes, indeed. That's why all his friends admire him so much for the resolute way he's gone on, conquering pain and grief and physical disabilities."

"Yes, it is splendid."

"The only thing I can't understand is this sudden outpouring of affection for this girl. She may, of course, have had some remarkable qualities."

"Probably not," said Miss Marple placidly.

"You don't think so?"

"I don't think her qualities entered into it."

Sir Henry said, "He isn't just a nasty old man, you know."

"Oh, no, no!" Miss Marple got quite pink. "I wasn't implying that for a minute. What I was trying to say was—very badly, I know—that he was just looking for a nice bright girl to take his dead daughter's place, and then this girl saw her opportunity and played it for all she was worth! That sounds rather uncharitable, I know, but I have seen so many cases of the kind. The young maidservant at Mr. Harbottle's, for instance. A very ordinary girl, but quiet, with nice manners. His sister was called away to nurse a dying relative, and when she got back she found the girl completely above herself, sitting down in the drawing room laughing and talking and not wearing her cap or apron. Miss Harbottle spoke to her very sharply, and the girl was impertinent, and then old Mr. Harbottle left her quite dumfounded by saying that he thought she had kept house for him long enough and that he was making other arrangements.

"Such a scandal as it created in the village, but poor Miss Harbottle had to go and live most uncomfortably in rooms in Eastbourne. People said things, of course, but I believe there was no familiarity of any kind. It was simply that the old man found it much pleasanter to have a young, cheerful girl telling him how clever and amusing he was than to have his sister continually pointing out his faults to him, even if she was a good, economical manager."

There was a moment's pause and then Miss Marple resumed, "And there was Mr. Badger, who had the chemist's shop. Made a lot of fuss over the young lady who worked in his cosmetics section. Told his wife they must look on her as a daughter and have her to live in the house. Mrs. Badger didn't see it that way at all."

Sir Henry said, "If she'd only been a girl in his own rank of life—a friend's child—"

Miss Marple interrupted him. "Oh, but that wouldn't have been nearly as satisfactory from his point of view. It's like King Cophetua and the beggar maid. If you're really rather a lonely tired old man, and if, perhaps, your own family have been neglecting you"—she paused for a second—

"well, to befriend someone who will be overwhelmed with your magnificence—to put it rather melodramatically, but I hope you see what I mean—well, that's much more interesting. It makes you feel a much greater person—a beneficent monarch! The recipient is more likely to be dazzled, and that, of course, is a pleasant feeling for you." She paused and said, "Mr. Badger, you know, bought the girl in his shop some really fantastic presents—a diamond bracelet and a most expensive radio. Took out a lot of his savings to do it. However, Mrs. Badger, who was a much more astute woman than poor Miss Harbottle—marriage, of course, helps—took the trouble to find out a few things. And when Mr. Badger discovered that the girl was carrying on with a very undesirable young man connected with the racecourses, and had actually pawned the bracelet to give him the money—well, he was completely disgusted and the affair passed over quite safely. And he gave Mrs. Badger a diamond ring the following Christmas."

Her pleasant, shrewd eyes met Sir Henry's. He wondered if what she had been saying was intended as a hint.

He said, "Are you suggesting that if there had been a young man in Ruby Keene's life, my friend's attitude towards her might have altered?"

"It probably would, you know. I dare say in a year or two he might have liked to arrange for her marriage himself; though more likely he wouldn't—gentlemen are usually rather selfish. But I certainly think that if Ruby Keene had had a young man she'd have been careful to keep very quiet about it."

"And the young man might have resented that?"

"I suppose that is the most plausible solution. It struck me, you know, that her cousin, the young woman who was at Gossington this morning, looked definitely angry with the dead girl. What you've told me explains why. No doubt she was looking forward to doing very well out of the business."

"Rather a cold-blooded character, in fact?"

"That's too harsh a judgment, perhaps. The poor thing has had to earn her living, and you can't expect her to sentimentalize because a well-to-do man and woman—as you have described Mr. Gaskell and Mrs. Jefferson—are going to be done out of a further large sum of money to which they have really no particular moral right. I should say Miss Turner was a hard-headed, ambitious young woman with a good temper and considerable *joie de vivre*. A little," added Miss Marple, "like Jessie Golden, the baker's daughter."

"What happened to her?" asked Sir Henry.

"She trained as a nursery governess and married the son of the house, who was home on leave from India. Made him a very good wife, I believe."

Sir Henry pulled himself clear of these fascinating side issues. He said, "Is there any reason, do you think, why my friend Conway Jefferson should suddenly have developed this 'Cophetua complex,' if you like to call it that?"

"There might have been."

"In what way?"

Miss Marple said, hesitating a little, "I should think—it's only a suggestion, of course—that perhaps his son-in-law and daughter-in-law might have wanted to get married again."

"Surely he couldn't have objected to that?"

"Oh, no, not objected. But, you see, you must look at it from his point of view. He has a terrible shock and loss; so have they. The three bereaved people live together and the link between them is the loss they have all sustained. But Time, as my dear mother used to say, is a great healer. Mr. Gaskell and Mrs. Jefferson are young. Without knowing it themselves, they may have begun to feel restless, to resent the bonds that tied them to their past sorrow. And so, feeling like that, old Mr. Jefferson would have become conscious of a sudden lack of sympathy without knowing its cause. It's usually that. Gentlemen so easily feel neglected. With Mr. Harbottle it was Miss Harbottle going away. And with the Badgers it was Mrs. Badger taking such an interest in spiritualism and always going out to séances."

"I must say," said Sir Henry ruefully, "that I do dislike the way you reduce us all to a general common denominator."

Miss Marple shook her head sadly. "Human nature is very much the same anywhere, Sir Henry."

Sir Henry said distastefully, "Mr. Harbottle! Mr. Badger! And poor Conway! I hate to intrude the personal note, but have you any parallel for my humble self in your village?"

"Well, of course, there is Briggs."

"Who's Briggs?"

"He was the head gardener up at Old Hall. Quite the best man they ever had. Knew exactly when the undergardeners were slacking off—quite uncanny it was! He managed with only three men and a boy, and the place was kept better than it had been with six. And took several Firsts with his sweet peas. He's retired now."

"Like me," said Sir Henry.

"But he still does a little jobbing, if he likes the people."

"Ah," said Sir Henry. "Again like me. That's what I'm doing now. Jobbing. To help an old friend."

"Two old friends."

"Two?" Sir Henry looked a little puzzled.

Miss Marple said, "I suppose you meant Mr. Jefferson. But I wasn't thinking of him. I was thinking of Colonel and Mrs. Bantry."

"Yes, yes, I see." He asked sharply, "Was that why you alluded to Dolly Bantry as 'poor dear' at the beginning of our conversation?"

"Yes. She hasn't begun to realize things yet. I know, because I've had more experience. You see, Sir Henry, it seems to me that there's a great possibility of this crime being the kind of crime that never does get solved. Like the Brighton trunk murders. But if that happens it will be absolutely disastrous for the Bantrys. Colonel Bantry, like nearly all retired military men, is really abnormally sensitive. He reacts very quickly to public opinion. He won't notice it for some time, and then it will begin to go home to him. A slight here, and a snub there, and invitations that are refused, and excuses that are made, and then, little by little, it will dawn upon him, and he'll retire into his shell and get terribly morbid and miserable."

"Let me be sure I understand you rightly, Miss Marple. You mean that, because the body was found in his house, people will think that he had something to do with it?"

"Of course they will! I've no doubt they're saying so already. They'll say so more and more. And people will cold-shoulder the Bantrys and avoid them. That's why the truth has got to be found out and why I was willing to come here with Mrs. Bantry. An open accusation is one thing and quite easy for a soldier to meet. He's indignant and he has a chance of fighting. But this other whispering business will break him—will break them both. So, you see, Sir Henry, we've got to find out the truth."

Sir Henry said, "Any ideas as to why the body should have been found in his house? There must be an explanation of that. Some connection."

"Oh, of course."

"The girl was last seen here about twenty minutes to eleven. By midnight, according to the medical evidence, she was dead. Gossington's about twenty miles from here. Good road for sixteen of those miles, until one turns off the main road. A powerful car could do it in well under half an hour. Practically any car could average thirty-five. But why anyone should either kill her here and take her body out to Gossington or should take her out to Gossington and strangle her there, I don't know."

"Of course you don't, because it didn't happen."

"Do you mean that she was strangled by some fellow who took her out in a car, and he then decided to push her into the first likely house in the neighborhood?"

"I don't think anything of the kind. I think there was a very careful plan made. What happened was that the plan went wrong."

Sir Henry stared at her. "Why did the plan go wrong?"

Miss Marple said rather apologetically, "Such curious things happen, don't they? If I were to say that this particular plan went wrong because human beings are so much more vulnerable and sensitive than anyone thinks, it wouldn't sound sensible, would it? But that's what I believe and—" She broke off. "Here's Mrs. Bantry now."

XII

Mrs. Bantry was with Adelaide Jefferson. The former came up to Sir Henry and exclaimed, "You!"

"I, myself." He took both her hands and pressed them warmly. "I can't tell you how distressed I am at all this, Mrs. B."

Mrs. Bantry said mechanically, "Don't call me Mrs. B!" and went on, "Arthur isn't here. He's taking it all rather seriously. Miss Marple and I have come here to sleuth. Do you know Mrs. Jefferson?"

"Yes, of course."

He shook hands. Adelaide Jefferson said, "Have you seen my father-in-law?"

"Yes, I have."

"I'm glad. We're anxious about him. It was a terrible shock."

Mrs. Bantry said, "Let's go out on the terrace and have drinks and talk about it all."

The four of them went out and joined Mark Gaskell, who was sitting at the extreme end of the terrace by himself.

After a few desultory remarks and the arrival of the drinks, Mrs. Bantry plunged straight into the subject with her usual zest for direct action.

"We can talk about it, can't we?" she said. "I mean we're all old friends —except Miss Marple, and she knows all about crime. And she wants to help."

Mark Gaskell looked at Miss Marple in a somewhat puzzled fashion. He said doubtfully, "Do you—er—write detective stories?"

The most unlikely people, he knew, wrote detective stories. And Miss Marple, in her old-fashioned spinster's clothes, looked a singularly unlikely person.

"Oh, no, I'm not clever enough for that."

"She's wonderful," said Mrs. Bantry impatiently. "I can't explain now, but she is. . . . Now, Addie. I want to know all about things. What was she really like, this girl?"

"Well—" Adelaide Jefferson paused, glanced across at Mark and half laughed. She said, "You're so direct."

"Did you like her?"

"No, of course I didn't."

"What was she really like?" Mrs. Bantry shifted her inquiry to Mark Gaskell.

Mark said deliberately, "Common or garden gold digger. And she knew her stuff. She'd got her hooks into Jeff all right."

Both of them called their father-in-law "Jeff."

Sir Henry thought, looking disapprovingly at Mark, Indiscreet fellow. Shouldn't be so outspoken.

He had always disapproved a little of Mark Gaskell. The man had charm, but he was unreliable—talked too much, was occasionally boastful—not quite to be trusted, Sir Henry thought. He had sometimes wondered if Conway Jefferson thought so too.

"But couldn't you do something about it?" demanded Mrs. Bantry.

Mark said dryly, "We might have, if we'd realized it in time."

He shot a glance at Adelaide and she colored faintly. There had been reproach in that glance.

She said, "Mark thinks I ought to have seen what was coming."

"You left the old boy alone too much, Addie. Tennis lessons and all the rest of it."

"Well, I had to have some exercise." She spoke apologetically. "Anyway, I never dreamed—"

"No," said Mark, "neither of us ever dreamed. Jeff has always been such a sensible, levelheaded old boy."

Miss Marple made a contribution to the conversation. "Gentlemen," she said with her old maid's way of referring to the opposite sex as though it were a species of wild animal, "are frequently not so levelheaded as they seem."

"I'll say you're right," said Mark. "Unfortunately, Miss Marple, we didn't realize that. We wondered what the old boy saw in that rather insipid and meretricious little bag of tricks. But we were pleased for him to be kept happy and amused. We thought there was no harm in her. No harm in her! I wish I'd wrung her neck."

"Mark," said Addie, "you really must be careful what you say."

He grinned at her engagingly. "I suppose I must. Otherwise people will think I actually did wring her neck. Oh, well, I suppose I'm under suspicion anyway. If anyone had an interest in seeing that girl dead, it was Addie and myself."

"Mark," cried Mrs. Jefferson, half laughing and half angry, "you really mustn't!"

"All right, all right," said Mark Gaskell pacifically. "But I do like speaking my mind. Fifty thousand pounds our esteemed father-in-law was proposing to settle upon that half-baked, nitwitted little slypuss."

"Mark, you mustn't! She's dead!"

"Yes, she's dead, poor little devil. And after all, why shouldn't she use the weapons that Nature gave her? Who am I to judge? Done plenty of rotten things myself in my life. No, let's say Ruby was entitled to plot and scheme, and we were mugs not to have tumbled to her game sooner."

Sir Henry said, "What did you say when Conway told you he proposed to adopt the girl?"

Mark thrust out his hands. "What could we say? Addie, always the little lady, retained her self-control admirably. Put a brave face upon it. I endeavored to follow her example."

"I should have made a fuss!" said Mrs. Bantry.

"Well, frankly speaking, we weren't entitled to make a fuss. It was Jeff's money. We weren't his flesh and blood. He'd always been damned good to us. There was nothing for it but to bite on the bullet." He added reflectively, "But we didn't love little Ruby."

Adelaide Jefferson said, "If only it had been some other kind of girl. Jeff had two godchildren, you know. If it had been one of them—well, one would have understood it." She added with a shade of resentment, "And Jeff's always seemed so fond of Peter."

"Of course," said Mrs. Bantry. "I always have known Peter was your first husband's child, but I'd quite forgotten it. I've always thought of him as Mr. Jefferson's grandson."

"So have I," said Adelaide. Her voice held a note that made Miss Marple turn in her chair and look at her.

"It was Josie's fault," said Mark. "Josie brought her here."

Adelaide said, "Oh, but surely you don't think it was deliberate, do you? Why, you've always liked Josie so much."

"Yes, I did like her. I thought she was a good sport."

"It was sheer accident, her bringing the girl down."

"Josie's got a good head on her shoulders, my girl."

"Yes, but she couldn't foresee—"

Mark said, "No, she couldn't. I admit it. I'm not really accusing her of planning the whole thing. But I've no doubt she saw which way the wind was blowing long before we did, and kept very quiet about it."

Adelaide said with a sigh, "I suppose one can't blame her for that."

Mark said, "Oh, we can't blame anyone for anything!"

Mrs. Bantry asked, "Was Ruby Keene very pretty?"

Mark stared at her. "I thought you'd seen—"

Mrs. Bantry said hastily, "Oh, yes, I saw her—her body. But she'd been strangled, you know, and one couldn't tell—" She shivered.

Mark said thoughtfully, "I don't think she was really pretty at all. She certainly wouldn't have been without any make-up. A thin ferrety little face, not much chin, teeth running down her throat, nondescript sort of nose—"

"It sounds revolting," said Mrs. Bantry.

"Oh, no, she wasn't. As I say, with make-up she managed to give quite an effect of good looks. . . . Don't you think so, Addie?"

"Yes, rather chocolate-box, pink-and-white business. She had nice blue eyes."

"Yes, innocent-baby stare, and the heavily blacked lashes brought out the blueness. Her hair was bleached, of course. It's true, when I come to think of it, that in coloring—artificial coloring, anyway—she had a kind of spurious resemblance to Rosamund—my wife, you know. I dare say that's what attracted the old man's attention to her." He sighed. "Well, it's a bad business. The awful thing is that Addie and I can't help being glad, really, that she's dead." He quelled a protest from his sister-in-law, "It's no good, Addie. I know what you feel. I feel the same. And I'm not going to pretend! But at the same time, if you know what I mean, I really am most awfully concerned for Jeff about the whole business. It's hit him very hard. I—"

He stopped and stared toward the doors leading out of the lounge onto the terrace. "Well, well. See who's here. . . . What an unscrupulous woman you are, Addie."

Mrs. Jefferson looked over her shoulder, uttered an exclamation and got up, a slight color rising in her face. She walked quickly along the terrace and went up to a tall, middle-aged man with a thin brown face who was looking uncertainly about him.

Mrs. Bantry said, "Isn't that Hugo McLean?"

Mark Gaskell said, "Hugo McLean it is. Alias William Dobbin."

Mrs. Bantry murmured, "He's very faithful, isn't he?"

"Doglike devotion," said Mark. "Addie's only got to whistle and Hugo comes trotting along from any odd corner of the globe. Always hopes that someday she'll marry him. I dare say she will."

Miss Marple looked beamingly after them. She said, "I see. A romance?"

"One of the good old-fashioned kind," Mark assured her. "It's been going on for years. Addie's that kind of woman." He added meditatively, "I suppose Addie telephoned him this morning. She didn't tell me she had."

Edwards came discreetly along the terrace and paused at Mark's elbow.

"Excuse me, sir. Mr. Jefferson would like you to come up."

"I'll come at once." Mark sprang up. He nodded to them, said, "See you later," and went off.

Sir Henry leaned forward to Miss Marple. He said, "Well, what do you think of the principal beneficiaries of the crime?"

Miss Marple said thoughtfully, looking at Adelaide Jefferson as she stood talking to her old friend, "I should think, you know, that she was a very devoted mother."

"Oh, she is," said Mrs. Bantry. "She's simply devoted to Peter."

"She's the kind of woman," said Miss Marple, "that everyone likes. The kind of woman that could go on getting married again and again. I don't mean a man's woman—that's quite different."

"I know what you mean," said Sir Henry.

"What you both mean," said Mrs. Bantry, "is that she's a good listener."

Sir Henry laughed. He said, "And Mark Gaskell?"

"Ah," said Miss Marple. "He's a downy fellow."

"Village parallel, please?"

"Mr. Cargill, the builder. He bluffed a lot of people into having things done to their houses they never meant to do. And how he charged them for it! But he could always explain his bill away plausibly. A downy fellow. He married money. So did Mr. Gaskell, I understand."

"You don't like him."

"Yes, I do. Most women would. But he can't take me in. He's a very attractive person, I think. But a little unwise, perhaps, to talk as much as he does."

"'Unwise' is the word," said Sir Henry. "Mark will get himself into trouble if he doesn't look out."

A tall dark young man in white flannels came up the steps to the terrace and paused just for a minute, watching Adelaide Jefferson and Hugo McLean.

"And that," said Sir Henry obligingly, "is X, whom we might describe as an interested party. He is the tennis and dancing pro, Raymond Starr, Ruby Keene's partner."

Miss Marple looked at him with interest. She said, "He's very nice-looking, isn't he?"

"I suppose so."

"Don't be absurd, Sir Henry," said Mrs. Bantry. "There's no supposing about it. He is good-looking."

Miss Marple murmured, "Mrs. Jefferson has been taking tennis lessons, I think she said."

"Do you mean anything by that, Jane, or don't you?"

Miss Marple had no chance of replying to this downright question. Young Peter Carmody came across the terrace and joined them.

He addressed himself to Sir Henry. "I say, are you a detective too? I saw you talking to the superintendent—the fat one is a superintendent, isn't he?"

"Quite right, my son."

"And somebody told me you were a frightfully important detective from London. The head of Scotland Yard or something like that."

"The head of Scotland Yard is usually a complete dud in books, isn't he?"

"Oh, no; not nowadays. Making fun of the police is very old-fashioned. Do you know who did the murder yet?"

"Not yet, I'm afraid."

"Are you enjoying this very much, Peter?" asked Mrs. Bantry.

"Well, I am rather. It makes a change, doesn't it? I've been hunting round to see if I could find any clues, but I haven't been lucky. I've got a souvenir though. Would you like to see it? Fancy, mother wanted me to throw it away. I do think one's parents are rather trying sometimes."

He produced from his pocket a small matchbox. Pushing it open, he disclosed the precious contents.

"See, it's a fingernail. Her fingernail! I'm going to label it Fingernail of the Murdered Woman and take it back to school. It's a good souvenir, don't you think?"

"Where did you get it?" asked Miss Marple.

"Well, it was a bit of luck, really. Because of course I didn't know she was going to be murdered then. It was before dinner last night. Ruby caught her nail in Josie's shawl and it tore it. Mums cut it off for her and gave it to me and said put it in the wastepaper basket, and I meant to, but I put it in my pocket instead, and this morning I remembered and looked to see if it was still there, and it was, so now I've got it as a souvenir."

"Disgusting," said Mrs. Bantry.

Peter said politely, "Oh, do you think so?"

"Got any other souvenirs?" asked Sir Henry.

"Well, I don't know. I've got something that might be."

"Explain yourself, young man."

Peter looked at him thoughtfully. Then he pulled out an envelope. From the inside of it he extracted a piece of brown tape-like substance.

"It's a bit of that chap George Bartlett's shoelace," he explained. "I saw his shoes outside the door this morning and I bagged a bit just in case."

"In case what?"

"In case he should be the murderer, of course. He was the last person to see her, and that's always frightfully suspicious, you know. . . . Is it nearly dinnertime, do you think? I'm frightfully hungry. It always seems such a long time between tea and dinner. . . . Hullo, there's Uncle Hugo. I didn't know mums had asked him to come down. I suppose she sent for him. She always does if she's in a jam. Here's Josie coming. . . . Hi, Josie!"

Josephine Turner, coming along the terrace, stopped and looked rather startled to see Mrs. Bantry and Miss Marple.

Mrs. Bantry said pleasantly, "How d'you do, Miss Turner. We've come to do a bit of sleuthing."

Josie cast a guilty glance round. She said, lowering her voice, "It's awful. Nobody knows yet. I mean it isn't in the papers yet. I suppose everyone will be asking me questions, and it's so awkward. I don't know what I ought to say."

Her glance went rather wistfully toward Miss Marple, who said, "Yes, it will be a very difficult situation for you, I'm afraid."

Josie warmed to this sympathy. "You see, Mr. Prestcott said to me, 'Don't talk about it.' And that's all very well, but everyone is sure to ask me and you can't offend people, can you? Mr. Prestcott said he hoped I'd feel able to carry on as usual, and he wasn't very nice about it, so, of course, I want to do my best. And I really don't see why it should all be blamed on me."

Sir Henry said, "Do you mind me asking you a frank question?"

"Oh, do ask me anything you like," said Josie a little insincerely.

"Has there been any unpleasantness between you and Mrs. Jefferson and Mr. Gaskell over all this?"

"Over the murder, do you mean?"

"No, I don't mean the murder."

Josie stood twisting her fingers together. She said rather sullenly, "Well, there has and there hasn't, if you know what I mean. Neither of them has said anything. But I think they blame it on me—Mr. Jefferson taking such a fancy to Ruby, I mean. It wasn't my fault, though, was it? These things happen, and I never dreamt of such a thing happening beforehand, not for a moment. I—I was quite dumfounded." Her words rang out with what seemed undeniable sincerity.

Sir Henry said kindly, "I'm sure you were. But once it had happened?"

Josie's chin went up. "Well, it was a piece of luck, wasn't it? Everyone's got the right to have a piece of luck sometimes."

She looked from one to the other of them in a slightly defiant, questioning manner, and then went on across the terrace and into the hotel.

Peter said judicially, "I don't think she did it."

Miss Marple murmured, "It's interesting, that piece of fingernail. It had been worrying me, you know—how to account for her nails."

"Nails?" asked Sir Henry.

"The dead girl's nails," explained Mrs. Bantry. "They were quite short and, now that Jane says so, of course it was a little unlikely. A girl like that usually has absolute talons!"

Miss Marple said, "But of course if she tore one off, then she might clip the others close so as to match. Did they find nail parings in her room, I wonder?"

Sir Henry looked at her curiously. He said, "I'll ask Superintendent Harper when he gets back."

"Back from where?" asked Mrs. Bantry. "He hasn't gone over to Gossington, has he?"

Sir Henry said gravely, "No. There's been another tragedy. Blazing car in a quarry."

Miss Marple caught her breath. "Was there someone in the car?"

"I'm afraid so, yes."

Miss Marple said thoughtfully, "I expect that will be the Girl Guide who's missing—Patience—no, Pamela Reeves."

Sir Henry stared at her. "Now why on earth do you think that?"

Miss Marple got rather pink. "Well, it was given out over the air that she was missing from her home since last night. And her home was Daneleigh Vale—that's not very far from here—and she was last seen at the Girl Guide rally up on Danebury Downs. That's very close indeed. In fact, she'd have to pass through Danemouth to get home. So it does rather fit in, doesn't it? I mean it looks as though she might have seen—or perhaps heard—something that no one was supposed to see and hear. If so, of course, she'd be a source of danger to the murderer and she'd have to be removed. Two things like that must be connected, don't you think?"

Sir Henry said, his voice dropping a little, "You think a second murder?"

"Why not?" Her quiet, placid gaze met his. "When anyone has committed one murder he doesn't shrink from another, does he? Nor even from a third."

"A third? You don't think there will be a third murder?"

"I think it's just possible. Yes, I think it's highly possible."

"Miss Marple," said Sir Henry, "you frighten me. Do you know who is going to be murdered?"

Miss Marple said, "I've a very good idea."

XIII

Colonel Melchett and Superintendent Harper looked at each other. Harper had come over to Much Benham for a consultation.

Melchett said gloomily, "Well, we know where we are—or rather where we aren't!"

"Where we aren't expresses it better, sir."

"We've got two deaths to take into account," said Melchett. "Two murders. Ruby Keene and the child, Pamela Reeves. Not much to identify her by, poor kid, but enough. One shoe escaped burning and has been identified as hers, and a button from her Girl Guide uniform. A fiendish business, superintendent."

Superintendent Harper said very quietly, "I'll say you're right, sir."

"I'm glad to say Haydock is quite certain she was dead before the car was set on fire. The way she was lying thrown across the seat shows that. Probably knocked on the head, poor kid."

"Or strangled, perhaps."

"You think so?"

"Well, sir, there are murderers like that."

"I know. I've seen the parents—the poor girl's mother's beside herself. Damned painful, the whole thing. The point for us to settle is: are the two murders connected?"

The superintendent ticked off the points on his fingers.

"Attended rally of Girl Guides on Danebury Downs. Stated by companions to be normal and cheerful. Did not return with three companions by the bus to Medchester. Said to them that she was going into Danemouth to Woolworth's and would take the bus home from there. That's likely enough—Woolworth's in Danemouth is a big affair—the girl lived in the back country and didn't get many chances of going into town. The main road into Danemouth from the downs does a big round inland; Pamela Reeves took a short cut over two fields and a footpath and lane which would bring her into Danemouth near the Majestic Hotel. The lane, in fact, actually passes the hotel on the west side. It's possible, therefore, that she overheard or saw something—something concerning Ruby Keene—which would have proved dangerous to the murderer—say, for instance, that she heard him arranging to meet Ruby Keene at eleven that evening. He realizes that this schoolgirl has overheard and he has to silence her."

Colonel Melchett said, "That's presuming, Harper, that the Ruby Keene crime was premeditated, not spontaneous."

Superintendent Harper agreed. "I believe it was, sir. It looks as though it would be the other way—sudden violence, a fit of passion or jealousy—but I'm beginning to think that that's not so. I don't see, otherwise, how you can account for the death of the child. If she was a witness of the actual crime it would be late at night, round about eleven P.M., and what would she be doing round about the Majestic Hotel at that time of night? Why, at nine o'clock her parents were getting anxious because she hadn't returned."

"The alternative is that she went to meet someone in Danemouth unknown to her family and friends, and that her death is quite unconnected with the other death."

"Yes, sir, and I don't believe that's so. Look how even the old lady, old Miss Marple, tumbled to it at once that there was a connection. She asked at once if the body in the burnt car was the body of the Girl Guide. Very smart old lady, that. These old ladies are, sometimes. Shrewd, you know. Put their fingers on the vital spot."

"Miss Marple has done that more than once," said Colonel Melchett dryly.

"And besides, sir, there's the car. That seems to me to link up her death definitely with the Majestic Hotel. It was Mr. George Bartlett's car."

Again the eyes of the two men met. Melchett said, "George Bartlett? Could be! What do you think?"

Again Harper methodically recited various points. "Ruby Keene was last seen with George Bartlett. He says she went to her room—borne out by the dress she was wearing being found there—but did she go to her room and change in order to go out with him? Had they made a date to go out together earlier—discussed it, say, before dinner—and did Pamela Reeves happen to overhear?"

Colonel Melchett said, "He didn't report the loss of his car until the following morning, and he was extremely vague about it then; pretended that he couldn't remember exactly when he had last noticed it."

"That might be cleverness, sir. As I see it, he's either a very clever gentleman pretending to be a silly ass, or else—well, he is a silly ass."

"What we want," said Melchett, "is motive. As it stands, he had no motive whatever for killing Ruby Keene."

"Yes, that's where we're stuck every time. Motive. All the reports from the Palais de Danse at Brixwell are negative, I understand."

"Absolutely! Ruby Keene had no special boy friend. Slack's been into the matter thoroughly. Give Slack his due; he is thorough."

"That's right, sir. 'Thorough' is the word."

"If there was anything to ferret out he'd have ferreted it out. But there's nothing there. He got a list of her most frequent dancing partners—all vetted and found correct. Harmless fellows, and all able to produce alibis for that night."

"Ah," said Superintendent Harper. "Alibis. That's what we're up against."

Melchett looked at him sharply. "Think so? I've left that side of the investigation to you."

"Yes, sir. It's been gone into—very thoroughly. We applied to London for help over it."

"Well?"

"Mr. Conway Jefferson may think that Mr. Gaskell and young Mrs. Jefferson are comfortably off, but that is not the case. They're both extremely hard up."

"Is that true?"

"Quite true, sir. It's as Mr. Conway Jefferson said; he made over considerable sums of money to his son and daughter when they married. That was a number of years ago though. Mr. Frank Jefferson fancied himself as knowing good investments. He didn't invest in anything absolutely wildcat, but he was unlucky and showed poor judgment more than once. His holdings have gone steadily down. I should say that Mrs. Jefferson found it very difficult to make both ends meet and send her son to a good school."

"But she hasn't applied to her father-in-law for help?"

"No, sir. As far as I can make out she lives with him and, consequently, has no household expenses."

"And his health is such that he wasn't expected to live long?"

"That's right, sir. Now for Mr. Mark Gaskell. He's a gambler, pure and simple. Got through his wife's money very soon. Has got himself tangled up rather badly just at present. He needs money badly, and a good deal of it."

"Can't say I liked the looks of him much," said Colonel Melchett. "Wild-looking sort of fellow, what? And he's got a motive, all right. Twenty-five thousand pounds it meant to him, getting that girl out of the way. Yes, it's a motive all right."

"They both had a motive."

"I'm not considering Mrs. Jefferson."

"No, sir, I know you're not. And, anyway, the alibi holds for both of them. They couldn't have done it. Just that."

"You've got a detailed statement of their movements that evening?"

"Yes, I have. Take Mr. Gaskell first. He dined with his father-in-law and Mrs. Jefferson, had coffee with them afterward when Ruby Keene joined them. Then said he had to write letters and left them. Actually, he took his car and went for a spin down to the front. He told me quite frankly he couldn't stick playing bridge for a whole evening. The old boy's mad on it. So he made letters an excuse. Ruby Keene remained with the others. Mark Gaskell returned when she was dancing with Raymond. After the dance Ruby came and had a drink with them, then she went off with young Bartlett, and Gaskell and the others cut for partners and started their bridge. That was at twenty minutes to eleven, and he didn't leave the table until after midnight. That's quite certain, sir. Everyone says so—the family, the waiters, everyone. Therefore, he couldn't have done it. And Mrs. Jefferson's alibi is the same. She, too, didn't leave the table. They're out, both of them—out."

Colonel Melchett leaned back, tapping the table with a paper cutter.

Superintendent Harper said, "That is, assuming the girl was killed before midnight."

"Haydock said she was. He's a very sound fellow in police work. If he says a thing, it's so."

"There might be reasons—health, physical idiosyncrasy or something."

"I'll put it to him." Melchett glanced at his watch, picked up the telephone receiver and asked for a number. He said, "Haydock ought to be in now. Now, assuming that she was killed after midnight—"

Harper said, "Then there might be a chance. There was some coming and going afterward. Let's assume that Gaskell had asked the girl to meet him outside somewhere—say at twenty past twelve. He slips away for a minute or two, strangles her, comes back, and disposes of the body later—in the early hours of the morning."

Melchett said, "Takes her by car twenty miles to put her in Bantry's library? Dash it all, it's not a likely story."

"No, it isn't," the superintendent admitted at once.

The telephone rang. Melchett picked up the receiver. "Hullo, Haydock, is that you? Ruby Keene. Would it be possible for her to have been killed after midnight?"

"I told you she was killed between ten and midnight."

"Yes, I know, but one could stretch it a bit, what?"

"No, you couldn't stretch it. When I say she was killed before midnight I mean before midnight, and don't try and tamper with the medical evidence."

"Yes, but couldn't there be some physiological what not? You know what I mean?"

"I know that you don't know what you're talking about. The girl was perfectly healthy and not abnormal in any way, and I'm not going to say she was just to help you fit a rope round the neck of some wretched fellow whom you police wallahs have got your knife into. Now, don't protest. I know your ways. And, by the way, the girl wasn't strangled willingly—that is to say, she was drugged first. Powerful narcotic. She died of strangulation, but she was drugged first." Haydock rang off.

Melchett said gloomily, "Well, that's that."

Harper said, "Thought I'd found another likely starter, but it petered out."

"What's that? Who?"

"Strictly speaking, he's your pigeon, sir. Name of Basil Blake. Lives near Gossington Hall."

"Impudent young jackanapes!" The colonel's brow darkened as he remembered Basil Blake's outrageous rudeness. "How's he mixed up in it?"

"Seems he knew Ruby Keene. Dined over at the Majestic quite often, danced with the girl. Do you remember what Josie said to Raymond when Ruby was discovered to be missing, 'She isn't with that film man, is she?' I've found out it was Blake she meant. He's employed with the Lenville Studios, you know. Josie has nothing to go upon except a belief that Ruby was rather keen on him."

"Very promising, Harper, very promising."

"Not so good as it sounds, sir. Basil Blake was at a party at the studios that night. You know the sort of thing. Starts at eight with cocktails and goes on and on until the air's too thick to see through and everyone passes out. According to Inspector Slack, who's questioned him, he left the show round about midnight. At midnight Ruby Keene was dead."

"Anyone bear out his statement?"

"Most of them, I gather, sir, were rather—er—far gone. The—er—young woman now at the bungalow, Miss Dinah Lee, says that statement is correct."

"Doesn't mean a thing."

"No, sir, probably not. Statements taken from other members of the party bear Mr. Blake's statement out, on the whole, though ideas as to time are somewhat vague."

"Where are these studios?"

"Lenville, sir, thirty miles southwest of London."

"H'm—about the same distance from here?"

"Yes, sir."

Colonel Melchett rubbed his nose. He said in a rather dissatisfied tone, "Well, it looks as though we could wash him out."

"I think so, sir. There is no evidence that he was seriously attracted by Ruby Keene. In fact"—Superintendent Harper coughed primly—"he seems fully occupied with his own young lady."

Melchett said, "Well, we are left with X, an unknown murderer—so unknown Slack can't find a trace of him. Or Jefferson's son-in-law, who might have wanted to kill the girl, but didn't have a chance to do so. Daughter-in-law ditto. Or George Bartlett, who has no alibi, but, unfortunately, no motive either. Or with young Blake, who has an alibi and no motive. And that's the lot! No, stop. I suppose we ought to consider the dancing fellow, Raymond Starr. After all, he saw a lot of the girl."

Harper said slowly, "Can't believe he took much interest in her—or else he's a thundering good actor. And, for all practical purposes, he's got an alibi too. He was more or less in view from twenty minutes to eleven until midnight, dancing with various partners. I don't see that we can make a case against him."

"In fact," said Colonel Melchett, "we can't make a case against anybody."

"George Bartlett's our best hope," Harper said. "If we could only hit on a motive."

"You've had him looked up?"

"Yes, sir. Only child. Coddled by his mother. Came into a good deal of money on her death a year ago. Getting through it fast. Weak rather than vicious."

"May be mental," said Melchett hopefully.

Superintendent Harper nodded. He said, "Has it struck you, sir, that that may be the explanation of the whole case?"

"Criminal lunatic, you mean?"

"Yes, sir. One of those fellows who go about strangling young girls. Doctors have a long name for it."

"That would solve all our difficulties," said Melchett.

"There's only one thing I don't like about it," said Superintendent Harper.

"What?"

"It's too easy."

"H'm—yes, perhaps. So, as I said at the beginning, where are we?"

"Nowhere, sir," said Superintendent Harper.

XIV

CONWAY JEFFERSON STIRRED in his sleep and stretched. His arms were flung out, long, powerful arms into which all the strength of his body seemed to be concentrated since his accident. Through the curtains the morning light glowed softly. Conway Jefferson smiled to himself. Always, after a night of rest, he woke like this, happy, refreshed, his deep vitality renewed. Another day! So, for a minute, he lay. Then he pressed the special bell by his hand. And suddenly a wave of remembrance swept over him. Even as Edwards, deft and quiet-footed, entered the room a groan was wrung from his master.

Edwards paused with his hand on the curtains. He said, "You're not in pain, sir?"

Conway Jefferson said harshly, "No. Go on, pull 'em."

The clear light flooded the room. Edwards, understanding, did not glance at his master.

His face grim, Conway Jefferson lay remembering and thinking. Before his eyes he saw again the pretty, vapid face of Ruby. Only in his mind he did not use the adjective "vapid." Last night he would have said "innocent." A naïve, innocent child!

And now?

A great weariness came over Conway Jefferson. He closed his eyes. He murmured below his breath, "Margaret." It was the name of his dead wife.

"I like your friend," said Adelaide Jefferson to Mrs. Bantry.

The two women were sitting on the terrace.

"Jane Marple's a very remarkable woman," said Mrs. Bantry.

"She's nice too," said Addie, smiling.

"People call her a scandalmonger," said Mrs. Bantry, "but she isn't really."

"Just a low opinion of human nature?"

"You could call it that."

"It's rather refreshing," said Adelaide Jefferson, "after having had too much of the other thing."

Mrs. Bantry looked at her sharply.

Addie explained herself. "So much high thinking—idealization of an unworthy object!"

"You mean Ruby Keene?"

Addie nodded. "I don't want to be horrid about her. There wasn't any harm in her. Poor little rat, she had to fight for what she wanted. She wasn't bad. Common and rather silly and quite good-natured, but a decided little gold digger. I don't think she schemed or planned. It was just that she was quick to take advantage of a possibility. And she knew just how to appeal to an elderly man who was lonely."

"I suppose," said Mrs. Bantry thoughtfully, "that Conway was lonely."

Addie moved restlessly. She said, "He was this summer." She paused and then burst out, "Mark will have it that it was all my fault! Perhaps it was; I don't know."

She was silent for a minute, then, impelled by some need to talk, she went on speaking in a difficult, almost reluctant way. "I—I've had such an odd sort of life. Mike Carmody, my first husband, died so soon after we were married it—it knocked me out. Peter, as you know, was born after his death. Frank Jefferson was Mike's great friend. So I came to see a lot of him. He was Peter's godfather—Mike had wanted that. I got very fond of him and—oh, sorry for him too."

"Sorry?" queried Mrs. Bantry with interest.

"Yes, just that. It sounds odd. Frank had always had everything he wanted. His father and his mother couldn't have been nicer to him. And yet—how can I say it?—you see, old Mr. Jefferson's personality is so strong. If you live with it you can't somehow have a personality of your own. Frank felt that.

"When we were married he was very happy—wonderfully so. Mr. Jefferson was very generous. He settled a large sum of money on Frank; said he wanted his children to be independent and not have to wait for his death. It was so nice of him—so generous. But it was much too sudden. He ought really to have accustomed Frank to independence little by little.

"It went to Frank's head. He wanted to be as good a man as his father, as clever about money and business, as farseeing and successful. And of course he wasn't. He didn't exactly speculate with the money, but he invested in the wrong things at the wrong time. It's frightening, you know, how soon money goes if you're not clever about it. The more Frank dropped, the more eager he was to get it back by some clever deal. So things went from bad to worse."

"But, my dear," said Mrs. Bantry, "couldn't Conway have advised him?"

"He didn't want to be advised. The one thing he wanted was to do well on his own. That's why we never let Mr. Jefferson know. When Frank died there was very little left; only a tiny income for me. And I—I didn't let his father know either. You see"—she turned abruptly—"it would have seemed like betraying Frank to him. Frank would have hated it so. Mr. Jefferson was ill for a long time. When he got well he assumed that I was a very-well-off widow. I've never undeceived him. It's been a point of honor. He knows I'm very careful about money, but he just approves of that, thinks I'm a thrifty sort of woman. And of course Peter and I have lived with him practically ever since, and he's paid for all our living expenses. So I've never had to worry." She said slowly, "We've been like a family all these years, only—only, you see—or don't you see?—I've never been Frank's widow to him; I've been Frank's wife."

Mrs. Bantry grasped the implication. "You mean he's never accepted their deaths?"

"No. He's been wonderful. But he's conquered his own terrible tragedy by refusing to recognize death. Mark is Rosamund's husband and I'm Frank's wife, and though Frank and Rosamund aren't exactly here with us they are still existent."

Mrs. Bantry said softly, "It's a wonderful triumph of faith."

"I know. We've gone on, year after year. But suddenly, this summer, something went wrong in me. I felt—felt rebellious.

"It's an awful thing to say, but I didn't want to think of Frank any more! All that was over—my love and companionship with him, and my grief when he died. It was something that had been and wasn't any longer.

"It's awfully hard to describe. It's like wanting to wipe the slate clean and start again. I wanted to be me—Addie, still reasonably young and strong and able to play games and swim and dance—just a person. Even Hugo—you know Hugo McLean?—he's a dear and wants to marry me, but of course I've never really thought of it, but this summer I did begin to think of it—not seriously, only vaguely."

She stopped and shook her head.

"And so I suppose it's true. I neglected Jeff. I don't mean really neglected him, but my mind and thoughts weren't with him. When Ruby, as I saw, amused him, I was rather glad. It left me freer to go and do my own things. I never dreamed—of course I never dreamed—that he would be so—so infatuated with her!"

Mrs. Bantry asked, "And when you did find out?"

"I was dumfounded—absolutely dumfounded! And, I'm afraid, angry too."

"I'd have been angry," said Mrs. Bantry.

"There was Peter, you see. Peter's whole future depends on Jeff. Jeff practically looked on him as a grandson, or so I thought, but of course he wasn't a grandson. He was no relation at all. And to think that he was going to be disinherited!" Her firm, well-shaped hands shook a little where they lay in her lap. "For that's what it felt like. And for a vulgar gold-digging little simpleton! Oh, I could have killed her!"

She stopped, stricken. Her beautiful hazel eyes met Mrs. Bantry's in a pleading horror. She said, "What an awful thing to say!"

Hugo McLean, coming quietly up behind them, asked, "What's an awful thing to say?"

"Sit down, Hugo. You know Mrs. Bantry, don't you?"

McLean had already greeted the older lady. He said, now, in a slow, persevering way, "What was an awful thing to say?"

Addie Jefferson said, "That I'd like to have killed Ruby Keene."

Hugo McLean reflected a minute or two. Then he said, "No, wouldn't say that if I were you. Might be misunderstood." His eyes, steady, reflective gray eyes, looked at her meaningly. He said, "You've got to watch your step, Addie." There was a warning in his voice.

When Miss Marple came out of the hotel and joined Mrs. Bantry a few minutes later, Hugo McLean and Adelaide Jefferson were walking down the path to the sea together.

Seating herself, Miss Marple remarked, "He seems very devoted."

"He's been devoted for years! One of those men."

"I know. Like Major Bury. He hung round an Anglo-Indian widow for quite ten years. A joke among her friends! In the end she gave in, but, unfortunately, ten days before they were to have been married she ran away with the chauffeur. Such a nice woman, too, and usually so well balanced."

"People do do very odd things," agreed Mrs. Bantry. "I wish you'd been here just now, Jane. Addie Jefferson was telling me all about herself—how her husband went through all his money, but they never let Mr. Jefferson know. And then, this summer, things felt different to her—"

Miss Marple nodded. "Yes. She rebelled, I suppose, against being made to live in the past. After all, there's a time for everything. You can't sit in the house with the blinds down forever. I suppose Mrs. Jefferson just pulled them up and took off her widow's weeds, and her father-in-law, of course, didn't like it. Felt left out in the cold, though I don't suppose for a minute he realized who put her up to it. Still, he certainly wouldn't like it. And so, of course, like old Mr. Badger when his wife took up spiritualism, he was just ripe for what happened. Any fairly nice-looking young girl who listened prettily would have done."

"Do you think," said Mrs. Bantry, "that that cousin, Josie, got her down deliberately—that it was a family plot?"

Miss Marple shook her head. "No, I don't think so at all. I don't think Josie has the kind of mind that could foresee people's reactions. She's rather dense in that way. She's got one of those shrewd, limited, practical minds that never do foresee the future and are usually astonished by it."

"It seems to have taken everyone by surprise," said Mrs. Bantry. "Addie —and Mark Gaskell, too, apparently."

Miss Marple smiled. "I dare say he had his own fish to fry. A bold fellow with a roving eye! Not the man to go on being a sorrowing widower for years, no matter how fond he may have been of his wife. I should think they were both restless under old Mr. Jefferson's yoke of perpetual remembrance. Only," added Miss Marple cynically, "it's easier for gentlemen, of course."

At that very moment Mark was confirming this judgment on himself in a talk with Sir Henry Clithering.

With characteristic candor Mark had gone straight to the heart of things.

"It's just dawned on me," he said, "that I'm Favorite Suspect Number One to the police! They've been delving into my financial troubles. I'm broke, you know; or very nearly. If dear old Jeff dies according to schedule in a month or two, and Addie and I divide the dibs also according to schedule, all will be well.

"Matter of fact, I owe rather a lot. If the crash comes, it will be a big one! If I can stave it off, it will be the other way round; I shall come out on top and be very rich."

Sir Henry Clithering said, "You're a gambler, Mark."

"Always have been. Risk everything, that's my motto! Yes, it's a lucky thing for me that somebody strangled that poor kid. I didn't do it. I'm not a strangler. I don't really think I could ever murder anybody. I'm too easy-going. But I don't suppose I can ask the police to believe that! I must look to them like the answer to the criminal investigator's prayer! Motive, on the spot, not burdened with high moral scruples! I can't imagine why I'm not in the jug already. That superintendent's got a very nasty eye."

"You've got that useful thing, an alibi."

"An alibi is the fishiest thing on God's earth! No innocent person ever has an alibi! Besides, it all depends on the time of death, or something like that, and you may be sure if three doctors say the girl was killed at midnight, at least six will be found who will swear positively that she was killed at five in the morning—and where's my alibi then?"

"Well, you are able to joke about it."

"Damned bad taste, isn't it?" said Mark cheerfully. "Actually, I'm rather scared. One is, with murder! And don't think I'm not sorry for old Jeff. I am. But it's better this way—bad as the shock was—than if he'd found her out."

"What do you mean, found her out?"

Mark winked. "Where did she go off to last night? I'll lay you any odds you like she went to meet a man. Jeff wouldn't have liked that. He wouldn't have liked it at all. If he'd found she was deceiving him—that she wasn't the prattling little innocent she seemed—well, my father-in-law is an odd man. He's a man of great self-control, but that self-control can snap. And then, look out!"

Sir Henry glanced at him curiously. "Are you fond of him or not?"

"I'm very fond of him, and at the same time I resent him. I'll try and explain. Conway Jefferson is a man who likes to control his surroundings. He's a benevolent despot, kind, generous and affectionate, but his is the tune and the others dance to his piping."

Mark Gaskell paused.

"I loved my wife. I shall never feel the same for anyone else. Rosamund was sunshine and laughter and flowers, and when she was killed I felt just like a man in the ring who's had a knockout blow. But the referee's been counting a good long time now. I'm a man, after all. I like women. I don't want to marry again—not in the least. Well, that's all right. I've had to be discreet, but I've had my good times all right. Poor Addie hasn't. Addie's a really nice woman. She's the kind of woman men want to marry. Give her half a chance and she would marry again, and be very happy and make the chap happy too.

"But old Jeff saw her always as Frank's wife and hypnotized her into seeing herself like that. He doesn't know it, but we've been in prison. I broke out, on the quiet, a long time ago. Addie broke out this summer, and it gave him a shock. It broke up his world. Result, Ruby Keene."

Irrepressibly he sang:

"But she is in her grave, and oh!
The difference to me!

"Come and have a drink, Clithering."

It was hardly surprising, Sir Henry reflected, that Mark Gaskell should be an object of suspicion to the police.

XV

Doctor Metcalf was one of the best-known physicians in Danemouth. He had no aggressive bedside manner, but his presence in the sickroom had an invariably cheering effect. He was middle-aged, with a quiet pleasant voice. He listened carefully to Superintendent Harper and replied to his questions with gentle precision.

Harper said, "Then I can take it, Doctor Metcalf, that what I was told by Mrs. Jefferson was substantially correct?"

"Yes, Mr. Jefferson's health is in a precarious state. For several years now the man has been driving himself ruthlessly. In his determination to live like other men he has lived at a far greater pace than the normal man of his age. He has refused to rest, to take things easy, to go slow, or any of the other phrases with which I and his other medical advisers have tendered our opinion. The result is that the man is an overworked engine. Heart, lungs, blood pressure—they're all overstrained."

"You say Mr. Jefferson has resolutely refused to listen?"

"Yes. I don't know that I blame him. It's not what I say to my patients, superintendent, but a man may as well wear out as rust out. A lot of my colleagues do that, and take it from me, it's not a bad way. In a place like Danemouth one sees most of the other thing. Invalids clinging to life, terrified of overexerting themselves, terrified of a breath of drafty air, of a stray germ, of an injudicious meal."

"I expect that's true enough," said Superintendent Harper. "What it amounts to, then, is this: Conway Jefferson is strong enough, physically speaking—or I suppose I mean muscularly speaking. Just what can he do in the active line, by the way?"

"He has immense strength in his arms and shoulders. He was a very powerful man before his accident. He is extremely dexterous in his handling of his wheeled chair, and with the aid of crutches he can move himself about a room—from his bed to the chair, for instance."

"Isn't it possible for a man injured as Mr. Jefferson was to have artificial legs?"

"Not in his case. There was a spine injury."

"I see. Let me sum up again. Jefferson is strong and fit in the muscular sense. He feels well and all that?"

Metcalf nodded.

"But his heart is in a bad condition; any overstrain or exertion, or a shock or a sudden fright, and he might pop off. Is that it?"

"More or less. Overexertion is killing him slowly because he won't give in when he feels tired. That aggravates the cardiac condition. It is unlikely that exertion would kill him suddenly. But a sudden shock or fright might easily do so. That is why I expressly warned his family."

Superintendent Harper said slowly, "But in actual fact a shock didn't kill him. I mean, doctor, that there couldn't have been a much worse shock than this business, and he's still alive."

Doctor Metcalf shrugged his shoulders. "I know. But if you'd had my experience, superintendent, you'd know that case history shows the impossibility of prognosticating accurately. People who ought to die of shock and exposure don't die of shock and exposure, et cetera, et cetera. The human frame is tougher than one can imagine possible. Moreover, in my experience, a physical shock is more often fatal than a mental shock. In plain language, a door banging suddenly would be more likely to kill Mr. Jefferson than the discovery that a girl he was fond of had died in a particularly horrible manner."

"Why is that, I wonder?"

"The breaking of a piece of bad news nearly always sets up a defense reaction. It numbs the recipient. They are unable, at first, to take it in. Full realization takes a little time. But the banged door, someone jumping out of a cupboard, the sudden onslaught of a motor as you cross a road—all those things are immediate in their action. The heart gives a terrified leap—to put it in layman's language."

Superintendent Harper said slowly, "But as far as anyone would know, Mr. Jefferson's death might easily have been caused by the shock of the girl's death?"

"Oh, easily." The doctor looked curiously at the other. "You don't think—"

"I don't know what I think," said Superintendent Harper vexedly.

"But you'll admit, sir, that the two things would fit in very prettily together," he said a little later to Sir Henry Clithering. "Kill two birds with one stone. First the girl, and the fact of her death takes off Mr. Jefferson, too, before he's had any opportunity of altering his will."

"Do you think he will alter it?"

"You'd be more likely to know that, sir, than I would. What do you say?"

"I don't know. Before Ruby Keene came on the scene I happen to know that he had left his money between Mark Gaskell and Mrs. Jefferson. I don't see why he should now change his mind about that. But of course he might do so."

Superintendent Harper agreed.

"You never know what bee a man is going to get in his bonnet; especially when he doesn't feel there's any moral obligation in the disposal of his fortune. No blood relations in this case."

Sir Henry said, "He is fond of the boy—of young Peter."

"D'you think he regards him as a grandson? You'd know that better than I would, sir."

Sir Henry said slowly, "No, I don't think so."

"There's another thing I'd like to ask you, sir. It's a thing I can't judge for myself. But they're friends of yours, and so you'd know. I'd like very much to know just how fond Mr. Jefferson is of Mr. Gaskell and young Mrs. Jefferson. Nobody doubts that he was much attached to them both, but he was attached to them, as I see it, because they were, respectively, the husband and the wife of his daughter and his son. But supposing, for instance, one of them had married again?"

Sir Henry reflected. He said, "It's an interesting point you raise there.

I don't know. I'm inclined to suspect—this is a mere opinion—that it would have altered his attitude a good deal. He would have wished them well, borne no rancor, but I think—yes, I rather think that he would have taken very little more interest in them."

Superintendent Harper nodded. "In both cases, sir?"

"I think so, yes. In Mr. Gaskell's, almost certainly, and I rather think in Mrs. Jefferson's also, but that's not nearly so certain. I think he was fond of her for her own sake."

"Sex would have something to do with that," said Superintendent Harper sapiently. "Easier for him to look on her as a daughter than to look on Mr. Gaskell as a son. It works both ways. Women accept a son-in-law as one of the family easily enough, but there aren't many times when a woman looks on her son's wife as a daughter." Superintendent Harper went on, "Mind if we walk along this path, sir, to the tennis court? I see Miss Marple's sitting there. I want to ask her to do something for me. As a matter of fact, I want to rope you both in."

"In what way, superintendent?"

"To get at stuff that I can't get at myself. I want you to tackle Edwards for me, sir."

"Edwards? What do you want from him?"

"Everything you can think of. Everything he knows and what he thinks. About the relations between the various members of the family, his angle on the Ruby Keene business. Inside stuff. He knows better than anyone the state of affairs. And he wouldn't tell me. But he'll tell you. Because you're a gentleman and a friend of Mr. Jefferson's."

Sir Henry said grimly, "I've been sent for, urgently, to get at the truth. I mean to do my utmost." He added, "Where do you want Miss Marple to help you?"

"With some girls. Some of those Girl Guides. We've rounded up half a dozen or so—the ones who were most friendly with Pamela Reeves. It's possible that they may know something. You see, I've been thinking. It seems to me that if that girl was going to Woolworth's she would have tried to persuade one of the other girls to go with her. So I think it's possible that Woolworth's was only an excuse. If so, I'd like to know where the girl was really going. She may have let slip something. If so, I feel Miss Marple's the person to get it out of these girls. I'd say she knows a thing or two about girls."

"It sounds to me the kind of village domestic problem that is right up Miss Marple's street. She's very sharp, you know."

The superintendent smiled. He said, "I'll say you're right. Nothing much gets past her."

Miss Marple looked up at their approach and welcomed them eagerly. She listened to the superintendent's request and at once acquiesced.

"I should like to help you very much, superintendent, and I think that perhaps I could be of some use. What with the Sunday school, you know, and Brownies and our Guides, and the orphanage quite near—I'm on the committee, you know, and often run in to have a little talk with the matron—and then servants—I usually have very young maids. Oh, yes, I've quite a lot of experience in when a girl is speaking the truth and when she's holding something back."

"In fact, you're an expert," said Sir Henry.

Miss Marple flashed him a reproachful glance and said, "Oh, please don't laugh at me, Sir Henry."

"I shouldn't dream of laughing at you. You've had the laugh on me too many times."

"One does see so much evil in a village," murmured Miss Marple in an explanatory voice.

"By the way," said Sir Henry, "I've cleared up one point you asked me about. The superintendent tells me that there were nail clippings in Ruby's wastepaper basket."

Miss Marple said thoughtfully, "There were? Then that's that—"

"Why did you want to know, Miss Marple?" asked the superintendent.

Miss Marple said, "It was one of the things that—well, that seemed wrong when I looked at the body. The hands were wrong somehow, and I couldn't at first think why. Then I realized that girls who are very much made up, and all that, usually have very long fingernails. Of course, I know that girls everywhere do bite their nails; it's one of those habits that are very hard to break oneself of. But vanity often does a lot to help. Still, I presumed that this girl hadn't cured herself. And then the little boy—Peter, you know—he said something which showed that her nails had been long, only she caught one and broke it. So then, of course, she might have trimmed off the rest to make an even appearance, and I asked about clippings and Sir Henry said he'd find out."

Sir Henry remarked, "You said just now 'one of the things that seemed wrong when I looked at the body.' Was there something else?"

Miss Marple nodded vigorously. "Oh, yes!" she said. "There was the dress. The dress was all wrong."

Both men looked at her curiously.

"Now, why?" said Sir Henry.

"Well, you see, it was an old dress. Josie said so, definitely, and I could see for myself that it was shabby and rather worn. Now, that's all wrong."

"I don't see why."

Miss Marple got a little pink. "Well, the idea is, isn't it, that Ruby Keene changed her dress and went off to meet someone on whom she presumably had what my young nephews call a 'crush'?"

The superintendent's eyes twinkled a little. "That's the theory. She'd got a date with someone—a boy friend, as the saying goes."

"Then why," demanded Miss Marple, "was she wearing an old dress?"

The superintendent scratched his head thoughtfully. He said, "I see your point. You think she'd wear a new one?"

"I think she'd wear her best dress. Girls do."

Sir Henry interposed, "Yes, but look here, Miss Marple. Suppose she was going outside to this rendezvous. Going in an open car, perhaps, or walking in some rough going. Then she'd not want to risk messing a new frock and she'd put on an old one."

"That would be the sensible thing to do," agreed the superintendent.

Miss Marple turned on him. She spoke with animation, "The sensible thing to do would be to change into trousers and a pullover, or into tweeds. That, of course—I don't want to be snobbish, but I'm afraid it's unavoidable—that's what a girl of—of our class would do.

"A well-bred girl," continued Miss Marple, warming to her subject, "is always very particular to wear the right clothes for the right occasion. I mean, however hot the day was, a well-bred girl would never turn up at a point-to-point in a silk flowered frock."

"And the correct wear to meet a lover?" demanded Sir Henry.

"If she were meeting him inside the hotel or somewhere where evening dress was worn, she'd wear her best evening frock, of course, but outside she'd feel she'd look ridiculous in evening dress and she'd wear her most attractive sports wear."

"Granted, Fashion Queen, but the girl Ruby—"

Miss Marple said, "Ruby, of course, wasn't—well, to put it bluntly, Ruby wasn't a lady. She belonged to the class that wear their best clothes, however unsuitable to the occasion. Last year, you know, we had a picnic outing at Scrantor Rocks. You'd be surprised at the unsuitable clothes the girls wore. Foulard dresses and patent-leather shoes and quite elaborate hats, some of them. For climbing about over rocks and in gorse and heather. And the young men in their best suits. Of course, hiking's different again. That's practically a uniform, and girls don't seem to realize that shorts are very unbecoming unless they are very slender."

The superintendent said slowly, "And you think that Ruby Keene—"

"I think that she'd have kept on the frock she was wearing—her best pink one. She'd only have changed it if she'd had something newer still."

Superintendent Harper said, "And what's your explanation, Miss Marple?"

Miss Marple said, "I haven't got one—yet. But I can't help feeling that it's important."

XVI

INSIDE THE WIRE cage, the tennis lesson that Raymond Starr was giving had come to an end. A stout middle-aged woman uttered a few appreciative squeaks, picked up a sky-blue cardigan and went off toward the hotel. Raymond called out a few gay words after her. Then he turned toward the bench where the three onlookers were sitting. The balls dangled in a net in his hand, his racket was under one arm. The gay, laughing expression on his face was wiped off as though by a sponge from a slate. He looked tired and worried.

Coming toward them he said, "That's over."

Then the smile broke out again, that charming, boyish, expressive smile that went so harmoniously with his sun-tanned face and dark, lithe grace.

Sir Henry found himself wondering how old the man was. Twenty-five, thirty, thirty-five? It was impossible to say.

Raymond said, shaking his head a little, "She'll never be able to play, you know."

"All this must," said Miss Marple, "be very boring for you."

Raymond said simply, "It is sometimes. Especially at the end of the summer. For a time the thought of the pay buoys one up, but even that fails to stimulate imagination in the end."

Superintendent Harper got up. He said abruptly, "I'll call for you in half an hour's time, Miss Marple, if that will be all right?"

"Perfectly, thank you. I shall be ready."

Harper went off. Raymond stood looking after him. Then he said, "Mind if I sit here for a bit?"

"Do," said Sir Henry. "Have a cigarette?" He offered his case, wondering as he did so why he had a slight feeling of prejudice against Raymond Starr. Was it simply because he was a professional tennis coach and dancer? If so, it wasn't the tennis, it was the dancing. The English, Sir Henry decided, had a distrust for any man who danced too well. This fellow moved with too much grace. Ramon—Raymond—which was his name? Abruptly, he asked the question.

The other seemed amused.

"Ramon was my original professional name. Ramon and Josie—Spanish effect, you know. Then there was rather a prejudice against foreigners, so I became Raymond—very British."

Miss Marple said, "And is your real name something quite different?"

He smiled at her. "Actually my real name is Ramon. I had an Argentine grandmother, you see." And that accounts for that swing from the hips, thought Sir Henry parenthetically. "But my first name is Thomas. Painfully prosaic."

He turned to Sir Henry. "You come from Devonshire, don't you, sir? From Stane? My people lived down that way. At Alsmonston."

Sir Henry's face lit up. "Are you one of the Alsmonston Starrs? I didn't realize that."

"No, I don't suppose you would." There was a slight bitterness in his voice.

Sir Henry said, "Bad luck—er—all that."

"The place being sold up after it had been in the family for three hundred years? Yes, it was rather! Still, our kind have to go, I suppose! We've outlived our usefulness. My elder brother went to New York. He's in publishing—doing well. The rest of us are scattered up and down the earth. I'll say it's hard to get a job nowadays when you've nothing to say for yourself except that you've had a public-school education. Sometimes, if you're lucky, you get taken on as a reception clerk at a hotel. The tie and the manner are an asset there. The only job I could get was showman in a plumbing establishment. Selling superb peach and lemon colored porcelain baths. Enormous showrooms, but as I never knew the price of the damned things or how soon we could deliver them, I got fired.

"The only things I could do were dance and play tennis. I got taken on at a hotel on the Riviera. Good pickings there. I suppose I was doing well. Then I overheard an old colonel—real old colonel, incredibly ancient, British to the backbone and always talking about Poona. He went up to the manager and said at the top of his voice: 'Where's the gigolo? I want to get hold of the gigolo. My wife and daughter want to dance, yer know. Where is the feller? What does he sting yer for? It's the gigolo I want.' "

Raymond said, "Silly to mind. But I did. I chucked it. Came here. Less pay, but pleasanter. Mostly teaching tennis to rotund women who will never, never be able to play. That and dancing with the wallflower daughters of rich clients! Oh, well, it's life, I suppose. Excuse today's hard-luck story."

He laughed. His teeth flashed out white, his eyes crinkled up at the corners. He looked suddenly healthy and happy and very much alive.

Sir Henry said, "I'm glad to have a chat with you. I've been wanting to talk with you."

"About Ruby Keene? I can't help you, you know. I don't know who killed her. I knew very little about her. She didn't confide in me."

Miss Marple said, "Did you like her?"

"Not particularly. I didn't dislike her." His voice was careless, uninterested.

Sir Henry said, "So you've no suggestions?"

"I'm afraid not. I'd have told Harper if I had. It just seems to me one of those things! Petty, sordid little crime, no clues, no motive."

"Two people had a motive," said Miss Marple.

Sir Henry looked at her sharply.

"Really?" Raymond looked surprised.

Miss Marple looked insistently at Sir Henry, and he said rather unwillingly, "Her death probably benefits Mrs. Jefferson and Mr. Gaskell to the amount of fifty thousand pounds."

"What?" Raymond looked really startled—more than startled, upset. "Oh, but that's absurd—absolutely absurd. Mrs. Jefferson—neither of them—could have had anything to do with it. It would be incredible to think of such a thing."

Miss Marple coughed. She said gently, "I'm afraid, you know, you're rather an idealist."

"I?" He laughed. "Not me! I'm a hard-boiled cynic."

"Money," said Miss Marple, "is a very powerful motive."

"Perhaps," Raymond said hotly. "But that either of those two would strangle a girl in cold blood—" He shook his head. Then he got up. "Here's Mrs. Jefferson now. Come for her lesson. She's late." His voice sounded amused. "Ten minutes late!"

Adelaide Jefferson and Hugo McLean were walking rapidly down the path toward them.

With a smiling apology for her lateness, Addie Jefferson went onto the court. McLean sat down on the bench. After a polite inquiry whether Miss Marple minded a pipe, he lit it and puffed for some minutes in silence, watching critically the two white figures about the tennis court.

He said at last, "Can't see what Addie wants to have lessons for. Have a game, yes. No one enjoys it better than I do. But why lessons?"

"Wants to improve her game," said Sir Henry.

"She's not a bad player," said Hugo. "Good enough, at all events. Dash it all, she isn't aiming to play at Wimbledon." He was silent for a minute or two. Then he said, "Who is this Raymond fellow? Where do they come from, these pros? Fellow looks like a Dago to me."

"He's one of the Devonshire Starrs," said Sir Henry.

"What? Not really?"

Sir Henry nodded. It was clear that this news was unpleasing to Hugo McLean. He scowled more than ever.

He said, "Don't know why Addie sent for me. She seems not to have turned a hair over this business. Never looked better. Why send for me?"

Sir Henry asked with some curiosity, "When did she send for you?"

"Oh—er—when all this happened."

"How did you hear? Telephone or telegram?"

"Telegram."

"As a matter of curiosity, when was it sent off?"

"Well, I don't know exactly."

"What time did you receive it?"

"I didn't exactly receive it. It was telephoned on to me, as a matter of fact."

"Why, where were you?"

"Fact is, I'd left London the afternoon before. I was staying at Danebury Head."

"What? Quite near here?"

"Yes, rather funny, wasn't it? Got the message when I got in from a round of golf and came over here at once."

Miss Marple gazed at him thoughtfully. He looked hot and uncomfortable. She said, "I've heard it's very pleasant at Danebury Head and not very expensive."

"No, it's not expensive. I couldn't afford it if it was. It's a nice little place."

"We must drive over there one day," said Miss Marple.

"Eh? What? Oh—er—yes, I should." He got up. "Better take some exercise, get an appetite." He walked away stiffly.

"Women," said Sir Henry, "treat their devoted admirers very badly."

Miss Marple smiled, but made no answer.

"Does he strike you as rather a dull dog?" asked Sir Henry. "I'd be interested to know."

"A little limited in his ideas, perhaps," said Miss Marple. "But with possibilities, I think—oh, definitely possibilities."

Sir Henry, in his turn, got up. "It's time for me to go and do my stuff. I see Mrs. Bantry is on her way to keep you company."

Mrs. Bantry arrived breathless and sat down with a gasp. She said, "I've been talking to chambermaids. But it isn't any good. I haven't found out a thing more! Do you think that girl can really have been carrying on with someone without everybody in the hotel knowing all about it?"

"That's a very interesting point, dear. I should say definitely not. Somebody knows, depend upon it, if it's true. But she must have been very clever about it."

Mrs. Bantry's attention had strayed to the tennis court. She said approvingly, "Addie's tennis is coming on a lot. Attractive young man, that tennis pro. Addie's quite nice-looking. She's still an attractive woman. I shouldn't be at all surprised if she married again."

"She'll be quite a rich woman, too, when Mr. Jefferson dies," said Miss Marple.

"Oh, don't always have such a nasty mind, Jane. Why haven't you solved this mystery yet? We don't seem to be getting on at all. I thought you'd know at once." Mrs. Bantry's tone held reproach.

"No, no, dear, I didn't know at once—not for some time."

Mrs. Bantry turned startled and incredulous eyes on her. "You mean you know now who killed Ruby Keene?"

"Oh, yes," said Miss Marple. "I know that!"

"But, Jane, who is it? Tell me at once."

Miss Marple shook her head very firmly and pursed up her lips. "I'm sorry, Dolly, but that wouldn't do at all."

"Why wouldn't it do?"

"Because you're so indiscreet. You would go round telling everyone—or if you didn't tell, you'd hint."

"No, indeed, I wouldn't. I wouldn't tell a soul."

"People who use that phrase are always the last to live up to it. It's no good, dear. There's a long way to go yet. A great many things that are quite obscure. You remember when I was so against letting Mrs. Partridge collect for the Red Cross and I couldn't say why. The reason was that her nose had twitched in just the same way that that maid of mine,

Alice, twitched her nose when I sent her out to pay the accounts. Always paid them a shilling or so short and said it could go on to next week, which, of course, was exactly what Mrs. Partridge did, only on a much larger scale. Seventy-five pounds it was she embezzled."

"Never mind Mrs. Partridge," said Mrs. Bantry.

"But I had to explain to you. And if you care, I'll give you a hint. The trouble in this case is that everybody has been much too credulous and believing. You simply cannot afford to believe everything that people tell you. When there's anything fishy about, I never believe anyone at all. You see, I know human nature so well."

Mrs. Bantry was silent for a minute or two. Then she said in a different tone of voice, "I told you, didn't I, that I didn't see why I shouldn't enjoy myself over this case? A real murder in my own house! The sort of thing that will never happen again."

"I hope not," said Miss Marple.

"Well, so do I really. Once is enough. But it's my murder, Jane. I want to enjoy myself over it."

Miss Marple shot a glance at her.

Mrs. Bantry said belligerently, "Don't you believe that?"

Miss Marple said sweetly, "Of course, Dolly, if you tell me so."

"Yes, but you never believe what people tell you, do you? You've just said so. Well, you're quite right." Mrs. Bantry's voice took on a sudden bitter note. She said, "I'm not altogether a fool. You may think, Jane, that I don't know what they're saying all over St. Mary Mead—all over the county! They're saying, one and all, that there's no smoke without fire; that if the girl was found in Arthur's library, then Arthur must know something about it. They're saying that the girl was Arthur's mistress; that she was his illegitimate daughter; that she was blackmailing him; they're saying anything that comes into their heads. And it will go on like that! Arthur won't realize it at first; he won't know what's wrong. He's such a dear old stupid that he'd never believe people would think things like that about him. He'll be cold-shouldered and looked at askance —whatever that means!—and it will dawn on him little by little, and suddenly he'll be horrified and cut to the soul, and he'll fasten up like a clam and just endure, day after day.

"It's because of all that's going to happen to him that I've come here to ferret out every single thing about it that I can! This murder's got to be solved! If it isn't, then Arthur's whole life will be wrecked, and I won't have that happen. I won't! I won't! I won't!" She paused for a minute and said, "I won't have the dear old boy go through hell for something he didn't do. That's the only reason I came to Danemouth and left him alone at home—to find out the truth."

"I know, dear," said Miss Marple. "That's why I'm here too."

XVII

In a quiet hotel room Edwards was listening deferentially to Sir Henry Clithering.

"There are certain questions I would like to ask you, Edwards, but I want you first to understand quite clearly my position here. I was at one time commissioner of the police at Scotland Yard. I am now retired into private life. Your master sent for me when this tragedy occurred. He begged me to use my skill and experience in order to find out the truth."

Sir Henry paused.

Edwards, his pale, intelligent eyes on the other's face, inclined his head. He said, "Quite so, Sir Henry."

Clithering went on slowly and deliberately, "In all police cases there is necessarily a lot of information that is held back. It is held back for various reasons—because it touches on a family skeleton, because it is considered to have no bearing on the case, because it would entail awkwardness and embarrassment to the parties concerned."

Again Edwards said, "Quite so, Sir Henry."

"I expect, Edwards, that by now you appreciate quite clearly the main points of this business. The dead girl was on the point of becoming Mr. Jefferson's adopted daughter. Two people had a motive in seeing that this should not happen. Those two people are Mr. Gaskell and Mrs. Jefferson."

The valet's eyes displayed a momentary gleam. He said, "May I ask if they are under suspicion, sir?"

"They are in no danger of arrest, if that is what you mean. But the police are bound to be suspicious of them and will continue to be so until the matter is cleared up."

"An unpleasant position for them, sir."

"Very unpleasant. Now to get at the truth, one must have all the facts of the case. A lot depends, must depend, on the reactions, the words and gestures, of Mr. Jefferson and his family. How did they feel, what did they show, what things were said? I am asking you, Edwards, for inside information—the kind of inside information that only you are likely to have. You know your master's moods. From observation of them you probably know what caused them. I am asking this, not as a policeman but as a friend of Mr. Jefferson's. That is to say, if anything you tell me is not, in my opinion, relevant to the case, I shall not pass it on to the police." He paused.

Edwards said quietly, "I understand you, sir. You want me to speak quite frankly; to say things that, in the ordinary course of events, I should not say, and that—excuse me, sir—you wouldn't dream of listening to."

Sir Henry said, "You're a very intelligent fellow, Edwards. That's exactly what I do mean."

Edwards was silent for a minute or two, then he began to speak. "Of course I know Mr. Jefferson fairly well by now. I've been with him quite a number of years. And I see him in his 'off' moments, not only in his 'on' ones. Sometimes, sir, I've questioned in my own mind whether it's good for anyone to fight fate in the way Mr. Jefferson has fought. It's taken a terrible toll of him, sir. If, sometimes, he could have given way, been an unhappy, lonely, broken old man—well, it might have been better for him in the end. But he's too proud for that! He'll go down fighting—that's his motto.

"But that sort of thing leads, Sir Henry, to a lot of nervous reaction. He looks a good-tempered gentleman. I've seen him in violent rages when he could hardly speak for passion. And the one thing that roused him, sir, was deceit."

"Are you saying that for any particular reason, Edwards?"

"Yes, sir, I am. You asked me, sir, to speak quite frankly."

"That is the idea."

"Well, then, Sir Henry, in my opinion the young woman that Mr. Jefferson was so taken up with wasn't worth it. She was, to put it bluntly, a common little piece. And she didn't care tuppence for Mr. Jefferson. All that play of affection and gratitude was so much poppycock. I don't say there was any harm in her, but she wasn't, by a long way, what Mr. Jefferson thought her. It was funny, that, sir, for Mr. Jefferson was a shrewd gentleman; he wasn't often deceived over people. But there, a gentleman isn't himself in his judgment when it comes to a young woman being in question. Young Mrs. Jefferson, you see, whom he'd always depended upon a lot for sympathy, had changed a good deal this summer. He noticed it and he felt it badly. He was fond of her, you see. Mr. Mark he never liked much."

Sir Henry interjected, "And yet he had him with him constantly?"

"Yes, but that was for Miss Rosamund's sake. Mrs. Gaskell, that was. She was the apple of his eye. He adored her. Mr. Mark was Miss Rosamund's husband. He always thought of him like that."

"Supposing Mr. Mark had married someone else?"

"Mr. Jefferson, sir, would have been furious."

Sir Henry raised his eyebrows. "As much as that?"

"He wouldn't have shown it, but that's what it would have been."

"And if Mrs. Jefferson had married again?"

"Mr. Jefferson wouldn't have liked that either, sir."

"Please go on, Edwards."

"I was saying, sir, that Mr. Jefferson fell for this young woman. I've often seen it happen with the gentlemen I've been with. Comes over them like a kind of disease. They want to protect the girl, and shield her, and shower benefits upon her, and nine times out of ten the girl is very well able to look after herself and has a good eye to the main chance."

"So you think Ruby Keene was a schemer?"

"Well, Sir Henry, she was quite inexperienced, being so young, but she had the makings of a very fine schemer indeed when she'd once got well into her swing, so to speak. In another five years she'd have been an expert at the game."

Sir Henry said, "I'm glad to have your opinion of her. It's valuable. Now, do you recall any incidents in which this matter was discussed between Mr. Jefferson and the members of his family?"

"There was very little discussion, sir. Mr. Jefferson announced what he had in mind and stifled any protests. That is, he shut up Mr. Mark, who was a bit outspoken. Mrs. Jefferson didn't say much—she's a quiet lady—only urged him not to do anything in a great hurry."

Sir Henry nodded. "Anything else? What was the girl's attitude?"

With marked distaste the valet said, "I should describe it, Sir Henry, as jubilant."

"Ah, jubilant, you say? You had no reason to believe, Edwards, that"—he sought about for a phrase suitable to Edwards—"that—er—her affections were engaged elsewhere?"

"Mr. Jefferson was not proposing marriage, sir. He was going to adopt her."

"Cut out the 'elsewhere' and let the question stand."

The valet said slowly, "There was one incident, sir. I happened to be a witness of it."

"That is gratifying. Tell me."

"There is probably nothing in it, sir. It was just that one day, the young woman chancing to open her handbag, a small snapshot fell out. Mr. Jefferson pounced on it and said, 'Hullo, kitten, who's this, eh?'

"It was a snapshot, sir, of a young man, a dark young man with rather untidy hair, and his tie very badly arranged.

"Miss Keene pretended that she didn't know anything about it. She said, 'I've no idea, Jeffie. No idea at all. I don't know how it could have got into my bag. I didn't put it there.'

"Now, Mr. Jefferson, sir, wasn't quite a fool. That story wasn't good enough. He looked angry, his brows came down heavy, and his voice was gruff when he said, 'Now then, kitten, now then. You know who it is right enough.'

"She changed her tactics quick, sir. Looked frightened. She said, 'I do recognize him now. He comes here sometimes and I've danced with him. I don't know his name. The silly idiot must have stuffed his photo into my bag one day. These boys are too silly for anything!' She tossed her head and giggled and passed it off. But it wasn't a likely story, was it? And I don't think Mr. Jefferson quite believed it. He looked at her once or twice after that in a sharp way, and sometimes, if she'd been out, he asked her where she'd been."

Sir Henry said, "Have you ever seen the original of the photo about the hotel?"

"Not to my knowledge, sir. Of course I am not much downstairs in the public apartments."

Sir Henry nodded. He asked a few more questions, but Edwards could tell him nothing more.

In the police station at Danemouth Superintendent Harper was interviewing Jessie Davis, Florence Small, Beatrice Henniker, Mary Price and Lilian Ridgeway.

They were girls much of an age, differing slightly in mentality. They ranged from "county" to farmers' and shopkeepers' daughters. One and all, they told the same story. Pamela Reeves had been just the same as usual; she had said nothing to any of them except that she was going to Woolworth's and would go home by a later bus.

In the corner of Superintendent Harper's office sat an elderly lady. The girls hardly noticed her. If they did they may have wondered who she was. She was certainly no police matron. Possibly they assumed that she, like them, was a witness to be questioned.

The last girl was shown out. Superintendent Harper wiped his forehead and turned round to look at Miss Marple. His glance was inquiring, but not hopeful.

Miss Marple, however, spoke crisply, "I'd like to speak to Florence Small."

The superintendent's eyebrows rose, but he nodded and touched a bell. A constable appeared.

Harper said, "Florence Small."

The girl reappeared, ushered in by the constable. She was the daughter of a well-to-do farmer—a tall girl with fair hair, a rather foolish mouth and frightened brown eyes. She was twisting her hands and looked nervous.

Superintendent Harper looked at Miss Marple, who nodded.

The superintendent got up. He said, "This lady will ask you some questions."

He went out, closing the door behind him.

Florence looked uneasily at Miss Marple. Her eyes looked rather like those of one of her father's calves.

Miss Marple said, "Sit down, Florence."

Florence Small sat down obediently. Unrecognized by herself, she felt suddenly more at home, less uneasy. The unfamiliar and terrorizing atmosphere of a police station was replaced by something more familiar—the accustomed tone of command of somebody whose business it was to give orders.

Miss Marple said, "You understand, Florence, that it's of the utmost importance that everything about poor Pamela's doings on the day of her death should be known?"

Florence murmured that she quite understood.

"And I'm sure you want to do your best to help?"

Florence's eyes were wary as she said of course she did.

"To keep back any piece of information is a very serious offense," said Miss Marple.

The girl's fingers twisted nervously in her lap. She swallowed once or twice.

"I can make allowances," went on Miss Marple, "for the fact that you are naturally alarmed at being brought into contact with the police. You are afraid, too, that you may be blamed for not having spoken sooner. Possibly you are afraid that you may also be blamed for not stopping Pamela at the time. But you've got to be a brave girl and make a clean breast of things. If you refuse to tell what you know now, it will be a very serious matter indeed—very serious—practically perjury—and for that, as you know, you can be sent to prison."

"I—I don't—"

Miss Marple said sharply, "Now don't prevaricate, Florence! Tell me all about it at once! Pamela wasn't going to Woolworth's, was she?"

Florence licked her lips with a dry tongue and gazed imploringly at Miss Marple, like a beast about to be slaughtered.

"Something to do with the films, wasn't it?" asked Miss Marple.

A look of intense relief mingled with awe passed over Florence's face. Her inhibitions left her. She gasped, "Oh, yes!"

"I thought so," said Miss Marple. "Now I want you to tell me all the details, please."

Words poured from Florence in a gush.

"Oh, I've been ever so worried. I promised Pam, you see, I'd never say a word to a soul. And then, when she was found, all burned up in that car—oh, it was horrible and I thought I should die—I felt it was all my fault. I ought to have stopped her. Only I never thought, not for a minute, that it wasn't all right. And then I was asked if she'd been quite as usual that day and I said 'Yes' before I'd had time to think. And not having said anything then, I didn't see how I could say anything later. And after all, I didn't know anything—not really—only what Pam told me."

"What did Pam tell you?"

"It was as we were walking up the lane to the bus on the way to the rally. She asked me if I could keep a secret, and I said yes, and she made me swear not to tell. She was going into Danemouth for a film test after the rally! She'd met a film producer—just back from Hollywood, he was. He wanted a certain type, and he told Pam she was just what he was looking for. He warned her, though, not to build on it. You couldn't tell, he said, not until you saw how a person photographed. It might be no good at all. It was a kind of Bergner part, he said. You had to have someone quite young for it. A schoolgirl, it was, who changes places with a revue artist and has a wonderful career. Pam's acted in plays at school and she's awfully good. He said he could see she could act, but she'd have to have some intensive training. It wouldn't be all beer and skittles, he told her; it would be hard work. Did she think she could stick it?"

Florence Small stopped for breath. Miss Marple felt rather sick as she listened to the glib rehash of countless novels and screen stories. Pamela Reeves, like most other girls, would have been warned against talking to strangers, but the glamour of the films would have obliterated all that.

"He was absolutely businesslike about it all," continued Florence. "Said if the test was successful she'd have a contract, and he said that as she was young and inexperienced she ought to let a lawyer look at it before she signed it. But she wasn't to pass on that he'd said that. He asked her if she'd have trouble with her parents, and Pam said she probably would, and he said, 'Well, of course that's always a difficulty with anyone as young as you are, but I think if it was put to them that this was a wonderful chance that wouldn't happen once in a million times, they'd see reason.' But anyway, he said, it wasn't any good going into that until they knew the result of the test. She mustn't be disappointed if it failed. He told her about Hollywood and about Vivien Leigh—how she'd suddenly taken London by storm, and how these sensational leaps into fame did happen. He himself had come back from America to work with the Lenville Studios and put some pep into the English film companies."

Miss Marple nodded.

Florence went on, "So it was all arranged. Pam was to go into Danemouth after the rally and meet him at his hotel and he'd take her along to the studios—they'd got a small testing studio in Danemouth, he told her. She'd have her test and she could catch the bus home afterward. She could say she'd been shopping, and he'd let her know the result of the test in a few days, and if it was favorable Mr. Harmsteiter, the boss, would come along and talk to her parents.

"Well, of course, it sounded too wonderful! I was green with envy! Pam got through the rally without turning a hair—we always call her a regular poker face. Then, when she said that she was going into Danemouth to Woolworth's, she just winked at me.

"I saw her start off down the footpath." Florence began to cry. "I ought to have stopped her! I ought to have stopped her! I ought to have known a thing like that couldn't be true! I ought to have told someone! Oh, dear, I wish I was dead!"

"There, there." Miss Marple patted her on the shoulder. "It's quite all right. No one will blame you, Florence. You've done the right thing in telling me."

She devoted some minutes to cheering the child up.

Five minutes later she was telling the girl's story to Superintendent Harper.

The latter looked very grim. "The clever devil!" he said. "I'll cook his goose for him! This puts rather a different aspect on things."

"Yes, it does."

Harper looked at her sideways. "It doesn't surprise you?"

"I expected something of the kind," Miss Marple said.

Superintendent Harper said curiously, "What put you on to this particular girl? They all looked scared to death and there wasn't a pin to choose between them, as far as I could see."

Miss Marple said gently, "You haven't had as much experience with girls telling lies as I have. Florence looked at you very straight, if you remember, and stood very rigid and just fidgeted with her feet like the others. But you didn't watch her as she went out of the door. I knew at once then that she'd got something to hide. They nearly always relax too soon. My little maid Janet always did. She'd explain quite convincingly that the mice had eaten the end of a cake and give herself away by smirking as she left the room."

"I'm very grateful to you," said Harper. He added thoughtfully, "Lenville Studios, eh?"

Miss Marple said nothing. She rose to her feet.

"I'm afraid," she said, "I must hurry away. So glad to have been able to help you."

"Are you going back to the hotel?"

"Yes, to pack up. I must go back to St. Mary Mead as soon as possible. There's a lot for me to do there."

XVIII

Miss Marple passed out through the French windows of her drawing room, tripped down her neat garden path, through a garden gate, in through the vicarage garden gate, across the vicarage garden and up to the drawing-room window, where she tapped gently on the pane.

The vicar was busy in his study composing his Sunday sermon, but the vicar's wife, who was young and pretty, was admiring the progress of her offspring across the hearthrug.

"Can I come in, Griselda?"

"Oh, do, Miss Marple. Just look at David! He gets so angry because he can only crawl in reverse. He wants to get to something, and the more he tries the more he goes backwards into the coalbox!"

"He's looking very bonny, Griselda."

"He's not bad, is he?" said the young mother, endeavoring to assume an indifferent manner. "Of course I don't bother with him much. All the books say a child should be left alone as much as possible."

"Very wise, dear," said Miss Marple. "Ahem–I came to ask if there was anything special you are collecting for at the moment?"

The vicar's wife turned somewhat astonished eyes upon her. "Oh, heaps of things," she said cheerfully. "There always are." She ticked them off on her fingers. "There's the Nave Restoration Fund, and St. Giles' Mission, and our Sale of Work next Wednesday, and the Unmarried Mothers, and a Boy Scouts Outing, and the Needlework Guild, and the Bishop's Appeal for Deep-Sea Fishermen."

"Any of them will do," said Miss Marple. "I thought I might make a little round–with a book, you know–if you would authorize me to do so."

"Are you up to something? I believe you are. Of course I authorize you. Make it the Sale of Work; it would be lovely to get some real money instead of those awful sachets and comic penwipers and depressing children's frocks and dusters all done up to look like dolls. . . . I suppose," continued Griselda, accompanying her guest to the window, "that you wouldn't like to tell me what it's all about?"

"Later, my dear," said Miss Marple, hurrying off.

With a sigh the young mother returned to the hearthrug and, by way of carrying out her principles of stern neglect, butted her son three times in the stomach, so that he caught hold of her hair and pulled it with gleeful yells. They then rolled over and over in a grand rough and tumble until the door opened and the vicarage maid announced to the most influential parishioner, who didn't like children, "Missus is in here."

Whereupon Griselda sat up and tried to look dignified and more what a vicar's wife should be.

Miss Marple, clasping a small black book with penciled entries in it, walked briskly along the village street until she came to the crossroads. Here she turned to the left and walked past the Blue Boar until she came to Chatsworth, alias "Mr. Booker's new house."

She turned in at the gate, walked up to the front door and knocked on it briskly.

The door was opened by the blond young woman named Dinah Lee. She was less carefully made up than usual and, in fact, looked slightly dirty. She was wearing gray slacks and an emerald jumper.

"Good morning," said Miss Marple briskly and cheerfully. "May I just come in for a minute?"

She pressed forward as she spoke, so that Dinah Lee, who was somewhat taken aback at the call, had no time to make up her mind.

"Thank you so much," said Miss Marple, beaming amiably at her and sitting down rather gingerly on a period bamboo chair. "Quite warm for the time of year, is it not?" went on Miss Marple, still exuding geniality.

"Yes, rather. Oh, quite," said Miss Lee.

At a loss how to deal with the situation, she opened a box and offered it to her guest.

"Er—have a cigarette?"

"Thank you so much, but I don't smoke. I just called, you know, to see if I could enlist your help for our Sale of Work next week."

"Sale of Work?" said Dinah Lee, as one who repeats a phrase in a foreign language.

"At the vicarage," said Miss Marple. "Next Wednesday."

"Oh!" Miss Lee's mouth fell open. "I'm afraid I couldn't—"

"Not even a small subscription—half a crown perhaps?" Miss Marple exhibited her little book.

"Oh—er—well, yes, I dare say I could manage that." The girl looked relieved and turned to hunt in her handbag.

Miss Marple's sharp eyes were looking round the room. She said, "I see you've no hearthrug in front of the fire."

Dinah Lee turned round and stared at her. She could not but be aware of the very keen scrutiny the old lady was giving her, but it aroused in her no other emotion than slight annoyance.

Miss Marple recognized that. She said, "It's rather dangerous, you know. Sparks fly out and mark the carpet."

Funny old tabby, thought Dinah, but she said quite amiably, if somewhat vaguely, "There used to be one. I don't know where it's got to."

"I suppose," said Miss Marple, "it was the fluffy woolly kind?"

"Sheep," said Dinah. "That's what it looked like." She was amused now. An eccentric old bean, this. She held out a half crown. "Here you are," she said.

"Oh, thank you, my dear." Miss Marple took it and opened the little book. "Er—what name shall I write down?"

Dinah's eyes grew suddenly hard and contemptuous. Nosy old cat, she thought. That's all she came for—prying around for scandal.

She said clearly and with malicious pleasure, "Miss Dinah Lee."

Miss Marple looked at her steadily. She said, "This is Mr. Basil Blake's cottage, isn't it?"

"Yes, and I'm Miss Dinah Lee!" Her voice rang out challengingly, her head went back, her blue eyes flashed.

Very steadily Miss Marple looked at her. She said, "Will you allow me to give you some advice, even though you may consider it impertinent?"

"I shall consider it impertinent. You had better say nothing."

"Nevertheless," said Miss Marple, "I am going to speak. I want to advise you, very strongly, not to continue using your maiden name in the village."

Dinah stared at her. She said, "What—what do you mean?"

Miss Marple said earnestly, "In a very short time you may need all the sympathy and good will you can find. It will be important to your husband, too, that he shall be thought well of. There is a prejudice in old-fashioned country districts against people living together who are not married. It has amused you both, I dare say, to pretend that that is what you are doing. It kept people away, so that you weren't bothered with what I expect you would call 'old frumps.' Nevertheless, old frumps have their uses."

Dinah demanded, "How did you know we are married?"

Miss Marple smiled a deprecating smile. "Oh, my dear," she said.

Dinah persisted, "No, but how did you know? You didn't—you didn't go to Somerset House?"

A momentary flicker showed in Miss Marple's eyes. "Somerset House? Oh, no. But it was quite easy to guess. Everything, you know, gets round in a village. The—er—the kind of quarrels you have—typical of early days of marriage. Quite—quite unlike an illicit relationship. It has been said, you know—and I think quite truly—that you can only really get under anybody's skin if you are married to them. When there is no—no legal bond, people are much more careful; they have to keep assuring themselves how happy and halcyon everything is. They have, you see, to justify themselves. They dare not quarrel! Married people, I have noticed, quite enjoy their battles and the—er—appropriate reconciliations." She paused, twinkling benignly.

"Well, I—" Dinah stopped and laughed. She sat down and lit a cigarette. "You're absolutely marvelous!" she said. Then she went on, "But why do you want us to own up and admit to respectability?"

Miss Marple's face was grave now. She said, "Because any minute now your husband may be arrested for murder."

XIX

For an interval Dinah stared at Miss Marple. Then she said incredulously, "Basil? Murder? Are you joking?"

"No, indeed. Haven't you seen the papers?"

Dinah caught her breath. "You mean that girl at the Majestic Hotel. Do you mean they suspect Basil of killing her?"

"Yes."

"But it's nonsense!"

There was the whir of a car outside, the bang of a gate. Basil Blake flung open the door and came in, carrying some bottles. He said, "Got the gin and the vermouth. Did you—" He stopped and turned incredulous eyes on the prim, erect visitor.

Dinah burst out breathlessly, "Is she mad? She says you're going to be arrested for the murder of that girl Ruby Keene."

"Oh, God!" said Basil Blake. The bottles dropped from his arms onto the sofa. He reeled to a chair and dropped down in it and buried his face in his hands. He repeated, "Oh, my God! Oh, my God!"

Dinah darted over to him. She caught his shoulders. "Basil, look at me! It isn't true! I know it isn't true! I don't believe it for a moment!"

His hand went up and gripped hers. "Bless you, darling."

"But why should they think— You didn't even know her, did you?"

"Oh, yes, he knew her," said Miss Marple.

Basil said fiercely, "Be quiet, you old hag! . . . Listen, Dinah, darling. I hardly knew her at all. Just ran across her once or twice at the Majestic. That's all—I swear that's all!"

Dinah said, bewildered, "I don't understand. Why should anyone suspect you, then?"

Basil groaned. He put his hands over his eyes and rocked to and fro.

Miss Marple said, "What did you do with the hearthrug?"

His reply came mechanically, "I put it in the dustbin."

Miss Marple clucked her tongue vexedly. "That was stupid—very stupid. People don't put good hearthrugs in dustbins. It had spangles in it from her dress, I suppose?"

"Yes, I couldn't get them out."

Dinah cried, "What are you talking about?"

Basil said sullenly, "Ask her. She seems to know all about it."

"I'll tell you what I think happened, if you like," said Miss Marple. "You can correct me, Mr. Blake, if I go wrong. I think that after having had a violent quarrel with your wife at a party and after having had, perhaps, rather too much—er—to drink, you drove down here. I don't know what time you arrived."

Basil Blake said sullenly, "About two in the morning. I meant to go up to town first; then, when I got to the suburbs, I changed my mind. I thought Dinah might come down here after me. So I drove down here. The place was all dark. I opened the door and turned on the light and I saw—and I saw—" He gulped and stopped.

Miss Marple went on, "You saw a girl lying on the hearthrug. A girl in a white evening dress, strangled. I don't know whether you recognized her then—"

Basil Blake shook his head violently. "I couldn't look at her after the first glance; her face was all blue, swollen; she'd been dead some time and she was there—in my living room!" He shuddered.

Miss Marple said gently, "You weren't, of course, quite yourself. You were in a fuddled state and your nerves are not good. You were, I think, panic-stricken. You didn't know what to do—"

"I thought Dinah might turn up any minute. And she'd find me there with a dead body—a girl's dead body—and she'd think I'd killed her. Then I got an idea. It seemed—I don't know why—a good idea at the time. I thought: 'I'll put her in old Bantry's library. Damned pompous old stick, always looking down his nose, sneering at me as artistic and effeminate. Serve the pompous old brute right,' I thought. 'He'll look a fool when a dead lovely is found on his hearthrug.'" He added with a pathetic eagerness to explain, "I was a bit drunk, you know, at the time. It really seemed positively amusing to me. Old Bantry with a dead blonde."

"Yes, yes," said Miss Marple. "Little Tommy Bond had very much the same idea. Rather a sensitive boy, with an inferiority complex, he said teacher was always picking on him. He put a frog in the clock and it jumped out at her. You were just the same," went on Miss Marple, "only, of course, bodies are more serious matters than frogs."

Basil groaned again. "By the morning I'd sobered up. I realized what I'd done. I was scared stiff. And then the police came here—another damned pompous ass of a chief constable. I was scared of him, and the only way I could hide it was by being abominably rude. In the middle of it all, Dinah drove up."

Dinah looked out of the window. She said, "There's a car driving up now. There are men in it."

"The police, I think," said Miss Marple.

Basil Blake got up. Suddenly he became quite calm and resolute. He even smiled. He said, "So I'm for it, am I? All right, Dinah, sweet, keep your head. Get onto old Sims—he's the family lawyer—and go to mother and tell her about our marriage. She won't bite. And don't worry. I didn't do it. So it's bound to be all right, see, sweetheart?"

There was a tap on the cottage door. Basil called, "Come in."

Inspector Slack entered with another man. He said, "Mr. Basil Blake?"

"Yes."

"I have a warrant here for your arrest on the charge of murdering Ruby Keene on the night of September twentieth last. I warn you that anything you say may be used at your trial. You will please accompany me now. Full facilities will be given you for communicating with your solicitor."

Basil nodded. He looked at Dinah, but did not touch her. He said, "So long, Dinah."

Cool customer, thought Inspector Slack.

He acknowledged the presence of Miss Marple with a half bow and a "Good morning," and thought to himself, Smart old pussy; she's on to it. Good job we've got that hearthrug. That and finding out from the car-park man at the studio that he left that party at eleven instead of midnight. Don't think those friends of his meant to commit perjury. They were bottled, and Blake told 'em firmly the next day it was twelve o'clock when he left, and they believed him. Well, his goose is cooked good and proper. Mental, I expect. Broadmoor, not hanging. First the Reeves kid, probably strangled her, drove her out to the quarry, walked back into Danemouth, picked up his own car in some side lane, drove to this party, then back to Danemouth, brought Ruby Keene out here, strangled her, put her in old Bantry's library, then probably got the wind up about the car in the quarry, drove there, set it on fire and got back here. Mad—sex and blood lust—lucky this girl's escaped. What they call recurring mania, I expect.

Alone with Miss Marple, Dinah Blake turned to her. She said, "I don't know who you are, but you've got to understand this: Basil didn't do it."

Miss Marple said, "I know he didn't. I know who did do it. But it's not going to be easy to prove. I've an idea that something you said just now may help. It gave me an idea—the connection I'd been trying to find. Now, what was it?"

XX

"I'M HOME, ARTHUR!" declared Mrs. Bantry, announcing the fact like a royal proclamation as she flung open the study door.

Colonel Bantry immediately jumped up, kissed his wife and declared heartily, "Well, well, that's splendid!"

The colonel's words were unimpeachable, the manner very well done, but an affectionate wife of as many years' standing as Mrs. Bantry was not deceived.

She said immediately, "Is anything the matter?"

"No, of course not, Dolly. What should be the matter?"

"Oh, I don't know," said Mrs. Bantry vaguely. "Things are so queer, aren't they?"

She threw off her coat as she spoke, and Colonel Bantry picked it up carefully and laid it across the back of the sofa.

All exactly as usual, yet not as usual. Her husband, Mrs. Bantry thought, seemed to have shrunk. He looked thinner, stooped more, there were pouches under his eyes, and those eyes were not ready to meet hers.

He went on to say, still with that affectation of cheerfulness, "Well, how did you enjoy your time at Danemouth?"

"Oh, it was great fun. You ought to have come, Arthur."

"Couldn't get away, my dear. Lot of things to attend to here."

"Still, I think the change would have done you good. And you like the Jeffersons?"

"Yes, yes, poor fellow. Nice chap. All very sad."

"What have you been doing with yourself since I've been away?"

"Oh, nothing much; been over the farms, you know. Agreed that Anderson shall have a new roof. Can't patch it up any longer."

"How did the Radfordshire Council meeting go?"

"I—well, as a matter of fact, I didn't go."

"Didn't go? But you were taking the chair."

"Well, as a matter of fact, Dolly, seems there was some mistake about that. Asked me if I'd mind if Thompson took it instead."

"I see," said Mrs. Bantry. She peeled off a glove and threw it deliberately into the wastepaper basket. Her husband went to retrieve it and she stopped him, saying sharply, "Leave it. I hate gloves."

Colonel Bantry glanced at her uneasily.

Mrs. Bantry said sternly, "Did you go to dinner with the Duffs on Thursday?"

"Oh, that? It was put off. Their cook was ill."

"Stupid people," said Mrs. Bantry. She went on, "Did you go to the Naylors' yesterday?"

"I rang up and said I didn't feel up to it; hoped they'd excuse me. They quite understood."

"They did, did they?" said Mrs. Bantry grimly.

She sat down by the desk and absent-mindedly picked up a pair of gardening scissors. With them she cut off the fingers, one by one, of her second glove.

"What are you doing, Dolly?"

"Feeling destructive," said Mrs. Bantry. She got up. "Where shall we sit after dinner, Arthur? In the library?"

"Well—er—I don't think so—eh? Very nice in here—or the drawing room."

"I think," said Mrs. Bantry, "that we'll sit in the library."

Her steady eye met his. Colonel Bantry drew himself up to his full height. A sparkle came into his eye. He said, "You're right, my dear. We'll sit in the library!"

Mrs. Bantry put down the telephone receiver with a sigh of annoyance. She had rung up twice, and each time the answer had been the same. Miss Marple was out.

Of a naturally impatient nature, Mrs. Bantry was never one to acquiesce in defeat. She rang up, in rapid succession, the vicarage, Mrs. Price Ridley, Miss Hartnell, Miss Wetherby and, as a last resort, the fishmonger, who, by reason of his advantageous geographical position, usually knew where everybody was in the village. The fishmonger was sorry, but he had not seen Miss Marple at all in the village that morning. She had not been her usual round.

"Where can the woman be?" demanded Mrs. Bantry impatiently, aloud.

There was a deferential cough behind her. The discreet Lorrimer murmured, "You were requiring Miss Marple, madam? I have just observed her approaching the house."

Mrs. Bantry rushed to the front door, flung it open and greeted Miss Marple breathlessly, "I've been trying to get you everywhere. Where have you been?" She glanced over her shoulder. Lorrimer had discreetly vanished. "Everything's too awful! People are beginning to cold-shoulder Arthur. He looks years older. We must do something, Jane. You must do something!"

Miss Marple said, "You needn't worry, Dolly," in a rather peculiar voice.

Colonel Bantry appeared from the study door. "Ah, Miss Marple. Good morning. Glad you've come. My wife's been ringing you up like a lunatic."

"I thought I'd better bring you the news," said Miss Marple as she followed Mrs. Bantry into the study.

"News?"

"Basil Blake has just been arrested for the murder of Ruby Keene."

"Basil Blake?" cried the colonel.

"But he didn't do it," said Miss Marple.

Colonel Bantry took no notice of this statement. It is doubtful if he even heard it. "Do you mean to say he strangled that girl and then brought her along and put her in my library?"

"He put her in your library," said Miss Marple, "but he didn't kill her."

"Nonsense. If he put her in my library, of course he killed her! The two things go together!"

"Not necessarily. He found her dead in his own cottage."

"A likely story," said the colonel derisively. "If you find a body—why, you ring up the police, naturally, if you're an honest man."

"Ah," said Miss Marple, "but we haven't all got such iron nerves as you have, Colonel Bantry. You belong to the old school. This younger generation is different."

"Got no stamina," said the colonel, repeating a well-worn opinion of his.

"Some of them," said Miss Marple, "have been through a bad time. I've heard a good deal about Basil. When he was only eighteen, he went into a burning house and brought out four children, one after another. He went back for a dog, although they told him it wasn't safe. The building fell in on him. They got him out, but his chest was badly crushed and he had to lie in plaster for a long time after that. That's when he got interested in designing."

"Oh!" The colonel coughed and blew his nose. "I—er—never knew that."

"He doesn't talk about it," said Miss Marple.

"Er—quite right. Proper spirit. Must be more in the young chap than I thought. Shows you ought to be careful in jumping to conclusions." Colonel Bantry looked ashamed. "But all the same"—his indignation revived—"what did he mean, trying to fasten a murder on me?"

"I don't think he saw it like that," said Miss Marple. "He thought of it more as a—as a joke. You see, he was rather under the influence of alcohol at the time."

"Bottled, was he?" said Colonel Bantry, with an Englishman's sympathy for alcoholic excess. "Oh, well, can't judge a fellow by what he does when he's drunk. When I was at Cambridge, I remember I put a certain utensil —well—well, never mind. Deuce of a row there was about it."

He chuckled, then checked himself sternly. He looked at Miss Marple with eyes that were shrewd and appraising.

He said, "You don't think he did the murder, eh?"

"I'm sure he didn't."

"And you think you know who did?"

Miss Marple nodded.

Mrs. Bantry, like an ecstatic Greek chorus, said, "Isn't she wonderful?" to an unhearing world.

"Well, who was it?"

Miss Marple said, "I was going to ask you to help me. I think if we went up to Somerset House we should have a very good idea."

XXI

Sir Henry's face was very grave. He said, "I don't like it."

"I am aware," said Miss Marple, "that it isn't what you call orthodox. But it is so important, isn't it, to be quite sure—to 'make assurance doubly sure,' as Shakespeare has it? I think, if Mr. Jefferson would agree—"

"What about Harper? Is he to be in on this?"

"It might be awkward for him to know too much. But there might be a hint from you. To watch certain persons—have them trailed, you know."

Sir Henry said slowly, "Yes, that would meet the case."

Superintendent Harper looked piercingly at Sir Henry Clithering. "Let's get this quite clear, sir. You're giving me a hint?"

Sir Henry said, "I'm informing you of what my friend has just informed me—he didn't tell me in confidence—that he purposes to visit a solicitor in Danemouth tomorrow for the purpose of making a new will."

The superintendent's bushy eyebrows drew downward over his steady eyes. He said, "Does Mr. Conway Jefferson propose to inform his son-in-law and daughter-in-law of that fact?"

"He intends to tell them about it this evening."

"I see." The superintendent tapped his desk with a penholder. He repeated again, "I see."

Then the piercing eyes bored once more into the eyes of the other man. Harper said, "So you're not satisfied with the case against Basil Blake?"

"Are you?"

The superintendent's mustaches quivered. He said, "Is Miss Marple?"

The two men looked at each other.

Then Harper said, "You can leave it to me. I'll have men detailed. There will be no funny business, I can promise you that."

Sir Henry said, "There is one more thing. You'd better see this." He unfolded a slip of paper and pushed it across the table.

This time the superintendent's calm deserted him. He whistled. "So that's it, is it? That puts an entirely different complexion on the matter. How did you come to dig up this?"

"Women," said Sir Henry, "are eternally interested in marriages."

"Especially," said the superintendent, "elderly single women."

Conway Jefferson looked up as his friend entered. His grim face relaxed into a smile. He said, "Well, I told 'em. They took it very well."

"What did you say?"

"Told 'em that, as Ruby was dead, I felt that the fifty thousand I'd originally left her should go to something that I could associate with her memory. It was to endow a hostel for young girls working as professional dancers in London. Damned silly way to leave your money—surprised they swallowed it—as though I'd do a thing like that." He added meditatively, "You know, I made a fool of myself over that girl. Must be turning into a silly old man. I can see it now. She was a pretty kid, but most of what I saw in her I put there myself. I pretended she was another Rosamund. Same coloring, you know. But not the same heart or mind. Hand me that paper; rather an interesting bridge problem."

Sir Henry went downstairs. He asked a question of the porter.

"Mr. Gaskell, sir? He's just gone off in his car. Had to go to London."

"Oh! I see. Is Mrs. Jefferson about?"

"Mrs. Jefferson, sir, has just gone up to bed."

Sir Henry looked into the lounge and through to the ballroom. In the lounge, Hugo McLean was doing a crossword puzzle and frowning a good deal over it. In the ballroom, Josie was smiling valiantly into the face of a stout, perspiring man as her nimble feet avoided his destructive tread. The stout man was clearly enjoying his dance. Raymond, graceful and weary, was dancing with an anemic-looking girl with adenoids, dull brown hair and an expensive and exceedingly unbecoming dress.

Sir Henry said under his breath, "And so to bed," and went upstairs.

It was three o'clock. The wind had fallen, the moon was shining over the quiet sea. In Conway Jefferson's room there was no sound except his own heavy breathing as he lay half propped up on pillows.

There was no breeze to stir the curtains at the window, but they stirred. For a moment they parted and a figure was silhouetted against the moonlight. Then they fell back into place. Everything was quiet again, but there was someone else inside the room. Nearer and nearer to the bed the intruder stole. The deep breathing on the pillow did not relax. There was no sound, or hardly any sound. A finger and thumb were ready to pick up a fold of skin; in the other hand the hypodermic was ready. And then, suddenly, out of the shadows a hand came and closed over the hand that held the needle; the other arm held the figure in an iron grasp.

An unemotional voice, the voice of the law, said, "No, you don't! I want that needle!"

The light switched on, and from his pillows Conway Jefferson looked grimly at the murderer of Ruby Keene.

XXII

Sir Henry Clithering said, "Speaking as Watson, I want to know your methods, Miss Marple."

Superintendent Harper said, "I'd like to know what put you on to it first."

Colonel Melchett said, "You've done it again, by Jove, Miss Marple. I want to hear all about it from the beginning."

Miss Marple smoothed the pure silk of her best evening gown. She flushed and smiled and looked very self-conscious.

She said, "I'm afraid you'll think my 'methods,' as Sir Henry calls them, are terribly amateurish. The truth is, you see, that most people—and I don't exclude policemen—are far too trusting for this wicked world. They believe what is told them. I never do. I'm afraid I always like to prove a thing for myself."

"That is the scientific attitude," said Sir Henry.

"In this case," continued Miss Marple, "certain things were taken for granted from the first, instead of just confining oneself to the facts. The facts, as I noted them, were that the victim was quite young and that she bit her nails and that her teeth stuck out a little—as young girls' so often do if not corrected in time with a plate—and children are very naughty about their plates and take them out when their elders aren't looking.

"But that is wandering from the point. Where was I? Oh, yes, looking down at the dead girl and feeling sorry, because it is always sad to see a young life cut short, and thinking that whoever had done it was a very wicked person. Of course it was all very confusing, her being found in Colonel Bantry's library, altogether too like a book to be true. In fact, it made the wrong pattern. It wasn't, you see, meant, which confused us a lot. The real idea had been to plant the body on poor young Basil Blake—a much more likely person—and his action in putting it in the colonel's library delayed things considerably and must have been a source of great annoyance to the real murderer.

"Originally, you see, Mr. Blake would have been the first object of suspicion. They'd have made inquiries at Danemouth, found he knew the girl, then found he had tied himself up with another girl, and they'd have assumed that Ruby came to blackmail him or something like that, and that he'd strangled her in a fit of rage. Just an ordinary, sordid, what I call night-club type of crime!

"But that, of course, all went wrong, and interest became focused much too soon on the Jefferson family—to the great annoyance of a certain person.

"As I've told you, I've got a very suspicious mind. My nephew Raymond tells me, in fun, of course—that I have a mind like a sink. He says that most Victorians have. All I can say is that the Victorians knew a good deal about human nature.

"As I say, having this rather insanitary—or surely sanitary?—mind, I looked at once at the money angle of it. Two people stood to benefit by this girl's death—you couldn't get away from that. Fifty thousand pounds is a lot of money; especially when you are in financial difficulties, as both these people were. Of course they both seemed very nice, agreeable people; they didn't seem likely people, but one never can tell, can one?

"Mrs. Jefferson, for instance—everyone liked her. But it did seem clear that she had become very restless that summer and that she was tired of the life she led, completely dependent on her father-in-law. She knew, because the doctor had told her, that he couldn't live long, so that was all right—to put it callously—or it would have been all right if Ruby Keene hadn't come along. Mrs. Jefferson was passionately devoted to her son, and some women have a curious idea that crimes committed for the sake of their offspring are almost morally justified. I have come across that attitude once or twice in the village. 'Well, 'twas all for Daisy, you see, miss,' they say, and seem to think that that makes doubtful conduct quite all right. Very lax thinking.

"Mr. Mark Gaskell, of course, was a much more likely starter, if I may use such a sporting expression. He was a gambler and had not, I fancied, a very high moral code. But for certain reasons I was of the opinion that a woman was concerned in this crime.

"As I say, with my eye on motive the money angle seemed very suggestive. It was annoying, therefore, to find that both these people had alibis for the time when Ruby Keene, according to the medical evidence, had met her death. But soon afterward, there came the discovery of the burnt-out car with Pamela Reeves' body in it, and then the whole thing leaped to the eye. The alibis, of course, were worthless.

"I now had two halves of the case, and both quite convincing, but they did not fit. There must be a connection, but I could not find it. The one person whom I knew to be concerned in the crime hadn't got a motive.

"It was stupid of me," said Miss Marple meditatively. "If it hadn't been for Dinah Lee I shouldn't have thought of it—the most obvious thing in the world. The vital records at Somerset House! Marriage! It wasn't a question of only Mr. Gaskell or Mrs. Jefferson; there was the further possibility of marriage. If either of those two was married, or even was likely to marry, then the other party to the marriage contract was involved too. Raymond, for instance, might think he had a pretty good chance of marrying a rich wife. He had been very assiduous to Mrs. Jefferson, and it was his charm, I think, that awoke her from her long widowhood. She had been quite content just being a daughter to Mr. Jefferson. Like Ruth and Naomi—only Naomi, if you remember, took a lot of trouble to arrange a suitable marriage for Ruth.

"Besides Raymond, there was Mr. McLean. She liked him very much, and it seemed highly possible that she would marry him in the end. He wasn't well off and he was not far from Danemouth on the night in question. So, it seemed, didn't it," said Miss Marple, "as though anyone might have done it? But, of course, really, in my own mind, I knew. You couldn't get away, could you, from those bitten nails?"

"Nails?" said Sir Henry. "But she tore her nail and cut the others."

"Nonsense," said Miss Marple. "Bitten nails and close-cut nails are quite different! Nobody could mistake them who knew anything about girls' nails—very ugly, bitten nails, as I always tell the girls in my class. Those nails, you see, were a fact. And they could only mean one thing. The body in Colonel Bantry's library wasn't Ruby Keene at all.

"And that brings you straight to the one person who must be concerned. Josie! Josie identified the body. She knew—she must have known—that it wasn't Ruby Keene's body. She said it was. She was puzzled—completely puzzled—at finding that body where it was. She practically betrayed that fact. Why? Because she knew—none better—where it ought to have been found! In Basil Blake's cottage. Who directed our attention to Basil? Josie, by saying to Raymond that Ruby might have been with the film man. And before that, by slipping a snapshot of him into Ruby's handbag. Josie! Josie, who was shrewd, practical, hard as nails and all out for money.

"Since the body wasn't the body of Ruby Keene, it must be the body of someone else. Of whom? Of the other girl who was also missing. Pamela Reeves! Ruby was eighteen. Pamela sixteen. They were both healthy, rather immature, but muscular girls. But why, I asked myself, all this hocus-pocus? There could be only one reason—to give certain persons an alibi. Who had alibis for the supposed time of Ruby Keene's death? Mark Gaskell, Mrs. Jefferson and Josie.

"It was really quite interesting, you know, tracing out the course of events, seeing exactly how the plan had worked out. Complicated and yet simple. First of all, the selection of the poor child, Pamela; the approach to her from the film angle. A screen test; of course the poor child couldn't resist it. Not when it was put up to her as plausibly as Mark Gaskell put it. She comes to the hotel, he is waiting for her, he takes her in by the side door and introduces her to Josie—one of their make-up experts! That poor child—it makes me quite sick to think of it! Sitting in Josie's bathroom while Josie bleaches her hair and makes up her face and varnishes her fingernails and toenails. During all this the drug was given. In an ice-cream soda, very likely. She goes off into a coma. I imagine that they put her into one of the empty rooms opposite. They were only cleaned once a week, remember.

"After dinner Mark Gaskell went out in his car—to the sea front, he said. That is when he took Pamela's body to the cottage, arranged it, dressed in one of Ruby's old dresses, on the hearthrug. She was still unconscious, but not dead, when he strangled her with the belt of the frock. Not nice, no, but I hope and pray she knew nothing about it. Really, I feel quite pleased to think of him hanging. . . . That must have been just after ten o'clock. Then back at top speed and into the lounge where Ruby Keene, still alive, was dancing her exhibition dance with Raymond.

"I should imagine that Josie had given Ruby instructions beforehand. Ruby was accustomed to doing what Josie told her. She was to change, go into Josie's room and wait. She, too, was drugged; probably in the after-dinner coffee. She was yawning, remember, when she talked to young Bartlett.

"Josie came up later with Raymond to 'look for her,' but nobody but Josie went into Josie's room. She probably finished the girl off then—with an injection, perhaps, or a blow on the back of the head. She went down, danced with Raymond, debated with the Jeffersons where Ruby could be and finally went up to bed. In the early hours of the morning she dressed the girl in Pamela's clothes, carried the body down the side stairs and out—she was a strong, muscular young woman—fetched George Bartlett's car, drove two miles to the quarry, poured petrol over the car and set it alight. Then she walked back to the hotel, probably timing her arrival there for eight or nine o'clock—up early in her anxiety about Ruby!"

"An intricate plot," said Colonel Melchett.

"Not more intricate than the steps of a dance," said Miss Marple.

"I suppose not."

"She was very thorough," said Miss Marple. "She even foresaw the discrepancy of the nails. That's why she managed to break one of Ruby's nails on her shawl. It made an excuse for pretending that Ruby had clipped her nails close."

Harper said, "Yes, she thought of everything. And the only real proof you had was a schoolgirl's bitten nails."

"More than that," said Miss Marple. "People will talk too much. Mark Gaskell talked too much. He was speaking of Ruby and he said, 'her teeth ran down her throat.' But the dead girl in Colonel Bantry's library had teeth that stuck out."

Conway Jefferson said rather grimly, "And was the last dramatic finale your idea, Miss Marple?"

"Well, it was, as a matter of fact. It's so nice to be sure, isn't it?"

"Sure is the word," said Conway Jefferson grimly.

"You see," said Miss Marple, "once those two knew that you were going to make a new will, they'd have to do something. They'd already committed two murders on account of the money. So they might as well commit a third. Mark, of course, must be absolutely clear, so he went off to London and established an alibi by dining at a restaurant with friends and going on to a night club. Josie was to do the work. They still wanted Ruby's death to be put down to Basil's account, so Mr. Jefferson's death must be thought due to his heart failing. There was digitalis, so the superintendent tells me, in the syringe. Any doctor would think death from heart trouble quite natural in the circumstances. Josie had loosened one of the stone balls on the balcony and she was going to let it crash down afterward. His death would be put down to the shock of the noise."

Melchett said, "Ingenious devil."

Sir Henry said, "So the third death you spoke of was to be Conway Jefferson?"

Miss Marple shook her head. "Oh, no, I meant Basil Blake. They'd have got him hanged if they could."

"Or shut up in Broadmoor," said Sir Henry.

Through the doorway floated Adelaide Jefferson. Hugo McLean followed her. The latter said, "I seem to have missed most of this! Haven't got the hang of it yet. What was Josie to Mark Gaskell?"

Miss Marple said, "His wife. They were married a year ago. They were keeping it dark until Mr. Jefferson died."

Conway Jefferson grunted. He said, "Always knew Rosamund had married a rotter. Tried not to admit it to myself. She was fond of him. Fond of a murderer! Well, he'll hang, as well as the woman. I'm glad he went to pieces and gave the show away."

Miss Marple said, "She was always the strong character. It was her plan throughout. The irony of it is that she got the girl down here herself, never dreaming that she would take Mr. Jefferson's fancy and ruin all her own prospects."

Jefferson said, "Poor lass. Poor little Ruby."

Adelaide laid her hand on his shoulder and pressed it gently. She looked almost beautiful tonight. She said, with a little catch in her breath, "I want to tell you something, Jeff. At once. I'm going to marry Hugo."

Conway Jefferson looked up at her for a moment. He said gruffly, "About time you married again. Congratulations to you both. By the way, Addie, I'm making a new will tomorrow."

She nodded. "Oh, yes. I know."

Jefferson said, "No, you don't. I'm settling ten thousand pounds on you. Everything else goes to Peter when I die. How does that suit you, my girl?"

"Oh, Jeff!" Her voice broke. "You're wonderful!"

"He's a nice lad. I'd like to see a good deal of him in—in the time I've got left."

"Oh, you shall!"

"Got a great feeling for crime, Peter has," said Conway Jefferson meditatively. "Not only has he got the fingernail of the murdered girl—one of the murdered girls, anyway—but he was lucky enough to have a bit of Josie's shawl caught in with the nail. So he's got a souvenir of the murderess too! That makes him very happy!"

Hugo and Adelaide passed by the ballroom. Raymond came up to them.

Adelaide said rather quickly, "I must tell you my news. We're going to be married."

The smile on Raymond's face was perfect—a brave, pensive smile.

"I hope," he said, ignoring Hugo and gazing into her eyes, "that you will be very, very happy."

They passed on and Raymond stood looking after them.

"A nice woman," he said to himself. "A very nice woman. And she would have had money too. The trouble I took to mug up that bit about the Devonshire Starrs. Oh, well, my luck's out. Dance, dance, little gentleman!"

And Raymond returned to the ballroom.

The Murder at the Vicarage

I

It is difficult to know quite where to begin this story, but I have fixed my choice on a certain Wednesday at luncheon at the Vicarage. The conversation, though in the main irrelevant to the matter in hand, yet contained one or two suggestive incidents which influenced later developments.

I had just finished carving some boiled beef (remarkably tough by the way), and on resuming my seat I remarked, in a spirit most unbecoming to my cloth, that anyone who murdered Colonel Protheroe would be doing the world at large a service.

My young nephew, Dennis, said instantly:

"That'll be remembered against you when the old boy is found bathed in blood. Mary will give evidence, won't you, Mary? And describe how you brandished the carving knife in a vindictive manner."

Mary, who is in service at the Vicarage as a stepping stone to better things and higher wages, merely said, in a loud businesslike voice, "Greens," and thrust a cracked dish at him in a truculent manner.

My wife said in a sympathetic voice, "Has he been very trying?"

I did not reply at once, for Mary, setting the greens on the table with a bang, proceeded to thrust a dish of singularly moist and unpleasant dumplings under my nose. I said, "No, thank you," and she deposited the dish with a clatter on the table and left the room.

"It is a pity that I am such a shocking housekeeper," said my wife with a tinge of genuine regret in her voice.

I was inclined to agree with her. My wife's name is Griselda—a highly suitable name for a parson's wife. But there the suitability ends. She is not in the least meek.

I have always been of the opinion that a clergyman should be unmarried. Why I should have urged Griselda to marry me at the end of twenty-four hours' acquaintance is a mystery to me. Marriage, I have always held, is a serious affair, to be entered into only after long deliberation and forethought, and suitability of tastes and inclinations is the most important consideration.

Griselda is nearly twenty years younger than myself. She is most distractingly pretty and quite incapable of taking anything seriously. She is incompetent in every way and extremely trying to live with. She treats the Parish as a kind of huge joke arranged for her amusement. I have endeavoured to form her mind and failed. I am more than ever convinced that celibacy is desirable for the clergy. I have frequently hinted as much to Griselda, but she has only laughed.

"My dear," I said. "If you would only exercise a little care—"

"I do sometimes," said Griselda. "But on the whole I think things go worse when I'm trying. I'm evidently not a housekeeper by nature. I find it better to leave things to Mary and just make up my mind to be uncomfortable and have nasty things to eat."

"And what about your husband, my dear?" I said reproachfully and, proceeding to follow the example of the devil in quoting Scripture for his own ends, I added, " 'She looketh to the ways of her household.' "

"Think how lucky you are not to be torn to pieces by lions," said Griselda quickly interrupting. "Or burnt at the stake. Bad food and lots of dust and dead wasps is really nothing to make a fuss about. Tell me more about Colonel Protheroe. At any rate the early Christians were lucky enough not to have churchwardens."

"Pompous old brute," said Dennis. "No wonder his first wife ran away from him."

"I don't see what else she could do," said my wife.

"Griselda," I said sharply. "I will not have you speaking in that way."

"Darling," said my wife affectionately. "Tell me about him. What was the trouble? Was it Mr. Hawes' becking and nodding and crossing himself every other minute?"

Hawes is our new curate. He has been with us just over three weeks. He has High Church views and fasts on Fridays. Colonel Protheroe is a great opposer of ritual in any form.

"Not this time. He did touch on it in passing. No, the whole trouble arose out of Mrs. Price Ridley's wretched pound note."

Mrs. Price Ridley is a devout member of my congregation. Attending early service on the anniversary of her son's death, she put a pound note into the offertory bag. Later, reading the amount of the collection posted up, she was pained to observe that one ten-shilling note was the highest item mentioned.

She complained to me about it, and I pointed out, very reasonably, that she must have made a mistake.

"We're none of us so young as we were," I said, trying to turn it off tactfully. "And we must pay the penalty of advancing years."

Strangely enough my words only seemed to incense her further. She said that things had a very odd look and that she was surprised I didn't think so also. And she flounced away and, I gather, took her troubles to Colonel Protheroe. Protheroe is the kind of man who enjoys making a fuss on every conceivable occasion. He made a fuss. It is a pity he made it on a Wednesday. I teach in the Church Day School on Wednesday mornings, a proceeding that causes me acute nervousness and leaves me unsettled for the rest of the day.

"Well, I suppose he must have some fun," said my wife, with the air of trying to sum up the position impartially. "Nobody flutters round him and calls him the dear Vicar, and embroiders awful slippers for him, and gives him bedsocks for Christmas. Both his wife and his daughter are fed to the teeth with him. I suppose it makes him happy to feel important somewhere."

"He needn't be offensive about it," I said with some heat. "I don't think he quite realized the implications of what he was saying. He wants to go over all the Church accounts—in case of defalcations—that was the word he used. Defalcations! Does he suspect me of embezzling the Church funds?"

"Nobody would suspect you of anything, darling," said Griselda. "You're so transparently above suspicion that really it would be a marvellous opportunity. I wish you'd embezzle the Society for the Preservation of the Gospel funds. I hate missionaries—I always have."

I would have reproved her for that sentiment, but Mary entered at that moment with a partially cooked rice pudding. I made a mild protest, but Griselda said that the Japanese always ate half cooked rice and had marvellous brains in consequence.

"I daresay," she said, "that if you had a rice pudding like this every day till Sunday, you'd preach the most marvellous sermon."

"Heaven forbid," I said with a shudder.

"Protheroe's coming over tomorrow evening and we're going over the accounts together," I went on. "I must finish preparing my talk for the Church of England Men's Society today. Looking up a reference I became so engrossed in Canon Shirley's 'Reality' that I haven't got on as well as I should. What are you doing this afternoon, Griselda?"

"My duty," said Griselda. "My duty as the Vicaress. Tea and scandal at four-thirty."

"Who is coming?"

Griselda ticked them off on her fingers with a glow of virtue on her face.

"Mrs. Price Ridley, Miss Wetherby, Miss Hartnell and that terrible Miss Marple."

"I rather like Miss Marple," I said. "She has, at least, a sense of humour."

"She's the worst cat in the village," said Griselda. "And she always knows every single thing that happens—and draws the worst inferences from it."

Griselda, as I have said, is much younger than I am. At my time of life, one knows that the worst is usually true.

"Well, don't expect me in for tea, Griselda," said Dennis.

"Beast!" said Griselda.

"Yes, but look here, the Protheroes really did ask me for tennis today."

"Beast!" said Griselda again.

Dennis beat a prudent retreat, and Griselda and I went together into my study.

"I wonder what we shall have for tea," said Griselda seating herself on my writing table. "Dr. Stone and Miss Cram, I suppose, and perhaps Mrs. Lestrange. By the way, I called on her yesterday, but she was out. Yes, I'm sure we shall have Mrs. Lestrange for tea. It's so mysterious, isn't it, her arriving like this and taking a house down here, and hardly ever going outside it? Makes one think of detective stories. You know—'*Who was she, the mysterious woman with the pale beautiful face? What was her past history? Nobody knew. There was something faintly sinister about her.*' I believe Dr. Haydock knows something about her."

"You read too many detective stories, Griselda," I observed mildly.

"What about you?" she retorted. "I was looking everywhere for 'The Stain on the Stairs' the other day when you were in here writing a sermon. And at last I came in to ask you if you'd seen it anywhere, and what did I find?"

I had the grace to blush.

"I picked it up at random. A chance sentence caught my eye and—"

"I know those chance sentences," said Griselda. She quoted impressively, "'*And then a very curious thing happened—Griselda rose, crossed the room and kissed her elderly husband affectionately.*'"

She suited the action to the word.

"Is that a very curious thing?" I inquired.

"Of course it is," said Griselda. "Do you realize, Len, that I might have married a Cabinet Minister, a Baronet, a rich Company Promoter, three subalterns and a n'er-do-weel with attractive manners, and that instead I chose you? Didn't it astonish you very much?"

"At the time it did," I replied. "I have often wondered why you did it."

Griselda sighed.

"It made me feel so powerful," she murmured. "The others thought me simply wonderful, and of course it would have been very nice for them to have me. But I'm everything you most dislike and disapprove of, and yet you couldn't withstand me! My vanity couldn't hold out against that. It's so much nicer to be a secret and delightful sin to anybody than to be a feather in his cap. I make you frightfully uncomfortable and stir you up the wrong way the whole time, and yet you adore me madly. You do adore me madly, don't you?"

"Naturally, I am very fond of you, my dear."

"Oh! Len, you adore me. Do you remember that day when I stayed up in town and sent you a wire you never got because the postmistress's sister was having twins and she forgot to send it round? The state you got into, and you telephoned Scotland Yard and made the most frightful fuss."

There are things one hates being reminded of. I had really been strangely foolish on the occasion in question. I said:

"If you don't mind, dear, I want to get on with the C.E.M.S."

Griselda gave a sigh of intense irritation, ruffled my hair up on end, smoothed it down again, said:

"You don't deserve me. You really don't. I'll have an affair with the artist. I will—really and truly. And then think of the scandal in the parish."

"There's a good deal already," I said mildly.

Griselda laughed, blew me a kiss, and departed through the window.

II

GRISELDA IS A very irritating woman. On leaving the luncheon table, I had felt myself to be in a good mood for preparing a really forceful address for the Church of England Men's Society. Now I felt restless and disturbed.

Just when I was really settling down to it, Lettice Protheroe drifted in.

I use the word "drifted" advisedly. I have read novels in which young people are described as bursting with energy—*joie de vivre,* the magnificent vitality of youth. Personally, all the young people I come across have the air of amiable wraiths.

Lettice was particularly wraith-like this afternoon. She is a pretty girl, very tall and fair and completely vague. She drifted through the French window, absently pulled off the yellow beret she was wearing, and murmured vaguely with a kind of far-away surprise:

"Oh! it's you."

There is a path from Old Hall through the woods which comes out by our garden gate, so that most people coming from there come in at that gate and up to the study window instead of going a long way round by the road and coming to the front door. I was not surprised at Lettice coming in this way, but I did a little resent her attitude.

If you come to a Vicarage, you ought to be prepared to find a Vicar.

She came in and collapsed in a crumpled heap in one of my big arm chairs. She plucked aimlessly at her hair, staring at the ceiling.

"Is Dennis anywhere about?"

"I haven't seen him since lunch. I understood he was going to play tennis at your place."

"Oh!" said Lettice. "I hope he isn't. He won't find anybody there."

"He said you'd asked him."

"I believe I did. Only that was Friday. And today's Tuesday."

"It's Wednesday," I said.

"Oh! how dreadful," said Lettice. "That means that I've forgotten to go to lunch with some people for the third time."

Fortunately it didn't seem to worry her much.

"Is Griselda anywhere about?"

"I expect you'll find her in the studio in the garden—sitting to Lawrence Redding."

"There's been quite a shemozzle about him," said Lettice. "With Father, you know. Father's dreadful."

"What was the she— whatever it was, about?" I inquired.

"About his painting me. Father found out about it. Why shouldn't I be painted in my bathing dress? If I go on a beach in it, why shouldn't I be painted in it?"

Lettice paused and then went on.

"It's really absurd—Father forbidding a young man the house. Of course, Lawrence and I simply shriek about it. I shall come and be done here in your studio."

"No, my dear," I said. "Not if your father forbids it."

"Oh! dear," said Lettice sighing. "How tiresome everyone is. I feel shattered. Definitely. If only I had some money I'd go away, but without it I can't. If only Father would be decent and die, I should be all right."

"You must not say things like that, Lettice."

"Well, if he doesn't want me to want him to die, he shouldn't be so horrible over money. I don't wonder Mother left him. Do you know for years I believed she was dead. What sort of a young man did she run away with? Was he nice?"

"It was before your father came to live here."

"I wonder what's become of her. I expect Anne will have an affair with someone soon. Anne hates me—she's quite decent to me, but she hates me. She's getting old and she doesn't like it. That's the age you break out, you know."

I wondered if Lettice was going to spend the entire afternoon in my study.

"You haven't seen my gramophone records, have you?" she asked.

"No."

"How tiresome. I know I've left them somewhere. And I've lost the dog. And my wrist watch is somewhere, only it doesn't much matter because it won't go. Oh! dear, I am so sleepy. I can't think why, because I didn't get up till eleven. But life's very shattering, don't you think? Oh! dear, I must go. I'm going to see Dr. Stone's barrow at three o'clock."

I glanced at the clock and remarked that it was now five and twenty to four.

"Oh! is it? How dreadful if they've waited or if they've gone without me. I suppose I'd better go down and do something about it."

She got up and drifted out again murmuring over her shoulder,

"You'll tell Dennis, won't you?"

I said "Yes" mechanically, only realizing too late that I had no idea what it was I was to tell Dennis. But I reflected that in all probability it did not matter. I fell to cogitating on the subject of Dr. Stone, a well known archæologist who had recently come to stay at the Blue Boar, while he superintended the excavation of a barrow situated on Colonel Protheroe's property. There had already been several disputes between him and the Colonel. I was amused at his appointment to take Lettice to see the operations.

It occurred to me that Lettice Protheroe was something of a minx. I wondered how she would get on with the archæologist's secretary, Miss Cram. Miss Cram is a healthy young woman of twenty-five, noisy in manner, with a high colour, fine animal spirits and a mouth that always seems to have more than its full share of teeth.

Village opinion is divided as to whether she is no better than she should be, or else a young woman of iron virtue who purposes to become Mrs. Stone at an early opportunity. She is in every way a great contrast to Lettice.

I could imagine that the state of things at Old Hall might not be too happy. Colonel Protheroe had married again some five years previously. The second Mrs. Protheroe was a remarkably handsome woman in a rather unusual style. I had always guessed that the relations between her and her stepdaughter were not too happy.

I had one more interruption. This time, it was my curate, Hawes. He wanted to know the details of my interview with Protheroe. I told him that the Colonel had deplored his "Romish tendencies," but that the real purpose of his visit had been on quite another matter. At the same time, I entered a protest of my own, and told him plainly that he must conform to my ruling. On the whole, he took my remarks very well.

I felt rather remorseful, when he had gone, for not liking him better. These irrational likes and dislikes that one takes to people are, I am sure, very unchristian.

With a sigh, I realized that the hands of the clock on my writing table pointed to a quarter to five, a sign that it was really half past four, and I made my way to the drawing room.

Four of my parishioners were assembled there with teacups. Griselda sat behind the tea table trying to look natural in her environment, but only succeeding in looking more out of place than usual.

I shook hands all round and sat down between Miss Marple and Miss Wetherby.

Miss Marple is a white-haired old lady with a gentle appealing manner —Miss Wetherby is a mixture of vinegar and gush. Of the two Miss Marple is much the more dangerous.

"We were just talking," said Griselda in a honey-sweet voice, "about Dr. Stone and Miss Cram."

A ribald rhyme concocted by Dennis shot through my head.

"Miss Cram doesn't give a damn."

I had a sudden yearning to say it out loud and observe the effect, but fortunately I refrained.

Miss Wetherby said tersely:

"No nice girl would do it," and shut her thin lips disapprovingly.

"Do what?" I inquired.

"Be a secretary to an unmarried man," said Miss Wetherby in a horrified tone.

"Oh! my dear," said Miss Marple. "I think married ones are the worst. Remember poor Mollie Carter."

"Married men living apart from their wives are, of course, notorious," said Miss Wetherby.

"And even some of the ones living with their wives," murmured Miss Marple. "I remember—"

I interrupted these unsavoury reminiscences.

"But surely," I said, "in these days a girl can take a post in just the same way as a man does."

"To come away to the country? And stay at the same hotel?" said Mrs. Price Ridley in a severe voice.

Miss Wetherby murmured to Miss Marple in a low voice:

"And all the bedrooms on the same floor. . . ."

They exchanged glances.

Miss Hartnell, who is weather-beaten and jolly and much dreaded by the poor, observed in a loud, hearty voice:

"The poor man will be caught before he knows where he is. He's as innocent as a babe unborn, you can see that."

Curious what turns of phrase we employ. None of the ladies present would have dreamed of alluding to an actual baby till it was safely in the cradle, visible to all.

"Disgusting, I call it," continued Miss Hartnell with her usual tactlessness. "The man must be at least twenty-five years older than she is."

Three female voices rose at once making disconnected remarks about the Choir Boys' Outing, the regrettable incident at the last Mothers' Meeting, and the draughts in the Church. Miss Marple twinkled at Griselda.

"Don't you think," said my wife, "that Miss Cram may just like having an interesting job, and that she considers Dr. Stone just as an employer?"

There was a silence. Evidently none of the four ladies agreed. Miss Marple broke the silence by patting Griselda on the arm.

"My dear," she said, "you are very young. The young have such innocent minds."

Griselda said indignantly that she hadn't got at all an innocent mind.

"Naturally," said Miss Marple, unheeding of the protest, "you think the best of everyone."

"Do you really think she wants to marry that bald-headed, dull man?"

"I understand he is quite well off," said Miss Marple. "Rather a violent temper, I'm afraid. He had quite a serious quarrel with Colonel Protheroe the other day."

Everyone leaned forward interestedly.

"Colonel Protheroe accused him of being an ignoramus."

"How like Colonel Protheroe, and how absurd," said Mrs. Price Ridley.

"Very like Colonel Protheroe, but I don't know about it being absurd," said Miss Marple. "You remember the woman who came down here and said she represented Welfare, and after taking subscriptions she was never heard of again, and proved to have nothing whatever to do with Welfare. One is so inclined to be trusting and take people at their own valuation."

I should never have dreamed of describing Miss Marple as trusting.

"There's been some fuss about that young artist, Mr. Redding, hasn't there?" asked Miss Wetherby.

Miss Marple nodded.

"Colonel Protheroe turned him out of the house. It appears he was painting Lettice in her bathing dress."

Suitable sensation!

"I always thought there was something between them," said Mrs. Price Ridley. "That young fellow is always mouching off up there. Pity the girl hasn't got a mother. A stepmother is never the same thing."

"I daresay Mrs. Protheroe does her best," said Miss Hartnell.

"Girls are so sly," deplored Mrs. Price Ridley.

"Quite a romance, isn't it?" said the softer hearted Miss Wetherby. "He's a very good-looking young fellow."

"But loose," said Miss Hartnell. "Bound to be. An artist! Paris! Models! The Altogether!"

"Painting her in her bathing dress," said Mrs. Price Ridley. "Not quite nice."

"He's painting me too," said Griselda.

"But not in your bathing dress, dear," said Miss Marple.

"It might be worse," said Griselda solemnly.

"Naughty girl," said Miss Hartnell, taking the joke broad-mindedly. Everybody else looked slightly shocked.

"Did dear Lettice tell you of the trouble?" asked Miss Marple of me.

"Tell me?"

"Yes. I saw her pass through the garden and go round to the study window."

Miss Marple always sees everything. Gardening is as good as a smoke screen, and the habit of observing birds through powerful glasses can always be turned to account.

"She mentioned it, yes," I admitted.

"Mr. Hawes looked worried," said Miss Marple. "I hope he hasn't been working too hard."

"Oh!" cried Miss Wetherby excitedly. "I quite forgot. I knew I had some news for you. I saw Dr. Haydock coming out of Mrs. Lestrange's cottage."

Everyone looked at each other.

"Perhaps she's ill," suggested Mrs. Price Ridley.

"It must have been very sudden, if so," said Miss Hartnell. "For I saw her walking round her garden at three o'clock this afternoon, and she seemed in perfect health."

"She and Dr. Haydock must be old acquaintances," said Mrs. Price Ridley. "He's been very quiet about it."

"It's curious," said Miss Wetherby, "that he's never mentioned it."

"As a matter of fact—" said Griselda in a low, mysterious voice, and stopped.

Everyone leaned forward excitedly.

"I happen to know," said Griselda impressively. "Her husband was a missionary. Terrible story. He was eaten, you know. Actually eaten. And she was forced to become the Chief's head wife. Dr. Haydock was with an expedition and rescued her."

For a moment excitement was rife, then Miss Marple said reproachfully, but with a smile:

"Naughty girl!"

She tapped Griselda reprovingly on the arm.

"Very unwise thing to do, my dear. If you make up these things, people are quite likely to believe them. And sometimes that leads to complications."

A distinct frost had come over the assembly. Two of the ladies rose to take their departure.

"I wonder if there *is* anything between young Lawrence Redding and Lettice Protheroe," said Miss Wetherby. "It certainly looks like it. What do you think, Miss Marple?"

Miss Marple seemed thoughtful.

"I shouldn't have said so myself. Not Lettice. Quite another person, I should have said."

"But Colonel Protheroe must have thought—"

"He has always struck me as rather a stupid man," said Miss Marple. "The kind of man who gets the wrong idea into his head and is obstinate about it. Do you remember Joe Bucknell who used to keep the Blue Boar? Such a to-do about his daughter carrying on with young Bailey. And all the time it was that minx of a wife of his."

She was looking full at Griselda as she spoke, and I suddenly felt a wild surge of anger.

"Don't you think, Miss Marple," I said, "that we're all inclined to let our tongues run away with us too much? Charity thinketh no evil, you know. Inestimable harm may be done by the foolish wagging of tongues in ill-natured gossip."

"Dear Vicar," said Miss Marple, "you are so unworldly. I'm afraid that, observing human nature for as long as I have done, one gets not to expect very much from it. I daresay idle tittle-tattle is very wrong and unkind, but it is so often true, isn't it?"

That last Parthian shot went home.

III

"NASTY OLD CAT," said Griselda as soon as the door was closed.

She made a face in the direction of the departing visitors and then looked at me and laughed.

"Len, do you really suspect me of having an affair with Lawrence Redding?"

"My dear, of course not."

"But you thought Miss Marple was hinting at it. And you rose to my defence simply beautifully. Like—like an angry tiger."

A momentary uneasiness assailed me. A clergyman of the Church of England ought never to put himself in the position of being described as an angry tiger. However, I trusted that Griselda exaggerated.

"I felt the occasion could not pass without a protest," I said. "But Griselda, I wish you would be a little more careful in what you say."

"Do you mean the cannibal story?" she asked. "Or the suggestion that Lawrence was painting me in the nude? If they only knew that he was painting me in a thick cloak with a very high fur collar—the sort of thing that you could go quite purely to see the Pope in—not a bit of sinful flesh showing anywhere! In fact, it's all marvellously pure. Lawrence never even attempts to make love to me—I can't think why."

"Surely, knowing that you're a married woman—"

"Don't pretend to come out of the Ark, Len. You know very well that an attractive young woman with an elderly husband is a kind of gift from heaven to a young man. There must be some other reason— It's not that I'm unattractive—I'm not."

"Surely you don't want him to make love to you?"

"N-n-o," said Griselda with more hesitation than I thought becoming.

"If he's in love with Lettice Protheroe—"

"Miss Marple didn't seem to think he was."

"Miss Marple may be mistaken."

"She never is. That kind of old cat is always right." She paused a minute and then said, with a quick, sidelong glance at me, "You do believe me, don't you? I mean, that there's nothing between Lawrence and me."

"My dear Griselda," I said surprised. "Of course."

My wife came across and kissed me.

"I wish you weren't so terribly easy to deceive, Len. You'd believe me whatever I said."

"I should hope so. But, my dear, I do beg of you to guard your tongue and be careful what you say. These women are singularly deficient in humour, remember, and take everything seriously."

"What they need," said Griselda, "is a little immorality in their lives. Then they wouldn't be so busy looking for it in other people's."

On this she left the room, and, glancing at my watch, I hurried out to pay some visits that ought to have been made earlier in the day.

The Wednesday evening service was sparsely attended as usual, but when I came out through the Church, after disrobing in the Vestry, it was empty save for a woman who stood staring up at one of our windows. We have some rather fine old stained glass, and indeed the Church itself is well worth looking at. She turned at my footsteps, and I saw that it was Mrs. Lestrange.

We both hesitated a moment and then I said:

"I hope you like our little church."

"I've been admiring the screen," she said.

Her voice was pleasant, low yet very distinct with a clear-cut enunciation. She added:

"I'm so sorry to have missed your wife yesterday."

We talked a few minutes longer about the church. She was evidently a cultured woman who knew something of church history and architecture. We left the building together and walked down the road, since one way to the Vicarage led past her house. As we arrived at the gate, she said pleasantly:

"Come in, won't you? And tell me what you think of what I have done."

I accepted the invitation. Little Gates had formerly belonged to an Anglo-Indian Colonel, and I could not help feeling relieved by the disappearance of the brass tables and the Burmese idols. It was furnished now very simply but in exquisite taste. There was a sense of harmony and rest about it.

Yet I wondered more and more what had brought such a woman as Mrs. Lestrange to St. Mary Mead. She was so very clearly a woman of the world that it seemed a strange taste to bury herself in a country village.

In the clear light of her drawing room I had an opportunity of observing her closely for the first time.

She was a very tall woman. Her hair was gold with a tinge of red in it. Her eyebrows and eyelashes were dark, whether by art or by nature I could not decide. If she was, as I thought, made up, it was done very artistically. There was something Sphinxlike about her face when it was in repose, and she had the most curious eyes I have ever seen—they were almost golden in shade.

Her clothes were perfect, and she had all the ease of manner of a well-bred woman, and yet there was something about her that was incongruous and baffling. You felt that she was a mystery. The word Griselda had used occurred to me—*sinister*. Absurd, of course, and yet—was it so absurd? The thought sprang unbidden into my mind:

"This woman would stick at nothing."

Our talk was on most normal lines—pictures, books, old churches. Yet somehow I got very strongly the impression that there was something else—something of quite a different nature that Mrs. Lestrange wanted to say to me.

I caught her eyes on me once or twice, looking at me with a curious hesitancy, as though she were unable to make up her mind. She kept the talk, I noticed, strictly to impersonal subjects. She made no mention of a husband, or of friends or relations.

But all the time there was that strange, urgent appeal in her glance. It seemed to say, "Shall I tell you? I want to. Can't you help me?"

Yet in the end it died away—or perhaps it had all been my fancy. I had the feeling that I was being dismissed. I rose and took my leave. As I went out of the room, I glanced back and saw her staring after me with a puzzled, doubtful expression. On an impulse I came back.

"If there is anything I can do—"

She said doubtfully, "It's very kind of you—"

We were both silent. Then she said:

"I wish I knew. It's very difficult. No, I don't think anyone can help me. But thank you for offering to do so."

That seemed final, so I went. But as I did so, I wondered. We are not used to mysteries in St. Mary Mead.

So much is this the case that as I emerged from the gate I was pounced upon. Miss Hartnell is very good at pouncing in a heavy and cumbrous way.

"I saw you!" she exclaimed with ponderous humour. "And I *was* so excited. Now you can tell us all about it."

"About what?"

"The mysterious lady! Is she a widow or has she a husband somewhere?"

"I really couldn't say. She didn't tell me."

"How very peculiar. One would think she would be certain to mention something casually. It almost looks, doesn't it, as though she had a reason for not speaking?"

"I really don't see that."

"Ah! but as dear Miss Marple says, you are so unworldly, dear Vicar. Tell me, has she known Dr. Haydock long?"

"She didn't mention him, so I don't know."

"Really? But what did you talk about then?"

"Pictures, music, books," I said truthfully.

Miss Hartnell, whose only topics of conversation are the purely personal, looked suspicious and unbelieving. Taking advantage of a momentary hesitation on her part as to how to proceed next, I bade her good night and walked rapidly away.

I called in at a house farther down the village and returned to the Vicarage by the garden gate, passing, as I did so, the danger point of Miss Marple's garden. However, I did not see how it was humanly possible for the news of my visit to Mrs. Lestrange to have yet reached her ears, so I felt reasonably safe.

As I latched the gate, it occurred to me that I would just step down to the shed in the garden which young Lawrence Redding was using as a studio, and see for myself how Griselda's portrait was progressing.

I append a rough sketch here which will be useful in the light of after happenings, only sketching in such details as are necessary.

I had no idea there was anyone in the studio. There had been no voices from within to warn me, and I suppose that my own footsteps made no noise upon the grass.

I opened the door and then stopped awkwardly on the threshold. For

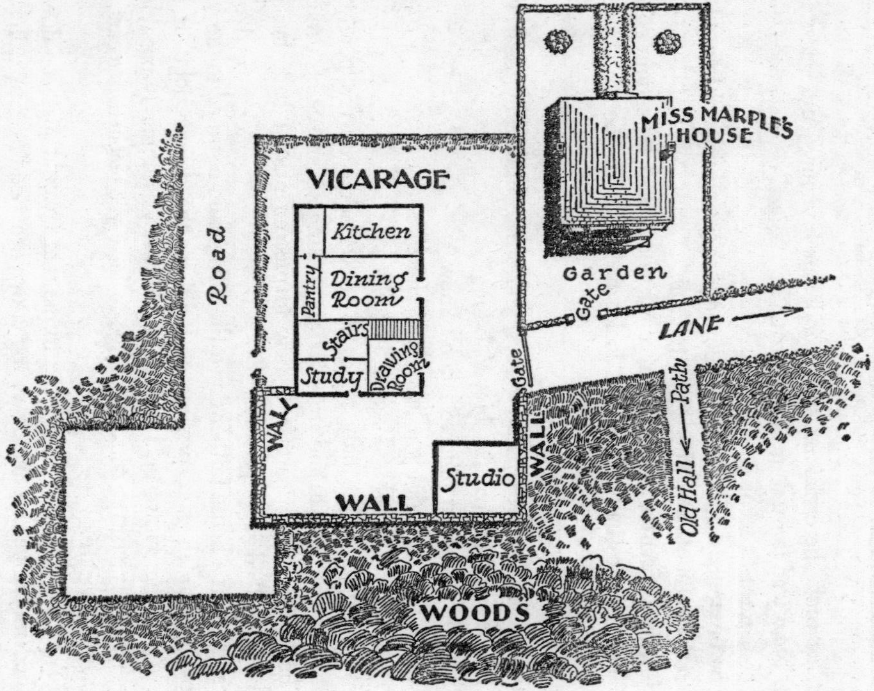
MISS MARPLE'S HOUSE
Garden
Gate
LANE
VICARAGE
Kitchen
Pantry
Dining Room
Stairs
Study
Drawing Room
Road
Gate
WALL
WALL
WALL
Studio
Path
Old Hall
WOODS

there were two people in the studio, and the man's arms were round the woman and he was kissing her passionately.

The two people were the artist, Lawrence Redding, and Mrs. Protheroe.

I backed out precipitately and beat a retreat to my study. There I sat down in a chair, took out my pipe, and thought things over. The discovery had come as a great shock to me. Especially since my conversation with Lettice that afternoon, I had felt fairly certain that there was some kind of understanding growing up between her and the young man. Moreover, I was convinced that she herself thought so. I felt positive that she had no idea of the artist's feelings for her stepmother.

A nasty tangle. I paid a grudging tribute to Miss Marple. She had not been deceived, but had evidently suspected the true state of things with a fair amount of accuracy. I had entirely misread her meaning glance at Griselda.

I had never dreamed of considering Mrs. Protheroe in the matter. There has always been rather a suggestion of Cæsar's wife about Mrs. Protheroe—a quiet, self-contained woman whom one would not suspect of any great depths of feeling.

I had got to this point in my meditations when a tap on my study window roused me. I got up and went to it. Mrs. Protheroe was standing outside. I opened the window and she came in, not waiting for an invitation on my part. She crossed the room in a breathless sort of way and dropped down on the sofa.

I had the feeling that I had never really seen her before. The quiet, self-contained woman that I knew had vanished. In her place was a quick-breathing, desperate creature. For the first time I realized that Anne Protheroe was beautiful.

She was a brown-haired woman with a pale face and very deep-set grey eyes. She was flushed now and her breast heaved. It was as though a statue had suddenly come to life. I blinked my eyes at the transformation.

"I thought it best to come," she said. "You—you saw just now?"

I bowed my head.

She said very quietly, "We love each other."

And even in the middle of her evident distress and agitation she could not keep a little smile from her lips. The smile of a woman who sees something very beautiful and wonderful.

I still said nothing, and she added presently:

"I suppose to you that seems very wrong?"

"Can you expect me to say anything else, Mrs. Protheroe?"

"No—no; I suppose not."

I went on, trying to make my voice as gentle as possible:

"You are a married woman—"

She interrupted me.

"Oh! I know—I know. Do you think I haven't gone over all that again and again? I'm not a bad woman really—I'm not. And things aren't—aren't—as you might think they are."

I said gravely, "I'm glad of that."

She asked rather timorously:

"Are you going to tell my husband?"

I said rather drily:

"There seems to be a general idea that a clergyman is incapable of behaving like a gentleman. That is not true."

She threw me a grateful glance.

"I'm so unhappy. Oh! I'm so dreadfully unhappy. I can't go on. I simply can't go on. And I don't know what to do." Her voice rose with a slightly hysterical note in it. "You don't know what my life is like. I've been miserable with Lucius from the beginning. No woman could be happy with him. I wish he were dead. It's awful, but I do. I'm desperate. I tell you, I'm desperate."

She started and looked over at the window.

"What was that? I thought I heard someone? Perhaps it's Lawrence."

I went over to the window, which I had not closed, as I had thought. I stepped out and looked down the garden, but there was no one in sight. Yet I was almost convinced that I, too, had heard someone. Or perhaps it was her certainty that had convinced me.

When I re-entered the room she was leaning forward, drooping her head down. She looked the picture of despair. She said again:

"I don't know what to do. I don't know what to do."

I came and sat down beside her. I said the things I thought it was my duty to say, and tried to say them with the necessary conviction, uneasily conscious all the time that that same morning I had given voice to the sentiment that a world without Colonel Protheroe in it would be improved for the better.

Above all, I begged her to do nothing rash. To leave her home and her husband was a very serious step.

I don't suppose I convinced her. I have lived long enough in the world to know that arguing with anyone in love is next door to useless, but I do think my words brought to her some measure of comfort.

When she rose to go, she thanked me, and promised to think over what I had said.

Nevertheless, when she had gone, I felt very uneasy. I felt that hitherto I had misjudged Anne Protheroe's character. She impressed me now as a very desperate woman, the kind of woman who would stick at nothing, once her emotions were aroused. And she was desperately, wildly, madly in love with Lawrence Redding, a man several years younger than herself.

I didn't like it.

IV

I HAD ENTIRELY forgotten that we had asked Lawrence Redding to dinner that night. When Griselda burst in and scolded me, pointing out that it lacked two minutes to dinner time, I was quite taken aback.

"I hope everything will be all right," Griselda called up the stairs after me. "I've thought over what you said at lunch, and I've really thought of some quite good things to eat."

I may say, in passing, that our evening meal amply bore out Griselda's assertion that things went much worse when she tried than when she didn't. The menu was ambitious in conception, and Mary seemed to have taken a perverse pleasure in seeing how best she could alternate undercooking and overcooking. Some oysters which Griselda had ordered, and which would seem to be beyond the reach of incompetence, we were unfortunately not able to sample, as we had nothing in the house to open them with—an omission which was discovered only when the moment for eating them arrived.

I had rather doubted whether Lawrence Redding would put in an appearance. He might very easily have sent an excuse. However, he arrived punctually enough, and the four of us went in to dinner.

Lawrence Redding has an undeniably attractive personality. He is, I suppose, about thirty years of age. He has dark hair, but his eyes are of a brilliant, almost startling blue. He is the kind of young man who does everything well. He is good at games, an excellent shot, a good amateur, and can tell a first-rate story. He is capable of making any party go. He has, I think, Irish blood in his veins. He is not, at all, one's idea of the typical artist. Yet I believe he is a clever painter in the modern style. I know very little of painting myself.

It was only natural that on this particular evening he should appear a shade distrait. On the whole, he carried off things very well. I don't think Griselda or Dennis noticed anything wrong. Probably I should not have noticed anything myself if I had not known beforehand.

Griselda and Dennis were particularly gay—full of jokes about Dr. Stone and Miss Cram—the Local Scandal! It suddenly came home to me with something of a pang that Dennis is nearer Griselda's age than I am. He calls me Uncle Len but her Griselda. It gave me, somehow, a lonely feeling.

I must, I think, have been upset by Mrs. Protheroe. I'm not usually given to such unprofitable reflections.

Griselda and Dennis went rather far now and then, but I hadn't the heart to check them. I have always thought it a pity that the mere presence of a clergyman should have a damping effect.

Lawrence took a gay part in the conversation. Nevertheless I was aware of his eyes continually straying to where I sat, and I was not surprised when after dinner he manœuvred to get me into the study.

As soon as we were alone, his manner changed. His face became grave and anxious. He looked almost haggard.

"You've surprised our secret, sir," he said. "What are you going to do about it?"

I could speak far more plainly to Redding than I could to Mrs. Protheroe, and I did so. He took it very well.

"Of course," he said when I had finished. "You're bound to say all this. You're a parson. I don't mean that in any way offensively. As a matter of fact, I think you're probably right. But this isn't the usual sort of thing between Anne and me."

I told him that people had been saying that particular phrase since the dawn of time, and a queer little smile creased his lips.

"You mean everyone thinks their case is unique? Perhaps so. But one thing you must believe."

He assured me that so far—"there was nothing wrong in it." Anne, he said, was one of the truest and most loyal women that ever lived. What was going to happen he didn't know.

"If this were only a book," he said gloomily, "the old man would die—and a good riddance to everybody."

I reproved him.

"Oh! I didn't mean I was going to stick him in the back with a knife, though I'd offer my best thanks to anyone else who did so. There's not a soul in the world who's got a good word to say for him. I rather wonder the first Mrs. Protheroe didn't do him in. I met her once, years ago, and she looked quite capable of it. One of those calm, dangerous women. He goes blustering along, stirring up trouble everywhere, mean as the devil, and with a particularly nasty temper. You don't know what Anne has had to stand from him. If I had a penny in the world I'd take her away without any more ado."

Then I spoke to him very earnestly. I begged him to leave St. Mary Mead. By remaining there, he could only bring greater unhappiness on Anne Protheroe than was already her lot. People would talk; the matter would get to Colonel Protheroe's ears—and things would be made infinitely worse for her.

Lawrence protested.

"Nobody knows a thing about it except you, padre."

"My dear young man, you underestimate the detective instinct of village life. In St. Mary Mead everyone knows your most intimate affairs. There is no detective in England equal to a spinster lady of uncertain age with plenty of time on her hands."

He said easily that that was all right. Everyone thought it was Lettice.

"Has it occurred to you," I asked, "that possibly Lettice might think so herself?"

He seemed quite surprised by the idea. Lettice, he said, didn't care a hang about him. He was sure of that.

"She's a queer sort of girl," he said. "Always seems in a kind of dream, and yet underneath I believe she's really rather practical. I believe all that vague stuff is a pose. Lettice knows jolly well what she's doing. And there's a funny vindictive streak in her. The queer thing is that she hates Anne. Simply loathes her. And yet Anne's been a perfect angel to her always."

I did not, of course, take his word for this last. To infatuated young men, their inamorata always behaves like an angel. Still, to the best of my observation, Anne had always behaved to her stepdaughter with kindness and fairness. I had been surprised myself that afternoon at the bitterness of Lettice's tone.

We had to leave the conversation there, because Griselda and Dennis burst in upon us and said I was not to make Lawrence behave like an old fogy.

"Oh! dear," said Griselda, throwing herself into an arm chair. "How I would like a thrill of some kind. A murder—or even a burglary."

"I don't suppose there's anyone much worth burgling," said Lawrence, trying to enter into her mood. "Unless we stole Miss Hartnell's false teeth."

"They do click horribly," said Griselda. "But you're wrong about there being no one worth while. There's some marvellous old silver at Old Hall. Trencher salts and a Charles II Tazza—all kinds of things like that. Worth thousands of pounds, I believe."

"The old man would probably shoot you with an army revolver," said Dennis. "Just the sort of thing he'd enjoy doing."

"Oh! we'd get in first and hold him up," said Griselda. "Who's got a revolver?"

"I've got a Mauser pistol," said Lawrence.

"Have you? How exciting! Why do you have it?"

"Souvenir of the War," said Lawrence briefly.

"Old Protheroe was showing the silver to Stone today," volunteered Dennis. "Old Stone was pretending to be no end interested in it."

"I thought they'd quarrelled about the barrow," said Griselda.

"Oh! they've made that up," said Dennis. "I can't think what people want to grub about in barrows for, anyway."

"That man Stone puzzles me," said Lawrence. "I think he must be very absent-minded. You'd swear sometimes he knew nothing about his own subject."

"That's love," said Dennis. "Sweet Gladys Cram, you are no sham. Your teeth are white and fill me with delight. Come, fly with me, my bride to be. And at the Blue Boar, on the bedroom floor—"

"That's enough, Dennis," I said.

"Well," said Lawrence Redding, "I must be off. Thank you very much, Mrs. Clement, for a very pleasant evening."

Griselda and Dennis saw him off. Dennis returned to the study alone. Something had happened to ruffle the boy. He wandered about the room aimlessly, frowning and kicking the furniture.

Our furniture is so shabby already that it can hardly be damaged further, but I felt impelled to utter a mild protest.

"Sorry," said Dennis.

He was silent for a moment and then burst out:

"What an absolutely rotten thing gossip is!"

I was a little surprised. Dennis does not usually take that attitude.

"What's the matter?" I asked.

"I don't know whether I ought to tell you."

I was more and more surprised.

"It's such an absolutely rotten thing," Dennis said again. "Going round and saying things. Not even saying them. Hinting them. No, I'm damned —sorry—if I'll tell you! It's too absolutely rotten."

I looked at him curiously but I did not press him further. I wondered very much, though. It is very unlike Dennis to take anything to heart.

Griselda came in at that moment.

"Miss Wetherby's just rung up," she said. "Mrs. Lestrange went out at a quarter past eight and hasn't come in yet. Nobody knows where she's gone."

"Why should they know?"

"But it isn't to Dr. Haydock's. Miss Wetherby does know that, because she telephoned to Miss Hartnell who lives next door to him and who would have been sure to see her."

"It is a mystery to me," I said, "how anyone ever gets any nourishment in this place. They must eat their meals standing up by the window so as to be sure of not missing anything."

"And that's not all," said Griselda bubbling with pleasure. "They've found out about the Blue Boar. Dr. Stone and Miss Cram have got rooms next door to each other BUT—" she waved an impressive forefinger—"no communicating door!"

"That," I said, "must be very disappointing to everybody."

At which Griselda laughed.

Thursday started badly. Two of the ladies of my parish elected to quarrel about the church decorations. I was called in to adjudicate between two middle-aged ladies, each of whom was literally trembling with rage. If it had not been so painful, it would have been quite an interesting physical phenomenon.

Then I had to reprove two of our choir boys for persistent sweet sucking during the hours of divine service, and I had an uneasy feeling that I was not doing the job as whole-heartedly as I should have done.

Then our organist, who is distinctly "touchy," had taken offence and had to be smoothed down.

And four of my poorer parishioners declared open rebellion against Miss Hartnell who came to me bursting with rage about it.

I was just going home when I met Colonel Protheroe. He was in high good humour having sentenced three poachers, in his capacity as magistrate.

"Firmness," he shouted in his stentorian voice. He is slightly deaf and raises his voice accordingly as deaf people often do. "That's what's needed nowadays—firmness! Make an example. That rogue Archer came out yesterday and is vowing vengeance against me, I hear. Impudent scoundrel. Threatened men live long, as the saying goes. I'll show him what his vengeance is worth, next time I catch him taking my pheasants. Lax!

We're too lax nowadays! I believe in showing a man up for what he is. You're always being asked to consider a man's wife and children. Damned nonsense. Fiddlesticks. Why should a man escape the consequences of his acts just because he whines about his wife and children? It's all the same to me—no matter what a man is—doctor, lawyer, clergyman, poacher, drunken wastrel—if you catch him on the wrong side of the law, let the law punish him. You agree with me, I'm sure."

"You forget," I said. "My calling obliges me to respect one quality above all others—the quality of mercy."

"Well, I'm a just man. No one can deny that."

I did not speak and he said sharply:

"Why don't you answer? A penny for your thoughts, man."

I hesitated, then I decided to speak.

"I was thinking," I said, "that, when my time comes, I should be sorry if the only plea I had to offer was that of justice. Because it might mean that only justice would be meted out to me."

"Pah! What we need is a little militant Christianity. I've always done my duty, I hope. Well, no more of that. I'll be along this evening as I said. We'll make it a quarter past six instead of six, if you don't mind. I've got to see a man in the village."

"That will suit me quite well."

He flourished his stick and strode away. Turning, I ran into Hawes. I thought he looked distinctly ill this morning. I had meant to upbraid him mildly for various matters, in his province, which had been muddled or shelved, but seeing his white, strained face, I felt that the man was ill.

I said as much and he denied it, but not very vehemently. Finally he confessed that he was not feeling too fit, and appeared ready to accept my advice of going home to bed.

I had a hurried lunch and went out to do some visits. Griselda had gone to London by the cheap Thursday train.

I came in about a quarter to four with the intention of sketching the outline of my Sunday sermon, but Mary told me that Mr. Redding was waiting for me in the study.

I found him pacing up and down with a worried face. He looked white and haggard.

He turned abruptly at my entrance.

"Look here, sir. I've been thinking over what you said yesterday. I've had a sleepless night thinking about it. You're right. I've got to cut and run."

"My dear boy," I said.

"You were right in what you said about Anne. I'll only bring trouble on her by staying here. She's—she's too good for anything else. I see I've got to go. I've made things hard enough for her as it is, Heaven help me."

"I think you have made the only decision possible," I said. "I know that it is a hard one, but believe me, it will be for the best in the end."

I could see that he thought that that was the kind of thing easily said by someone who didn't know what he was talking about.

"You'll look after Anne? She needs a friend."

"You can rest assured that I will do everything in my power."

"Thank you, sir." He wrung my hand. "You're a good sort, padre. I shall see her to say good-bye this evening, and I shall probably pack up and go tomorrow. No good prolonging the agony. Thanks for letting me have the shed to paint in. I'm sorry not to have finished Mrs. Clement's portrait."

"Don't worry about that, my dear boy. Good-bye, and God bless you."

When he had gone I tried to settle down to my sermon, but with very poor success. I kept thinking of Lawrence and Anne Protheroe.

I had rather an unpalatable cup of tea, cold and black, and at half past five the telephone rang. I was informed that Mr. Abbott of Lower Farm was dying and would I please come at once.

I rang up Old Hall immediately, for Lower Farm was nearly two miles away and I could not possibly get back by six-fifteen. I have never succeeded in learning to ride a bicycle.

I was told, however, that Colonel Protheroe had just started out in the car, so I departed, leaving word with Mary that I had been called away but would try to be back by six-thirty or soon after.

V

IT WAS NEARER seven than half past six when I approached the Vicarage gate on my return. Before I reached it, it swung open and Lawrence Redding came out. He stopped dead on seeing me and I was immediately struck by his appearance. He looked like a man who was on the point of going mad. His eyes stared in a peculiar manner; he was deathly white, and he was shaking and twitching all over.

I wondered for a moment whether he could have been drinking, but repudiated the idea immediately.

"Hullo," I said, "have you been to see me again? Sorry I was out. Come back now. I've got to see Protheroe about some accounts—but I daresay we shan't be long."

"Protheroe," he said. He began to laugh. "Protheroe? You're going to see Protheroe? Oh! you'll see Protheroe all right. Oh! my God—yes."

I stared. Instinctively I stretched out a hand towards him. He drew sharply aside.

"No," he almost cried out. "I've got to get away—to think. I've got to think. I must think."

He broke into a run and vanished rapidly down the road towards the village leaving me staring after him, my first idea of drunkenness recurring.

Finally I shook my head, and went on to the Vicarage. The front door is always left open, but nevertheless I rang the bell. Mary came wiping her hands on her apron.

"So you're back at last," she observed.

"Is Colonel Protheroe here?" I asked.

"In the study. Been here since a quarter past six."

"And Mr. Redding's been here?"

"Come a few minutes ago. Asked for you. I told him you'd be back any minute and that Colonel Protheroe was waiting in the study, and he said he'd wait too and went there. He's there now."

"No, he isn't," I said. "I've just met him going down the road."

"Well, I didn't hear him leave. He can't have stayed more than a couple of minutes. The mistress isn't back from town yet."

I nodded absent-mindedly. Mary beat a retreat to the kitchen quarters and I went down the passage and opened the study door.

After the dusk of the passage, the evening sunshine that was pouring into the room made my eyes blink. I took a step or two across the floor and then stopped dead.

For a moment I could hardly take in the meaning of the scene before me.

Colonel Protheroe was lying sprawled across my writing table in a horrible, unnatural position. There was a pool of some dark fluid on the desk by his head, and it was slowly dripping onto the floor with a horrible drip, drip, drip.

I pulled myself together and went across to him. His skin was cold to the touch. The hand that I raised fell back lifeless. The man was dead—shot through the head.

I went to the door and called Mary. When she came I ordered her to run as fast as she could and fetch Dr. Haydock, whose house is next door to mine. I told her there had been an accident.

Then I went back and closed the door to await the doctor's coming.

Fortunately Mary found him at home. Haydock is a good fellow, a big, fine, strapping fellow, with an honest, rugged face.

His eyebrows went up when I pointed silently across the room. But like a true doctor he showed no signs of emotion. He bent over the dead man, examining him rapidly. Then he straightened himself and looked across at me.

"Well?" I asked.

"He's dead right enough—been dead half an hour, I should say."

"Suicide?"

"Out of the question, man. Look at the position of the wound. Besides, if he shot himself, where's the weapon?"

True enough, there was no sign of any such thing.

"We'd better not mess around with anything," said Haydock. "I'd better ring up the police."

He picked up the receiver and spoke into it. He gave the facts as curtly as possible and then replaced the telephone and came across to where I was sitting.

"This is a rotten business. How did you come to find him?"

I explained.

"A rotten business," he repeated.

"Is—is it murder?" I asked rather faintly.

"Looks like it. Mean to say, what else can it be? Extraordinary business. Wonder who had a down on the poor old fellow. Of course I know he wasn't popular, but one isn't often murdered for that reason—worse luck."

"There's one rather curious thing," I said. "I was telephoned for this afternoon to go to a dying parishioner. When I got there everyone was very surprised to see me. The sick man was very much better than he had been for some days, and his wife flatly denied telephoning for me at all."

Haydock drew his brows together.

"That's suggestive—very. You were being got out of the way. Where's your wife?"

"Gone up to London for the day."

"And the maid?"

"In the kitchen—right at the other side of the house."

"Where she wouldn't be likely to hear anything that went on in here.

It's a nasty business. Who knew that Protheroe was coming here this evening?"

"He referred to the fact this morning in the village street, at the top of his voice as usual."

"Meaning that the whole village knew it! Which they always do in any case. Know of anyone who had a grudge against him?"

The thought of Lawrence Redding's white face and staring eyes came to my mind. I was spared answering by a noise of shuffling feet in the passage outside.

"The police," said my friend, and rose to his feet.

Our police force was represented by Constable Hurst, looking very important but slightly worried.

"Good evening, gentlemen," he greeted us. "The Inspector will be here any minute. In the meantime I'll follow out his instructions. I understand Colonel Protheroe's been found shot—in the Vicarage."

He paused and directed a look of cold suspicion at me which I tried to meet with a suitable bearing of conscious innocence.

He moved over to the writing table and announced:

"Nothing to be touched till the Inspector comes."

For the convenience of my readers, I append a sketch plan of the room.

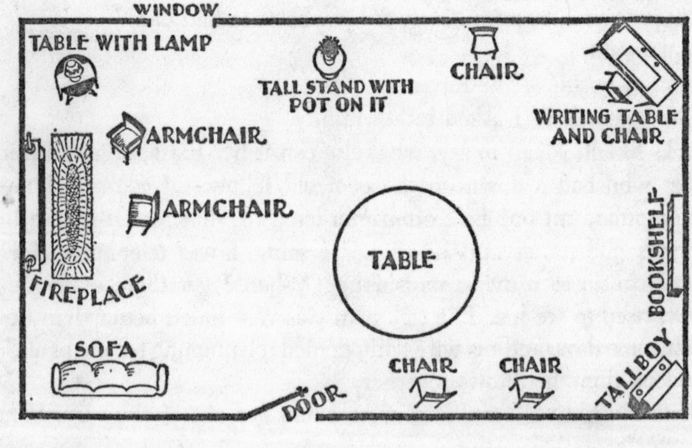

He got out his notebook, moistened his pencil and looked expectantly at both of us.

I repeated my story of discovering the body. When he had got it all down, which took some time, he turned to the doctor.

"In your opinion, Dr. Haydock, what was the cause of death?"

"Shot through the head at close quarters."

"And the weapon?"

"I can't say with certainty until we get the bullet out. But I should say in all probability the bullet was fired from a pistol of small calibre—say a Mauser .25."

I started, remembering our conversation of the night before, and Lawrence Redding's admission. The police constable brought his cold fishlike eye round on me.

"Did you speak, sir?"

I shook my head. Whatever suspicions I might have, they were no more than suspicions, and as such to be kept to myself.

"When, in your opinion, did the tragedy occur?"

The doctor hesitated for a minute before he answered. Then he said:

"The man has been dead just over half an hour, I should say. Certainly not longer."

Hurst turned to me.

"Did the girl hear anything?"

"As far as I know she heard nothing," I said. "But you had better ask her."

But at this moment Inspector Slack arrived, having come by car from Much Benham, two miles away.

All that I can say of Inspector Slack is that never did a man more determinedly strive to contradict his name. He was a dark man, restless and energetic in manner, with black eyes that snapped ceaselessly. His manner was rude and overbearing in the extreme.

He acknowledged our greetings with a curt nod, seized his subordinate's notebook, perused it, exchanged a few curt words with him in an undertone, then strode over to the body.

"Everything's been messed up and pulled about, I suppose," he said.

"I've touched nothing," said Haydock.

"No more have I," I said.

The Inspector busied himself for some time peering at the things on the table and examining the pool of blood.

"Ah!" he said in a tone of triumph. "Here's what we want. Clock overturned when he fell forward. That'll give us the time of the crime. Twenty-two minutes past six. What time did you say death occurred, doctor?"

"I said about half an hour, but—"

The Inspector consulted his watch.

"Five minutes past seven. I got word about ten minutes ago, at five minutes to seven. Discovery of the body was at about a quarter to seven. I understand you were fetched immediately. Say you examined it at ten minutes to— Why, that brings it to the identical second almost!"

"I don't guarantee the time absolutely," said Haydock. "That is an approximate estimate."

"Good enough, sir, good enough."

I had been trying to get a word in.

"About that clock—"

"If you'll excuse me, sir, I'll ask you any questions I want to know. Time's short. What I want is absolute silence."

"Yes, but I'd like to tell you—"

"Absolute silence," said the Inspector, glaring at me ferociously.

I gave him what he asked for.

He was still peering about the writing table.

"What was he sitting here for," he grunted. "Did he want to write a note? Hullo—what's this?"

He held up a piece of note paper triumphantly. So pleased was he with his find that he permitted us to come to his side and examine it with him.

It was a piece of Vicarage note paper, and it was headed at the top 6.20.

DEAR CLEMENT (it began)

Sorry I cannot wait any longer, but I must . . .

Here the writing tailed off in a scrawl.

"Plain as a pike staff," said Inspector Slack triumphantly. "He sits down here to write this; an enemy comes softly in through the window and shoots him as he writes. What more do you want?"

"I'd just like to say—" I began.

"Out of the way, if you please, sir. I want to see if there are footprints."

He went down on his hands and knees, moving towards the open window.

"I think you ought to know—" I said obstinately.

The Inspector rose. He spoke without heat, but firmly:

"We'll go into all that later. I'd be obliged if you gentlemen will clear out of here. Right out, if you please."

We permitted ourselves to be shooed out like children.

Hours seemed to have passed—yet it was only a quarter past seven.

"Well," said Haydock. "That's that. When that conceited ass wants me, you can send him over to the surgery. So long."

"The mistress is back," said Mary, making a brief appearance from the kitchen. Her eyes were round and agog with excitement. "Come in about five minutes ago."

I found Griselda in the drawing room. She looked frightened, but excited.

I told her everything and she listened attentively.

"The letter is headed 6.20," I ended. "And the clock fell over and has stopped at 6.22."

"Yes," said Griselda. "But that clock, didn't you tell him that it was always kept a quarter of an hour fast?"

"No," I said. "I didn't. He wouldn't let me. I tried my best."

Griselda was frowning in a puzzled manner.

"But, Len," she said. "That makes the whole thing perfectly extraordinary. Because when that clock said twenty past six it was really five minutes past, and at five minutes past I don't suppose Colonel Protheroe had even arrived at the house."

VI

WE PUZZLED OVER the business of the clock for some time, but we could make nothing of it. Griselda said I ought to make another effort and tell Inspector Slack about it, but on that point I was feeling what I can only describe as "mulish."

Inspector Slack had been abominably and most unnecessarily rude. I was looking forward to a moment when I could produce my valuable contribution and effect his discomfiture. I would then say in a tone of mild reproach:

"If you had only listened to me, Inspector Slack—"

I expected that he would at least speak to me before he left the house, but to our surprise we learned from Mary that he had departed, having locked up the study door and issued orders that no one was to attempt to enter the room.

Griselda suggested going up to Old Hall.

"It will be so awful for Anne Protheroe—with the police and everything," she said. "Perhaps I might be able to do something for her."

I cordially approved of this plan, and Griselda set off with instructions that she was to telephone to me if she thought that I could be of any use or comfort to either of the ladies.

I now proceeded to ring up the Sunday School teachers who were coming at 7.45 for their weekly preparation class. I thought that under the circumstances it would be better to put them off.

Dennis was the next person to arrive on the scene, having just returned from a tennis party. The fact that murder had taken place at the Vicarage seemed to afford him acute satisfaction.

"Fancy being right on the spot in a murder case," he exclaimed. "I've always wanted to be right in the midst of one. Why have the police locked up the study? Wouldn't one of the other door keys fit it?"

I refused to allow anything of the sort to be attempted. Dennis gave in with a bad grace. After extracting every possible detail from me he went out into the garden to look for footprints, remarking cheerfully that it was lucky it was only old Protheroe, whom everyone disliked.

His cheerful callousness rather grated on me, but I reflected that I was perhaps being hard on the boy. At Dennis' age a detective story is one of the best things in life, and to find a real detective story, complete with corpse, waiting on one's own front doorstep, so to speak, is bound to send a healthy minded boy into the seventh heaven of enjoyment. Death means very little to a boy of sixteen.

Griselda came back in about an hour's time. She had seen Anne Protheroe, having arrived just after the Inspector had broken the news to her.

On hearing that Mrs. Protheroe had last seen her husband in the village about a quarter to six, and that she had no light of any kind to throw upon the matter, he had taken his departure, explaining that he would return on the morrow for a fuller interview.

"He was quite decent in his way," said Griselda grudgingly.

"How did Mrs. Protheroe take it?" I asked.

"Well—she was very quiet—but then she always is."

"Yes," I said. "I can't imagine Anne Protheroe going into hysterics."

"Of course it was a great shock. You could see that. She thanked me for coming and said she was very grateful, but that there was nothing I could do."

"What about Lettice?"

"She was out playing tennis somewhere. She hadn't got home yet."

There was a pause and then Griselda said:

"You know, Len, she was really very queer—very queer indeed."

"The shock," I suggested.

"Yes—I suppose so. And yet—" Griselda furrowed her brows perplexedly.

"It wasn't like that somehow. She didn't seem so much bowled over as—well—terrified."

"Terrified?"

"Yes—not showing it, you know. At least not meaning to show it. But a queer, watchful look in her eyes. I wonder if she has a sort of idea who did kill him. She asked again and again if anyone were suspected."

"Did she?" I said thoughtfully.

"Yes. Of course Anne's got marvellous self-control, but one could see that she was terribly upset. More so than I would have thought, for after all it wasn't as though she were so devoted to him. I should have said she rather disliked him, if anything."

"Death alters one's feelings sometimes," I said.

"Yes, I suppose so."

Dennis came in and was full of excitement over a footprint he had found in one of the flower beds. He was sure that the police had overlooked it, and that it would turn out to be the turning point of the mystery.

I spent a troubled night. Dennis was up and about and out of the house long before breakfast, to "study the latest developments," as he said.

Nevertheless it was not he, but Mary, who brought us the morning's sensational bit of news.

We had just sat down to breakfast when she burst into the room, her cheeks red and her eyes shining, and addressed us with her customary lack of ceremony.

"Would you believe it? The baker's just told me. They've arrested young Mr. Redding."

"Arrested Lawrence," cried Griselda incredulously. "Impossible. It must be some stupid mistake."

"No mistake about it, Mum," said Mary with a kind of gloating exultation. "Mr. Redding, he went there himself and gave himself up. Last night last thing. Went right in, threw down the pistol on the table and, 'I did it,' he says. Just like that."

She looked at us both, nodded her head vigorously, and withdrew, satisfied with the effect she had produced. Griselda and I stared at each other.

"Oh! it isn't true," said Griselda. "It can't be true."

She noticed my silence and said, "Len, you don't think it's true?"

I found it hard to answer her. I sat silent, thoughts whirling through my head.

"He must be mad," said Griselda. "Absolutely mad. Or do you think they were looking at the pistol together and it suddenly went off?"

"That doesn't sound at all a likely thing to happen."

"But it must have been an accident of some kind. Because there's not a shadow of a motive. What earthly reason could Lawrence have for killing Colonel Protheroe?"

I could have answered that question very decidedly, but I wished to spare Anne Protheroe as far as possible. There might still be a chance of keeping her name out of it.

"Remember, they had had a quarrel," I said.

"About Lettice and her bathing dress. Yes, but that's absurd. And even if he and Lettice were engaged secretly, well, that's not a reason for killing her father."

"We don't know what the true facts of the case may be, Griselda."

"You do believe it, Len! Oh! how can you! I tell you, I'm sure Lawrence never touched a hair of his head."

"Remember, I met him just outside the gate. He looked like a madman."

"Yes, but—oh! it's impossible."

"There's the clock, too," I said. "This explains the clock. Lawrence must have put it back to 6.22 with the idea of making an alibi for himself. Look how Inspector Slack fell into the trap."

"You're wrong, Len. Lawrence knew about that clock being fast. 'Keeping the Vicar up to time!' he used to say. Lawrence would never have made the mistake of putting it back to 6.22. He'd have put the hands somewhere possible—like a quarter to seven."

"He mayn't have known what time Protheroe got here. Or he may have simply forgotten about the clock being fast."

Griselda disagreed.

"No, if you were committing a murder, you'd be awfully careful about things like that."

"You don't know, my dear," I said mildly. "You've never done one."

Before Griselda could reply, a shadow fell across the breakfast table, and a very gentle voice said:

"I hope I am not intruding. You must forgive me. But in the sad circumstances—the very sad circumstances—"

It was our neighbour, Miss Marple. Accepting our polite disclaimers, she stepped in through the window and I drew up a chair for her. She looked faintly flushed and quite excited.

"Very terrible, is it not? Poor Colonel Protheroe. Not a very pleasant man, perhaps, and not exactly popular, but it's none the less sad for that. And actually shot in the Vicarage study, I understand?"

I said that that had indeed been the case.

"But the dear Vicar was not here at the time?" Miss Marple questioned of Griselda.

I explained where I had been.

"Mr. Dennis is not with you this morning?" said Miss Marple glancing round.

"Dennis," said Griselda, "fancies himself as an amateur detective. He is very excited about a footprint he found in one of the flower beds and I fancy has gone off to tell the police about it."

"Dear, dear," said Miss Marple. "Such a to-do, is it not? And Mr. Dennis thinks he knows who committed the crime. Well, I suppose we all think we know."

"You mean it is obvious?" said Griselda.

"No, dear, I didn't mean that at all. I daresay everyone thinks it is somebody different. That is why it is so important to have proofs. I, for instance, am quite convinced I know who did it. But I must admit I haven't one shadow of proof. One must, I know, be very careful of what one says at a time like this—criminal libel, don't they call it? I had made up my mind to be most careful with Inspector Slack. He sent word he would come and see me this morning, but now he has just 'phoned up to say it won't be necessary after all."

"I suppose, since the arrest, it isn't necessary," I said.

"The arrest?" Miss Marple leaned forward, her cheeks pink with excitement. "I didn't know there had been an arrest."

It is so seldom that Miss Marple is worse informed than we are that I had taken it for granted that she would know the latest developments.

"It seems we have been talking at cross purposes," I said. "Yes, there has been an arrest—Lawrence Redding."

"Lawrence Redding?" Miss Marple seemed very surprised. "Now I should not have thought—"

Griselda interrupted vehemently.

"I can't believe it even now. No, not though he has actually confessed."

"Confessed?" said Miss Marple. "You say he has confessed? Oh! dear, I see I have been sadly at sea—yes, sadly at sea."

"I can't help feeling it must have been some kind of an accident," said Griselda. "Don't you think so, Len? I mean his coming forward to give himself up looks like that."

Miss Marple leant forward eagerly.

"He gave himself up, you say?"

"Yes."

"Oh!" said Miss Marple, with a deep sigh. "I am so glad—so very glad."

I looked at her in some surprise.

"It shows a true state of remorse, I suppose," I said.

"Remorse?" Miss Marple looked very surprised. "Oh! but surely dear, dear Vicar, you don't think that he is guilty?"

It was my turn to stare.

"But since he has confessed—"

"Yes, but that just proves it, doesn't it? I mean that he had nothing to do with it."

"No," I said. "I may be dense, but I can't see that it does. If you have not committed a murder, I cannot see the object of pretending you have."

"Oh! of course, there's a reason," said Miss Marple. "Naturally. There's always a reason, isn't there? And young men are so hot-headed and often prone to believe the worst."

She turned to Griselda.

"Don't you agree with me, my dear?"

"I—I don't know," said Griselda. "It's difficult to know what to think. I can't see any reason for Lawrence behaving like a perfect idiot."

"If you had seen his face last night—" I began.

"Tell me," said Miss Marple.

I described my homecoming while she listened attentively.

When I had finished she said:

"I know that I am very often rather foolish and don't take in things as I should, but I really do not see your point. It seems to me that if a young man had made up his mind to the great wickedness of taking a fellow creature's life, he would not appear distraught about it afterwards. It would be a premeditated and cold-blooded action and, though the murderer might be a little flurried and possibly might make some small mistake, I do not think it likely he would fall into a state of agitation such as you describe. It is difficult to put oneself in such a position, but I cannot imagine getting into a state like that myself."

"We don't know the circumstances," I argued. "If there was a quarrel, the shot may have been fired in a sudden gust of passion, and Lawrence might afterwards have been appalled at what he had done. Indeed, I prefer to think that that is what did actually occur."

"I know, dear Mr. Clement, that there are many ways we prefer to look at things. But one must actually take facts as they are, must one not? And it does not seem to me that the facts bear the interpretation you put upon them. Your maid distinctly stated that Mr. Redding was only in the house a couple of minutes, not long enough, surely, for a quarrel such as you describe. And then again, I understand the Colonel was shot through the back of the head while he was writing a letter—at least that is what my maid told me."

"Quite true," said Griselda. "He seems to have been writing a note to say he couldn't wait any longer. The note was dated 6.20, and the clock on the table was overturned and had stopped at 6.22, and that's just what has been puzzling Len and myself so frightfully."

She explained our custom of keeping the clock a quarter of an hour fast.

"Very curious," said Miss Marple. "Very curious indeed. But the note seems to me even more curious still. I mean—"

She stopped and looked round. Lettice Protheroe was standing outside the window. She came in, nodding to us and murmuring, "Morning."

She dropped into a chair and said, with rather more animation than usual, "They've arrested Lawrence, I hear."

"Yes," said Griselda. "It's been a great shock to us."

"I never really thought anyone would murder Father," said Lettice. She was obviously taking a pride in letting no hint of distress or emotion escape her. "Lots of people wanted to, I'm sure. There are times when I'd have liked to do it myself."

"Won't you have something to eat or drink, Lettice?" asked Griselda.

"No, thank you. I just drifted round to see if you'd got my beret here—a queer little yellow one. I think I left it in the study the other day."

"If you did, it's there still," said Griselda. "Mary never tidies anything."

"I'll go and see," said Lettice rising. "Sorry to be such a bother, but I seem to have lost everything else in the hat line."

"I'm afraid you can't get it now," I said. "Inspector Slack has locked the room up."

"Oh! what a bore. Can't we get in through the window?"

"I'm afraid not. It is latched in the inside. Surely, Lettice, a yellow beret won't be much good to you at present?"

"You mean mourning and all that? I shan't bother about mourning. I think it's an awfully archaic idea. It's a nuisance about Lawrence—yes, it's a nuisance."

She got up and stood frowning abstractedly.

"I suppose it's all on account of me and my bathing dress. So silly, the whole thing."

Griselda opened her mouth to say something, but for some unexplained reason shut it again.

A curious smile came to Lettice's lips.

"I think," she said softly, "I'll go home and tell Anne about Lawrence being arrested."

She went out of the window again. Griselda turned to Miss Marple.

"Why did you step on my foot?"

The old lady was smiling.

"I thought you were going to say something, my dear. And it is often so much better to let things develop on their own lines. I don't think, you know, that that child is half so vague as she pretends to be. She's got a very definite idea in her head, and she's acting upon it."

Mary gave a loud knock on the dining-room door and entered hard upon it.

"What is it?" said Griselda. "And Mary, you must remember not to knock on doors. I've told you about it before."

"Thought you might be busy," said Mary. "Colonel Melchett's here. Wants to see the master."

Colonel Melchett is Chief Constable of the County. I rose at once.

"I thought you wouldn't like my leaving him in the hall, so I put him in the drawing room," went on Mary. "Shall I clear?"

"Not yet," said Griselda. "I'll ring."

She turned to Miss Marple and I left the room.

VII

Colonel Melchett is a dapper little man with a habit of snorting suddenly and unexpectedly. He has red hair and rather keen, bright-blue eyes.

"Good morning, Vicar," he said. "Nasty business, eh? Poor old Protheroe. Not that I liked him. I didn't. Nobody did for that matter. Nasty bit of work for you, too. Hope it hasn't upset your Missus?"

I said Griselda had taken it very well.

"That's lucky. Rotten thing to happen in one's house. I must say I'm surprised at young Redding—doing it the way he did. No sort of consideration for anyone's feelings."

A wild desire to laugh came over me, but Colonel Melchett evidently saw nothing odd in the idea of a murderer being considerate, so I held my peace.

"I must say I was rather taken aback when I heard the fellow had marched in and given himself up," continued Colonel Melchett, dropping on to a chair.

"How did it happen, exactly?"

"Last night. About ten o'clock. Fellow rolls in, throws down a pistol and says, 'Here I am. I did it.' Just like that."

"What account does he give of the business?"

"Precious little. He was warned, of course, about making a statement. But he merely laughed. Said he came here to see you—found Protheroe here. They had words and he shot him. Won't say what the quarrel was about. Look here, Clement—just between you and me—do you know anything about it? I've heard rumours—about his being forbidden the house and all that. What was it—did he seduce the daughter, or what? We don't want to bring the girl into it more than we can help, for everybody's sake. Was that the trouble?"

"No," I said. "You can take it from me that it was something quite different, but I can't say more at the present juncture."

He nodded and rose.

"I'm glad to know. There's a lot of talk. Too many women in this part of the world. Well, I must get along. I've got to see Haydock. He was called out to some case or other, but he ought to be back by now. I don't mind telling you I'm sorry about Redding. He always struck me as a decent young chap. Perhaps they'll think out some kind of defence for him. After-effects of War, shell shock, or something. Especially if no very adequate motive turns up. I must be off. Like to come along?"

I said I would like to very much, and we went out together.

Haydock's house is next door to mine. His servant said the doctor had just come in, and showed us into the dining room, where Haydock was sitting down to a steaming plate of eggs and bacon.

He greeted us with an amiable nod.

"Sorry I had to go out. Confinement case. I've been up most of the night, over your business. I've got the bullet for you."

He shoved a little box along the table. Melchett examined it.

".25?"

Haydock nodded.

"I'll keep the technical details for the inquest," he said. "All you want to know is that death was practically instantaneous. Silly young fool, what did he want to do it for? Amazing, by the way, that nobody heard the shot."

"Yes," said Melchett; "that surprises me."

"The kitchen window gives on the other side of the house," I said.

"With the study door, the pantry door, and the kitchen door all shut, I doubt if you would hear anything, and there was no one but the maid in the house."

"H'm," said Melchett. "It's odd, all the same. I wonder the old lady—what's her name—Marple didn't hear it. The study window was open."

"Perhaps she did," said Haydock.

"I don't think she did," said I. "She was over at the Vicarage just now and she didn't mention anything of the kind, which I'm certain she would have done if there had been anything to tell."

"May have heard it and paid no attention to it—thought it was a car backfiring."

It struck me that Haydock was looking much more jovial and good-humoured this morning. He seemed like a man who was decorously trying to subdue unusually good spirits.

"Or what about a silencer?" he added. "That's quite likely. Nobody would hear anything then."

Melchett shook his head.

"Slack didn't find anything of the kind, and he asked Redding, and Redding didn't seem to know what he was talking about at first, and then denied point-blank using anything of the kind. And I suppose one can take his word for it."

"Yes, indeed, poor devil."

"Damned young fool," said Colonel Melchett. "Sorry, Clement. But he really is! Somehow one can't get used to thinking of him as a murderer."

"Any motive?" asked Haydock, taking a final draught of coffee and pushing back his chair.

"He says they quarrelled, and he lost his temper and shot him."

"Hoping for manslaughter, eh?" The doctor shook his head. "That story doesn't hold water. He stole up behind him as he was writing and shot him through the head. Precious little 'quarrel' about that."

"Anyway, there wouldn't have been time for a quarrel," I said, remembering Miss Marple's words. "To creep up, shoot him, alter the clock hands back to 6.22, and leave again would have taken him all his time. I shall never forget his face when I met him outside the gate, or the way he said, 'You want to see Protheroe— Oh! you'll see him all right!' That in itself ought to have made me suspicious of what had just taken place a few minutes before."

Haydock stared at me.

"What do you mean—what had just taken place? When do you think Redding shot him?"

"A few minutes before I got to the house."

The doctor shook his head.

"Impossible. Plumb impossible. He'd been dead much longer than that."

"But, my dear man," cried Colonel Melchett. "You said yourself that half an hour was only an approximate estimate."

"Half an hour, thirty-five minutes, twenty-five minutes, twenty minutes—possibly, but less, no. Why, the body would have been warm when I got to it."

We stared at each other. Haydock's face had changed. It had gone suddenly grey and old. I wondered at the change in him.

"But look here, Haydock." The Colonel found his voice. "If Redding admits shooting him at a quarter to seven—"

Haydock sprang to his feet.

"I tell you it's impossible," he roared. "If Redding says he killed Protheroe at a quarter to seven, then Redding lies. Hang it all, I tell you I'm a doctor, and I know. The blood had begun to congeal."

"If Redding is lying—" began Melchett. He stopped, shook his head.

"We'd better go down to the police station and see him," he said.

VIII

We were rather silent on our way down to the police station. Haydock drew behind a little and murmured to me.

"You know I don't like the look of this. I don't like it. There's something here we don't understand."

He looked thoroughly worried and upset.

Inspector Slack was at the police station, and presently we found ourselves face to face with Lawrence Redding.

He looked pale and strained but quite composed—marvellously so, I thought, considering the circumstances. Melchett snorted and hummed, obviously nervous.

"Look here, Redding," he said. "I understand you made a statement to Inspector Slack here. You state you went to the Vicarage at approximately a quarter to seven, found Protheroe there, quarrelled with him, shot him and came away. I'm not reading it over to you, but that's the gist of it."

"Yes."

"I'm going to ask you a few questions. You've already been told that you needn't answer them unless you choose. Your solicitor—"

Lawrence interrupted.

"I've nothing to hide. I killed Protheroe."

"Ah! well—" Melchett snorted. "How did you happen to have a pistol with you?"

Lawrence hesitated.

"It was in my pocket."

"You took it with you to the Vicarage?"

"Yes."

"Why?"

"I always take it."

He had hesitated again before answering, and I was absolutely sure that he was not speaking the truth.

"Why did you put the clock back?"

"The clock?"

He seemed puzzled.

"Yes, the hands pointed to 6.22."

A look of fear sprang up in his face.

"Oh! that—yes. I—I altered it."

Haydock spoke suddenly.

"Where did you shoot Colonel Protheroe?"

"In the study at the Vicarage."

"I mean in what part of the body?"

"Oh!—I—through the head I think. Yes, through the head."

"Aren't you sure?"

"Since you know, I can't see why it is necessary to ask me."

It was a feeble kind of bluster. There was some commotion outside. A constable without a helmet brought in a note.

"For the Vicar. It says very urgent on it."

I tore it open and read:

"Please—please—come to me. I don't know what to do. It is all too awful. I want to tell someone. Please come immediately, and bring anyone you like with you. ANNE PROTHEROE."

I gave Melchett a meaning glance. He took the hint. We all went out together. Glancing over my shoulder I had a glimpse of Lawrence Redding's face. His eyes were rivetted on the paper in my hand, and I have hardly ever seen such a terrible look of anguish and despair in any human being's face.

I remembered Anne Protheroe sitting on my sofa and saying, "I'm a desperate woman"; and my heart grew heavy within me. I saw now the possible reason for Lawrence Redding's heroic self-accusation.

Melchett was speaking to Slack.

"Have you got any line on Redding's movements earlier in the day? There's some reason to think he shot Protheroe earlier than he says. Get on to it, will you?"

He turned to me and, without a word, I handed him Anne Protheroe's letter. He read it and pursed up his lips in astonishment. Then he looked at me inquiringly.

"Is this what you were hinting at this morning?"

"Yes. I was not sure then if it was my duty to speak. I am quite sure now." And I told him of what I had seen that night in the studio.

The Colonel had a few words with the Inspector, and then we set off for Old Hall. Dr. Haydock came with us.

A very correct butler opened the door, with just the right amount of gloom in his bearing.

"Good morning," said Melchett. "Will you ask Mrs. Protheroe's maid to tell her we are here and would like to see her; and then return here and answer a few questions."

The butler hurried away, and presently returned with the news that he had dispatched the message.

"Now, let's hear something about yesterday," said Colonel Melchett. "Your master was in to lunch?"

"Yes, sir."

"And in his usual spirits?"

"As far as I could see; yes, sir."

"What happened after that?"

"After luncheon Mrs. Protheroe went to lie down, and the Colonel went to his study. Miss Lettice went out to a tennis party in the two-seater. Colonel and Mrs. Protheroe had tea at four-thirty, in the drawing room. The car was ordered for five-thirty to take them to the village. Immediately after they had left, Mr. Clement rang up"—he bowed to me. "I told him they had started."

"H'm," said Colonel Melchett. "When was Mr. Redding last here?"

"On Tuesday afternoon, sir."

"I understand that there was a disagreement between them?"

"I believe so, sir. The Colonel gave me orders that Mr. Redding was not to be admitted in future."

"Did you overhear the quarrel at all?" asked Colonel Melchett bluntly.

"Colonel Protheroe, sir, had a very loud voice, especially when it was raised in anger. I was unable to help overhearing a few words here and there."

"Enough to tell you the cause of the dispute?"

"I understood, sir, that it had to do with a portrait Mr. Redding had been painting—a portrait of Miss Lettice."

Melchett grunted.

"Did you see Mr. Redding when he left?"

"Yes, sir; I let him out."

"Did he seem angry?"

"No, sir; if I may say so, he seemed rather amused."

"Ah! He didn't come to the house yesterday?"

"No, sir."

"Anyone else come?"

"Not yesterday, sir."

"Well, the day before?"

"Mr. Dennis Clement came in the afternoon. And Dr. Stone was here for some time. And there was a lady in the evening."

"A lady?" Melchett was surprised. "Who was she?"

The butler couldn't remember her name. It was a lady he had not seen before. Yes, she had given her name, and when he told her that the family were at dinner, she had said that she would wait. So he had shown her into the little morning room.

She had asked for Colonel Protheroe, not Mrs. Protheroe. He had told the Colonel, and the Colonel had gone to the morning room directly dinner was over.

How long had the lady stayed? He thought about half an hour. The Colonel himself had let her out. Ah! yes, he remembered her name now. The lady had been a Mrs. Lestrange.

This was a surprise.

"Curious," said Melchett. "Really very curious."

But we pursued the matter no further, for at that moment a message came that Mrs. Protheroe would see us.

Anne was in bed. Her face was pale and her eyes very bright. There was a look on her face that puzzled me—a kind of grim determination.

She spoke to me.

"Thank you for coming so promptly," she said. "I see you've understood what I meant by bringing anyone you liked with you."

She paused.

"It's best to get it over quickly, isn't it?" she said. She gave a queer, half-pathetic little smile. "I suppose you're the person I ought to say it to, Colonel Melchett. You see, it was I who killed my husband."

Colonel Melchett said gently:

"My dear Mrs. Protheroe—"

"Oh! it's quite true. I suppose I've said it rather bluntly, but I never can go into hysterics over anything. I've hated him for a long time, and yesterday I shot him."

She lay back on the pillows and closed her eyes.

"That's all. I suppose you'll arrest me and take me away. I'll get up and dress as soon as I can. At the moment I am feeling rather sick."

"Are you aware, Mrs. Protheroe, that Mr. Lawrence Redding has already accused himself of committing the crime?"

Anne opened her eyes and nodded brightly.

"I know. Silly boy. He's very much in love with me, you know. It was frightfully noble of him—but very silly."

"He knew that it was you who had committed the crime?"

"Yes."

"How did he know?"

She hesitated.

"Did you tell him?"

Still she hesitated. Then at last she seemed to make up her mind.

"Yes—I told him."

She twitched her shoulders with a movement of irritation.

"Can't you go away now? I've told you. I don't want to talk about it any more."

"Where did you get the pistol, Mrs. Protheroe?"

"The pistol? Oh! it was my husband's. I got it out of the drawer of his dressing table."

"I see. And you took it with you to the Vicarage?"

"Yes. I knew he would be there—"

"What time was this?"

"It must have been after six—quarter—twenty past—something like that."

"You took the pistol meaning to shoot your husband?"

"No—I—I meant it for myself."

"I see. But you went to the Vicarage?"

"Yes. I went along to the window. There were no voices. I looked in. I saw my husband. Something came over me—and I fired."

"And then?"

"Then? Oh! then I went away."

"And told Mr. Redding what you had done?"

Again I noticed the hesitation in her voice before she said, "Yes."

"Did anybody see you entering or leaving the Vicarage?"

"No—at least, yes. Old Miss Marple. I talked to her a few minutes. She was in her garden."

She moved restlessly on the pillows.

"Isn't that enough? I've told you. Why do you want to go on bothering me?"

Dr. Haydock moved to her side and felt her pulse.

He beckoned to Melchett.

"I'll stay with her," he said in a whisper, "while you make the necessary arrangements. She oughtn't to be left. Might do herself a mischief."

Melchett nodded.

We left the room and descended the stairs. I saw a thin, cadaverous looking man come out of the adjoining room and, on impulse, I remounted the stairs.

"Are you Colonel Protheroe's valet?"

The man looked surprised.

"Yes, sir."

"Do you know whether your late master kept a pistol anywhere?"

"Not that I know of, sir."

"Not in one of the drawers of his dressing table? Think, man."

The valet shook his head decisively.

"I'm quite sure he didn't, sir. I'd have seen it if so. Bound to."

I hurried down the stairs after the others.

Mrs. Protheroe had lied about the pistol.

Why?

IX

After leaving a message at the police station, the Chief Constable announced his intention of paying a visit to Miss Marple.

"You'd better come with me, Vicar," he said. "I don't want to give a member of your flock hysterics. So lend the weight of your soothing presence."

I smiled. For all her fragile appearance, Miss Marple is capable of holding her own with any policeman or chief constable in existence.

"What's she like?" asked the Colonel as we rang the bell. "Anything she says to be depended upon or otherwise?"

I considered the matter.

"I think she is quite dependable," I said cautiously. "That is, in so far as she is talking of what she has actually seen. Beyond that, of course, when you get on to what she thinks—well, that is another matter. She has a powerful imagination, and systematically thinks the worst of everyone."

"The typical elderly spinster, in fact," said Melchett with a laugh. "Well, I ought to know the breed by now. Gad, the tea parties down here!"

We were admitted by a very diminutive maid and shown into a small drawing room.

"A bit crowded," said Colonel Melchett, looking round. "But plenty of good stuff. A lady's room, eh, Clement?"

I agreed, and at that moment the door opened and Miss Marple made her appearance.

"Very sorry to bother you, Miss Marple," said the Colonel when I had introduced him, putting on his bluff, military manner, which he had an idea was attractive to elderly ladies. "Got to do my duty, you know."

"Of course, of course," said Miss Marple. "I quite understand. Won't you sit down? And might I offer you a little glass of cherry brandy? My own making. A receipt of my grandmother's."

"Thank you very much, Miss Marple. Very kind of you. But I think I won't. Nothing till lunch time, that's my motto. Now, I want to talk to you about this sad business—very sad business indeed. Upset us all, I'm sure. Well, it seems possible that, owing to the position of your house and garden, you may have been able to tell us something we want to know about yesterday evening."

"As a matter of fact, I was in my little garden from five o'clock onwards yesterday, and of course from there—well, one simply cannot help seeing anything that is going on next door."

"I understand, Miss Marple, that Mrs. Protheroe passed this way yesterday evening?"

"Yes, she did. I called out to her, and she admired my roses."

"Could you tell us about what time that was?"

"I should say it was just a minute or two after a quarter past six. Yes, that's right. The church clock had just chimed the quarter."

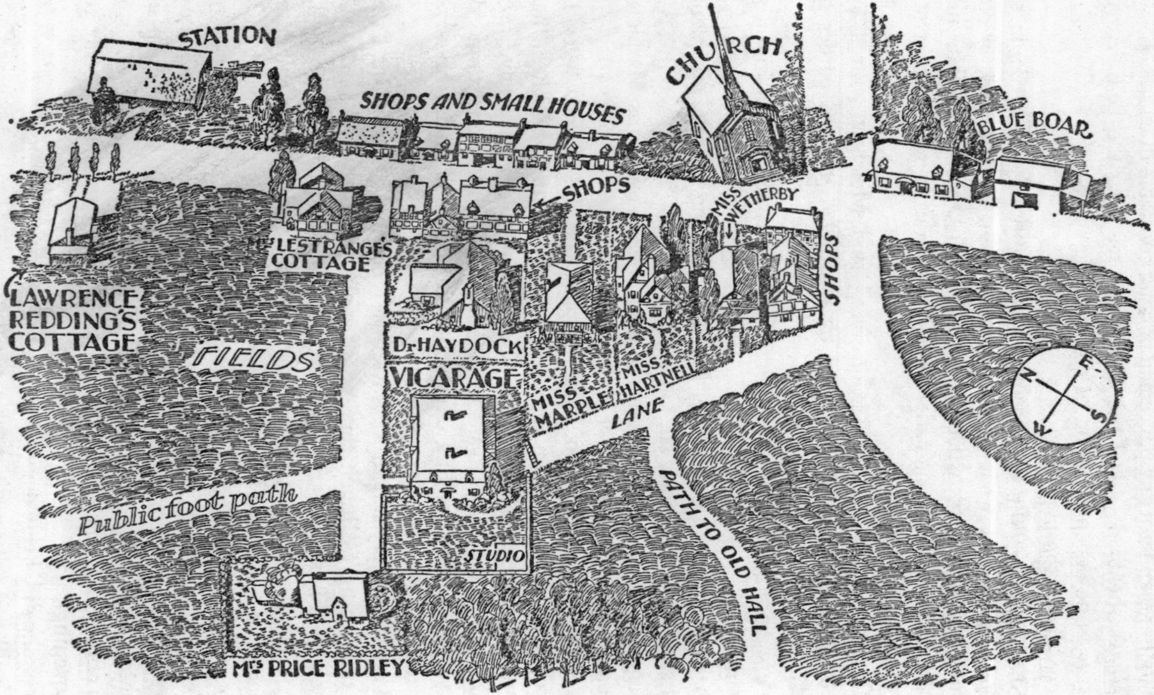
STATION
SHOPS AND SMALL HOUSES
CHURCH
BLUE BOAR
SHOPS
MISS WETHERBY
SHOPS
Mrs LESTRANGE'S COTTAGE
LAWRENCE REDDING'S COTTAGE
FIELDS
Dr HAYDOCK
VICARAGE
MISS MARPLE
MISS HARTNELL
LANE
N
E
S
W
Public foot path
STUDIO
PATH TO OLD HALL
Mrs PRICE RIDLEY

"Very good. What happened next?"

"Well, Mrs. Protheroe said she was calling for her husband at the Vicarage, so that they could go home together. She had come along the lane, you understand, and she went into the Vicarage by the back gate and across the garden."

"She came from the lane?"

"Yes, I'll show you."

Full of eagerness, Miss Marple led us out into the garden, and pointed out the lane that ran along by the bottom of her garden.

"The path opposite with the stile leads to the Hall," she explained. "That was the way they were going home together. Mrs. Protheroe came from the village."

"Perfectly, perfectly," said Colonel Melchett. "And she went across to the Vicarage, you say?"

"Yes. I saw her turn the corner of the house. I suppose the Colonel wasn't there yet, because she came back almost immediately, and went down the lawn to the studio—that building there. The one the Vicar lets Mr. Redding use as a studio."

"I see. And—you didn't happen to hear a shot, Miss Marple?"

"I didn't hear a shot then," said Miss Marple.

"But you did hear one some time?"

"Yes, I think there was a shot somewhere in the woods. But quite five or ten minutes afterwards—and, as I say, out in the woods. At least, I think so. It couldn't have been—surely it couldn't have been—"

She stopped, pale with excitement.

"Yes, yes, we'll come to all that presently," said Colonel Melchett. "Please go on with your story. Mrs. Protheroe went down to the studio?"

"Yes, she went inside and waited. Presently Mr. Redding came along the lane from the village. He came to the Vicarage gate, looked all round—"

"And saw you, Miss Marple."

"As a matter of fact, he didn't see me," said Miss Marple flushing slightly. "Because, you see, just at that minute I was bending right over—trying to get up one of those nasty dandelions, you know. So difficult. And then he went through the gate and down to the studio."

"He didn't go near the house?"

"Oh! no, he went straight to the studio. Mrs. Protheroe came to the door to meet him, and then they both went inside."

Here Miss Marple contributed a singularly eloquent pause.

"Perhaps she was sitting to him?" I suggested.

"Perhaps," said Miss Marple.

"And they came out—when?"

"About ten minutes later."

"That was roughly?"

"The church clock had chimed the half hour. They strolled out through the garden gate and along the lane, and, just at that minute, Dr. Stone came down the path leading to the Hall, and climbed over the stile and joined them. They all walked towards the village together. At the end of the lane, I think, but I can't be quite sure, they were joined by Miss Cram. I think it must have been Miss Cram, because her skirts were so short."

"You must have very good eyesight, Miss Marple, if you can observe as far as that."

"I was observing a bird," said Miss Marple. "A golden-crested wren, I think he was. A sweet little fellow. I had my glasses out, and that's how I happened to see Miss Cram (if it was Miss Cram, and I think so) join them."

"Ah! well, that may be so," said Colonel Melchett. "Now, since you seem very good at observing, did you happen to notice, Miss Marple, what sort of expression Mrs. Protheroe and Mr. Redding had as they passed along the lane?"

"They were smiling and talking," said Miss Marple. "They seemed very happy to be together, if you know what I mean."

"They didn't seem upset or disturbed in any way?"

"Oh! no. Just the opposite."

"Deuced odd," said the Colonel. "There's something deuced odd about the whole thing."

Miss Marple suddenly took our breath away by remarking in a placid voice:

"Has Mrs. Protheroe been saying that she committed the crime now?"

"Upon my soul," said the Colonel. "How did you come to guess that, Miss Marple?"

"Well, I rather thought it might happen," said Miss Marple. "I think dear Lettice thought so too. She's really a very sharp girl. Not always very scrupulous, I'm afraid. So Anne Protheroe says she killed her husband. Well, well. I don't think it's true. No, I'm almost sure it isn't true. Not with a woman like Anne Protheroe. Although one never can be quite sure about anyone, can one? At least that's what I've found. When does she say she shot him?"

"At twenty minutes past six. Just after speaking to you."

Miss Marple shook her head slowly and pityingly. The pity was, I think, for two full grown men being so foolish as to believe such a story. At least that is what we felt like.

"What did she shoot him with?"

"A pistol."

"Where did she find it?"

"She brought it with her."

"Well, that she didn't do," said Miss Marple with unexpected decision. "I can swear to that. She'd no such thing with her."

"You mightn't have seen it."

"Of course I should have seen it."

"If it had been in her handbag."

"She wasn't carrying a handbag."

"Well, it might have been concealed—er—upon her person."

Miss Marple directed a glance of sorrow and scorn upon him.

"My dear Colonel Melchett. You know what young women are nowadays. Not ashamed to show exactly how the creator made them. She hadn't so much as a handkerchief in the top of her stocking."

Melchett was obstinate.

"You must admit that it all fits in," he said. "The time, the overturned clock pointing to 6.22—"

Miss Marple turned on me.

"Do you mean you haven't told him about that clock yet?"

"What about the clock, Clement?"

I told him. He showed a good deal of annoyance.

"Why on earth didn't you tell Slack this last night?"

"Because," I said, "he wouldn't let me."

"Nonsense, you ought to have insisted."

"Probably," I said, "Inspector Slack behaves quite differently to you than he does to me. I had no earthly chance of insisting."

"It's an extraordinary business altogether," said Melchett. "If a third person comes along and claims to have done this murder, I shall go into a lunatic asylum."

"If I might be allowed to suggest—" murmured Miss Marple.

"Well?"

"If you were to tell Mr. Redding what Mrs. Protheroe has done, and then explain that you don't really believe it is her; and then if you were to go to Mrs. Protheroe and tell her that Mr. Redding is all right—why then, they might each of them tell you the truth. And the truth is helpful, though I daresay they don't know very much themselves, poor things."

"It's all very well, but they are the only two people who had a motive for making away with Protheroe."

"Oh! I wouldn't say that, Colonel Melchett," said Miss Marple.

"Why, can you think of anyone else?"

"Oh! yes, indeed. Why," she counted on her fingers, "one, two, three, four, five, six—yes, and a possible seven. I can think of at least seven people who might be very glad to have Colonel Protheroe out of the way."

The Colonel looked at her feebly.

"Seven people? In St. Mary Mead?"

Miss Marple nodded brightly.

"Mind you, I name no names," she said. "That wouldn't be right. But I'm afraid there's a lot of wickedness in the world. A nice, honourable, upright soldier like you doesn't know about these things, Colonel Melchett."

I thought the Chief Constable was going to have apoplexy.

X

His remarks on the subject of Miss Marple as we left the house were far from complimentary.

"I really believe that wizened-up old maid thinks she knows everything there is to know. And hardly been out of this village all her life. Preposterous. What can she know of life?"

I said mildly that, though doubtless Miss Marple knew next to nothing of life with a capital L, she knew practically everything that went on in St. Mary Mead.

Melchett admitted that grudgingly. She was a valuable witness—particularly valuable from Mrs. Protheroe's point of view.

"I suppose there's no doubt about what she says, eh?"

"If Miss Marple says she had no pistol with her, you can take it for granted that it is so," I said. "If there was the least possibility of such a thing, Miss Marple would have been on to it like a knife."

"That's true enough. We'd better go and have a look at the studio."

The so-called studio was a mere rough shed with a skylight. There were no windows, and the door was the only means of entrance or egress.

Satisfied on this score, Melchett announced his intention of visiting the Vicarage with the Inspector.

I nodded.

"I'm going to the police station now."

As I entered through the front door, a murmur of voices caught my ear. I opened the drawing-room door.

On the sofa beside Griselda, conversing animatedly, sat Miss Gladys Cram. Her legs, which were encased in particularly shiny pink stockings, were crossed, and I had every opportunity of observing that she wore pink striped silk knickers.

"Hullo, Len," said Griselda.

"Good morning, Mr. Clement," said Miss Cram. "Isn't the news about the Colonel reely too awful? Poor old gentleman."

"Miss Cram," said my wife, "very kindly came in to offer to help us with the Guides. We asked for helpers last Sunday, you remember."

I did remember, and I was convinced, and so, I knew from her tone, was Griselda, that the idea of enrolling herself among them would never have occurred to Miss Cram but for the exciting incident which had taken place at the Vicarage.

"I was only just saying to Mrs. Clement," went on Miss Cram, "you could have struck me all of a heap when I heard the news. A murder? I said. In this quiet, one-horse village—for quiet it is, you must admit—not so much as a picture house, and as for Talkies! And then when I heard it was Colonel Protheroe—why, I simply couldn't believe it. He didn't seem the kind, somehow, to get murdered."

I don't know what Miss Cram considers are the necessary qualifications for being murdered. It has never struck me that the murdered belong to a special class, but doubtless she had some idea in her golden shingled head.

"And so," said Griselda, "Miss Cram came round to find out all about it."

I feared this plain speaking might offend the lady, but she merely flung her head back and laughed uproariously, showing every tooth she possessed.

"That's too bad. You're a sharp one, aren't you, Mrs. Clement? But it's only natural, isn't it, to want to hear the ins and outs of a case like this? And I'm sure I'm willing enough to help with the Guides in any way you like. Exciting, that's what it is. I've been stagnating for a bit of fun. I have; reely I have. Not that my job isn't a very good one, well paid, and Dr. Stone quite the gentleman in every way. But a girl wants a bit of life out of office hours, and, except for you, Mrs. Clement, who is there in the place to talk to, except a lot of old cats?"

"There's Lettice Protheroe," I said.

Gladys Cram tossed her head.

"She's too high and mighty for the likes of me. Fancies herself the County, and wouldn't demean herself by noticing a girl who had to work for her living. Not but what I *did* hear her talking of earning her living herself. And who'd employ her, I should like to know? Why, she'd be fired in less than a week. Unless she went as one of those mannequins, all dressed up and sidling about. She could do that, I expect."

"She'd make a very good mannequin," said Griselda. "She's got such a lovely figure." There's nothing of the cat about Griselda. "When was she talking of earning her own living?"

Miss Cram seemed momentarily discomfited, but recovered herself with her usual archness.

"That would be telling, wouldn't it?" she said. "But she did say so. Things not very happy at home, I fancy. Catch me living at home with a stepmother. I wouldn't sit down under it for a minute."

"Ah! but you're so high spirited and independent," said Griselda gravely, and I looked at her with suspicion.

Miss Cram was clearly pleased.

"That's right. That's me all over. Can be led, not driven. A palmist told me that not so very long ago. No, I'm not one to sit down and be bullied. And I've made it clear all along to Dr. Stone that I must have my regular times off. These scientific gentlemen, they think a girl's a kind of machine—half the time they just don't notice her or remember she's there."

"Do you find Dr. Stone pleasant to work with? It must be an interesting job if you are interested in archæology."

"Of course, I don't know much about it," confessed the girl. "It still seems to me that digging up people that are dead and have been dead for hundreds of years isn't—well, it seems a bit nosey, doesn't it? And there's Dr. Stone so wrapped up in it all that half the time he'd forget his meals if it wasn't for me."

"Is he at the barrow this morning?" asked Griselda.

Miss Cram shook her head.

"A bit under the weather this morning," she explained. "Not up to doing any work. That means a holiday for little Gladys."

"I'm sorry," I said.

"Oh! it's nothing much. There's not going to be a second death. But do tell me, Mr. Clement, I hear you've been with the police all the morning. What do they think?"

"Well," I said slowly. "There is still a little—uncertainty."

"Ah!" cried Miss Cram. "Then they don't think it is Mr. Lawrence Redding after all. So handsome, isn't he? Just like a movie star. And such a nice smile when he says good morning to you. I really couldn't believe my ears when I heard the police had arrested him. Still one always hears they're very stupid—the country police."

"You can hardly blame them in this instance," I said. "Mr. Redding came in and gave himself up."

"What?" the girl was clearly dumfounded. "Well—of all the poor fish! If I'd committed the murder, I wouldn't go straight off and give myself up. I should have thought Lawrence Redding would have had more sense. To give in like that! What did he kill Protheroe for? Did he say? Was it just a quarrel?"

"It's not absolutely certain that he did kill him," I said.

"But surely—if he says he has—why really, Mr. Clement, he ought to know."

"He ought to, certainly," I agreed. "But the police are not satisfied with his story."

"But why should he say he'd done it if he hasn't?"

That was a point on which I had no intention of enlightening Miss Cram. Instead I said rather vaguely:

"I believe that in all prominent murder cases, the police receive numerous letters from people accusing themselves of the crime."

Miss Cram's reception of this piece of information was:

"They must be chumps!" in a tone of wonder and scorn.

She added, "I'd never do a thing like that."

"I'm sure you wouldn't," I said.

"Well," she said with a sigh. "I suppose I must be trotting along." She rose. "Mr. Redding accusing himself of the murder will be a bit of news for Dr. Stone."

"Is he interested?" asked Griselda.

Miss Cram furrowed her brows perplexedly.

"He's a queer one. You never can tell with him. All wrapped up in the past. He'd a hundred times rather look at a nasty old bronze knife out of one of those humps of ground than he would see the knife Crippen cut up his wife with, supposing he had a chance to."

"Well," I said. "I must confess I agree with him."

Miss Cram's eyes expressed incomprehension and slight contempt. Then, with reiterated good-byes, she took her departure.

"Not such a bad sort, really," said Griselda as the door closed behind her. "Terribly common, of course, but one of those big, bouncing, good-humoured girls that you can't dislike. I wonder what really brought her here?"

"Curiosity."

"Yes, I suppose so. Now, Len, tell me all about it. I'm simply dying to hear."

I sat down and recited faithfully all the happenings of the morning, Griselda interpolating the narrative with little exclamations of surprise and interest.

"So it was Anne Lawrence was after all along! Not Lettice. How blind we've all been. That must have been what old Miss Marple was hinting at yesterday. Don't you think so?"

"Yes," I said, averting my eyes.

Mary entered.

"There's a couple of men here—come from a newspaper, so they say. Do you want to see them?"

"No," I said. "Certainly not. Refer them to Inspector Slack at the police station."

Mary nodded and turned away.

"And when you've got rid of them," I said, "come back here. There's something I want to ask you."

Mary nodded again.

It was some few minutes before she returned.

"Had a job getting rid of them," she said. "Persistent. You never saw anything like it. Wouldn't take 'no' for an answer."

"I expect we shall be a good deal troubled with them," I said. "Now, Mary, what I want to ask you is this: Are you quite certain you didn't hear the shot yesterday evening?"

"The shot what killed him? No, of course I didn't. If I had of done, I should have gone in to see what had happened."

"Yes, but—" I was remembering Miss Marple's statement that she had heard a shot "in the wood." I changed the form of my question. "Did you hear any other shot—one down in the wood, for instance?"

"Oh! that." The girl paused. "Yes, now I come to think of it, I believe I did. Not a lot of shots, just one. Queer sort of bang it was."

"Exactly," I said. "Now what time was that?"

"Time?"

"Yes, time."

"I couldn't say, I'm sure. Well after tea time. I do know that."

"Can't you get a little nearer than that?"

"No, I can't. I've got my work to do, haven't I? I can't go on looking at clocks the whole time—and it wouldn't be much good anyway—the alarum loses a good three quarters every day, and what with putting it on, and one thing and another, I'm never exactly sure what time it is."

This perhaps explains why our meals are never punctual. They are sometimes too late and sometimes bewilderingly early.

"Was it long before Mr. Redding came?"

"No, it wasn't long. Ten minutes—a quarter of an hour—not longer than that."

I nodded my head, satisfied.

"Is that all?" said Mary. "Because what I mean to say is, I've got the joint in the oven and the pudding boiling over as likely as not."

"That's all right. You can go."

She left the room and I turned to Griselda.

"Is it quite out of the question to induce Mary to say 'sir' or 'ma'am'?"

"I have told her. She doesn't remember. She's just a raw girl, remember."

"I am perfectly aware of that," I said. "But raw things do not necessarily remain raw for ever. I feel a tinge of cooking might be induced in Mary."

"Well, I don't agree with you," said Griselda. "You know how little we can afford to pay a servant. If once we got her smartened up at all, she'd leave. Naturally. And get higher wages. But as long as Mary can't cook and has these awful manners—well, we're safe; nobody else would have her."

I perceived that my wife's methods of housekeeping were not so entirely haphazard as I had imagined. A certain amount of reasoning underlay them. Whether it was worth while having a maid at the price of her not being able to cook, and having a habit of throwing dishes and remarks at one with the same disconcerting abruptness was a debatable matter.

"And anyway," continued Griselda, "you must make allowances for her manners being worse than usual just now. You can't expect her to feel exactly sympathetic about Colonel Protheroe's death when he jailed her young man."

"Did he jail her young man?"

"Yes, for poaching. You know, that man Archer. Mary has been walking out with him for two years."

"I didn't know that."

"Darling Len, you never know anything."

"It's queer," I said, "that everyone says the shot came from the wood."

"I don't think it's queer at all," said Griselda. "You see, one so often does hear shots in the wood. So, naturally, when you do hear a shot, you just assume as a matter of course that it is in the wood. It probably just sounds a bit louder than usual. Of course, if you were in the next room, you'd realize that it was in the house, but from Mary's kitchen, with the window right the other side of the house, I don't believe you'd ever think of such a thing."

The door opened again.

"Colonel Melchett's back," said Mary. "And that police Inspector with him, and they say they'd be glad if you'd join them. They're in the study."

XI

I SAW AT a glance that Colonel Melchett and Inspector Slack had not been seeing eye to eye about the case. Melchett looked flushed and annoyed, and the Inspector looked sulky.

"I'm sorry to say," said Melchett, "that Inspector Slack doesn't agree with me in considering young Redding innocent."

"If he didn't do it, what does he go and say he did it for?" asked Slack sceptically.

"Mrs. Protheroe acted in an exactly similar fashion, remember, Slack."

"That's different. She's a woman, and women act in that silly way. I'm not saying she did it, for a moment. She heard he was accused, and she trumped up a story. I'm used to that sort of game. You wouldn't believe the fool things I've known women do. But Redding's different. He's got his head screwed on all right. And if he admits he did it, well, I say he did do it. It's his pistol—you can't get away from that. And, thanks to this business of Mrs. Protheroe, we know the motive. That was the weak point before, but now we know it—why, the whole thing's plain sailing."

"You think he can have shot him earlier? At six-thirty, say?"

"He can't have done that."

"You've checked up his movements?"

The Inspector nodded.

"He was in the village near the Blue Boar at ten past six. From there he came along the back lane where you say the lady next door saw him—she doesn't miss much, I should say,—and kept his appointment with Mrs. Protheroe in the studio in the garden. They left there together just after six-thirty and went along the lane to the village, being joined by Dr.

Stone. He corroborates that all right—I've seen him. They all stood talking just by the post office for a few minutes; then Mrs. Protheroe went into Miss Hartnell's to borrow a gardening magazine. That's all right, too. I've seen Miss Hartnell. Mrs. Protheroe remained there talking to her till just on seven o'clock, when she exclaimed at the lateness of the hour and said she must get home."

"What was her manner?"

"Very easy and pleasant, Miss Hartnell said. She seemed in good spirits—Miss Hartnell is quite sure there was nothing on her mind."

"Well, go on."

"Redding, he went with Dr. Stone to the Blue Boar, and they had a drink together. He left there at twenty minutes to seven, went rapidly along the village street and down the road to the Vicarage. Lots of people saw him."

"Not down the back lane this time?" commented the Colonel.

"No—he came to the front, asked for the Vicar, heard Colonel Protheroe was there, went in—and shot him—just as he said he did! That's the truth of it and we needn't look further."

Melchett shook his head.

"There's the doctor's evidence. You can't get away from that. Protheroe was shot not later than six-thirty."

"Oh! doctors!" Inspector Slack looked contemptuous. "If you're going to believe doctors. Take out all your teeth—that's what they do nowadays—and then say they're very sorry, but all the time it was appendicitis. Doctors!"

"This isn't a question of diagnosis. Dr. Haydock was absolutely positive on the point. You can't go against the medical evidence, Slack."

"And there's my evidence for what it is worth," I said, suddenly recalling a forgotten incident. "I touched the body and it was cold. That I can swear to."

"You see, Slack?" said Melchett.

Inspector Slack gave in with a good grace.

"Well, of course, if that's so. But there it was—a beautiful case. Mr. Redding only too anxious to be hanged, so to speak."

"That, in itself strikes me as a little unnatural," observed Colonel Melchett.

"Well, there's no accounting for tastes," said the Inspector. "There's a lot of gentlemen went a bit balmy after the War. Now, I suppose, it means starting again at the beginning." He turned on me. "Why you went out of your way to mislead me about the clock, sir, I can't think. Obstructing the ends of justice, that's what that was."

I was stung.

"I tried to tell you on three separate occasions," I said. "And each time you shut me up and refused to listen."

"That's just a way of speaking, sir. You could have told me perfectly well if you had had a mind to. The clock and the note seemed to tally perfectly. Now, according to you, the clock was all wrong. I never knew such a case. What's the sense of keeping a clock a quarter of an hour fast anyway?"

"It is supposed," I said, "to induce punctuality."

The Inspector snorted.

"I don't think we need go farther into that now, Inspector," said Colonel Melchett tactfully. "What we want now is the true story from both Mrs. Protheroe and young Redding. I telephoned to Haydock and asked him to bring Mrs. Protheroe over here with him. They ought to be here in about a quarter of an hour. I think it would be as well to have Redding here first."

"I'll get on to the station," said Inspector Slack, and took up the telephone.

He spoke down it.

"And now," he said replacing the receiver, "we'll get to work on this room."

He looked at me in a meaning fashion.

"Perhaps," I said, "you'd like me out of the way."

The Inspector immediately opened the door for me. Melchett called out:

"Come back when young Redding arrives, will you, Vicar? You're a friend of his, and you may have sufficient influence to persuade him to speak the truth."

I found my wife and Miss Marple with their heads together.

"We've been discussing all sorts of possibilities," said Griselda. "I wish you'd solve the case, Miss Marple, like you did the way Miss Wetherby's gill of picked shrimps disappeared. And all because it reminded you of something quite different about a sack of coals."

"You're laughing, my dear," said Miss Marple. "But after all, that is a very sound way of arriving at the truth. It's really what people call intuition and make such a fuss about. Intuition is like reading a word without having to spell it out. A child can't do that, because it has had so little experience. But a grown-up person knows the word because he's seen it often before. You catch my meaning, Vicar?"

"Yes," I said slowly. "I think I do. You mean that if a thing reminds you of something else—well, it's probably the same kind of thing."

"Exactly."

"And what precisely does the murder of Colonel Protheroe remind you of?"

Miss Marple sighed.

"That is just the difficulty. So many parallels come to the mind. For instance, there was Major Hargraves, a churchwarden and a man highly respected in every way. And all the time he was keeping a separate second establishment—a former housemaid, just think of it! And five children—actually five children—a terrible shock to his wife and daughter."

I tried hard to visualize Colonel Protheroe in the rôle of secret sinner, and failed.

"And then there was that laundry business," went on Miss Marple. "Miss Hartnell's opal pin—left most imprudently in a frilled blouse and sent to the laundry. And the woman who took it didn't want it in the least, and wasn't by any means a thief. She simply hid it in another woman's house and told the police she'd seen this other woman take it. Spite, you know, sheer spite. It's an astonishing motive—spite. A man in it, of course. There always is."

This time I failed to see any parallel, however remote. Miss Marple went on in a dreamy voice.

"And then there was poor Elwell's daughter—such a pretty, ethereal girl—tried to stifle her little brother. And there was the money for the Choir Boys' Outing (before your time, Vicar) actually taken by the organist. His wife was sadly in debt. Yes, this case makes one think of so many things—too many. It's very hard to arrive at the truth."

"I wish you would tell me," I said. "Who were the seven suspects?"

"The seven suspects?"

"You said you could think of seven people who would—well, be glad of Colonel Protheroe's death."

"Did I? Yes, I remember I did."

"Was that true?"

"Oh! certainly it was true. But I mustn't mention names. You can think of them quite easily yourself, I am sure."

"Indeed I can't. There is Lettice Protheroe, I suppose, since she probably comes into money on her father's death. But it is absurd to think of her in such a connection, and outside her I can think of nobody."

"And you, my dear?" said Miss Marple, turning to Griselda.

Rather to my surprise Griselda coloured up. Something very like tears started into her eyes. She clenched both her small hands.

"Oh!" she cried indignantly. "People are hateful—hateful. The things they say! The beastly things they say!"

I looked at her curiously. It is very unlike Griselda to be so upset. She noticed my glance and tried to smile.

"Don't look at me as though I were an interesting specimen you didn't understand, Len. Don't let's get heated and wander from the point. I don't believe that it was Lawrence or Anne, and Lettice is out of the question. There must be some clue or other that would help us."

"There is the note, of course," said Miss Marple. "You will remember my saying this morning that that struck me as exceedingly peculiar."

"It seems to fix the time of his death with remarkable accuracy," I said. "And yet, is that possible? Mrs. Protheroe would only have just left the study. She would hardly have had time to reach the studio. The only way in which I can account for it is that he consulted his own watch and that his watch was slow. That seems to me a feasible solution."

"I have another idea," said Griselda. "Suppose, Len, that the clock had already been put back—no, that comes to the same thing—how stupid of me!"

"It hadn't been altered when I left," I said. "I remember comparing it with my watch. Still, as you say, that has no bearing on the present matter."

"What do you think, Miss Marple?" asked Griselda.

The old lady shook her head.

"My dear, I confess I wasn't thinking about it from that point of view at all. What strikes me as so curious, and has done from the first, is the subject matter of that letter."

"I don't see that," I said. "Colonel Protheroe merely wrote that he couldn't wait any longer—"

"At twenty minutes past six?" said Miss Marple. "Your maid, Mary, had already told him that you wouldn't be in till half past six at the earliest, and he had appeared to be quite willing to wait until then. And yet, at twenty past six, he sits down and says he 'can't wait any longer.'"

I stared at the old lady, feeling an increased respect for her mental powers. Her keen wits had seen what we had failed to perceive. It was an odd thing—a very odd thing.

"If only," I said, "the letter hadn't been dated—"

Miss Marple nodded her head.

"Exactly," she said. "If it hadn't been dated!"

I cast my mind back, trying to recall that sheet of notepaper and the blurred scrawl, and at the top that neatly printed 6.20. Surely these figures were on a different scale to the rest of the letter.

I gave a gasp.

"Supposing," I said, "it wasn't dated. Supposing that round about 6.30 Colonel Protheroe got impatient and sat down to say he couldn't wait any longer. And as he was sitting there writing, someone came in through the window—"

"Or through the door," suggested Griselda.

"He'd hear the door and look up."

"Colonel Protheroe was rather deaf, you remember," said Miss Marple.

"Yes, that's true. He wouldn't hear it. Whichever way the murderer came, he stole up behind the Colonel and shot him. Then he saw the note and the clock and the idea came to him. He put 6.20 at the top of the letter and he altered the clock to 6.22. It was a clever idea. It gave him, or so he would think, a perfect alibi."

"And what we want to find," said Griselda, "is someone who has a cast iron alibi for 6.20, but no alibi at all for—well, that isn't so easy. One can't fix the time."

"We can fix it within very narrow limits," I said. "Haydock places 6.30 as the outside limit of time. I suppose one could perhaps shift it to 6.35, from the reasoning we have just been following out; it seems clear that Protheroe would not have got impatient before 6.30. I think we can say we do know pretty well."

"Then that shot I heard—yes, I suppose it is quite possible. And I thought nothing about it—nothing at all. Most vexing. And yet, now I try to recollect, it does seem to me that it was different from the usual sort of shot one hears. Yes, there was a difference."

"Louder?" I suggested.

No, Miss Marple didn't think it had been louder. In fact, she found it hard to say in what way it had been different, but she still insisted that it was.

I thought she was probably persuading herself of the fact rather than actually remembering it, but she had just contributed such a valuable new outlook to the problem that I felt highly respectful towards her.

She rose, murmuring that she must really get back—it had been so tempting just to run over and discuss the case with dear Griselda. I escorted her to the boundary wall and the back gate, and returned to find Griselda wrapped in thought.

"Still puzzling over that note?" I asked.

"No."

She gave a sudden shiver and shook her shoulders impatiently.

"Len, I've been thinking. How badly someone must have hated Anne Protheroe."

"Hated her?"

"Yes. Don't you see? There's no real evidence against Lawrence—all the evidence against him is what you might call accidental. He just happens to take it into his head to come here. If he hadn't—well, no one would have thought of connecting him with the crime. But Anne is different. Suppose someone knew that she was here at exactly 6.20—the clock and the time on the letter—everything pointing to her. I don't think it was only because of an alibi it was moved to that exact time—I think there was more in it than that—a direct attempt to fasten the business on her. If it hadn't been for Miss Marple saying she hadn't got the pistol with her, and noticing that she was only a moment before going down to the studio— Yes, if it hadn't been for that . . ." She shivered again. "Len—I feel that someone hated Anne Protheroe very much. I—I don't like it."

XII

I WAS SUMMONED to the study when Lawrence Redding arrived. He looked haggard and, I thought, suspicious. Colonel Melchett greeted him with something approaching cordiality.

"We want to ask you a few questions—here, on the spot," he said.

Lawrence sneered slightly.

"Isn't that a French idea? Reconstruction of the crime?"

"My dear boy," said Colonel Melchett. "Don't take that tone with us. Are you aware that someone else has also confessed to committing the crime which you pretend to have committed?"

The effect of these words on Lawrence was painful and immediate.

"S-s-omeone else?" he stammered. "Who—who?"

"Mrs. Protheroe," said Colonel Melchett, watching him.

"Absurd. She never did it. She couldn't have. It's impossible."

Melchett interrupted him.

"Strangely enough, we did not believe her story. Neither, I may say, do we believe yours. Dr. Haydock says positively that the murder could not have been committed at the time you say it was."

"Dr. Haydock says that?"

"Yes; so, you see, you are cleared whether you like it or not. And now we want you to help us, to tell us exactly what occurred."

Lawrence still hesitated.

"You're not deceiving me about—about Mrs. Protheroe? You really don't suspect her?"

"On my word of honour," said Colonel Melchett.

Lawrence drew a deep breath.

"I've been a fool," he said. "An absolute fool. How I could have thought for one minute that she did it—"

"Suppose you tell us all about it?" suggested the Chief Constable.

"There's not much to tell. I—I met Mrs. Protheroe that afternoon—"

He paused.

"We know all about that," said Melchett. "You may think that your feeling for Mrs. Protheroe and hers for you was a dead secret, but in reality it was known and commented upon. In any case everything is bound to come out now."

"Very well then. I expect you are right. I had promised the Vicar here" (he glanced at me) "to—to go right away. I met Mrs. Protheroe that evening in the studio at a quarter past six. I told her of what I had decided. She, too, agreed that it was the only thing to do. We—we said good-bye to each other.

"We left the studio, and almost at once Dr. Stone joined us. Anne managed to seem marvellously natural. I couldn't do it. I went off with Stone to the Blue Boar and had a drink. Then I thought I'd go home, but, when I got to the corner of this road, I changed my mind and decided to come along and see the Vicar. I felt I wanted someone to talk to about the matter.

"At the door, the maid told me the Vicar was out but would be in shortly, but that Colonel Protheroe was in the study waiting for him. Well, I didn't like to go away again—looked as though I were shirking meeting him. So I said I'd wait too, and I went into the study."

He stopped.

"Well?" said Colonel Melchett.

"Protheroe was sitting at the writing table—just as you found him. I went up to him. I saw that he was dead. Then I looked down and saw the pistol lying on the floor beside him. I picked it up—and at once saw that it was my pistol!

"That gave me a turn. My pistol! And then, straightway I leaped to one conclusion. Anne must have bagged my pistol some time or other—meaning it for herself if she couldn't bear things any longer. Perhaps she had had it with her today. After we parted in the village she must have come back here and—and—Oh! I suppose I was mad to think of it. But that's what I thought. I slipped the pistol in my pocket and came away. Just outside the Vicarage gate, I met the Vicar. He said something nice and normal about seeing Protheroe—suddenly I had a wild desire to laugh. His manner was so ordinary and everyday, and there was I all strung up. I remember shouting out something absurd and seeing his face change. I was nearly off my head, I believe. I went walking—walking—at last I couldn't bear it any longer. If Anne had done this ghastly thing, I was, at least, morally responsible. I went and gave myself up."

There was a silence when he had finished. Then the Colonel said in a businesslike voice:

"I would like to ask just one or two questions. First, did you touch or move the body in any way?"

"No, I didn't touch it at all. One could see he was dead without touching him."

"Did you notice a note lying on the blotter half concealed by his body?"

"No."

"Did you interfere in any way with the clock?"

"I never touched the clock. I seem to remember a clock lying overturned on the table, but I never touched it."

"Now as to this pistol of yours, when did you last see it?"

Lawrence Redding reflected.

"It's hard to say exactly."

"Where do you keep it?"

"Oh! in a litter of odds and ends in the sitting room in my cottage. On one of the shelves of the bookcase."

"You left it lying about carelessly?"

"Yes. I really didn't think about it. It was just there."

"So that anyone who came to your cottage could have seen it?"

"Yes."

"And you don't remember when you last saw it?"

Lawrence drew his brows together in a frown of recollection.

"I'm almost sure it was there the day before yesterday. I remember pushing it aside to get an old pipe. I think it was the day before yesterday—but it may have been the day before that."

"Who has been to your cottage lately?"

"Oh! crowds of people. Someone is always drifting in and out. I had a sort of tea party the day before yesterday. Lettice Protheroe, Dennis, and all their crowd. And then one or other of the old Pussies comes in now and again."

"Do you lock the cottage up when you go out?"

"No, why on earth should I? I've nothing to steal. And no one does lock his house up round here."

"Who looks after your wants there?"

"An old Mrs. Archer comes in every morning to 'do for me,' as it's called."

"Do you think she would remember when the pistol was there last?"

"I don't know. She might. But I don't fancy conscientious dusting is her strong point."

"It comes to this—that almost anyone might have taken that pistol?"

"It seems so—yes."

The door opened and Dr. Haydock came in with Anne Protheroe.

She started at seeing Lawrence. He, on his part, made a tentative step towards her.

"Forgive me, Anne," he said. "It was abominable of me to think what I did."

"I—" she faltered, then looked appealingly at Colonel Melchett. "It is true, what Dr. Haydock told me?"

"That Mr. Redding is cleared of suspicion? Yes. And now what about this story of yours, Mrs. Protheroe? Eh, what about it?"

She smiled rather shamefacedly.

"I suppose you think it dreadful of me?"

"Well, shall we say—very foolish? But that's all over. What I want now, Mrs. Protheroe, is the truth—the absolute truth."

She nodded gravely.

"I will tell you. I suppose you know about—about everything."

"Yes."

"I was to meet Lawrence—Mr. Redding—that evening at the studio. At a quarter past six. My husband and I drove into the village together. I had some shopping to do. As we parted he mentioned casually that he was going to see the Vicar. I couldn't get word to Lawrence, and I was rather uneasy. I—well, it was awkward meeting him in the Vicarage garden while my husband was at the Vicarage."

Her cheeks burned as she said this. It was not a pleasant moment for her.

"I reflected that perhaps my husband would not stay very long. To find this out, I came along the back lane and into the garden. I hoped no one would see me, but of course old Miss Marple had to be in her garden!

She stopped me and we said a few words, and I explained I was going to call for my husband. I felt I had to say something. I don't know whether she believed me or not. She looked rather—funny.

"When I left her, I went straight across to the Vicarage and round the corner of the house to the study window. I crept up to it very softly expecting to hear the sound of voices. But to my surprise there were none. I just glanced in, saw the room was empty, and hurried across the lawn and down to the studio where Lawrence joined me almost at once."

"You say the room was empty, Mrs. Protheroe?"

"Yes; my husband was not there."

"Extraordinary."

"You mean, M'am, that you didn't see him?" said the Inspector.

"No, I didn't see him."

Inspector Slack whispered to the Chief Constable, who nodded his head.

"Do you mind, Mrs. Protheroe, just showing us exactly what you did?"

"Not at all."

She rose; Inspector Slack pushed open the window for her, and she stepped out on the terrace and round the house to the left.

Inspector Slack beckoned me imperiously to go and sit at the writing table.

Somehow I didn't much like doing it. It gave me an uncomfortable feeling. But of course I complied.

Presently I heard footsteps outside; they paused for a minute, then retreated. Inspector Slack indicated to me that I could return to the other side of the room. Mrs. Protheroe re-entered through the window.

"Is that exactly how it was?" asked Colonel Melchett.

"I think exactly."

"Then can you tell us, Mrs. Protheroe, just exactly where the Vicar was in the room when you looked in?" asked Inspector Slack.

"The Vicar? I—no, I'm afraid I can't. I didn't see him."

Inspector Slack nodded.

"That's how you didn't see your husband. He was round the corner at the writing desk."

"Oh!" she paused. Suddenly her eyes grew round with horror. "It wasn't there that—that—"

"Yes, Mrs. Protheroe. It was while he was sitting there."

"Oh!" she shivered.

He went on with his questions.

"Did you know, Mrs. Protheroe, that Mr. Redding had a pistol?"

"Yes. He told me so once."

"Did you ever have that pistol in your possession?"

She shook her head.

"No."

"Did you know where he kept it?"

"I'm not sure. I think—yes, I think I've seen it on a shelf in his cottage. Didn't you keep it there, Lawrence?"

"When was the last time you were at the cottage, Mrs. Protheroe?"

"Oh! about three weeks ago. My husband and I had tea there with him."

"And you have not been there since?"

"No. I never went there. You see, it would probably cause a lot of talk in the village."

"Doubtless," said Colonel Melchett drily. "Where were you in the habit of seeing Mr. Redding, if I may ask?"

She blushed.

"He used to come up to the Hall. He was painting Lettice. We—we often met in the wood afterwards."

Colonel Melchett nodded.

"Isn't that enough?" Her voice was suddenly broken. "It's so awful—having to tell you all these things. And—and there wasn't anything wrong about it. There wasn't—indeed, there wasn't. We were just friends. We—we couldn't help caring for each other."

She looked pleadingly at Dr. Haydock, and that soft-hearted man stepped forward.

"I really think, Melchett," he said, "that Mrs. Protheroe has had enough. She's had a great shock—in more ways than one."

The Chief Constable nodded.

"There is really nothing more I want to ask you, Mrs. Protheroe," he said. "Thank you for answering my questions so frankly."

"Then—then I may go?"

He bowed his head in assent, but I noticed him make an almost imperceptible sign to Slack, which that worthy answered with a nod of understanding. Anne Protheroe was not yet completely cleared of suspicion. The evidence of the note was too strong.

"Is your wife in?" asked Haydock. "I think Mrs. Protheroe would like to see her."

"Yes," I said, "Griselda is in. You'll find her in the drawing room."

She and Haydock left the room together, and Lawrence Redding with them.

Colonel Melchett had pursed up his lips and was playing with a paper knife. Slack was looking at the note. It was then that I mentioned Miss Marple's theory.

Slack looked closely at it.

"My word," he said. "I believe the old lady's right. Look here, sir, don't you see?—these figures are written in different ink. That date was written with a fountain pen or I'll eat my boots!"

We were all rather excited.

"You've examined the note for finger prints, of course," said the Chief Constable.

"What do you think, Colonel? No finger prints on the note at all. Finger prints on the pistol those of Mr. Lawrence Redding. May have been some others once, before he went fooling round with it and carrying it around in his pocket, but there's nothing clear enough to get hold of now."

"At first the case looked very black against Mrs. Protheroe," said the Colonel thoughtfully. "Much blacker than against young Redding. There was that old woman Marple's evidence that she didn't have the pistol with her, but these elderly ladies are often mistaken."

I was silent, but I did not agree with him. I was quite sure that Anne Protheroe had had no pistol with her, since Miss Marple had said so. Miss Marple is not the type of elderly lady who makes mistakes. She has got an uncanny knack of being always right.

"What did get me was that nobody heard the shot. If it was fired then—somebody *must* have heard it—wherever they thought it came from. Slack, you'd better have a word with the maid."

Inspector Slack moved with alacrity towards the door.

"I shouldn't ask her if she heard a shot in the house," I said. "Because if you do, she'll deny it. Call it a shot in the wood. That's the only kind of shot she'll admit to hearing."

"I know how to manage them," said Inspector Slack, and disappeared.

"Miss Marple says she heard a shot later," said Colonel Melchett thoughtfully. "We must see if she can fix the time at all precisely. Of course it may be a stray shot that had nothing to do with the case."

"It may be, of course," I agreed.

The Colonel took a turn or two up and down the room.

"Do you know, Clement," he said suddenly, "I've a feeling that this is going to turn out a much more intricate and difficult business than any of us think. Dash it all, there's something behind it." He snorted. "Something we don't know about. We're only beginning, Clement. Mark my words, we're only beginning. All these things, the clock, the note, the pistol—they don't make sense as they stand."

I shook my head. They certainly didn't.

"But I'm going to get to the bottom of it. No calling in of Scotland Yard. Slack's a smart man. He's a very smart man. He's a kind of ferret. He'll nose his way through to the truth. He's done several very good things already and this case will be his *chef d'œuvre*. Some men would call in Scotland Yard. I shan't. We'll get to the bottom of this here in Downshire."

"I hope so, I'm sure," I said.

I tried to make my voice enthusiastic, but I had already taken such a dislike to Inspector Slack that the prospect of his success failed to appeal to me. A successful Slack would, I thought, be even more odious than a baffled one.

"Who has the house next door?" asked the Colonel suddenly.

"You mean at the end of the road? Mrs. Price Ridley."

"We'll go along to her after Slack has finished with your maid. She might just possibly have heard something. She isn't deaf or anything, is she?"

"I should say her hearing was remarkably keen. I'm going by the amount of scandal she has started by 'just happening to overhear accidentally.'"

"That's the kind of woman we want. Oh! here's Slack."

The Inspector had the air of one emerging from a severe tussle. He looked hot.

"Phew!" he said. "That's a tartar you've got, sir."

"Mary is essentially a girl of strong character," I replied.

"Doesn't like the police," he said. "I cautioned her–did what I could to put the fear of the Law into her, but no good. She stood right up to me."

"Spirited," I said, feeling more kindly towards Mary.

"But I pinned her down all right. She heard one shot–and one shot only. And it was a good long time after Colonel Protheroe came. I couldn't get her to name a time, but we fixed it at last by means of the fish. The fish was late, and she blew the boy up when he came, and he said it was barely half past six anyway, and it was just after that she heard the shot. Of course, that's not accurate, so to speak, but it gives us an idea."

"H'm," said Melchett.

"I don't think Mrs. Protheroe's in this after all," said Slack, with a note of regret in his voice. "She wouldn't have had time, to begin with, and then women never like fiddling about with firearms. Arsenic's more in their line. No, I don't think she did it. It's a pity!"

He sighed.

Melchett explained that he was going round to Mrs. Price Ridley's, and Slack approved.

"May I come with you?" I asked. "I'm getting interested."

I was given permission and we set forth. A loud "Hi" greeted us as we emerged from the Vicarage gate, and my nephew, Dennis, came running up the road from the village to join us.

"Look here," he said to the Inspector. "What about that footprint I told you about?"

"Gardener's," said Inspector Slack laconically.

"You don't think it might be someone else wearing the gardener's boots?"

"No, I don't," said Inspector Slack in a discouraging way.

It would take more than that to discourage Dennis, however.

He held out a couple of burnt matches.

"I found these by the Vicarage gate."

"Thank you," said Slack and put them in his pocket.

Matters appeared now to have reached a deadlock.

"You're not arresting Uncle Len, are you?" inquired Dennis facetiously.

"Why should I?" inquired Slack.

"There's a lot of evidence against him," declared Dennis. "You ask Mary. Only the day before the murder he was wishing Colonel Protheroe out of the world. Weren't you, Uncle Len?"

"Er—" I began.

Inspector Slack turned a slow, suspicious stare upon me, and I felt hot all over. Dennis is exceedingly tiresome. He ought to realize that a policeman seldom has a sense of humour.

"Don't be absurd, Dennis," I said irritably.

The innocent child opened his eyes in a stare of surprise.

"I say, it's only a joke," he said. "Uncle Len just said that anyone who murdered Colonel Protheroe would be doing the world a service."

"Ah!" said Inspector Slack, "that explains something the maid said."

Servants very seldom have any sense of humour either. I cursed Dennis heartily in my mind for bringing the matter up. That and the clock together will make the Inspector suspicious of me for life.

"Come on, Clement," said Colonel Melchett.

"Where are you going? Can I come too?" asked Dennis.

"No, you can't," I snapped.

We left him looking after us with a hurt expression. We went up to the neat front door of Mrs. Price Ridley's house, and the Inspector knocked and rang in what I can only describe as an official manner.

A pretty parlour maid answered the bell.

"Mrs. Price Ridley in?" inquired Melchett.

"No, sir." The maid paused and added, "She's just gone down to the police station."

This was a totally unexpected development. As we retraced our steps, Melchett caught me by the arm and murmured:

"If she's gone to confess to the crime too, I really shall go off my head."

XIII

I HARDLY THOUGHT it likely that Mrs. Price Ridley had anything so dramatic in view, but I did wonder what had taken her to the police station. Had she really got evidence of importance, or that she thought of importance, to offer? At any rate we should soon know.

We found Mrs. Price Ridley talking at a high rate of speed to a somewhat bewildered looking police constable. That she was extremely indignant I knew from the way the bow in her hat was trembling. Mrs. Price Ridley wears what, I believe, are known as "Hats for Matrons"—they make a specialty of them in our adjacent town of Much Benham. They perch easily on a superstructure of hair and are somewhat overweighted with large bows of ribbon. Griselda is always threatening to get a Matron's hat.

Mrs. Price Ridley paused in her flow of words upon our entrance.

"Mrs. Price Ridley?" inquired Colonel Melchett, lifting his hat.

"Let me introduce Colonel Melchett to you, Mrs. Price Ridley," I said. "Colonel Melchett is our Chief Constable."

Mrs. Price Ridley looked at me coldly, but produced the semblance of a gracious smile for the Colonel.

"We've just been round to your house, Mrs. Price Ridley," explained the Colonel, "and heard you had come down here."

Mrs. Price Ridley thawed altogether.

"Ah!" she said. "I'm glad some notice is being taken of the occurrence. Disgraceful, I call it. Simply disgraceful."

There is no doubt that murder is disgraceful, but it is not the word I should use to describe it myself. It surprised Melchett too, I could see.

"Have you any light to throw upon the matter?" he asked.

"That's your business. It's the business of the police. What do we pay rates and taxes for, I should like to know?"

One wonders how many times that query is uttered in a year!

"We're doing our best, Mrs. Price Ridley," said the Chief Constable.

"But the man here hadn't even heard of it till I told him about it!" cried the lady.

We all looked at the constable.

"Lady been rung up on the telephone," he said. "Annoyed. Matter of obscene language, I understand."

"Oh! I see." The Colonel's brow cleared. "We've been talking at cross purposes. You came down here to make a complaint, did you?"

Melchett is a wise man. He knows that, when it is a question of an irate middle-aged lady, there is only one thing to be done—to listen to her. When she has said all that she wants to say, there is a chance that she will listen to you.

Mrs. Price Ridley surged into speech.

"Such disgraceful occurrences ought to be prevented. They ought not to occur. To be rung up in one's own house and insulted—yes, insulted. I'm not accustomed to such things happening. Ever since the War there has been a loosening of moral fibre. Nobody minds what they say, and as to the clothes they wear—"

"Quite," said Colonel Melchett hastily. "What happened exactly?"

Mrs. Price Ridley took breath and started again.

"I was rung up—"

"When?"

"Yesterday afternoon—evening to be exact. About half past six. I went to the telephone, suspecting nothing. Immediately I was foully attacked, threatened—"

"What actually was said?"

Mrs. Price Ridley got slightly pink.

"That I decline to state."

"Obscene language," murmured the Constable in a ruminative bass.

"Was bad language used?" asked Colonel Melchett.

"It depends on what you call bad language."

"Could you understand it?" I asked.

"Of course I could understand it."

"Then it couldn't have been bad language," I said.

Mrs. Price Ridley looked at me suspiciously.

"A refined lady," I explained, "is naturally unacquainted with bad language."

"It wasn't that kind of thing," said Mrs. Price Ridley. "At first, I must admit, I was quite taken in. I thought it was a genuine message. Then the—er—person became abusive."

"Abusive?"

"Most abusive. I was quite alarmed."

"Used threatening language, eh?"

"Yes. I am not accustomed to being threatened."

"What did they threaten you with? Bodily damage?"

"Not exactly."

"I'm afraid, Mrs. Price Ridley, you must be more explicit. In what way were you threatened?"

This Mrs. Price Ridley seemed singularly reluctant to answer.

"I can't remember exactly. It was all so upsetting. But right at the end—when I was really very upset, this—this—wretch laughed."

"Was it a man's voice or a woman's?"

"It was a degenerate voice," said Mrs. Price Ridley with dignity. "I can only describe it as a kind of perverted voice. Now gruff, now squeaky. Really a very peculiar voice."

"Probably a practical joke," said the Colonel soothingly.

"A most wicked thing to do, if so. I might have had a heart attack."

"We'll look into it," said the Colonel. "Eh, Inspector? Trace the telephone call. You can't tell me more definitely exactly what was said, Mrs. Price Ridley?"

A struggle began in Mrs. Price Ridley's ample black bosom. The desire for reticence fought against a desire for vengeance. Vengeance triumphed.

"This, of course, will go no farther," she began.

"Of course not."

"This creature began by saying—I can hardly bring myself to repeat it—"

"Yes, yes," said Melchett encouragingly.

"*'You are a wicked, scandal-mongering old woman!'* Me, Colonel Melchett—a scandal-mongering old woman. *'But this time you've gone too far. Scotland Yard are after you for libel.'*"

"Naturally, you were alarmed," said Melchett, biting his moustache to conceal a smile.

"*'Unless you hold your tongue in future, it will be the worse for you—in more ways than one.'* I can't describe to you the menacing way that was said. I gasped, 'Who are you?' faintly—like that, and the voice answered, *'The Avenger.'* I gave a little shriek; it sounded so awful, and then—the person laughed. Laughed! Distinctly. And that was all. I heard him hang up the receiver. Of course I asked the exchange what number had been ringing me up, but they said they didn't know. You know what exchanges are. Thoroughly rude and unsympathetic."

"Quite," I said.

"I felt quite faint," continued Mrs. Price Ridley. "All on edge and so nervous that when I heard a shot in the wood I do declare I jumped almost out of my skin. That will show you."

"A shot in the wood," said Inspector Slack alertly.

"In my excited state, it simply sounded to me like a cannon going off. 'Oh!' I said, and sank down on the sofa in a state of prostration. Clara had to bring me a glass of damson gin."

"Shocking," said Melchett. "Shocking. All very trying for you. And the shot sounded very loud, you say? As though it were near at hand?"

"That was simply the state of my nerves."

"Of course. Of course. And what time was all this? To help us in tracing the telephone call, you know."

"About half past six."

"You can't give it us more exactly than that?"

"Well, you see, the little clock on my mantelpiece had just chimed the half hour, and I said 'Surely that clock is fast.' (It does gain, that clock.) And I compared it with the watch I was wearing and that only said ten minutes past, but then I put it to my ear and found it had stopped. So I thought, 'Well, if that clock *is* fast, I shall hear the church tower in a moment or two.' And then, of course, the telephone bell rang, and I forgot all about it."

She paused breathless.

"Well, that's near enough," said Colonel Melchett. "We'll have it looked into for you, Mrs. Price Ridley."

"Just think of it as a silly joke, and don't worry, Mrs. Price Ridley," I said.

She looked at me coldly. Evidently the incident of the pound note still rankled.

"Very strange things have been happening in this village lately," she said, addressing herself to Melchett. "Very strange things indeed. Colonel Protheroe was going to look into them, and what happened to him, poor man? Perhaps I shall be the next."

And on that she took her departure, shaking her head with a kind of ominous melancholy. Melchett muttered under his breath, "No such luck." Then his face grew grave, and he looked inquiringly at Inspector Slack.

That worthy nodded his head slowly.

"This about settles it, sir. That's three people who heard the shot. We've got to find out now who fired it. This business of Mr. Redding's has delayed us. But we've got several starting points. Thinking Mr. Redding was guilty, I didn't bother to look into them. But that's all changed now. And now one of the first things to do is to look up that telephone call."

"Mrs. Price Ridley's?"

The Inspector grinned.

"No—though I suppose we'd better make a note of that or else we shall have the old girl bothering in here again. No, I meant that fake call that got the Vicar out of the way."

"Yes," said Melchett. "That's important."

"And the next thing is to find out what everyone was doing that evening between six and seven. Everyone at Old Hall, I mean, and pretty well everyone in the village as well."

I gave a sigh.

"What wonderful energy you have, Inspector Slack."

"I believe in hard work. We'll begin by just noting down your own movements, Mr. Clement."

"Willingly. The telephone call came through about half past five."

"A man's voice, or a woman's?"

"A woman's. At least it sounded like a woman's. But of course I took it for granted it was Mrs. Abbott speaking."

"You didn't recognize it as being Mrs. Abbott's?"

"No, I can't say I did. I didn't notice the voice particularly, or think about it."

"And you started right away? Walked? Haven't you got a bicycle?"

"No."

"I see. So it took you—how long?"

"It's very nearly two miles, whichever way you go."

"Through Old Hall wood is the shortest way, isn't it?"

"Actually, yes. But it's not particularly good going. I went and came back by the footpath across the fields."

"The one that comes out opposite the Vicarage gate?"

"Yes."

"And Mrs. Clement?"

"My wife was in London. She arrived back by the 6.50 train."

"Right. The maid I've seen. That finishes with the Vicarage. I'll be off to Old Hall next. And then I want an interview with Mrs. Lestrange.

Queer, her going to see Protheroe the night before he was killed. A lot of queer things about this case."

I agreed.

Glancing at the clock, I realized that it was nearly lunch time. I invited Melchett to partake of pot luck with us, but he excused himself on the plea of having to go to the Blue Boar. The Blue Boar gives you a first-rate meal of the joint and two vegetable type. I thought his choice was a wise one. After her interview with the police, Mary would probably be feeling more temperamental than usual.

XIV

On my way home, I ran into Miss Hartnell, and she detained me at least ten minutes, declaiming in her deep bass voice against the improvidence and ungratefulness of the lower classes. The crux of the matter seemed to be that The Poor did not want Miss Hartnell in their houses. My sympathies were entirely on their side. I am debarred by my social standing from expressing my prejudices in the forceful manner they do. I soothed her as best I could and made my escape.

Haydock overtook me in his car at the corner of the Vicarage road.

"I've just taken Mrs. Protheroe home," he called.

He waited for me at the gate of his house.

"Come in a minute," he said.

I complied.

"This is an extraordinary business," he said as he threw his hat on a chair and opened the door into his surgery.

He sank down on a shabby leather chair, and stared across the room. He looked harried and perplexed.

I told him that we had succeeded in fixing the time of the shot. He listened with an almost abstracted air.

"That lets Anne Protheroe out," he said. "Well, well, I'm glad it's neither of those two. I like 'em both."

I believed him, and yet it occurred to me to wonder why, since, as he said, he liked them both, their freedom from complicity seemed to have had the result of plunging him in gloom. This morning he had looked like a man with a weight lifted from his mind; now he looked thoroughly rattled and upset.

And yet I was convinced that he meant what he said. He was fond of both Anne Protheroe and Lawrence Redding. Why, then, this gloomy absorption?

He roused himself with an effort.

"I meant to tell you about Hawes. All this business has driven him out of my mind."

"Is he really ill?"

"There's nothing radically wrong with him. You know, of course, that he's had *Encephalitis Lethargica*—sleeping sickness, as it's commonly called?"

"No," I said, very much surprised. "I didn't know anything of the kind. He never told me anything about it. When did he have it?"

"About a year ago. He recovered all right—as far as one ever recovers. It's a strange disease—has a queer moral effect. The whole character may change after it."

He was silent for a moment or two and then said:

"We think with horror now of the days when we burnt witches. I believe the day will come when we will shudder to think that we ever hanged criminals."

"You don't believe in capital punishment?"

"It's not so much that." He paused. "You know," he said slowly, "I'd rather have my job than yours."

"Why?"

"Because your job deals very largely with what we call right and wrong—and I'm not at all sure that there's any such thing. Suppose it's all a question of glandular secretion. Too much of one gland, too little of another—and you get your murderer, your thief, your habitual criminal. Clement, I believe the time will come when we'll be horrified to think of the long centuries in which we've indulged in what you may call moral reprobation, to think how we've punished people for disease—which they can't help, poor devils. You don't hang a man for having tuberculosis."

"He isn't dangerous to the community."

"In a sense he is. He infects other people. Or take a man who fancies he's the Emperor of China. You don't say 'how wicked of him.' I take your point about the community. The community must be protected. Shut up these people where they can't do any harm—even put them peacefully out of the way—yes, I'd go as far as that. But don't call it punishment. Don't bring shame on them and their innocent families."

I looked at him curiously.

"I've never heard you speak like this before."

"I don't usually air my theories abroad. Today I'm riding my hobby. You're an intelligent man, Clement, which is more than some parsons are. You won't admit, I daresay, that there's no such thing as what is technically termed 'Sin,' but you're broad-minded enough to consider the possibility of such a thing."

"It strikes at the root of all our accepted ideas," I said.

"Yes, we're a narrow-minded, self-righteous lot, only too keen to judge matters we know nothing about. I honestly believe crime is a case for the doctor, not the policeman and not the parson. In the future, perhaps, there won't be any such thing."

"You'll have cured it?"

"We'll have cured it. Rather a wonderful thought. Have you ever studied the statistics of crime? No—very few people have. I have, though. You'd be amazed at the amount there is of adolescent crime—glands again, you see. Young Neil, the Oxfordshire murderer, killed five little girls before he was suspected. Nice lad—never given any trouble of any kind. Lily Rose, the little Cornish girl, killed her uncle because he docked her of sweets. Hit him when he was asleep with a coal hammer. Went home and a fortnight later killed her elder sister who had annoyed her about some trifling matter. Neither of them hanged, of course. Sent to a home. May be all right later—may not. Doubt if the girl will. The only thing she cares about is seeing the pigs killed. Do you know when suicide is commonest? Fifteen to sixteen years of age. From self-murder to murder of someone else isn't a very long step. But it's not a moral lack—it's a physical one."

"What you say is terrible!"

"No—it's only new to you. New truths have to be faced. One's ideas adjusted. But sometimes—it makes life difficult."

He sat there frowning, yet with a strange look of weariness.

"Haydock," I said, "if you suspected—if you knew—that a certain person was a murderer, would you give that person up to the law, or would you be tempted to shield him?"

I was quite unprepared for the effect of my question. He turned on me angrily and suspiciously.

"What makes you say that, Clement? What's in your mind? Out with it, man."

"Why, nothing particular," I said rather taken aback. "Only—well, murder is in our minds just now. If by any chance you happened to discover the truth—I wondered how you would feel about it, that was all."

His anger died down. He stared once more straight ahead of him, like a man trying to read the answer to a riddle that perplexes him, yet which exists only in his own brain.

"If I suspected—if I knew—I should do my duty, Clement. At least, I hope so."

"The question is—which way would you consider your duty lay?"

He looked at me with inscrutable eyes.

"That question comes to every man some time in his life, I suppose, Clement. And every man has to decide it in his own way."

"You don't know?"

"No, I don't know. . . ."

I felt the best thing was to change the subject.

"That nephew of mine is enjoying this case thoroughly," I said. "Spends his entire time looking for footprints and cigarette ash."

Haydock smiled.

"What age is he?"

"Just sixteen. You don't take tragedies seriously at that age. It's all Sherlock Holmes and Arsène Lupin to you."

Haydock said thoughtfully:

"He's a fine looking boy. What are you going to do with him?"

"I can't afford a University education, I'm afraid. The boy himself wants to go into the Merchant Service. He failed for the Navy."

"Well—it's a hard life—but he might do worse. Yes, he might do worse."

"I must be going," I exclaimed, catching sight of the clock. "I'm nearly half an hour late for lunch."

My family were just sitting down when I arrived. They demanded a full account of the morning's activities, which I gave them, feeling, as I did so, that most of it was in the nature of an anticlimax.

Dennis, however, was highly entertained by the history of Mrs. Price Ridley's telephone call, and went into fits of laughter as I enlarged upon the nervous shock her system had sustained and the necessity for reviving her with damson gin.

"Serve the old cat right," he exclaimed. "She's got the worst tongue in the place. I wish I'd thought of ringing her up and giving her a fright. I say, Uncle Len, what about giving her a second dose?"

I hastily begged him to do nothing of the sort. Nothing is more dangerous than the well-meant efforts of the younger generation to assist you and show their sympathy.

Dennis' mood changed suddenly. He frowned and put on his man-of-the-world air.

"I've been with Lettice most of the morning," he said. "You know, Griselda, she's really very worried. She doesn't want to show it, but she is. Very worried indeed."

"I should hope so," said Griselda with a toss of her head.

Griselda is not too fond of Lettice Protheroe.

"I don't think you're ever quite fair to Lettice."

"Don't you?" said Griselda.

"Lots of people don't wear mourning."

Griselda was silent and so was I. Dennis continued:

"She doesn't talk to most people, but she does talk to me. She's awfully worried about the whole thing, and she thinks something ought to be done about it."

"She will find," I said, "that Inspector Slack shares her opinion. He is going up to Old Hall this afternoon, and will probably make the life of everybody there quite unbearable to them in his efforts to get at the truth."

"What do you think is the truth, Len?" asked my wife suddenly.

"It's hard to say, my dear. I can't say that at the moment I've any idea at all."

"Did you say that Inspector Slack was going to trace that telephone call —the one that took you to the Abbotts'?"

"Yes."

"But can he do it? Isn't it a very difficult thing to do?"

"I should not imagine so. The exchange will have a record of the calls."

"Oh!" My wife relapsed into thought.

"Uncle Len," said my nephew. "Why were you so ratty with me this morning for joking about your wishing Colonel Protheroe to be murdered?"

"Because," I said, "there is a time for everything. Inspector Slack has no sense of humour. He took your words quite seriously, will probably cross-examine Mary, and will get out a warrant for my arrest."

"Doesn't he know when a fellow's ragging?"

"No," I said. "He does not. He has attained to his present position through hard work and zealous attention to duty. That has left him no time for the minor recreations of life."

"Do you like him, Uncle Len?"

"No," I said. "I do not. From the first moment I saw him I disliked him intensely. But I have no doubt that he is a highly successful man in his profession."

"You think he'll find out who shot old Protheroe?"

"If he doesn't," I said, "it will not be for the want of trying."

Mary appeared and said:

"Mr. Hawes wants to see you. I've put him in the drawing room, and here's a note. Waiting for an answer. Verbal will do."

I tore open the note and read it.

DEAR MR. CLEMENT,

I should be so very grateful if you could come and see me this afternoon as early as possible. I am in great trouble and would like your advice.

Sincerely yours,

ESTELLE LESTRANGE.

"Say I will come round in about half an hour," I said to Mary.

Then I went into the drawing room to see Hawes.

XV

HAWES' APPEARANCE DISTRESSED me very much. His hands were shaking and his face kept twitching nervously. In my opinion he should have been in bed, and I told him so. He insisted that he was perfectly well.

"I assure you, sir, I never felt better. Never in my life."

This was so obviously wide of the truth that I hardly knew how to answer. I have a certain admiration for a man who will not give in to illness, but Hawes was carrying the thing rather too far.

"I called to tell you how sorry I was—that such a thing should happen in the Vicarage."

"Yes," I said. "It's not very pleasant."

"It's terrible—quite terrible. It seems they haven't arrested Mr. Redding after all?"

"No. That was a mistake. He made—er—rather a foolish statement."

"And the police are now quite convinced that he is innocent?"

"Perfectly."

"Why is that, may I ask? Is it—I mean, do they suspect anyone else?"

I should never have suspected that Hawes would take such a keen interest in the details of a murder case. Perhaps it is because it happened in the Vicarage. He appeared as eager as a reporter.

"I don't know that I am completely in Inspector Slack's confidence. So far as I know he does not suspect anyone in particular. He is at present engaged in making inquiries."

"Yes. Yes—of course. But who can one imagine doing such a dreadful thing?"

I shook my head.

"Colonel Protheroe was not a popular man, I know that. But murder! For murder—one would need a very strong motive."

"So I should imagine," I said.

"Who could have such a motive? Have the police any idea?"

"I couldn't say."

"He might have made enemies, you know. The more I think about it, the more I am convinced that he was the kind of man to have enemies. He had a reputation on the Bench for being very severe."

"I suppose he had."

"Why, don't you remember, sir? He was telling you yesterday morning about having been threatened by that man, Archer."

"Now I come to think of it, so he did," I said. "Of course, I remember. You were quite near us at the time."

"Yes, I overheard what he was saying. Almost impossible to help it with Colonel Protheroe. He had such a very loud voice, hadn't he? I remember being impressed by your own words, that when his time came, he might have justice meted out to him instead of mercy."

"Did I say that?" I asked frowning. My remembrance of my own words was slightly different.

"You said it very impressively, sir. I was struck by your words. Justice is a terrible thing. And to think the poor man was struck down shortly afterwards. It's almost as though you had a premonition."

"I had nothing of the sort," I said shortly. I rather dislike Hawes' tendency to mysticism. There is a touch of the visionary about him.

"Have you told the police about this man Archer, sir?"

"I know nothing about him."

"I mean, have you repeated to them what Colonel Protheroe said—about Archer having threatened him?"

"No," I said slowly. "I have not."

"But you are going to do so?"

I was silent. I dislike hounding a man down who has already got the forces of law and order against him. I held no brief for Archer. He is an inveterate poacher—one of those cheerful ne'er-do-weels that are to be found in any parish. Whatever he may have said in the heat of anger when he was sentenced I had no definite knowledge that he felt the same when he came out of prison.

"You heard the conversation," I said at last. "If you feel it your duty to go to the police with it, you must do so."

"It would come better from you, sir."

"Perhaps—but to tell the truth—well, I've no fancy for doing it. I might be helping to put the rope round the neck of an innocent man."

"But if he shot Colonel Protheroe—"

"Oh! if! There's no evidence of any kind that he did."

"His threats."

"Strictly speaking, the threats were not his but Colonel Protheroe's. Colonel Protheroe was threatening to show Archer what vengeance was worth next time he caught him."

"I don't understand your attitude, sir."

"Don't you?" I said wearily. "You're a young man. You're zealous in the cause of right. When you get to my age, you'll find that you like to give people the benefit of the doubt."

"It's not—I mean—"

He paused and I looked at him in surprise.

"You haven't any—any ideas of your own—as to the identity of the murderer, I mean?"

"Good heavens, no."

Hawes persisted.

"Or as to the—the motive?"

"No. Have you?"

"I? No, indeed. I just wondered. If Colonel Protheroe had—had confided in you in any way—mentioned anything . . ."

"His confidences, such as they were, were heard by the whole village street yesterday morning," I said drily.

"Yes. Yes—of course. And you don't think—about Archer?"

"The police will know all about Archer soon enough," I said. "If I'd heard him threaten Colonel Protheroe myself, that would be a different matter. But you may be sure that if he actually has threatened him, half the people in the village will have heard him, and the news will get to the police all right. You, of course, must do as you like about the matter."

But Hawes seemed curiously unwilling to do anything himself.

The man's whole attitude was nervous and queer. I recalled what Haydock had said about his illness. There, I supposed, lay the explanation.

He took his leave unwillingly, as though he had more to say, and didn't know how to say it.

Before he left, I arranged with him to take the Service for the Mothers' Union followed by the Meeting of District Visitors. I had several projects of my own for the afternoon.

Dismissing Hawes and his troubles from my mind, I started off for Mrs. Lestrange.

On the table in the hall lay the "Guardian" and the "Church Times" unopened.

As I walked I remembered that Mrs. Lestrange had had an interview with Colonel Protheroe the night before his death. It was possible that something had transpired in that interview which would throw light upon the problem of his murder.

I was shown straight into the little drawing room, and Mrs. Lestrange rose to meet me. I was struck anew by the marvellous atmosphere that this woman could create. She wore a dress of some dead black material that showed off the extraordinary fairness of her skin. There was something curiously dead about her face. Only the eyes were burningly alive. There was a watchful look in them today. Otherwise she showed no signs of animation.

"It was very good of you to come, Mr. Clement," she said as she shook hands. "I wanted to speak to you the other day. Then I decided not to do so. I was wrong."

"As I told you then, I shall be glad to do anything that can help you."

"Yes, you said that. And you said it as though you meant it. Very few people, Mr. Clement, in this world have ever sincerely wished to help me."

"I can hardly believe that, Mrs. Lestrange."

"It is true. Most people—most men, at any rate, are out for their own hand."

There was a bitterness in her voice.

I did not answer and she went on:

"Sit down, won't you?"

I obeyed, and she took a chair facing me. She hesitated a moment and then began to speak very slowly and thoughtfully, seeming to weigh each word as she uttered it.

"I am in a very peculiar position, Mr. Clement, and I want to ask your advice. That is, I want to ask your advice as to what I should do next. What is past is past and cannot be undone. You understand?"

Before I could reply, the maid who had admitted me opened the door and said, with a scared face:

"Oh! please, m'am, there's a police inspector here, and he says he must speak to you, please."

There was a pause. Mrs. Lestrange's face did not change. Only her eyes very slowly closed and opened again. She seemed to swallow once or twice, then she said in exactly the same clear, calm voice:

"Show him in, Hilda."

I was about to rise, but she motioned me back again with an imperious hand.

"If you do not mind—I should be much obliged if you would stay."

I resumed my seat.

"Certainly, if you wish it," I murmured, as Slack entered with a brisk regulation tread.

"Good afternoon, Madam," he began.

"Good afternoon, Inspector."

At this moment he caught sight of me and scowled. There is no doubt about it; Slack does not like me.

"You have no objection to the Vicar's presence, I hope?"

I suppose that Slack could not very well say he had.

"No-o," he said grudgingly. "Though, perhaps, it might be better—"

Mrs. Lestrange paid no attention to the hint.

"What can I do for you, Inspector?" she asked.

"It's this way, Madam. Murder of Colonel Protheroe. I'm in charge of the case and making inquiries."

Mrs. Lestrange nodded.

"Just as a matter of form, I'm asking everyone just where they were yesterday evening between the hours of six and seven. Just as a matter of form, you understand."

Mrs. Lestrange did not seem in the least discomposed.

"You want to know where I was yesterday evening between six and seven?"

"If you please, Madam."

"Let me see." She reflected a moment. "I was here. In this house."

"Oh!" I saw the Inspector's eyes flash. "And your maid—you have only one maid, I think, can confirm that statement?"

"No, it was Hilda's afternoon out."

"I see."

"So unfortunately you will have to take my word for it," said Mrs. Lestrange pleasantly.

"You seriously declare that you were at home all the afternoon?"

"You said between six and seven, Inspector. I was out for a walk early in the afternoon. I returned some time before five o'clock."

"Then if a lady—Miss Hartnell, for instance—were to declare that she came here about six o'clock, rang the bell, but could make no one hear and was compelled to go away again, you'd say she was mistaken, eh?"

"Oh! no," Mrs. Lestrange shook her head.

"But—"

"If your maid is in, she can say not at home. If one is alone and does not happen to want to see callers—well, the only thing to do is to let them ring."

Inspector Slack looked slightly baffled.

"Elderly women bore me dreadfully," said Mrs. Lestrange. "And Miss Hartnell is particularly boring. She must have rung at least half a dozen times before she went away."

She smiled sweetly at Inspector Slack.

The Inspector shifted his ground.

"Then if anyone were to say they'd seen you out and about then—"

"Oh! but they didn't, did they?" She was quick to sense his weak point. "No one saw me out, because I was in, you see."

"Quite so, Madam."

The Inspector hitched his chair a little nearer.

"Now I understand, Mrs. Lestrange, that you paid a visit to Colonel Protheroe at Old Hall the night before his death."

Mrs. Lestrange said calmly:

"That is so."

"Can you indicate to me the nature of that interview?"

"It concerned a private matter, Inspector."

"I'm afraid I must ask you to tell me the nature of that private matter."

"I shall not tell you anything of the kind. I will only assure you that nothing which was said at that interview could possibly have any bearing upon the crime."

"I don't think you are the best judge of that."

"At any rate, you will have to take my word for it, Inspector."

"In fact, I have to take your word about everything."

"It does seem rather like it," she agreed, still with the same smiling calm.

Inspector Slack grew very red.

"This is a serious matter, Mrs. Lestrange. I want the truth—" He banged his fist down on a table. "And I mean to get it."

Mrs. Lestrange said nothing at all.

"Don't you see, Madam, that you're putting yourself in a very fishy position?"

Still Mrs. Lestrange said nothing.

"You'll be required to give evidence at the inquest."

"Yes."

Just the monosyllable. Unemphatic, uninterested. The Inspector altered his tactics.

"You were acquainted with Colonel Protheroe?"

"Yes, I was acquainted with him."

"Well acquainted?"

There was a pause before she said:

"I had not seen him for several years."

"You were acquainted with Mrs. Protheroe?"

"No."

"You'll excuse me, but it was a very unusual time to make a call."

"Not from my point of view."

"What do you mean by that?"

She said clearly and distinctly:

"I wanted to see Colonel Protheroe alone. I did not want to see Mrs. Protheroe or Miss Protheroe. I considered this the best way of accomplishing my object."

"Why didn't you want to see Mrs. or Miss Protheroe?"

"That, Inspector, is my business."

"Then you refuse to say more?"

"Absolutely."

Inspector Slack rose.

"You'll be putting yourself in a nasty position, Madam, if you're not careful. All this looks bad—it looks very bad."

She laughed. I could have told Inspector Slack that this was not the kind of woman who is easily frightened.

"Well," he said, extricating himself with dignity, "don't say I haven't warned you, that's all. Good afternoon, Madam, and mind you, we're going to get at the truth."

He departed. Mrs. Lestrange rose and held out her hand.

"I am going to send you away—yes, it is better so. You see, it is too late for advice now. I have chosen my part."

She repeated, in a rather forlorn voice:

"I have chosen my part."

XVI

As I WENT out, I ran into Haydock on the doorstep. He glanced sharply after Slack, who was just passing through the gate, and demanded:

"Has he been questioning her?"

"Yes."

"He's been civil, I hope?"

Civility, to my mind, is an art which Inspector Slack has never learnt, but I presumed that according to his own lights, civil he had been, and anyway I didn't want to upset Haydock any further. He was looking worried and upset as it was. So I said he had been quite civil.

Haydock nodded and passed on into the house, and I went on down the village street where I soon caught up with the Inspector. I fancy that he was walking slowly on purpose. Much as he dislikes me, he is not the man to let dislike stand in the way of acquiring any useful information.

"Do you know anything about the lady?" he asked me point-blank.

I said I knew nothing whatever.

"She's never said anything about why she came here to live?"

"No."

"Yet you go and see her?"

"It is one of my duties to call on my parishioners," I replied, evading to remark that I had been sent for.

"H'm, I suppose it is." He was silent for a minute or two and then, unable to resist discussing his recent failure, he went on, "Fishy business, it looks to me."

"You think so?"

"If you ask me, I say 'blackmail.' Seems funny, when you think of what Colonel Protheroe was always supposed to be. But there, you never can tell. He wouldn't be the first churchwarden who'd led a double life."

Faint remembrances of Miss Marple's remarks on the same subject floated through my mind.

"You really think that's likely?"

"Well, it fits the facts, sir. Why did a smart, well dressed lady come down to this quiet little hole? Why did she go and see him at that funny time of day? Why did she avoid seeing Mrs. and Miss Protheroe? Yes, it all hangs together. Awkward for her to admit—blackmail's a punishable offence. But we'll get the truth out of her. For all we know it may have a very important bearing on the case. If Colonel Protheroe had some guilty secret in his life—something disgraceful—well, you can see for yourself what a field it opens up."

I suppose it did.

"I've been trying to get the butler to talk. He might have overheard some of the conversation between Colonel Protheroe and Lestrange. Butlers do sometimes. But he swears he hasn't the least idea of what the conversation was about. By the way, he got the sack through it. The Colonel went for him, being angry at his having let her in. The butler retorted by giving notice. Says he didn't like the place anyway, and had been thinking of leaving for some time."

"Really."

"So that gives us another person who had a grudge against the Colonel."

"You don't seriously suspect the man—what's his name by the way?"

"His name's Reeves, and I don't say I do suspect him. What I say is, you never know. I don't like that soapy, oily manner of his."

I wonder what Reeves would say of Inspector Slack's manner.

"I'm going to question the chauffeur now."

"Perhaps, then," I said, "you'll give me a lift in your car. I want a short interview with Mrs. Protheroe."

"What about?"

"The funeral arrangements."

"Oh!" Inspector Slack was slightly taken aback. "The inquest's tomorrow, Saturday."

"Just so. The funeral will probably be arranged for Tuesday."

Inspector Slack seemed to be a little ashamed of himself for his brusqueness. He held out an olive branch in the shape of an invitation to be present at the interview with the chauffeur, Manning.

Manning was a nice lad, not more than twenty-five or six years of age. He was inclined to be awed by the Inspector.

"Now then, my lad," said Slack, "I want a little information from you."

"Yes, sir," stammered the chauffeur. "Certainly, sir."

If he had committed the murder himself he could not have been more alarmed.

"You took your master to the village yesterday?"

"Yes, sir."

"What time was that?"

"Five-thirty."

"Mrs. Protheroe went too?"

"Yes, sir."

"You went straight to the village?"

"Yes, sir."

"You didn't stop anywhere on the way?"

"No, sir."

"What did you do when you got there?"

"The Colonel got out and told me he wouldn't want the car again. He'd walk home. Mrs. Protheroe had some shopping to do. The parcels were put in the car. Then she said that was all and I drove home."

"Leaving her in the village?"

"Yes, sir."

"What time was that?"

"A quarter past six, sir. A quarter past exactly."

"Where did you leave her?"

"By the church, sir."

"Had the Colonel mentioned at all where he was going?"

"He said something about having to see the vet—something to do with one of the horses."

"I see. And you drove straight back here?"

"Yes, sir."

"There are two entrances to Old Hall, by the South Lodge and by the North Lodge. I take it that going to the village you would go by the South Lodge?"

"Yes, sir, always."

"And you came back the same way?"

"Yes, sir."

"H'm. I think that's all. Ah! here's Miss Protheroe."

Lettice drifted towards us.

"I want the Fiat, Manning," she said. "Start her for me, will you?"

"Very good, Miss."

He went towards a two-seater and lifted the bonnet.

"Just a minute, Miss Protheroe," said Slack. "It's necessary that I should have a record of everybody's movements yesterday afternoon. No offence meant."

Lettice stared at him.

"I never know the time of anything," she said.

"I understand you went out soon after lunch yesterday."

She nodded.

"Where to, please?"

"To play tennis."

"Who with?"

"The Hartley Napiers."

"At Much Benham?"

"Yes."

"And you returned?"

"I don't know. I tell you I never know these things."

"You returned," I said, "about seven-thirty."

"That's right," said Lettice. "In the middle of the shemozzle. Anne having fits and Griselda supporting her."

"Thank you, Miss," said the Inspector. "That's all I want to know."

"How queer," said Lettice. "It seems so uninteresting."

She moved towards the Fiat.

The Inspector touched his forehead in a surreptitious manner.

"A bit wanting?" he suggested.

"Not in the least," I said. "But she likes to be thought so."

"Well, I'm off to question the maids now."

One cannot really like Slack, but one can admire his energy.

We parted company and I inquired of Reeves if I could see Mrs. Protheroe.

"She is lying down, sir, at the moment."

"Then I'd better not disturb her."

"Perhaps if you would wait, sir, I know that Mrs. Protheroe is anxious to see you. She was saying as much at luncheon."

He showed me into the drawing room, switching on the electric lights, since the blinds were down.

"A very sad business all this," I said.

"Yes, sir."

His voice was cold and respectful.

I looked at him. What feelings were at work under that impassive demeanour. Were there things that he knew and could have told us? There is nothing so inhuman as the mask of the good servant.

"Is there anything more, sir?"

Was there just a hint of anxiety to be gone behind that correct expression?

"There's nothing more," I said.

I had a very short time to wait before Anne Protheroe came to me. We discussed and settled a few arrangements and then:

"What a wonderfully kind man Dr. Haydock is," she exclaimed.

"Haydock is the best fellow I know."

"He has been amazingly kind to me. But he looks very sad, doesn't he?"

It had never occurred to me to think of Haydock as sad. I turned the idea over in my mind.

"I don't think I've ever noticed it," I said at last.

"I never have, until today."

"One's own troubles sharpen one's eyes sometimes," I said.

"That's very true."

She paused and then said:

"Mr. Clement, there's one thing I absolutely cannot make out. If my husband was shot immediately after I left him, how was it that I didn't hear the shot?"

"They have reason to believe that the shot was fired later."

"But the 6.20 on the note."

"Was possibly added by a different hand—the murderer's."

Her cheek paled.

"How horrible!"

"It didn't strike you that the date was not in his handwriting?"

"None of it looked like his handwriting."

There was some truth in this observation. It was a somewhat illegible scrawl, not so precise as Protheroe's writing usually was.

"You are sure they don't still suspect Lawrence?"

"I think he is definitely cleared."

"But Mr. Clement, who can it be? Lucius was not popular, I know, but I don't think he had any real enemies. Not—not that kind of enemy."

I shook my head.

"It's a mystery."

I thought wonderingly of Miss Marple's seven suspects. Who could they be?

After I took leave of Anne, I proceeded to put a certain plan of mine into action.

I returned from Old Hall by way of the private path. When I reached the stile, I retraced my steps, and, choosing a place where I fancied the undergrowth showed signs of being disturbed, I turned aside from the path and forced my way through the bushes. The wood was a thick one, with a good deal of tangled undergrowth. My progress was not very fast, and I suddenly became aware that someone else was moving among the bushes not very far from me. As I paused irresolutely, Lawrence Redding came into sight. He was carrying a large stone.

I suppose I must have looked surprised, for he suddenly burst out laughing.

"No," he said, "it's not a clue; it's a peace offering."

"A peace offering?"

"Well, a basis for negotiations, shall we say? I want an excuse for calling on your neighbour, Miss Marple, and I have been told that there is nothing she likes so much as a nice bit of rock or stone for the Japanese gardens she makes."

"Quite true," I said. "But what do you want with the old lady?"

"Just this. If there was anything to be seen yesterday evening Miss Marple saw it. I don't mean anything necessarily connected with the crime—that she would think connected with the crime. I mean some *outré* or bizarre incident, some simple little happening that might give us a clue to the truth. Something that she wouldn't think worth while mentioning to the police."

"It's possible, I suppose."

"It's worth trying anyhow. Clement, I'm going to get to the bottom of this business. For Anne's sake, if nobody's else. And I haven't any too much confidence in Slack—he's a zealous fellow, but zeal can't really take the place of brains."

"I see," I said, "that you are that favourite character of fiction, the amateur detective. I don't know that they really hold their own with the professional in real life."

He looked at me shrewdly and suddenly laughed.

"What are you doing in the wood, padre?"

I had the grace to blush.

"Just the same as I am doing, I dare swear. We've got the same idea, haven't we? How did the murderer come to the study? First way, along the lane and through the gate; second way, by the front door; third way—is there a third way? My idea was to see if there were any signs of the bushes being disturbed or broken anywhere near the wall of the Vicarage garden."

"That was just my idea," I admitted.

"I hadn't really got down to the job, though," continued Lawrence, "because it occurred to me that I'd like to see Miss Marple first, to make quite sure that no one did pass along the lane yesterday evening while we were in the studio."

I shook my head.

"She was quite positive that nobody did."

"Yes, nobody whom she would call anybody—sounds mad, but you see what I mean. But there might have been someone like a postman or a milkman or a butcher's boy—someone whose presence would be so natural that you wouldn't think of mentioning it."

"You've been reading G. K. Chesterton," I said, and Lawrence did not deny it.

"But don't you think there's just possibly something in the idea?"

"Well, I suppose there might be," I admitted.

Without further ado we made our way to Miss Marple's. She was working in the garden, and called out to us as we climbed over the stile.

"You see," murmured Lawrence, "she sees everybody."

She received us very graciously, and was much pleased with Lawrence's immense rock, which he presented with all due solemnity.

"It's very thoughtful of you, Mr. Redding. Very thoughtful indeed."

Emboldened by this, Lawrence embarked on his questions. Miss Marple listened attentively.

"Yes, I see what you mean, and I quite agree; it is the sort of thing no one mentions or bothers to mention. But I can assure you that there was nothing of the kind. Nothing whatever."

"You are sure, Miss Marple?"

"Quite sure."

"Did you see anyone go by the path into the wood that afternoon?" I asked. "Or come from it?"

"Oh! yes, quite a number of people. Dr. Stone and Miss Cram went that way—it's the nearest way to the Barrow for them. That was a little after two o'clock. And Dr. Stone returned that way—as you know, Mr. Redding, since he joined you and Mrs. Protheroe."

"By the way," I said, "that shot—the one you heard, Miss Marple. Mr. Redding and Mrs. Protheroe must have heard it too."

I looked inquiringly at Lawrence.

"Yes," he said frowning. "I believe I did hear some shots. Weren't there one or two shots?"

"I only heard one," said Miss Marple.

"It's only the vaguest impression in my mind," said Lawrence. "Curse it all, I wish I could remember. If only I'd known. You see I was so completely taken up with—with—"

He paused, embarrassed.

I gave a tactful cough. Miss Marple, with a touch of prudishness, changed the subject.

"Inspector Slack has been trying to get me to say whether I heard the shot after Mr. Redding and Mrs. Protheroe had left the studio or before. I've had to confess that I really could not say definitely, but I have the impression—which is growing stronger the more I think about it—that it was after."

"Then that lets the celebrated Dr. Stone out anyway," said Lawrence with a laugh. "Not that there has ever been the slightest reason why he should be suspected of shooting poor old Protheroe."

"Ah!" said Miss Marple. "But I always find it prudent to suspect everybody just a little. What I say is, you really never know, do you?"

This was typical of Miss Marple. I asked Lawrence if he agreed with her about the shot.

"I really can't say. You see, it was such an ordinary sound. I should be inclined to think it had been fired when we were in the studio. The sound would have been deadened and—and one would have noticed it less there."

For other reasons than the sound being deadened, I thought to myself!

"I must ask Anne," said Lawrence. "She may remember. By the way, there seems to me to be one curious fact that needs explanation. Mrs. Lestrange, the Mystery Lady of St. Mary Mead, paid a visit to old Protheroe after dinner on Wednesday night. And nobody seems to have any idea what it was all about. Old Protheroe said nothing to either his wife or Lettice."

"Perhaps the Vicar knows," said Miss Marple.

Now how did the woman know that I had been to visit Mrs. Lestrange that afternoon? The way she always knows things is uncanny.

I shook my head and said I could throw no light upon the matter.

"What does Inspector Slack think?" asked Miss Marple.

"He's done his best to bully the butler—but apparently the butler wasn't curious enough to listen at the door. So there it is—no one knows."

"I expect someone overheard something, though, don't you?" said Miss Marple. "I mean, somebody always does. I think that is where Mr. Redding might find out something."

"But Mrs. Protheroe knows nothing."

"I didn't mean Anne Protheroe," said Miss Marple. "I meant the women servants. They do so hate telling anything to the police. But a nice-looking young man—you'll excuse me, Mr. Redding—and one who has been unjustly suspected— Oh! I'm sure they'd tell him at once."

"I'll go and have a try this evening," said Lawrence with vigour. "Thanks for the hint, Miss Marple. I'll go after—well, after a little job the Vicar and I are going to do."

It occurred to me that we had better be getting on with it. I said goodbye to Miss Marple and we entered the wood once more.

First we went up the path till we came to a new spot, where it certainly looked as though someone had left the path on the right-hand side. Lawrence explained that he had already followed this particular trail and found it led nowhere, but he added that we might as well try again. He might have been wrong.

It was, however, as he had said. After about ten or twelve yards, any sign of broken and trampled leaves petered out. It was from this spot that Lawrence had broken back towards the path to meet me earlier in the afternoon.

We emerged on the path again and walked a little farther along it. Again we came to a place where the bushes seemed disturbed. The signs were very slight but, I thought, unmistakable. This time the trail was more promising. By a devious course, it wound steadily nearer to the Vicarage. Presently we arrived at where the bushes grew thickly up to the wall. The wall is a high one and ornamented with fragments of broken bottles on the top. If anyone had placed a ladder against it, we ought to find traces of their passage.

We were working our way slowly along the wall when a sound came to our ears of a breaking twig. I pressed forward, forcing my way through a thick tangle of shrubs—and came face to face with Inspector Slack.

"So it's you," he said. "And Mr. Redding. Now what do you think you two gentlemen are doing?"

Slightly crestfallen, we explained.

"Quite so," said the Inspector. "Not being the fools we're usually thought to be, I had the same idea myself. I've been here over an hour. Would you like to know something?"

"Yes," I said meekly.

"Whoever murdered Colonel Protheroe didn't come this way to do it! There's not a sign either on this side of the wall, nor the other. Whoever murdered Colonel Protheroe came through the front door. There's no other way he could have come."

"Impossible," I cried.

"Why impossible? Your door stands open. Anyone's only got to walk in. They can't be seen from the kitchen. They know you're safely out of the way; they know Mrs. Protheroe's in London; they know Mr. Dennis is at a tennis party. Simple as A.B.C. And they don't need to go or come through the village. Just opposite the Vicarage gate is a public footpath and, from it, you can turn into these same woods and come out whichever way you choose. Unless Mrs. Price Ridley were to come out of her front gate at that particular minute, it's all clear sailing. A great deal more so than climbing over walls. The side windows of the upper story of Mrs.

Price Ridley's house do overlook most of that wall. No, depend upon it, that's the way he came."

It really seemed as though he must be right.

XVII

INSPECTOR SLACK CAME round to see me the following morning. He is, I think, thawing towards me. In time, he may forget the incident of the clock.

"Well, sir," he greeted me. "I've traced that telephone call that you received."

"Indeed?" I said eagerly.

"It's rather odd. It was put through from the North Lodge of Old Hall. Now that Lodge is empty; the lodgekeepers have been pensioned off, and the new lodgekeepers aren't in yet. The place was empty and convenient—a window at the back was open. No finger prints on the instrument itself—it had been wiped clean. That's suggestive."

"How do you mean?"

"I mean that it shows that call was put through deliberately to get you out of the way. Therefore the murder was carefully planned in advance. If it had been just a harmless practical joke, the finger prints wouldn't have been wiped off so carefully."

"No, I see that."

"It also shows that the murderer was well acquainted with Old Hall and its surroundings. It wasn't Mrs. Protheroe who put that call through. I've accounted for every moment of her time that afternoon. There are half a dozen servants who can swear that she was at home up till five-thirty. Then the car came round and drove Colonel Protheroe and her to the village. The Colonel went to see Quinton, the vet, about one of the horses. Mrs. Protheroe did some ordering at the grocer's and at the fish shop, and from there came straight down the back lane where Miss Marple saw her. All the shops agree she carried no handbag with her. The old lady was right."

"She usually is," I said mildly.

"And Miss Protheroe was over at Much Benham at 5.30."

"Quite so," I said. "My nephew was there too."

"That disposes of her. The maids seem all right—a bit hysterical and upset, but what can you expect? Of course, I've got my eye on the butler—what with giving notice and all. But I don't think he knows anything about it."

"Your inquiries seem to have had rather a negative result, Inspector."

"They do and they do not, sir. There's one very queer thing has turned up—quite unexpectedly, I may say."

"Yes?"

"You remember the fuss that Mrs. Price Ridley, who lives next door to you, was kicking up yesterday morning? About being rung up on the telephone?"

"Yes?" I said.

"Well we traced the call just to calm her—and where on this earth do you think it was put through from?"

"A call office?" I hazarded.

"No, Mr. Clement. That call was put through from Mr. Lawrence Redding's cottage."

"What?" I exclaimed, surprised.

"Yes. A bit odd, isn't it? Mr. Redding had nothing to do with it. At that time, 6.35, he was on his way to the Blue Boar with Dr. Stone, in full view of the village. But there it is. Suggestive, eh? Someone walked into that empty cottage and used the telephone. Who was it? That's two queer telephone calls in one day. Makes you think there's some connection between them. I'll eat my hat if they weren't both put through by the same person."

"But with what object?"

"Well, that's what we've got to find out. There seems no particular point in the second one, but there must be a point somewhere. And you see the significance? Mr. Redding's house used to telephone from. Mr. Redding's pistol. All throwing suspicion on Mr. Redding."

"It would be more to the point to have put through the first call from his house," I objected.

"Ah! But I've been thinking that out. What did Mr. Redding do most afternoons? He went up to Old Hall and painted Miss Protheroe. And from his cottage, he'd go on his motor bicycle, passing through the North Gate. Now you see the point of the call being put through from there. The murderer is someone who didn't know about the quarrel, and that Mr. Redding wasn't going up to Old Hall any more."

I reflected a moment to let the Inspector's points sink into my brain. They seemed to me logical and unavoidable.

"Were there any finger prints on the receiver in Mr. Redding's cottage?" I asked.

"There were not," said the Inspector bitterly. "That dratted old woman who goes and does for him had been and dusted them off yesterday morning." He reflected wrathfully for a few minutes. "She's a stupid old fool anyway. Can't remember when she saw the pistol last. It might have been there on the morning of the crime or it might not. 'She couldn't say, she's sure.' They're all alike!

"Just as a matter of form, I went round and saw Dr. Stone," he went on. "I must say he was pleasant as could be about it. He and Miss Cram went up to that mound—or barrow—or whatever you call it, about half past two yesterday, and stayed there all the afternoon. Dr. Stone came back alone, and she came later. He says he didn't hear any shot, but admits he's absent-minded. But it all bears out what we think."

"Only," I said, "you haven't caught the murderer."

"H'm," said the Inspector. "It was a woman's voice you heard through the telephone. It was, in all probability, a woman's voice Mrs. Price Ridley heard. If only that shot hadn't come hard on the close of the telephone call—well, I'd know where to look."

"Where?"

"Ah! that's just what it's best not to say, sir."

Unblushingly, I suggested a glass of old port. I have some very fine old vintage port. Eleven o'clock in the morning is not the usual time for drinking port, but I did not think that mattered with Inspector Slack. It was, of course, cruel abuse of the vintage port, but one must not be squeamish about such things.

When Inspector Slack had polished off the second glass, he began to unbend and become genial. Such is the effect of that particular port.

"I don't suppose it matters with you, sir," he said. "You'll keep it to yourself? No letting it get round the parish."

I reassured him.

"Seeing as the whole thing happened in your house, it almost seems as though you had a right to know."

"Just what I feel myself," I said.

"Well, then, sir, what about the lady who called on Colonel Protheroe the night before the murder?"

"Mrs. Lestrange?" I cried, speaking rather loud in my astonishment.

The Inspector threw me a reproachful glance.

"Not so loud, sir. Mrs. Lestrange is the lady I've got my eye on. You remember what I told you—blackmail."

"Hardly a reason for murder. Wouldn't it be a case of killing the goose that laid the golden eggs? That is, assuming that your hypothesis is true, which I don't for a minute admit."

The Inspector winked at me in a common manner.

"Ah! she's the kind the gentlemen will always stand up for. Now look here, sir. Suppose she's successfully blackmailed the old gentleman in the past. After a lapse of years, she gets wind of him, comes down here and tries it on again. But in the meantime, things have changed. The law has taken up a very different stand. Every facility is given nowadays to people prosecuting for blackmail—names are not allowed to be reported in the press. Suppose Colonel Protheroe turns round and says he'll have the law on her. She's in a nasty position. They give a very severe sentence for blackmail. The boot's on the other leg. The only thing to do to save herself is to put him out good and quick."

I was silent. I had to admit that the case the Inspector had built up was plausible. Only one thing to my mind made it inadmissible—the personality of Mrs. Lestrange.

"I don't agree with you, Inspector," I said. "Mrs. Lestrange doesn't seem to me to be a potential blackmailer. She's—well, it's an old-fashioned word, but she's a—lady."

He threw me a pitying glance.

"Ah! well, sir," he said tolerantly. "You're a clergyman. You don't know half of what goes on. Lady indeed! You'd be surprised if you knew some of the things I know."

"I'm not referring to mere social position. Anyway I should imaigne Mrs. Lestrange to be a *déclassée*. What I mean is a question of—personal refinement."

"You don't see her with the same eyes as I do, sir. I may be a man—but I'm a police officer too. They can't get over me with their personal refinement. Why, that woman is the kind who could stick a knife into you without turning a hair."

Curiously enough, I could believe Mrs. Lestrange guilty of murder more easily than I could believe her capable of blackmail.

"But of course she can't have been telephoning to the old lady next door and shooting Colonel Protheroe at one and the same time," continued the Inspector.

The words were hardly out of his mouth when he slapped his leg ferociously.

"Got it," he exclaimed. "That's the point of the telephone call. Kind of alibi. Knew we'd connect it with the first one. I'm going to look into this. She may have bribed some village lad to do the phoning for her. He'd never think of connecting it with the murder."

The Inspector hurried off.

"Miss Marple wants to see you," said Griselda putting her head in. "She sent over a very incoherent note—all spidery and underlined. I couldn't read most of it. Apparently she can't leave home herself. Hurry up and go across and see her and find out what it is. I've got my old women coming in two minutes or I'd come myself. I do hate old women—they tell you about their bad legs, and sometimes insist on showing them to you. What luck that the inquest is this afternoon! You won't have to go and watch the Boys' Club Cricket Match."

I hurried off considerably exercised in my own mind as to the reason for this summons.

I found Miss Marple in what, I believe, is described as a fluster. She was very pink and slightly incoherent.

"My nephew," she explained. "My nephew, Raymond West, the author. He is coming down today. Such a to-do. I have to see to everything myself. You cannot trust a maid to air a bed properly, and we must, of course, have a meat meal tonight. Gentlemen require such a lot of meat, do they not? And drink. There certainly should be some drink in the house—and a siphon."

"If I can do anything—" I began.

"Oh! how very kind. But I did not mean that. There is plenty of time really. He brings his own pipe and tobacco, I am glad to say. Glad because it saves me from knowing which kind of cigarettes are right to buy. But rather sorry, too, because it takes so long for the smell to get out of the curtains. Of course, I open the window and shake them well very early every morning. Raymond gets up very late—I think writers often do. He writes very clever books, I believe, though people are not really nearly so unpleasant as he makes out. Clever young men know so little of life, don't you think?"

"Would you like to bring him to dinner at the Vicarage?" I asked, still unable to gather why I had been summoned.

"Oh! no, thank you," said Miss Marple. "It's very kind of you," she added.

"There was—er—something you wanted to see me about, I think," I suggested desperately.

"Oh! of course. In all the excitement it had gone right out of my head."

She broke off and called to her maid: "Emily—Emily. Not those sheets. The frilled ones with the monogram, and don't put them too near the fire."

She closed the door and returned to me on tiptoe.

"It's just rather a curious thing that happened last night," she explained. "I thought you would like to hear about it, though at the moment it doesn't seem to make sense. I felt very wakeful last night—wondering about all this sad business. And I got up and looked out of my window. And what do you think I saw?"

I looked inquiring.

"Gladys Cram," said Miss Marple, with great emphasis. "As I live, going into the wood with a suitcase."

"A suitcase?"

"Isn't it extraordinary? What should she want with a suitcase in the wood at twelve o'clock at night?"

We both stared at each other.

"You see," said Miss Marple. "I daresay it has nothing to do with the murder. But it is a Peculiar Thing. And just at present we all feel we must take notice of Peculiar Things."

"Perfectly amazing," I said. "Was she going to—er—sleep in the barrow by any chance?"

"She didn't, at any rate," said Miss Marple. "Because quite a short time afterwards she came back, and she hadn't got the suitcase with her."

We stared at each other again.

XVIII

THE INQUEST WAS held that afternoon (Saturday) at two o'clock at the Blue Boar. The local excitement was, I need hardly say, tremendous. There has been no murder in St. Mary Mead for at least fifteen years. And to have someone like Colonel Protheroe murdered actually in the Vicarage study is such a feast of sensation as rarely falls to the lot of a village population.

Various comments floated to my ears which I was probably not meant to hear.

"There's Vicar. Look pale, don't he? I wonder if he had a hand in it. 'Twas done at Vicarage, after all."

"How can you, Mary Adams? And him visiting Henry Abbott at the time."

"Ah! but they do say him and the Colonel had words. There's Mary Hill. Giving herself airs, she is, on account of being in service there. Hush, here's Coroner."

The Coroner was Dr. Roberts of our adjoining town of Much Benham. He cleared his throat, adjusted his eyeglasses, and looked important.

To recapitulate all the evidence would be merely tiresome. Lawrence Redding gave evidence of finding the body, and identified the pistol as belonging to him. To the best of his belief he had seen it on the Tuesday, two days previously. It was kept on a shelf in his cottage, and the door of the cottage was habitually unlocked.

Mrs. Protheroe gave evidence that she had last seen her husband at about a quarter to six, when they separated in the village street. She agreed to call for him at the Vicarage later. She had gone to the Vicarage about a quarter past six, by way of the back lane and the garden gate. She had heard no voices in the study, and had imagined that the room was empty, but her husband might have been sitting at the writing table, in which case she would not have seen him. As far as she knew, he had been in his usual health and spirits. She knew of no enemy who might have had a grudge against him.

I gave evidence next, told of my appointment with Protheroe and my summons to the Abbotts'. I described how I had found the body and my summoning of Dr. Haydock.

"How many people, Mr. Clement, were aware that Colonel Protheroe was coming to see you that evening?"

"A good many, I should imagine. My wife knew and my nephew, and Colonel Protheroe himself alluded to the fact that morning when I met him in the village. I should think several people might have overheard him, as, being slightly deaf, he spoke in a loud voice."

"It was then, a matter of common knowledge? Anyone might know?"

I agreed.

Haydock followed. He was an important witness. He described carefully and technically the appearance of the body and the exact injuries. It was his opinion that deceased had been shot while actually in the act of writing. He placed the time of death at approximately 6.20 to 6.30—certainly not later than 6.35. That was the outside limit. He was positive and emphatic on that point. There was no question of suicide; the wound could not have been self-inflicted.

Inspector Slack's evidence was discreet and abridged. He described his summons, and the circumstances under which he had found the body. The unfinished letter was produced and the time on it—6.20—noted. Also the clock. It was tacitly assumed that the time of death was 6.22. The police were giving nothing away. Anne Protheroe told me afterwards that she had been told to suggest a slightly earlier period of time than 6.20 for her visit.

Our maid, Mary, was the next witness and proved a somewhat truculent one. She hadn't heard anything and didn't want to hear anything. It wasn't as though gentlemen who came to see the Vicar usually got shot. They didn't. She'd got her own jobs to look after. Colonel Protheroe had arrived at a quarter past six exactly. No, she didn't look at the clock. She heard the church chime after she had shown him into the study. She didn't hear any shot. If there had been a shot she'd have heard it. Well, of course she knew there must have been a shot, since the gentleman was found shot—but there it was. She hadn't heard it.

The Coroner did not press the point. I realized that he and Colonel Melchett were working in agreement.

Mrs. Lestrange had been subpœnaed to give evidence, but a medical certificate, signed by Dr. Haydock, was produced saying she was too ill to attend.

There was only one other witness, a somewhat doddering old woman, the one who, in Slack's phrase, "did for" Lawrence Redding.

Mrs. Archer was shown the pistol and recognized it as the one she had seen in Mr. Redding's sitting room—"Over against the bookcase, he kept it, lying about." She had last seen it on the day of the murder. Yes—in answer to a further question,—she was quite sure it was there at lunch time on Thursday—quarter to one when she left.

I remembered what the Inspector had told me, and I was mildly surprised. However vague she might have been when he questioned her, she was quite positive about it now.

The Coroner summed up in a negative manner but with a good deal of firmness. The verdict was given almost immediately.

Murder by person or persons unknown.

As I left the room I was aware of a small army of young men with bright, alert faces, and a kind of superficial resemblance to each other. Several of them were already known to me by sight, as having haunted the Vicarage the last few days. Seeking to escape, I plunged back into the

Blue Boar, and was lucky enough to run straight into the archæologist, Dr. Stone. I clutched at him without ceremony.

"Journalists," I said briefly and expressively. "If you could deliver me from their clutches?"

"Why, certainly, Mr. Clement. Come upstairs with me."

He led the way up the narrow staircase and into his sitting room, where Miss Cram was sitting rattling the keys of a typewriter with a practised touch. She greeted me with a broad smile of welcome, and seized the opportunity to stop work.

"Awful, isn't it?" she said. "Not knowing who did it, I mean. Not but that I'm disappointed in an inquest. Tame, that's what I call it. Nothing what you might call spicy from beginning to end."

"You were there, then, Miss Cram?"

"I was there all right. Fancy your not seeing me. Didn't you see me? I feel a bit hurt about that. Yes, I do. A gentleman, even if he is a clergyman, ought to have eyes in his head."

"Were you present also?" I asked Dr. Stone, in an effort to escape from this playful badinage. Young women like Miss Cram always make me feel awkward.

"No, I'm afraid I feel very little interest in such things. I am a man very wrapped up in his own hobby."

"It must be a very interesting hobby," I said.

"You know something of it, perhaps?"

I was obliged to confess that I knew next to nothing.

Dr. Stone was not the kind of man whom a confession of ignorance daunts. The result was exactly the same as though I had said that the excavation of barrows was my only relaxation. He surged and eddied into speech. Long barrows, round barrows, stone age, bronze age, paleolithic, neolithic, kistvaens and cromlechs, it burst forth in a torrent. I had little to do save nod my head and look intelligent—and that last is perhaps over optimistic. Dr. Stone boomed on. He is a little man. His head is round and bald; his face is round and rosy, and he beams at you through very strong glasses. I have never known a man so enthusiastic on so little encouragement. He went into every argument for and against his own pet theory—which by the way, I quite failed to grasp!

He detailed at great length his difference of opinion with Colonel Protheroe.

"An opinionated boor," he said with heat. "Yes, yes, I know he is dead, and one should speak no ill of the dead. But death does not alter facts. An opinionated boor describes him exactly. Because he had read a few books, he set himself up as an authority—against a man who has made a lifelong study of the subject. My whole life, Mr. Clement, has been given up to this work. My whole life—"

He was spluttering with excitement. Gladys Cram brought him back to earth with a terse sentence.

"You'll miss your train if you don't look out," she observed.

"Oh!" The little man stopped in mid speech and dragged a watch from his pocket. "Bless my soul. Quarter to? Impossible."

"Once you start talking you never remember the time. What you'd do without me to look after you, I reelly don't know."

"Quite right, my dear, quite right." He patted her affectionately on the shoulder. "This is a wonderful girl, Mr. Clement. Never forgets anything. I consider myself extremely lucky to have found her."

"Oh! go on, Dr. Stone," said the lady. "You spoil me, you do."

I could not help feeling that I should be in a material position to add my support to the second school of thought—that which foresees lawful matrimony as the future of Dr. Stone and Miss Cram. I imagined that in her own way Miss Cram was rather a clever young woman.

"You'd better be getting along," said Miss Cram.

"Yes, yes, so I must."

He vanished into the room next door and returned carrying a suitcase.

"You are leaving?" I asked in some surprise.

"Just running up to town for a couple of days," he explained. "My old mother to see tomorrow, some business with my lawyers on Monday. On Tuesday I shall return. By the way, I suppose that Colonel Protheroe's death will make no difference to our arrangements. As regards the barrow, I mean. Mrs. Protheroe will have no objection to our continuing the work?"

"I should not think so."

As he spoke, I wondered who actually would be in authority at Old Hall. It was just possible that Protheroe might have left it to Lettice. I felt that it would be interesting to know the contents of Protheroe's will.

"Causes a lot of trouble in a family, a death does," remarked Miss Cram with a kind of gloomy relish. "You wouldn't believe what a nasty spirit there sometimes is."

"Well, I must really be going." Dr. Stone made ineffectual attempts to control the suitcase, a large rug and an unwieldy umbrella. I came to his rescue. He protested.

"Don't trouble—don't trouble. I can manage perfectly. Doubtless there will be somebody downstairs."

But down below there was no trace of a boots or anyone else. I suspect that they were being regaled at the expense of the Press. Time was getting on, so we set out together to the station, Dr. Stone carrying the suitcase, and I holding the rug and umbrella.

Dr. Stone ejaculated remarks in between panting breaths as we hurried along.

"Really too good of you—didn't mean—to trouble you. Hope we shan't miss—the train—Gladys is a good girl—really a wonderful girl—a very sweet nature—not too happy at home, I'm afraid—absolutely—the heart of a child—heart of a child, I do assure you—in spite of—difference in our ages—find a lot in common. . . ."

I felt that several well-known parallels would have occurred to Miss Marple, had she been there.

We saw Lawrence Redding's cottage just as we turned off to the station. It stands in an isolated position with no other house near it. I observed two young men of smart appearance standing on the doorstep, and a couple more peering in at the windows. It was a busy day for the Press.

"Nice fellow, young Redding," I remarked to see what my companion would say.

He was so out of breath by this time that he found it difficult to say anything, but he puffed out a word which I did not at first quite catch.

"Dangerous," he gasped when I asked him to repeat his remark.

"Dangerous?"

"Most dangerous. Innocent girls—know no better—taken in by a fellow like that—always hanging round women. No good."

From which I deduced that the only young man in the village had not passed unnoticed by the fair Gladys.

"Goodness," ejaculated Dr. Stone. "The train!"

We were close to the station by this time and we broke into a fast sprint. A down train was standing in the station and the up London train was just coming in.

At the door of the booking office we collided with a rather exquisite young man, and I recognized Miss Marple's nephew just arriving. He is, I think, a young man who does not like to be collided with. He prides himself on his poise and general air of detachment, and there is no doubt that vulgar contact is detrimental to poise of any kind. He staggered back. I apologized hastily and we passed in. Dr. Stone climbed on the train and I handed up his baggage just as the train gave an unwilling jerk and started.

I waved to him and then turned away. Raymond West had departed, but our local chemist, who rejoices in the name of Cherubim, was just setting out for the village. I walked beside him.

"Close shave that," he observed. "Well, how did the inquest go, Mr. Clement?"

I gave him the verdict.

"Oh! so that's what happened. I rather thought they'd adjourn the inquest. Where's Dr. Stone off to?"

I repeated what he had told me.

"Lucky not to miss the train. Not that you ever know on this line. I tell you, Mr. Clement, it's a crying shame. Disgraceful, that's what I call it. Train I came down by was ten minutes late. And that on a Saturday, with no traffic to speak off. And on Wednesday—no, Thursday—yes, Thursday it was—I remember it was the day of the murder because I meant to write a strongly worded complaint to the company—and the murder put it out of my head—yes, last Thursday. I had been to a meeting of the pharmaceutical society. How late do you think the 6.50 was? Half an hour. Half an hour exactly! What do you think of that? Ten minutes I don't mind. But if the train doesn't get in till twenty past seven, well, you can't get home before half past. What I say is, why call it the 6.50?"

"Quite so," I said, and, wishing to escape from the monologue, I broke away with the excuse that I had something to say to Lawrence Redding whom I saw approaching us on the other side of the road.

XIX

"Very glad to have met you," said Lawrence. "Come to my place."

We turned in at the little rustic gate, went up the path, and he drew a key from his pocket and inserted it in the lock.

"You keep the door locked now," I observed.

"Yes." He laughed rather bitterly. "Case of stable door when the steed is gone, eh? It is rather like that. You know, padre," he held the door open and I passed inside, "there's something about all this business that I don't like. It's too much of—how shall I put it?—an inside job. Someone knew about that pistol of mine. That means that the murderer, whoever he was, must have actually been in this house—perhaps even had a drink with me."

"Not necessarily," I objected. "The whole village of St. Mary Mead probably knows exactly where you keep your tooth brush and what kind of tooth powder you use."

"But why should it interest them?"

"I don't know," I said, "but it does. If you change your shaving cream it will be a topic of conversation."

"They must be very hard up for news."

"They are. Nothing exciting ever happens here."

"Well, it has now—with a vengeance."

I agreed.

"And who tells them all these things, anyway? Shaving cream and things like that?"

"Probably old Mrs. Archer."

"That old crone? She's practically a half wit, as far as I can make out."

"That's merely the camouflage of the poor," I explained. "They take refuge behind a mask of stupidity. You'll probably find that the old lady has all her wits about her. By the way, she seems very certain now that the pistol was in its proper place mid-day Thursday. What's made her so positive all of a sudden?"

"I haven't the least idea."

"Do you think she's right?"

"There again I haven't the least idea. I don't go round taking an inventory of my possessions every day."

I looked round the small living room. Every shelf and table was littered with miscellaneous articles. Lawrence lived in the midst of an artistic disarray that would have driven me quite mad.

"It's a bit of a job finding things sometimes," he said, observing my glance. "On the other hand, everything is handy—not tucked away."

"Nothing is tucked away, certainly," I agreed. "It might perhaps have been better if the pistol had been."

"Do you know, I rather expected the Coroner to say something of the sort. Coroners are such asses. I expected to be censured, or whatever they call it."

"By the way," I asked. "Was it loaded?"

Lawrence shook his head.

"I'm not quite so careless as that. It was unloaded, but there was a box of cartridges beside it."

"It was apparently loaded in all six chambers, and one shot had been fired."

Lawrence nodded.

"And whose hand fired it? It's all very well, sir, but unless the real murderer is discovered I shall be suspected of the crime to the day of my death."

"Don't say that, my boy."

"But I do say it."

He became silent, frowning to himself. He roused himself at last and said:

"But let me tell you how I got on last night. You know, old Miss Marple knows a thing or two."

"She is, I believe, rather unpopular on that account."

Lawrence proceeded to recount his story.

He had, following Miss Marple's advice, gone up to Old Hall. There, with Anne's assistance, he had had an interview with the parlour maid.

Anne had said simply:

"Mr. Redding wants to ask you a few questions, Rose."

Then she had left the room.

Lawrence had felt somewhat nervous. Rose, a pretty girl of twenty-five, gazed at him with a limpid gaze which he found rather disconcerting.

"It's—it's about Colonel Protheroe's death."

"Yes, sir?"

"I'm very anxious, you see, to get at the truth."

"Yes, sir."

"I feel that there may be—that someone might—that—that—there might be some incident—"

At this point Lawrence felt that he was not covering himself with glory, and heartily cursed Miss Marple and her suggestions.

"I wondered if you could help me?"

"Yes, sir?"

Rose's demeanour was still that of the perfect servant, polite, anxious to assist, and completely uninterested.

"Dash it all," said Lawrence. "Haven't you talked the thing over in the servants' hall?"

This method of attack flustered Rose slightly. Her perfect poise was shaken.

"In the servants' hall, sir?"

"Or the housekeeper's room, or the bootboy's dugout, or wherever you do talk? There must be some place."

Rose displayed a very faint disposition to giggle, and Lawrence felt encouraged.

"Look here, Rose, you're an awfully nice girl. I'm sure you must understand what I'm feeling like. I don't want to be hanged. I didn't murder your master, but a lot of people think I did. Can't you help me in any way?"

I can imagine at this point that Lawrence must have looked extremely appealing. His handsome head thrown back, his Irish blue eyes appealing. Rose softened and capitulated.

"Oh! sir, I'm sure—if any of us could help in any way. None of us think you did it, sir. Indeed we don't."

"I know, my dear girl, but that's not going to help me with the police."

"The police!" Rose tossed her head. "I can tell you, sir, we don't think much of that Inspector. Slack, he calls himself. The police indeed."

"All the same, the police are very powerful. Now, Rose, you say you'll do your best to help me. I can't help feeling that there's a lot we haven't got at yet. The lady, for instance, who called to see Colonel Protheroe the night before he died."

"Mrs. Lestrange?"

"Yes, Mrs. Lestrange. I can't help feeling there's something rather odd about that visit of hers."

"Yes, indeed, sir; that's what we all said."

"You did?"

"Coming the way she did. And asking for the Colonel. And of course there's been a lot of talk—nobody knowing anything about her down here. And Mrs. Simmons, she's the housekeeper, sir, she gave it as her opinion that she was a regular bad lot. But after hearing what Gladdie said, well, I didn't know what to think."

"What did Gladdie say?"

"Oh! nothing, sir. It was just—we were talking, you know."

Lawrence looked at her. He had the feeling of something kept back.

"I wonder very much what her interview with Colonel Protheroe was about."

"Yes, sir."

"I believe you know, Rose?"

"Me? Oh! no, sir. Indeed I don't. How could I?"

"Look here, Rose. You said you'd help me. If you overheard anything, anything at all—it mightn't seem important, but anything . . . I'd be so awfully grateful to you. After all, anyone might—might chance—just chance to overhear something."

"But I didn't, sir, really I didn't."

"Then somebody else did," said Lawrence acutely.

"Well, sir—"

"Do tell me, Rose."

"I don't know what Gladdie would say, I'm sure."

"She'd want you to tell me. Who is Gladdie, by the way?"

"She's the kitchen maid, sir. And you see, she'd just stepped out to speak to a friend, and she was passing the window—the study window—and the master was there with the lady. And of course he did speak very loud, the master did, always. And naturally, feeling a little curious—I mean—"

"Awfully natural," said Lawrence. "I mean one would simply have to listen."

"But of course she didn't tell anyone—except me. And we both thought it very odd. But Gladdie couldn't say anything, you see, because if it was known she'd gone out to meet a—a friend—well, it would have meant a lot of unpleasantness with Mrs. Pratt; that's the cook, sir. But I'm sure she'd tell you anything, sir, willing."

"Well, can I go to the kitchen and speak to her?"

Rose was horrified by the suggestion.

"Oh! no, sir, that would never do. And Gladdie's a very nervous girl anyway."

At last the matter was settled, after a lot of discussion over difficult points. A clandestine meeting was arranged in the shrubbery.

Here, in due course, Lawrence was confronted by the nervous Gladdie, whom he described as more like a shivering rabbit than anything human. Ten minutes were spent in trying to put the girl at her ease, the shivering Gladys explaining that she couldn't ever—that she didn't ought, that she didn't think Rose would have given her away, that anyway she hadn't meant no harm, indeed she hadn't, and that she'd catch it badly if Mrs. Pratt ever came to hear of it.

Lawrence reassured, cajoled, persuaded—at last Gladys consented to speak.

"If you'll be sure it'll go no further, sir."

"Of course it won't."

"And it won't be brought up against me in a court of law?"

"Never."

"And you won't tell the mistress?"

"Not on any account."

"If it were to get to Mrs. Pratt's ears—"

"It won't. Now tell me, Gladys."

"If you're sure it's all right?"

"Of course it is. You'll be glad some day you've saved me from being hanged."

Gladys gave a little shriek.

"Oh! indeed, I wouldn't like that, sir. Well, it's very little I heard—and that entirely by accident, as you might say—"

"I quite understand."

"But the master, he was evidently very angry. 'After all these years—' that's what he was saying—'you dare to come here. It's an outrage—' I couldn't hear what the lady said—but after a bit he said, 'I utterly refuse—utterly.' I can't remember everything—seemed as though they were at it hammer and tongs, she wanting him to do something and he refusing. 'It's a disgrace that you should have come down here,' that's one thing he said. And 'You shall not see her—I forbid it.' And that made me prick up my ears. Looked as though the lady wanted to tell Mrs. Protheroe a thing or two, and he was afraid about it. And I thought to myself 'Well, now, fancy the master. Him so particular. And maybe no beauty himself when all's said and done. Fancy!' I said. And 'Men are all alike,' I said to my friend later. Not that he'd agree. Argued, he did. But he did admit he was surprised at Colonel Protheroe—him being a churchwarden and handing round the plate and reading the lessons on Sundays. 'But there,' I said, 'that's very often the worst.' For that's what I've heard my mother say, many a time."

Gladdie paused, out of breath, and Lawrence tried tactfully to get back to where the conversation had started.

"Did you hear anything else?"

"Well, it's difficult to remember exactly, sir. It was all much the same. He said once or twice 'I don't believe it.' Just like that. 'Whatever Haydock says, I don't believe it.' "

"He said that, did he? 'Whatever Haydock says?' "

"Yes. And he said it was all a plot."

"You didn't hear the lady speak at all?"

"Only just at the end. She must have got up to go and come nearer the window. And I heard what she said. Made my blood run cold, it did. I'll never forget it. 'By this time tomorrow night, you may be dead,' she said. Wicked the way she said it. As soon as I heard the news: 'There,' I said to Rose. 'There!' "

Lawrence wondered. Principally he wondered how much of Gladys's story was to be depended upon. True, in the main, he suspected that it had been embellished and polished since the murder. In especial he doubted the accuracy of the last remark. He thought it highly possible that it owed its being to the fact of the murder.

He thanked Gladys, rewarded her suitably, reassured her as to her misdoings being made known to Mrs. Pratt, and left Old Hall with a good deal to think over.

One thing was clear; Mrs. Lestrange's interview with Colonel Protheroe had certainly not been a peaceful one, and it was one which he was anxious to keep from the knowledge of his wife.

I thought of Miss Marple's churchwarden with his separate establishment. Was this a case resembling that?

I wondered more than ever where Haydock came in. He had saved Mrs. Lestrange from having to give evidence at the inquest. He had done his best to protect her from the police.

How far would he carry that protection?

Supposing he suspected her of crime—would he still try and shield her?

She was a curious woman—a woman of very strong magnetic charm. I myself hated the thought of connecting her with the crime in any way.

Something in me said, "It can't be her!"

Why?

And an imp in my brain replied, "Because she's a very beautiful and attractive woman. That's why."

There is, as Miss Marple would say, a lot of human nature in all of us.

XX

When I got back to the Vicarage I found that we were in the middle of a domestic crisis.

Griselda met me in the hall and, with tears in her eyes, dragged me into the drawing room.

"She's going."

"Who's going?"

"Mary. She's given notice."

I really could not take the announcement in a tragic spirit.

"Well," I said, "we'll have to get another servant."

It seemed to me a perfectly reasonable thing to say. When one servant goes, you get another. I was at a loss to understand Griselda's look of reproach.

"Len—you are absolutely heartless. You don't care."

I didn't. In fact, I felt almost light hearted at the prospect of no more burnt puddings and undercooked vegetables.

"I'll have to look about for a girl, and find one, and train her," continued Griselda in a voice of acute self-pity.

"Is Mary trained?" I said.

"Of course she is."

"I suppose," I said, "that somebody has heard her address us as 'sir' or 'ma'am,' and has immediately wrested her from us as a paragon. All I can say is, they'll be disappointed."

"It isn't that," said Griselda. "Nobody else wants her. I don't see how they could. It's her feelings. They're upset because Lettice Protheroe said she didn't dust properly."

Griselda often comes out with surprising statements, but this seemed to me so surprising that I questioned it. It seemed to me the most unlikely thing in the world that Lettice Protheroe should go out of her way to interfere in our domestic affairs and reprove our maid for slovenly housework. It was completely un-Lettice like, and I said so.

"I don't see," I said, "what our dust has to do with Lettice Protheroe."

"Nothing at all," said my wife. "That's why it's so unreasonable. I wish you'd go and talk to Mary yourself. She's in the kitchen."

I had no wish to talk to Mary on the subject, but Griselda, who is very energetic and quick, fairly pushed me through the baize door into the kitchen before I had time to rebel.

Mary was peeling potatoes at the sink.

"Er—good afternoon," I said nervously.

Mary looked up and snorted, but made no other response.

"Mrs. Clement tells me that you wish to leave us," I said.

Mary condescended to reply to this.

"There's some things," she said darkly, "as no girl can be asked to put up with."

"Will you be more explicit, please?"

"Eh?"

"Will you tell me exactly what it is that has upset you?"

"Tell you that in two words, I can." (Here, I may say she vastly underestimated.) "People coming snooping round here when my back's turned. Poking round. And what business of hers, is it, how often the study is dusted or turned out? If you and the missus don't complain, it's nobody else's business. If I give satisfaction to you that's all that matters, I say."

Mary has never given satisfaction to me. I confess that I have a hankering after a room thoroughly dusted and tidied every morning. Mary's practice of flicking off the more obvious deposit on the surface of low tables is to my thinking grossly inadequate. However, I realized that at the moment it was no good to go into side issues.

"Had to go to that inquest, didn't I? Standing up before twelve men, a respectable girl like me! And who knows what questions you may be asked. I'll tell you this. I've never before been in a place where they had a murder in the house, and I never want to be again."

"I hope you won't," I said. "On the law of averages I should say it was very unlikely."

"I don't hold with the law. He was a magistrate. Many a poor fellow sent to jail for potting at a rabbit—and him with his pheasants and what not. And then, before he's so much as decently buried, that daughter of his comes round and says I don't do my work properly."

"Do you mean that Miss Protheroe has been here?"

"Found her here when I came back from the Blue Boar. In the study she was. And 'Oh' she says, 'I'm looking for my little yellow berry—a little yellow hat. I left it here the other day.' 'Well,' I says, 'I haven't seen no hat. It wasn't here when I done the room on Thursday morning,' I says. And 'Oh!' she says, 'but I daresay you wouldn't see it. You don't spend much time doing a room, do you?' And with that she draws her finger along the mantelshelf and looks at it. As though I had time on a morning like this to take off all them ornaments and put them back, with the police only unlocking the room the night before. 'If the Vicar and his lady are satisfied that's all that matters, I think, Miss,' I said. And she laughs and goes out of the window and says 'Oh! but are you sure they are?' "

"I see," I said.

"And there it is! A girl has her feelings! I'm sure I'd work my fingers to the bone for you and the Missus. And if she wants a new-fangled dish tried I'm always ready to try it."

"I'm sure you are," I said soothingly.

"But she must have heard something or she wouldn't have said what she did. And if I don't give satisfaction I'd rather go. Not that I take any notice of what Miss Protheroe says. She's not loved up at the Hall, I can tell you. Never a 'please' or a 'thank you,' and everything scattered right and left. I wouldn't set any store by Miss Lettice Protheroe myself, for all that Mr. Dennis is so set upon her. But she's the kind that can always twist a young gentleman round her little finger."

During all this, Mary had been extracting eyes from potatoes with such energy that they had been flying round the kitchen like hailstones. At this moment one hit me in the eye and caused a momentary pause in the conversation.

"Don't you think," I said, as I dabbed my eye with my handkerchief, "that you have been rather too inclined to take offence where none is meant? You know, Mary, your mistress will be very sorry to lose you."

"I've nothing against the mistress—or against you, sir, for that matter."

"Well, then, don't you think you're being rather silly?"

Mary sniffed.

"I was a bit upset like—after the inquest and all. And a girl has her feelings. But I wouldn't like to cause the mistress inconvenience."

"Then that's all right," I said.

I left the kitchen to find Griselda and Dennis waiting for me in the hall.

"Well?" exclaimed Griselda.

"She's staying," I said, and sighed.

"Len," said my wife. "You have been clever."

I felt rather inclined to disagree with her. I do not think I had been clever. It is my firm opinion that no servant could be a worse one than Mary. Any change, I consider, would have been a change for the better. But I like to please Griselda. I detailed the heads of Mary's grievance.

"How like Lettice," said Dennis. "She couldn't have left that yellow beret of hers here on Wednesday. She was wearing it for tennis on Thursday."

"That seems to me highly probable," I said.

"She never knows where she's left anything," said Dennis, with a kind of affectionate pride and admiration that I felt was entirely uncalled for. "She loses about a dozen things every day."

"A remarkably attractive trait," I observed.

Any sarcasm missed Dennis.

"She is attractive," he said, with a deep sigh. "People are always proposing to her—she told me so."

"They must be illicit proposals if they're made to her down here," I remarked. "We haven't got a bachelor in the place."

"There's Dr. Stone," said Griselda, her eyes dancing.

"He asked her to come and see the barrow the other day," I admitted.

"Of course he did," said Griselda. "She is attractive, Len. Even bald-headed archæologists feel it."

"Lots of S.A." said Dennis sapiently.

And yet Lawrence Redding is completely untouched by Lettice's charm. Griselda, however, explained that with the air of one who knew she was right.

"Lawrence has got lots of S.A. himself. That kind always likes the—how shall I put it—the Quaker type. Very restrained and diffident. The kind of women whom everybody calls cold. I think Anne is the only woman who could ever hold Lawrence. I don't think they'll ever tire of each other. All the same, I think he's been rather stupid in one way. He's rather made use of Lettice, you know. I don't think he ever dreamed she cared—he's awfully modest in some ways—but I have a feeling she does."

"She can't bear him," said Dennis positively. "She told me so."

I have never seen anything like the pitying silence with which Griselda received this remark.

I went into my study. There was, to my fancy, still a rather eerie feeling in the room. I knew that I must get over this. Once give in to that feeling, and I should probably never use the study again. I walked thoughtfully over to the writing table. Here Protheroe had sat, red-faced, hearty, self-righteous, and here, in a moment of time, he had been struck down. Here, where I was standing, an enemy had stood. . . .

And so—no more Protheroe. . . .

Here was the pen his fingers had held.

On the floor was a faint dark stain—the rug had been sent to the cleaner's, but the blood had soaked through.

I shivered.

"I can't use this room," I said aloud. "I can't use it."

Then my eye was caught by something—a mere speck of bright blue. I bent down. Between the floor and the desk I saw a small object. I picked it up.

I was standing staring at it in the palm of my hand when Griselda came in.

"I forgot to tell you, Len. Miss Marple wants us to go over tonight after dinner. To amuse the nephew. She's afraid of his being dull. I said we'd go."

"Very well, my dear."

"What are you looking at?"

"Nothing."

I closed my hand, and looking at my wife, observed:

"If you don't amuse Master Raymond West, my dear, he must be very hard to please."

My wife said, "Don't be ridiculous, Len," and turned pink.

She went out again, and I unclosed my hand.

In the palm of my hand was a blue lapis lazuli earring, set in seed pearls.

It was rather an unusual jewel, and I knew very well where I had seen it last.

XXI

I CANNOT SAY that I have at any time a great admiration for Mr. Raymond West. He is, I know, supposed to be a brilliant novelist, and has made quite a name as a poet. His poems have no capital letters in them, which is, I believe, the essence of modernity. His books are about unpleasant people leading lives of surpassing dullness.

He has a tolerant affection for "Aunt Jane," whom he alludes to in her presence as a "survival." She listens to his talk with a flattering interest, and if there is sometimes an amused twinkle in her eye I am sure he never notices it.

He fastened on Griselda at once with flattering abruptness. They discussed modern plays, and from there went on to modern schemes of decoration. Griselda affects to laugh at Raymond West, but she is, I think, susceptible to his conversation.

During my (dull) conversation with Miss Marple, I heard at intervals the reiteration "buried as you are down here."

It began at last to irritate me. I said suddenly:

"I suppose you consider us very much out of things down here?"

Raymond West waved his cigarette.

"I regard St. Mary Mead," he said authoritatively, "as a stagnant pool."

He looked at us, prepared for resentment at his statement; but somewhat, I think, to his chagrin, no one displayed annoyance.

"That is really not a very good simile, dear Raymond," said Miss Marple briskly. "Nothing, I believe, is so full of life under the microscope as a drop of water from a stagnant pool."

"Life—of a kind," admitted the novelist.

"It's all much the same kind, really, isn't it?" said Miss Marple.

"You compare yourself to a denizen of a stagnant pond, Aunt Jane?"

"My dear, you said something of the sort in your last book, I remember."

No clever young man likes having his works quoted against himself. Raymond West was no exception.

"That was entirely different," he snapped.

"Life is, after all, very much the same everywhere," said Miss Marple in her placid voice. "Getting born, you know, and growing up—and coming into contact with other people—getting jostled—and then marriage and more babies—"

"And finally death," said Raymond West. "And not death with a death certificate always. Death in life."

"Talking of death," said Griselda. "You know we've had a murder here?"

Raymond West waved murder away with his cigarette.

"Murder is so crude," he said. "I take no interest in it."

That statement did not take me in for a moment. They say all the world loves a lover—apply that saying to murder and you have an even more infallible truth. No one can fail to be interested in a murder. Simple people like Griselda and myself can admit the fact, but anyone like Raymond West has to pretend to be bored—at any rate for the first five minutes.

Miss Marple, however, gave her nephew away by remarking:

"Raymond and I have been discussing nothing else all through dinner."

"I take a great interest in all the local news," said Raymond hastily. He smiled benignly and tolerantly at Miss Marple.

"Have you a theory, Mr. West?" asked Griselda.

"Logically," said Raymond West, again flourishing his cigarette, "only one person could have killed Protheroe."

"Yes?" said Griselda.

We hung upon his words with flattering attention.

"The Vicar," said Raymond, and pointed an accusing finger at me.

I gasped.

"Of course," he reassured me, "I know you didn't do it. Life is never what it should be. But think of the drama—the fitness—Churchwarden murdered in the Vicar's study by the Vicar. Delicious!"

"And the motive?" I inquired.

"Oh! That's interesting." He sat up—allowed his cigarette to go out. "Inferiority complex, I think. Possibly too many inhibitions. I should like to write the story of the affair. Amazingly complex. Week after week, year after year, he's seen the man—at vestry meetings—at choir boys' outings—handing round the bag in church—bringing it to the altar. Always he dislikes the man—always he chokes down his dislike. It's unchristianlike, he won't encourage it. And so it festers underneath, and one day—"

He made a graphic gesture.

Griselda turned to me.

"Have you ever felt like that, Len?"

"Never," I said truthfully.

"Yet I hear you were wishing him out of the world not so long ago," remarked Miss Marple.

(That miserable Dennis! But my fault, of course, for ever making the remark.)

"I'm afraid I was," I said. "It was a stupid remark to make, but really I'd had a very trying morning with him."

"That's disappointing," said Raymond West. "Because, of course if your subconscious were really planning to do him in, it would never have allowed you to make that remark."

He sighed.

"My theory falls to the ground. This is probably a very ordinary murder—a revengeful poacher or something of that sort."

"Miss Cram came to see me this afternoon," said Miss Marple. "I met her in the village and I asked her if she would like to see my garden."

"Is she fond of gardens?" asked Griselda.

"I don't think so," said Miss Marple with a faint twinkle. "But it makes a very useful excuse for talk, don't you think?"

"What did you make of her?" asked Griselda. "I don't believe she's really so bad."

"She volunteered a lot of information—really a lot of information," said Miss Marple. "About herself, you know, and her people. They all seem to be dead or in India. Very sad. By the way, she has gone to Old Hall for the week-end."

"What?"

"Yes, it seems Mrs. Protheroe asked her—or she suggested it to Mrs. Protheroe—I don't quite know which way about it was. To do some secretarial work for her—there are so many letters to cope with. It turned out rather fortunately. Dr. Stone being away, she has nothing to do. What an excitement this barrow has been."

"Stone?" said Raymond. "Is that the archæologist fellow?"

"Yes, he is excavating a barrow. On the Protheroe property."

"He's a good man," said Raymond. "Wonderfully keen on his job. I met him at a dinner not long ago, and we had a most interesting talk. I must look him up."

"Unfortunately," I said, "he's just gone to London for the week-end. Why, you actually ran into him at the station this afternoon."

"I ran into you. You had a little fat man with you—with glasses on."

"Yes—Dr. Stone."

"But, my dear fellow—that wasn't Stone."

"Not Stone?"

"Not the archæologist. I know him quite well. The man wasn't Stone—not the faintest resemblance."

We stared at each other. In particular I stared at Miss Marple.

"Extraordinary," I said.

"The suitcase," said Miss Marple.

"But why?" said Griselda.

"It reminds me of the time the man went round pretending to be the gas inspector," murmured Miss Marple. "Quite a little haul, he got."

"An impostor," said Raymond West. "Now this is really interesting."

"The question is, has it anything to do with murder?" said Griselda.

"Not necessarily," I said. "But—" I looked at Miss Marple.

"It is," she said, "a Peculiar Thing. Another Peculiar Thing."

"Yes," I said rising. "I rather feel the Inspector ought to be told about this at once."

XXII

INSPECTOR SLACK'S ORDERS, once I had got him on the telephone, were brief and emphatic. Nothing was to "get about." In particular, Miss Cram was not to be alarmed. In the meantime, a search was to be instituted for the suitcase in the neighbourhood of the barrow.

Griselda and I returned home very excited over this new development. We could not say much with Dennis present, as we had faithfully promised Inspector Slack to breathe no word to anybody.

In any case, Dennis was full of his own troubles. He came into my study and began fingering things and shuffling his feet and looking thoroughly embarrassed.

"What is it, Dennis?" I said at last.

"Uncle Len. I don't want to go to sea."

I was astonished. The boy had been so very decided about his career up to now.

"But you were so keen on it."

"Yes, but I've changed my mind."

"What do you want to do?"

"I want to go into finance."

I was even more surprised.

"What do you mean—finance?"

"Just that. I want to go into the City."

"But my dear boy, I am sure you would not like the life. Even if I obtained a post for you in a bank—"

Dennis said that wasn't what he meant. He didn't want to go into a bank. I asked him what exactly he did mean, and of course, as I suspected, the boy didn't really know.

By "going into finance" he simply meant getting rich quickly, which, with the optimism of youth, he imagined was a certainty if one "went into the City." I disabused him of this notion as gently as I could.

"What's put it into your head?" I asked. "You were so satisfied with the idea of going to sea."

"I know, Uncle Len, but I've been thinking. I shall want to marry some day—and, I mean, you've got to be rich to marry a girl."

"Facts disprove your theory," I said.

"I know—but a real girl. I mean, a girl who's used to things."

It was very vague but I thought I knew what he meant.

"You know," I said gently, "all girls aren't like Lettice Protheroe."

He fired up at once.

"You're awfully unfair to her. You don't like her. Griselda doesn't either. She says she's tiresome."

From the feminine point of view, Griselda is quite right. Lettice is tiresome. I could quite realize, however, that a boy would resent the adjective.

"If only people made a few allowances. Why even the Hartley Napiers are going about grousing about her at a time like this! Just because she left their old tennis party a bit early. Why should she stay if she was bored? Jolly decent of her to go at all, I think."

"Quite a favour," I said, but Dennis suspected no malice. He was full of his own grievance on Lettice's behalf.

"She's awfully unselfish really. Just to show you, she made me stay. Naturally I wanted to go too. But she wouldn't hear of it. Said it was too bad on the Napiers. So, just to please her, I stopped on a quarter of an hour."

The young have very curious views on unselfishness.

"And now I hear Susan Hartley Napier is going about everywhere saying Lettice has rotten manners."

"If I were you," I said, "I shouldn't worry."

"It's all very well, but—"

He broke off.

"I'd—I'd do anything for Lettice."

"Very few of us can do anything for anyone else," I said. "However much we wish it, we are powerless."

"I wish I were dead," said Dennis.

Poor lad. Calf love is a virulent disease. I forebore to say any of the obvious and probably irritating things which come so easily to one's lips. Instead I said good night, and went up to bed.

I took the eight o'clock service the following morning, and when I returned found Griselda sitting at the breakfast table with an open note in her hand. It was from Anne Protheroe.

DEAR GRISELDA,

If you and the Vicar could come up and lunch here quietly today, I should be so very grateful. Something very strange has occurred and I should like Mr. Clement's advice.

Please don't mention this when you come, as I have said nothing to anyone.

With love,
Yours affectionately,
ANNE PROTHEROE.

"We must go, of course," said Griselda.

I agreed.

"I wonder what can have happened?"

I wondered too.

"You know," I said to Griselda, "I don't feel we are really at the end of this case yet."

"You mean not till someone has really been arrested?"

"No," I said. "I didn't mean that. I mean that there are ramifications, undercurrents, that we know nothing about. There are a whole lot of things to clear up before we get at the truth."

"You mean things that don't really matter, but that get in the way?"

"Yes, I think that expresses my meaning very well."

"I think we're all making a great fuss," said Dennis, helping himself to marmalade. "It's a jolly good thing old Protheroe is dead. Nobody liked him. Oh! I know the police have got to worry—it's their job. But I rather hope myself they'll never find out. I should hate to see Slack promoted, going about swelling with importance over his cleverness."

I am human enough to feel that I agreed over the matter of Slack's promotion. A man who goes about systematically rubbing people up the wrong way cannot hope to be popular.

"Dr. Haydock thinks rather like I do," went on Dennis. "He'd never give a murderer up to justice. He said so."

I think that that is the danger of Haydock's views. They may be sound in themselves—it is not for me to say—but they produce an impression on the young, careless mind which I am sure Haydock himself never meant to convey.

Griselda looked out of the window and remarked that there were reporters in the garden.

"I suppose they're photographing the study windows again," she said with a sigh.

We had suffered a good deal in this way. There was first the idle curiosity of the village—everyone had come to gape and stare. There were next the reporters armed with cameras, and the village again to watch the reporters. In the end we had to have a constable from Much Benham on duty outside the window.

"Well," I said, "the funeral is tomorrow morning. After that, surely, the excitement will die down."

I noticed a few reporters hanging about Old Hall when we arrived there. They accosted me with various queries, to which I gave the invariable answer (we had found it the best) that I had nothing to say.

We were shown by the butler into the drawing room, the sole occupant of which turned out to be Miss Cram—apparently in a state of high enjoyment.

"This is a surprise, isn't it?" she said as she shook hands. "I never should have thought of such a thing, but Mrs. Protheroe is kind, isn't she? And, of course, it isn't what you might call nice for a young girl to be staying alone at a place like the Blue Boar, reporters about and all. And, of course, it's not as though I haven't been able to make myself useful—you really need a secretary at a time like this, and Miss Protheroe doesn't do anything to help, does she?"

I was amused to notice that the old animosity against Lettice persisted, but that the girl had apparently become a warm partisan of Anne's. At the same time I wondered if the story of her coming here was strictly accurate. In her account, the initiative had come from Anne, but I wondered if that were really so. The first mention of disliking to be at the Blue Boar alone might have easily come from the girl herself. While keeping an open mind on the subject, I did not fancy that Miss Cram was strictly truthful.

At that moment Anne Protheroe entered the room.

She was dressed very quietly in black. She carried in her hand a Sunday paper, which she held out to me with a rueful glance.

"I've never had any experience of this sort of thing. It's pretty ghastly, isn't it? I saw a reporter at the inquest. I just said that I was terribly upset and had nothing to say, and then he asked me if I wasn't very anxious to find my husband's murderer, and I said 'Yes.' And then whether I had any suspicions and I said 'No.' And whether I didn't think the crime showed local knowledge, and I said it seemed to, certainly. And that was all. And now look at this!"

In the middle of the page was a photograph, evidently taken at least ten years ago—Heaven knows where they had dug it out. There were large headlines.

WIDOW DECLARES SHE WILL NEVER REST TILL SHE HAS HUNTED DOWN HUSBAND'S MURDERER.

Mrs. Protheroe, the widow of the murdered man, is certain that the murderer must be looked for locally. She has suspicions but no certainty. She declared herself prostrated with grief, but reiterated her determination to hunt down the murderer.

"It doesn't sound like me, does it?" said Anne.

"I daresay it might have been worse," I said handing back the paper.

"Impudent, aren't they?" said Miss Cram. "I'd like to see one of those fellows trying to get something out of me."

By the twinkle in Griselda's eye, I was convinced that she regarded this statement as being more literally true than Miss Cram intended it to appear.

Luncheon was announced and we went in. Lettice did not come in till half way through the meal, when she drifted into the empty place with a smile for Griselda and a nod for me. I watched her with some attention, for reasons of my own, but she seemed much the same vague creature as usual. Extremely pretty—that in fairness I had to admit. She was still not wearing mourning, but was dressed in a shade of pale green that brought out all the delicacy of her fair colouring.

After we had had coffee, Anne said quietly:

"I want to have a little talk with the Vicar. I will take him up to my sitting room."

At last I was to learn the reason of our summons. I rose and followed her up the stairs. She paused at the door of the room. As I was about to speak, she stretched out a hand to stop me. She remained listening, looking down towards the hall.

"Good. They are going out into the garden. No—don't go in there. We can go straight up."

Much to my surprise she led the way along the corridor to the extremity of the wing. Here a narrow, ladder-like staircase rose to the floor above and she mounted it, I following. We found ourselves in a dusty boarded passage. Anne opened a door and led me into a large, dim attic which was evidently used as a lumber room. There were trunks there, old broken furniture, a few stacked pictures, and the many countless odds and ends which a lumber room collects.

My surprise was so evident that she smiled faintly.

"First of all, I must explain. I am sleeping very lightly just now. Last night—or rather this morning about three o'clock—I was convinced that I heard someone moving about the house. I listened for some time, and at last got up and came out to see. Out on the landing I realized that the sounds came, not from down below, but from up above. I came along to the foot of these stairs. Again I thought I heard a sound. I called up 'Is anybody there?' But there was no answer, and I heard nothing more, so I assumed that my nerves had been playing tricks on me and went back to bed.

"However, early this morning, I came up here—simply out of curiosity. And I found this!"

She stooped down and turned round a picture that was leaning against the wall with the back of the canvas towards us.

I gave a gasp of surprise. The picture was evidently a portrait in oils, but the face had been hacked and cut in such a savage way as to render it unrecognizable. Moreover the cuts were clearly quite fresh.

"What an extraordinary thing," I said.

"Isn't it? Tell me, can you think of any explanation?"

I shook my head.

"There's a kind of savagery about it," I said, "that I don't like. It looks as though it had been done in a fit of maniacal rage."

"Yes, that's what I thought."

"What is the portrait?"

"I haven't the least idea. I have never seen it before. All these things were in the attic when I married Lucius and came here to live. I have never been through them or bothered about them."

"Extraordinary," I commented.

I stooped down and examined the other pictures. They were very much what you would expect to find—some very mediocre landscapes, some oleographs, and a few cheaply framed reproductions.

There was nothing else helpful. A large, old-fashioned trunk, of the kind that used to be called an "ark," had the initials E.P. upon it. I raised the lid. It was empty. Nothing else in the attic was the least suggestive.

"It really is a most amazing occurrence," I said. "It's so—senseless."

"Yes," said Anne. "That frightens me a little."

There was nothing more to see. I accompanied her down to her sitting room where she closed the door.

"Do you think I ought to do anything about it? Tell the police?"

I hesitated.

"It's hard to say on the face of it whether—"

"It has anything to do with the murder or not," finished Anne. "I know. That's what is so difficult. On the face of it, there seems no connection whatever."

"No," I said, "but it is another Peculiar Thing."

We both sat silent with puzzled brows.

"What are your plans, if I may ask?" I said presently.

She lifted her head.

"I'm going to live here for at least another six months!" She said it defiantly. "I don't want to. I hate the idea of living here. But I think it's the only thing to be done. Otherwise people will say that I ran away—that I had a guilty conscience."

"Surely not."

"Oh! yes, they will. Especially when—" She paused and then said: "When the six months are up—I am going to marry Lawrence." Her eyes met mine. "We're neither of us going to wait any longer."

"I supposed," I said, "that that would happen."

Suddenly she broke down, burying her head in her hands.

"You don't know how grateful I am to you—you don't know. We'd said good-bye to each other—he was going away. I feel—I feel not so awful about Lucius' death. If we'd been planning to go away together, and he'd died then—it would be so awful now. But you made us both see how wrong it would be. That's why I'm grateful."

"I, too, am thankful," I said gravely.

"All the same, you know," she sat up. "Unless the real murderer is found, they'll always think it was Lawrence. Oh! yes, they will. And especially when he marries me."

"My dear, Dr. Haydock's evidence made it perfectly clear—"

"What do people care about evidence? They don't even know about it. And medical evidence never means anything to outsiders anyway. That's another reason why I'm staying on here. Mr. Clement, I'm going to find out the truth."

Her eyes flashed as she spoke. She added:

"That's why I asked that girl here."

"Miss Cram?"

"Yes."

"You did ask her, then. I mean, it was your idea?"

"Entirely. Oh! as a matter of fact, she whined a bit. At the inquest—she was there when I arrived. No, I asked her here deliberately."

"But surely," I cried, "you don't think that that silly young woman could have had anything to do with the crime?"

"It's awfully easy to appear silly, Mr. Clement. It's one of the easiest things in the world."

"Then you really think—?"

"No. I don't. Honestly I don't. What I do think is that that girl knows something—or might know something. I wanted to study her at close quarters."

"And the very night she arrives, that picture is slashed," I said thoughtfully.

"You think she did it? But why? It seems so utterly absurd and impossible."

"It seems to me utterly impossible and absurd that your husband should have been murdered in my study," I said bitterly. "But he was."

"I know." She laid her hand on my arm. "It's dreadful for you. I do realize that, though I haven't said very much about it."

I took the blue lapis lazuli earring from my pocket and held it out to her.

"This is yours, I think?"

"Oh! yes." She held out her hand for it with a pleased smile. "Where did you find it?"

But I did not put the jewel into her outstretched hand.

"Would you mind," I said, "if I kept it a little longer?"

"Why, certainly." She looked puzzled and a little inquiring. I did not satisfy her curiosity.

Instead I asked her how she was situated financially.

"It is an impertinent question," I said. "But I really do not mean it as such."

"I don't think it's impertinent at all. You and Griselda are the best friends I have here. And I like that funny old Miss Marple. Lucius was very well off, you know. He left things pretty equally divided between me and Lettice. Old Hall goes to me, but Lettice is to be allowed to choose enough furniture to furnish a small house, and she is left a separate sum for the purpose of buying one, so as to even things up."

"What are her plans, do you know?"

Anne made a comical grimace.

"She doesn't tell them to me. I imagine she will leave here as soon as possible. She doesn't like me—she never has. I daresay it's my fault, though I've really always tried to be decent. But I suppose any girl resents a young stepmother."

"Are you fond of her?" I asked bluntly.

She did not reply at once, which convinced me that Anne Protheroe is a very honest woman.

"I was at first," she said. "She was such a pretty little girl. I don't think I am now. I don't know why. Perhaps it's because she doesn't like me. I like being liked, you know."

"We all do," I said, and Anne Protheroe smiled.

I had one more task to perform. That was to get a word alone with Lettice Protheroe. I managed that easily enough, catching sight of her in the deserted drawing room. Griselda and Gladys Cram were out in the garden.

I went in and shut the door.

"Lettice," I said, "I want to speak to you about something."

She looked up indifferently.

"Yes?"

I had thought beforehand what to say. I held out the lapis earring and said quietly:

"Why did you drop that in my study?"

I saw her stiffen for a moment—it was almost instantaneous. Her recovery was so quick that I myself could hardly have sworn to the movement. Then she said carelessly:

"I never dropped anything in your study. That's not mine. That's Anne's."

"I know that," I said.

"Well, why ask me then? Anne must have dropped it."

"Mrs. Protheroe has only been in my study once since the murder, and then she was wearing black and so would not have been likely to have had on a blue earring."

"In that case," said Lettice, "I suppose she must have dropped it before." She added, "That's only logical."

"It's very logical," I said. "I suppose you don't happen to remember when your stepmother was wearing these earrings last?"

"Oh!" She looked at me with a puzzled, trustful gaze. "Is it very important?"

"It might be," I said.

"I'll try and think." She sat there knitting her brows. I have never seen Lettice Protheroe look more charming than she did at that moment. "Oh! yes," she said suddenly. "She had them on on Thursday. I remember now."

"Thursday," I said slowly, "was the day of the murder. Mrs. Protheroe came to the studio in the garden that day, but, if you remember, in her evidence, she only came as far as the study window, not inside the room."

"Where did you find this?"

"Rolled underneath the desk."

"Then it looks, doesn't it," said Lettice coolly, "as though she hadn't spoken the truth?"

"You mean that she came right in and stood by the desk?"

"Well, it looks like it, doesn't it?"

Her eyes met mine calmly.

"If you want to know," she said calmly. "I never have thought she was speaking the truth."

"And I know you are not, Lettice."

"What do you mean?"

She was startled.

"I mean," I said, "that the last time I saw this earring was on Friday morning when I came up here with Colonel Melchett. It was lying with its fellow on your stepmother's dressing table. I actually handled them both."

"Oh!—" She wavered, then suddenly flung herself sideways over the arm of her chair and burst into tears. Her short, fair hair hung down almost touching the floor. It was a strange attitude—beautiful and unrestrained.

I let her sob for some moments in silence and then I said very gently:

"Lettice, why did you do it?"

"What?"

She sprang up, flinging her hair wildly back. She looked wild—almost terrified.

"What do you mean?"

"What made you do it? Was it jealousy? Dislike of Anne?"

"Oh!—Oh! yes." She pushed the hair back from her face and seemed suddenly to regain complete self-possession. "Yes, you can call it jealousy. I've always disliked Anne—ever since she came queening it here. I put the damned thing under the desk. I hoped it would get her into trouble. It would have done if you hadn't been such a Nosey Parker, fingering things on dressing tables. Anyway, it isn't a clergyman's business to go about helping the police."

It was a spiteful childish outburst. I took no notice of it. Indeed at that moment, she seemed a very pathetic child indeed.

Her childish attempt at vengeance against Anne seemed hardly to be taken seriously. I told her so, and added that I should return the earring to her and say nothing of the circumstances in which I had found it. She seemed rather touched by that.

"That's nice of you," she said.

She paused a minute and then said, keeping her face averted and evidently choosing her words with care:

"You know, Mr. Clement, I should—I should get Dennis away from here soon, if I were you. I—I think it would be better."

"Dennis?" I raised my eyebrows in slight surprise but with a trace of amusement too.

"I think it would be better," she added, still in the same awkward manner. "I'm sorry about Dennis. I didn't think he—anyway, I'm sorry."

We left it at that.

XXIII

ON THE WAY back, I proposed to Griselda that we should make a detour and go round by the barrow. I was anxious to see if the police were at work and, if so, what they had found. Griselda, however, had things to do at home, so I was left to make the expedition on my own.

I found Constable Hurst in charge of operations.

"No sign so far, sir," he reported, "and yet it stands to reason that this is the only place for a *cache*."

His use of the word *cache* puzzled me for the moment, as he pronounced it catch, but his real meaning occurred to me almost at once.

"Whatimeantersay is, sir, where else could the young woman be going, starting into the wood by that path? It leads to Old Hall, and it leads here, and that's about all."

"I suppose," I said, "that Inspector Slack would disdain such a simple course as asking the young lady straight out."

"Anxious not to put the wind up her," said Hurst. "Anything she writes to Stone or he writes to her may throw light on things—once she knows we're on to her, she'd shut up like that."

Like what exactly was left in doubt, but I personally doubted Miss Gladys Cram ever being shut up in the way described. It was impossible to imagine her as other than overflowing with conversation.

"When a man's an h'impostor, you want to know why he's an h'impostor," said Constable Hurst didactically.

"Naturally," I said.

"And the answer is to be found in this here barrow—or else why was he for ever messing about with it?"

"A *raison d'être* for prowling about," I suggested, but this bit of French was too much for the constable. He revenged himself for not understanding it by saying coldly:

"That's the h'amateur's point of view."

"Anyway you haven't found the suitcase," I said.

"We shall do, sir. Not a doubt of it."

"I'm not so sure," I said. "I've been thinking. Miss Marple said it was quite a short time before the girl reappeared empty-handed. In that case, she wouldn't have had time to get up here and back."

"You can't take any notice of what old ladies say. When they've seen something curious, and are waiting all eager like, why time simply flies for them. And anyway, no lady knows anything about time."

I often wonder why the whole world is so prone to generalize. Generalizations are seldom or ever true, and are usually utterly inaccurate. I have a poor sense of time myself (hence the keeping of my clock fast), and Miss Marple, I should say, has a very acute one. Her clocks keep time to the minute, and she herself is rigidly punctual on every occasion.

However I had no intention of arguing with Constable Hurst on the point. I wished him good afternoon and good luck, and went on my way.

It was just as I was nearing home that the idea came to me. There was nothing to lead up to it. It just flashed into my brain as a possible solution.

You will remember that on my first search of the path, the day after the murder, I had found the bushes disturbed in a certain place. They proved, or so I thought at the time, to have been disturbed by Lawrence, bent on the same errand as myself.

But I remembered that afterwards he and I together had come upon another faintly marked trail which proved to be that of the Inspector. On thinking it over, I distinctly remembered that the first trail (Lawrence's) had been much more noticeable than the second, as though more than one person had been passing that way. And I reflected that that was probably what had drawn Lawrence's attention to it in the first instance. Supposing that it had originally been made by either Dr. Stone or else Miss Cram?

I remembered, or else I imagined remembering, that there had been several withered leaves on broken twigs. If so, the trail could not have been made the afternoon of our search.

I was just approaching the spot in question. I recognized it easily enough, and once more forced my way through the bushes. This time I noticed fresh twigs broken. Someone had passed this way since Lawrence and myself.

I soon came to the place where I had encountered Lawrence. The faint trail, however, persisted farther, and I continued to follow it. Suddenly it widened out into a little clearing, which showed signs of recent upheaval. I say a clearing, because the denseness of the undergrowth was thinned out there, but the branches of the trees met overhead and the whole place was not more than a few feet across.

On the other side, the undergrowth grew densely again and it seemed quite clear that no one had forced a way through it recently. Nevertheless, it seemed to have been disturbed in one place.

I went across and kneeled down, thrusting the bushes aside with both hands. A glint of a shiny brown surface rewarded me. Full of excitement I thrust my arm in and with a good deal of difficulty I extracted a small brown suitcase.

I uttered an ejaculation of triumph. I had been successful. Coldly snubbed by Constable Hurst, I had yet proved right in my reasoning. Here without doubt was the suitcase carried by Miss Cram. I tried the hasp, but it was locked.

As I rose to my feet, I noticed a small brownish crystal lying on the ground. Almost automatically, I picked it up and slipped it into my pocket.

Then, grasping my find by the handle, I retraced my steps to the path.

As I climbed over the stile into the lane, an agitated voice near at hand called out.

"Oh! Mr. Clement. You've found it! How clever of you!"

Mentally registering the fact that, in the art of seeing without being seen, Miss Marple had no rival, I balanced my find on the palings between us.

"That's the one," said Miss Marple. "I'd know it anywhere."

This, I thought, was a slight exaggeration. There are thousands of cheap shiny suitcases all exactly alike. No one could recognize one, particularly one seen from such a distance away by moonlight, but I realized that the whole business of the suitcase was Miss Marple's particular triumph and, as such, she was entitled to a little pardonable exaggeration.

"It's locked, I suppose, Mr. Clement?"

"Yes. I'm just going to take it down to the police station."

"You don't think it would be better to telephone?"

Of course unquestionably it would be better to telephone. To stride through the village, suitcase in hand, would be to court a probably undesirable publicity.

So I unlatched Miss Marple's garden gate and entered the house by the French window, and from the sanctity of the drawing room, with the door shut, I telephoned my news.

The result was that Inspector Slack announced he would be up himself in a couple of jiffies.

When he arrived it was in his most cantankerous mood.

"So we've got it, have we?" he said. "You know, sir, you shouldn't keep things to yourself. If you've any reason to believe you know where the article in question was hidden, you ought to have reported it to the proper authorities."

"It was a pure accident," I said. "The idea just happened to occur to me."

"And that's a likely tale. Nearly three quarters of a mile of woodland, and you go right to the proper spot and lay your hand upon it."

I would have given Inspector Slack the steps in reasoning which led me to this particular spot, but he had achieved his usual result of putting my back up. I said nothing.

"Well!" said Inspector Slack, eyeing the suitcase with dislike and would-be indifference. "I suppose we might as well have a look at what's inside."

He had brought an assortment of keys and wire with him. The lock was a cheap affair. In a couple of seconds the case was open.

I don't know what we had expected to find—something sternly sensational, I imagine. But the first thing that met our eyes was a greasy plaid scarf. The Inspector lifted it out. Next came a faded dark blue overcoat, very much the worse for wear. A checked cap followed.

"A shoddy lot," said the Inspector.

A pair of boots, very down at heel and battered, came next. At the bottom of the suitcase was a parcel done up in newspaper.

"Fancy shirt, I suppose," said the Inspector bitterly, as he tore it open.

A moment later he had caught his breath in surprise.

For inside the parcel were some demure little silver objects and a round platter of the same metal.

Miss Marple gave a shrill exclamation of recognition.

"The trencher salts," she exclaimed. "Colonel Protheroe's trencher salts, and the Charles II tazza. Did you ever hear of such a thing!"

The Inspector had got very red.

"So that was the game," he muttered. "Robbery. But I can't make it out. There's been no mention of these things being missing."

"Perhaps they haven't discovered the loss," I suggested. "I presume these valuable things would not have been kept out in common use. Colonel Protheroe probably kept them locked away in a safe."

"I must investigate this," said the Inspector. "I'll go right up to Old Hall now. So that's why our Dr. Stone made himself scarce. What with the murder and one thing and another, he was afraid we'd get wind of his activities. As likely as not his belongings might have been searched. He got the girl to hide them in the wood with a suitable change of clothing. He meant to come back by a roundabout route and go off with them one night while she stayed here to disarm suspicion. Well, there's one thing to the good. This lets him out over the murder. He'd nothing to do with that. Quite a different game."

He repacked the suitcase and took his departure, refusing Miss Marple's offer of a glass of sherry.

"Well, that's one mystery cleared up," I said with a sigh. "What Slack says is quite true; there are no grounds for suspecting him of the murder. Everything's accounted for quite satisfactorily."

"It really would seem so," said Miss Marple. "Although one never can be quite certain, can one?"

"There's a complete lack of motive," I pointed out. "He'd got what he came for and was clearing out."

"Y–es."

She was clearly not quite satisfied, and I looked at her in some curiosity.

She hastened to answer my inquiring gaze with a kind of apologetic eagerness.

"I've no doubt I am quite wrong. I'm so stupid about these things. But I just wondered—I mean this silver is very valuable, is it not?"

"A tazza sold the other day for over a thousand pounds, I believe."

"I mean—it's not the value of the metal."

"No, it's what one might call a connoisseur's value."

"That's what I mean. The sale of such things would take a little time to arrange, or, even if it was arranged, it couldn't be carried through without secrecy. I mean—if the robbery were reported and a hue and cry were raised, well, the things couldn't be marketed at all."

"I don't quite see what you mean?" I said.

"I know I'm putting it badly." She became more flustered and apologetic. "But it seems to me that—that the things couldn't just have been abstracted, so to speak. The only satisfactory thing to do would be to replace these things with copies. Then, perhaps, the robbery wouldn't be discovered for some time."

"That's a very ingenious idea," I said.

"It would be the only way to do it, wouldn't it? And if so, of course, as you say, once the substitution had been accomplished, there wouldn't have been any reason for murdering Colonel Protheroe—quite the reverse."

"Exactly," I said. "That's what I said."

"Yes, but I just wondered—I don't know, of course—and Colonel Protheroe always talked a lot about doing things before he actually did do them, and of course sometimes never did them at all, but he did say—"

"Yes?"

"That he was going to have all his things valued—a man down from London. For probate—no, that's when you're dead—for insurance. Someone told him that was the thing to do. He talked about it a great deal, and the importance of having it done. Of course, I don't know if he had made any actual arrangement, but if he had . . ."

"I see," I said slowly.

"Of course, the moment the expert saw the silver, he'd know, and then Colonel Protheroe would remember having shown the things to Dr. Stone—I wonder if it was done then—legerdemain, don't they call it? So clever—and then, well, the fat would be in the fire, to use an old-fashioned expression."

"I see your idea," I said. "I think we ought to find out for certain."

I went once more to the telephone. In a few minutes I was through to Old Hall and speaking to Anne Protheroe.

"No, it's nothing very important. Has the Inspector arrived yet? Oh! well, he's on his way. Mrs. Protheroe, can you tell me if the contents of Old Hall were ever valued? What's that you say?"

Her answer came clear and prompt. I thanked her, replaced the receiver and turned to Miss Marple.

"That's very definite. Colonel Protheroe had made arrangements for a man to come down from London on Monday—tomorrow—to make a full valuation. Owing to the Colonel's death, the matter has been put off."

"Then there was a motive," said Miss Marple softly.

"A motive, yes. But that's all. You forget. When the shot was fired, Dr. Stone had just joined the others, or was climbing over the stile in order to do so."

"Yes," said Miss Marple thoughtfully. "So that rules him out."

XXIV

I RETURNED TO the Vicarage to find Hawes waiting for me in my study. He was pacing up and down nervously, and when I entered the room he started as though he had been shot.

"You must excuse me," he said, wiping his forehead. "My nerves are all to pieces lately."

"My dear fellow," I said, "you positively must get away for a change. We shall have you breaking down altogether, and that will never do."

"I can't desert my post. No, that is a thing I will never do."

"It's not a case of desertion. You are ill. I'm sure Haydock would agree with me."

"Haydock—Haydock. What kind of a doctor is he? An ignorant country practitioner."

"I think you're unfair to him. He has always been considered a very able man in his profession."

"Oh! perhaps. Yes, I daresay. But I don't like him. However, that's not what I came to say. I came to ask you if you would be kind enough to preach tonight instead of me. I—I really do not feel equal to it."

"Why, certainly. I will take the service for you."

"No, no. I wish to take the service. I am perfectly fit. It is only the idea of getting up in the pulpit, of all those eyes staring at me . . ."

He shut his eyes and swallowed convulsively.

It was clear to me that there was something very wrong indeed the matter with Hawes. He seemed aware of my thoughts, for he opened his eyes and said quickly.

"There is nothing really wrong with me. It is just these headaches—these awful racking headaches. I wonder if you could let me have a glass of water."

"Certainly," I said.

I went and fetched it myself from the tap. Ringing bells is a profitless form of exercise in our house.

I brought the water to him and he thanked me. He took from his pocket a small cardboard box and, opening it, extracted a rice paper capsule, which he swallowed with the aid of the water.

"A headache powder," he explained.

I suddenly wondered whether Hawes might have become addicted to drugs. It would explain a great many of his peculiarities.

"You don't take too many, I hope," I said.

"No—oh, no. Dr. Haydock warned me against that. But it is really wonderful. They bring instant relief."

Indeed he already seemed calmer and more composed.

He stood up.

"Then you will preach tonight? It's very good of you, sir."

"Not at all. And I insist on taking the service too. Get along home and rest. No, I won't have any argument. Not another word."

He thanked me again. Then he said, his eyes sliding past me to the window:

"You—you have been up at Old Hall today, haven't you, sir?"

"Yes."

"Excuse me—but were you sent for?"

I looked at him in surprise, and he flushed.

"I'm sorry, sir. I—I just thought some new development might have arisen, and that that was why Mrs. Protheroe had sent for you."

I had not the faintest intention of satisfying Hawes' curiosity.

"She wanted to discuss the funeral arrangements and one or two other small matters with me," I said.

"Oh! that was all. I see."

I did not speak. He fidgeted from foot to foot, and finally said:

"Mr. Redding came to see me last night. I—I can't imagine why."

"Didn't he tell you?"

"He—he just said he thought he'd look me up. Said it was a bit lonely in the evenings. He's never done such a thing before."

"Well, he's supposed to be pleasant company," I said smiling.

"What does he want to come and see me for? I don't like it." His voice rose shrilly. "He spoke of dropping in again. What does it all mean? What idea do you think he has got into his head?"

"Why should you suppose he has any ulterior motive?" I asked.

"I don't like it," repeated Hawes obstinately. "I've never gone against him in any way. I never suggested that he was guilty—even when he accused himself, I said it seemed most incomprehensible. If I've had suspicions of anybody, it's been of Archer—never of him. Archer is a totally different proposition—a godless, irreligious ruffian. A drunken blackguard."

"Don't you think you're being a little harsh?" I said. "After all, we really know very little about the man."

"A poacher, in and out of prison, capable of anything."

"Do you really think he shot Colonel Protheroe?" I asked curiously.

Hawes has an inveterate dislike of answering "yes" or "no." I have noticed it several times lately.

"Don't you think yourself, sir, that it's the only possible solution?"

"As far as we know," I said, "there's no evidence of any kind against him."

"His threats," said Hawes eagerly. "You forget about his threats."

"I am sick and tired of hearing about Archer's threats. As far as I can make out, there is no direct evidence that he ever made any."

"He was determined to be revenged on Colonel Protheroe. He primed himself with drink, and then shot him."

"That's pure supposition."

"But you will admit that it's perfectly probable?"

"No, I don't."

"Possible, then?"

"Possible, yes."

Hawes glanced at me sideways.

"Why don't you think it's probable?"

"Because," I said, "a man like Archer wouldn't think of shooting a man with a pistol. It's the wrong weapon."

Hawes seemed taken aback by my argument. Evidently it wasn't the objection he had expected.

"Do you really think the objection is feasible?" he asked doubtingly.

"To my mind it is a complete stumbling block to Archer's having committed the crime," I said.

In face of my positive assertion, Hawes said no more. He thanked me again and left.

I had gone as far as the front door with him, and on the hall table I saw four notes. They had certain characteristics in common. The handwriting was almost unmistakably feminine; they all bore the words "By hand, Urgent," and the only difference I could see was that one was noticeably dirtier than the rest.

Their similarity gave me a curious feeling of seeing—not double but quadruple.

Mary came out of the kitchen and caught me staring at them.

"Come by hand since lunch time," she volunteered. "All but one. I found that in the box."

I nodded, gathered them up and took them into the study.

The first one ran thus.

DEAR MR. CLEMENT,

Something has come to my knowledge which I feel you ought to know. It concerns the death of poor Colonel Protheroe. I should much appreciate your advice on the matter—whether to go to the police or not. Since my dear husband's death, I have such a shrinking from every kind of publicity. Perhaps you could run in and see me for a few minutes this afternoon,

Yours sincerely,

MARTHA PRICE RIDLEY.

I opened the second.

DEAR MR. CLEMENT,

I am so troubled—so exercised *in my mind—to know what I ought to do. Something has come to my ears that I feel may be important. I have such a* horror *of being mixed up with the police in any way. I am so disturbed and distressed. Would it be asking too much of you, dear Vicar, to drop in for a few minutes and solve my doubts and perplexities for me in the wonderful way you always do?*

Forgive my troubling you,

Yours very sincerely,

CAROLINE WETHERBY.

The third, I felt, I could almost have recited beforehand.

DEAR MR. CLEMENT,

Something most important has come to my ears. I feel you should be the first to know about it. Will you call in and see me this afternoon sometime? I will wait in for you.

This militant epistle was signed

AMANDA HARTNELL.

I opened the fourth missive. It has been my good fortune to be troubled with very few anonymous letters. An anonymous letter is, I think, the meanest and cruelest weapon there is. This one was no exception. It purported to be written by an illiterate person, but several things inclined me to disbelieve that assumption.

DEAR VICAR,

i think you ought to know what is Going On. Your lady has been seen coming out of Mr. Redding's cottage in a surreptitious manner. You know wot i mean. The two are Carrying On together. i think you ought to know.

A FRIEND.

I made a faint exclamation of disgust and, crumpling up the paper, tossed it into the open grate just as Griselda entered the room.

"What's that you're throwing down so contemptuously?" she asked.

"Filth," I said.

Taking a match from my pocket, I struck it and bent down. Griselda however, was too quick for me. She had stooped down and caught up the crumpled ball of paper and smoothed it out before I could stop her.

She read it, gave a little exclamation of disgust, and tossed it back to me, turning away as she did so. I lighted it and watched it burn.

Griselda had moved away. She was standing by the window looking out into the garden.

"Len," she said without turning round.

"Yes, my dear."

"I'd like to tell you something. Yes, don't stop me. I want to, please. When—when Lawrence Redding came here, I let you think that I had only known him slightly before. That wasn't true. I—I had known him rather well. In fact, before I met you, I had been rather in love with him. I think most people are with Lawrence. I was—well—absolutely silly about him at one time. I don't mean I wrote him compromising letters or anything idiotic like they do in books. But I was rather keen on him once."

"Why didn't you tell me?" I asked.

"Oh! because! I don't know exactly except that—well, you're foolish in some ways. Just because you're so much older than I am, you think that I—

well, that I'm likely to like other people. I thought you'd be tiresome, perhaps, about me and Lawrence being friends."

"You're very clever at concealing things," I said, remembering what she had told me in that room less than a week ago, and the ingenuous natural way she had talked.

"Yes, I've always been able to hide things. In a way, I like doing it."

Her voice held a childlike ring of pleasure in it.

"But it's quite true what I said. I didn't know about Anne, and I wondered why Lawrence was so different, not—well, really not noticing me. I'm not used to it."

There was a pause.

"You do understand, Len?" said Griselda anxiously.

"Yes," I said. "I understand."

But did I?

XXV

I FOUND IT hard to shake off the impression left by the anonymous letter. Pitch soils. However, I gathered up the other three letters, glanced at my watch and started out.

I wondered very much what this might be that had "come to the knowledge" of three ladies simultaneously. I took it to be the same piece of news. In this, I was to realize that my psychology was at fault.

I cannot pretend that my calls took me past the police station. My feet gravitated there of their own accord. I was anxious to know whether Inspector Slack had returned from Old Hall.

I found that he had and, further, that Miss Cram had returned with him. The fair Gladys was seated in the police station carrying off matters with a high hand. She denied absolutely having taken the suitcase to the wood.

"Just because one of these gossiping old cats has nothing better to do than look out of her window all night, you go and pitch upon me. She's been mistaken once, remember, when she said she saw me at the end of the lane on the afternoon of the murder, and if she was mistaken then, in daylight, how can she possibly have recognized me by moonlight?

"Wicked, it is, the way these old ladies go on down here. Say anything, they will. And me asleep in my bed as innocent as can be. You ought to be ashamed of yourselves, the lot of you."

"And supposing the landlady of the Blue Boar identifies the suitcase as yours, Miss Cram?"

"If she says anything of the kind, she's wrong. There's no name on it. Nearly everybody's got a suitcase like that. As for poor Dr. Stone, accusing him of being a common burglar! And he with a lot of letters after his name."

"You refuse to give us any explanation, then, Miss Cram?"

"No refusing about it. You've made a mistake, that's all. You and your meddlesome Marples. I won't say a word more—not without my solicitor present. I'm going this minute—unless you're going to arrest me."

For answer, the Inspector rose and opened the door for her, and, with a toss of the head, Miss Cram walked out.

"That's the line she takes," said Slack, coming back to his chair. "Absolute denial. And of course the old lady may have been mistaken. No jury would believe you could recognize anyone from that distance on a moonlit night. And of course, as I say, the old lady may have made a mistake."

"She may," I said, "but I don't think she did. Miss Marple is usually right. That's what makes her unpopular."

The Inspector grinned.

"That's what Hurst says. Lord, these villages!"

"What about the silver, Inspector?"

"Seemed to be perfectly in order. Of course that meant one lot or the other must be a fake. There's a very good man in Much Benham, an authority on old silver. I've phoned over to him and sent a car to fetch him. We'll soon know which is which. Either the burglary was an accomplished fact, or else it was only planned. Doesn't make a frightful lot of difference either way—I mean as far as we're concerned. Robbery's a small business compared with murder. These two aren't concerned with the murder. We'll maybe get a line on him through the girl—that's why I let her go without any more fuss."

"I wondered," I said.

"A pity about Mr. Redding. It's not often you find a man who goes out of his way to oblige you."

"I suppose not," I said smiling slightly.

"Women cause a lot of trouble," moralized the Inspector.

He sighed and then went on, somewhat to my surprise. "Of course there's Archer."

"Oh!" I said. "You've thought of him?"

"Why, naturally, sir, first thing. It didn't need any anonymous letters to put me on his track."

"Anonymous letters," I said sharply. "Did you get one then?"

"That's nothing new, sir. We get a dozen a day, at least. Oh! yes, we were put wise to Archer. As though the police couldn't look out for themselves! Archer's been under suspicion from the first. The trouble of it is, he's got an alibi. Not that it amounts to anything, but it's awkward to get over."

"What do you mean by its not amounting to anything?" I asked.

"Well, it appears he was with a couple of pals all the afternoon. Not, as I say, that that counts much. Men like Archer and his pals would swear to anything. There's no believing a word they say. We know that. But the public doesn't, and the jury's taken from the public, more's the pity. They know nothing, and ten to one believe everything that's said in the witness box, no matter who it is that says it. And of course Archer himself will swear till he's black in the face that he didn't do it."

"Not so obliging as Mr. Redding," I said with a smile.

"Not he," said the Inspector, making the remark as a plain statement of fact.

"It is natural, I suppose, to cling to life," I mused.

"You'd be surprised if you knew the murderers that have got off through the soft-heartedness of the jury," said the Inspector gloomily.

"But do you really think that Archer did it?" I asked.

It has struck me as curious all along that Inspector Slack never seems to have any personal views of his own on the murder. The easiness or difficulty of getting a conviction are the only points that seem to appeal to him.

"I'd like to be a bit surer," he admitted. "A finger print now, or a foot print, or seen in the vicinity about the time of the crime. Can't risk arresting him without something of that kind. He's been seen round Mr. Redding's house once or twice, but he'd say that was to speak to his mother. A decent body, she is. No, on the whole, I'm for the lady. If I could only get definite proof of blackmail—but you can't get definite proof of anything in this crime! It's theory, theory, theory. It's a sad pity that there's not a single spinster lady living along your road, Mr. Clement. I bet she'd have seen something if there had been."

His words reminded me of my calls, and I took leave of him. It was about the solitary instance when I had seen him in a genial mood.

My first call was on Miss Hartnell. She must have been watching for me from the window, for, before I had time to ring, she had opened the front door, and clasping my hand firmly in hers had led me over the threshold.

"So good of you to come. In here. More private."

We entered a microscopic room, about the size of a hencoop. Miss Hartnell shut the door and, with an air of deep secrecy, waved me to a seat (there were only three). I perceived that she was enjoying herself.

"I'm never one to beat about the bush," she said in her jolly voice, the latter slightly toned down to meet the requirements of the situation. "You know how things go the round in a village like this?"

"Unfortunately," I said, "I do."

"I agree with you. Nobody dislikes gossip more than I do. But there it is. I thought it my duty to tell the police Inspector that I'd called on Mrs. Lestrange the afternoon of the murder and that she was out. I don't expect to be thanked for doing my duty; I just do it. Ingratitude is what you meet with first and last in this life. Why only yesterday that impudent Mrs. Baker—"

"Yes, yes," I said hoping to avert the usual tirade. "Very sad, very sad. But you were saying."

"The lower classes don't know who are their best friends," said Miss Hartnell. "I always say a word in season when I'm visiting. Not that I'm ever thanked for it."

"You were telling the Inspector about your call upon Mrs. Lestrange," I prompted.

"Exactly—and, by the way, he didn't thank me. Said he'd ask for information when he wanted it—not those words exactly, but that was the spirit. There's a different class of men in the police force nowadays."

"Very probably," I said. "But you were going on to say something?"

"I decided that this time I wouldn't go near any wretched Inspector. After all, a clergyman is a gentleman—at least some are," she added.

I gathered that the qualification was not intended to include me.

"If I can help you in any way," I began.

"It's a matter of duty," said Miss Hartnell and closed her mouth with a snap. "I don't want to have to say these things. No one likes it less. But duty is duty."

I waited.

"I've been given to understand," went on Miss Hartnell, turning rather red, "that Mrs. Lestrange gives out that she was at home all the time—that she didn't answer the door because—well, because she didn't choose.

Such airs and graces. I only called as a matter of duty, and to be treated like that!"

"She has been ill," I said mildly.

"Ill? Fiddlesticks. You're too unworldly, Mr. Clement. There's nothing the matter with that woman. Too ill to attend the inquest indeed! Medical certificate from Dr. Haydock! She can wind him round her little finger; everyone knows that. Well, where was I?"

I didn't quite know. It is difficult with Miss Hartnell to know where narrative ends and vituperation begins.

"Oh! about calling on her that afternoon. Well, it's fiddlesticks to say she was in the house. She wasn't. I know."

"How can you possibly know?"

Miss Hartnell's face turned a little redder. In someone less truculent, her demeanour might have been called embarrassed.

"I'd knocked and rung," she explained. "Twice. If not three times. And it occurred to me suddenly that the bell might be out of order."

She was, I was glad to note, unable to look me in the face when saying this. The same builder builds all our houses, and the bells he installs are always clearly audible when standing on the mat outside the front door. Both Miss Hartnell and I knew this perfectly well, but I suppose decencies have to be preserved.

"Yes?" I murmured.

"I didn't want to push my card through the letter box. That would seem so rude, and, whatever I am, I am never rude."

She made this amazing statement without a tremor.

"So I thought I would just go round the house and—and tap on the window pane," she continued unblushingly. "I went all round the house and looked in at all the windows, but there was no one in the house at all."

I understood her perfectly. Taking advantage of the fact that the house was empty, Miss Hartnell had given unbridled rein to her curiosity and had gone round the house, examining the garden and peering in at all the windows to see as much as she could of the interior. She had chosen to tell her story to me, believing that I should be a more sympathetic and lenient audience than the police. The clergy are supposed to give the benefit of the doubt to their parishioners.

I made no comment on the situation. I merely asked a question:

"What time was this, Miss Hartnell?"

"As far as I can remember," said Miss Hartnell, "it must have been close on six o'clock. I went straight home afterwards, and I got in about ten past six, and Mrs. Protheroe came in somewhere round about the half hour, leaving Dr. Stone and Mr. Redding outside, and we talked about bulbs. And all the time the poor Colonel lying murdered. It's a sad world."

"It is sometimes a rather unpleasant one," I said.

I rose.

"And that is all you have to tell me?"

"I just thought it might be important."

"It might," I agreed.

And refusing to be drawn further, much to Miss Hartnell's disappointment, I took my leave.

Miss Wetherby, whom I visited next, received me in a kind of flutter.

"Dear Vicar, how truly kind. You've had tea? Really, you won't? A cushion for your back? It is so kind of you to come round so promptly. Always willing to put yourself out for others."

There was a good deal of this before we came to the point, and even then it was approached with a good deal of circumlocution.

"You must understand that I heard this on the best authority."

In St. Mary Mead, the best authority is always somebody else's servant.

"You can't tell me who told you?"

"I promised, dear Mr. Clement. And I always think a promise should be a sacred thing."

She looked very solemn.

"Shall we say a little bird told me? That is safe, isn't it?"

I longed to say, "It's damned silly." I rather wish I had. I should have liked to observe the effect on Miss Wetherby.

"Well, this little bird told that she saw a certain lady who shall be nameless."

"Another kind of bird?" I inquired.

To my great surprise Miss Wetherby went off into paroxysms of laughter and tapped me playfully on the arm saying:

"Oh! Vicar, you must not be so naughty."

When she had recovered, she went on.

"A certain lady, and where do you think this certain lady was going? She turned into the Vicarage road, but before she did so, she looked up and down the road in a most peculiar way—to see if anyone she knew were noticing her, I imagine."

"And the little bird?" I inquired.

"Paying a visit to the fishmonger's—in the room over the shop."

651Ø32 ZIHS8C

NWØ3Ø9 29JUL97

ETKT ETKT

14-B MSP

SEAT NUMBER DESTINATION

FQTV PERK

SPECIAL SERVICE

NORTHWEST
AIRLINES

PASSENGER'S NAME

RANK/LAURIE

NW3Ø2849713

NORTHWEST

WORLDPERKS®

Northwest's free travel program, WorldPerks, is the best program in the sky. Begin earning awards after only 20,000 miles. No other airline gives you free trips faster. Ask a Northwest agent or flight attendant for information on how you can begin earning miles on today's flight. Before you know it you'll be flying FREE.

I now know where maids go on their days out. I know there is one place they never go if they can help—anywhere in the open air.

"And the time," continued Miss Wetherby, leaning forward mysteriously, "was just before six o'clock."

"On which day?"

Miss Wetherby gave a little scream.

"The day of the murder, of course, didn't I say so?"

"I inferred it," I replied. "And the name of the lady?"

"Begins with an L," said Miss Wetherby nodding her head several times.

Feeling that I had got to the end of the information Miss Wetherby had to impart, I rose to my feet.

"You won't let the police cross-question me, will you?" said Miss Wetherby pathetically, as she clasped my hand in both of hers. "I do shrink from publicity. And to stand up in Court!"

"In special cases," I said, "they let witnesses sit down."

And I escaped.

There was still Mrs. Price Ridley to see. That lady put me in my place at once.

"I will not be mixed up in any police court business," she said firmly, after shaking my hand coldly. "You understand that. On the other hand, having come across a circumstance which needs explaining, I think it should be brought to the notice of the authorities."

"Does it concern Mrs. Lestrange?" I asked.

"Why should it?" demanded Mrs. Price Ridley coldly.

She had me at a disadvantage there.

"It's a very simple matter," she continued. "My maid, Clara, was standing at the front gate; she went down there for a minute or two—she says to get a breath of fresh air. Most unlikely, I should say. Much more probable that she was looking out for the fishmonger's boy—if he calls himself a boy—impudent young jackanapes, thinks because he's seventeen he can joke with all the girls. Anyway, as I say, she was standing at the gate and she heard a sneeze."

"Yes," I said waiting for more.

"That's all. I tell you she heard a sneeze. And don't start telling me I'm not so young as I once was and may have made a mistake, because it was Clara who heard it and she's only nineteen."

"But," I said, "why shouldn't she have heard a sneeze?"

Mrs. Price Ridley looked at me in obvious pity for my poorness of intellect.

"She heard a sneeze on the day of the murder at a time when there was no one in your house. Doubtless the murderer was concealed in the bushes waiting his opportunity. What you have to look for is a man with a cold in his head."

"Or a sufferer from hay fever," I suggested. "But as a matter of fact, Mrs. Price Ridley, I think that mystery has a very easy solution. Our maid, Mary, has been suffering from a severe cold in the head. In fact, her sniffing has tried us very much lately. It must have been her sneeze your maid heard."

"It was a man's sneeze," said Mrs. Price Ridley firmly. "And you couldn't hear your maid sneeze in your kitchen from our gate."

"You couldn't hear anyone sneezing in the study from your gate," I said. "Or at least I very much doubt it."

"I said the man might have been concealed in the shrubbery," said Mrs. Price Ridley. "Doubtless when Clara had gone in, he effected an entrance by the front door."

"Well, of course that's possible," I said.

I tried not to make my voice consciously soothing, but I must have failed, for Mrs. Price Ridley glared at me suddenly.

"I am accustomed not to be listened to, but I might mention also that to leave a tennis racquet carelessly flung down on the grass without a press completely ruins it. And tennis racquets are very expensive nowadays."

There did not seem to be rhyme or reason in this flank attack. It bewildered me utterly.

"But perhaps you don't agree," said Mrs. Price Ridley.

"Oh! I do—certainly."

"I am glad. Well, that is all I have to say. I wash my hands of the whole affair."

She leaned back and closed her eyes like one weary of this world. I thanked her and said good-bye.

On the doorstep, I ventured to ask Clara about her mistress's statement.

"It's quite true, sir, I heard a sneeze. And it wasn't an ordinary sneeze—not by any means."

Nothing about a crime is ever ordinary. The shot was not an ordinary kind of shot. The sneeze was not a usual kind of sneeze. It was, I presume, a special murderer's sneeze. I asked the girl what time this had been, but she was very vague—some time between a quarter and half past six she thought. Anyway, "it was before the mistress had the telephone call and was took bad."

I asked her if she had heard a shot of any kind. And she said the shots had been something awful. After that, I placed very little credence in her statements.

I was just turning in at my own gate when I decided to pay a friend a visit.

Glancing at my watch, I saw that I had just time for it before taking Evensong. I went down the road to Haydock's house. He came out on the doorstep to meet me.

I noticed afresh how worried and haggard he looked. This business seemed to have aged him out of all knowledge.

"I'm glad to see you," he said. "What's the news?"

I told him the latest Stone development.

"A high class thief," he commented. "Well, that explains a lot of things. He'd read up his subject, but he made slips from time to time to me. Protheroe must have caught him out once. You remember the row they had. What do they think about the girl? Is she in it too?"

"Opinion as to that is undecided," I said. "For my own part, I think the girl is all right. She's such a prize idiot," I added.

"Oh! I wouldn't say that. She's rather shrewd, is Miss Gladys Cram. A remarkably healthy specimen. Not likely to trouble members of my profession."

I told him that I was worried about Hawes, and that I was anxious that he should get away for a real rest and change.

Something evasive came into his manner when I said this. His answer did not ring quite true.

"Yes," he said slowly. "I suppose that would be the best thing. Poor chap. Poor chap."

"I thought you didn't like him."

"I don't—not much. But I'm sorry for a lot of people I don't like." He added, after a minute or two, "I'm even sorry for Protheroe. Poor fellow—nobody ever liked him much. Too full of his own rectitude and too self-assertive. It's an unlovable mixture. He was always the same—even as a young man."

"I didn't know you knew him then?"

"Oh! yes. When he lived in Westmoreland, I had a practice not far away. That's a long time ago now. Nearly twenty years."

I sighed. Twenty years ago Griselda was five years old. Time is an odd thing.

"Is that all you came to say to me, Clement?"

I looked up with a start. Haydock was watching me with keen eyes.

"There's something else, isn't there?" he said.

I nodded.

I had been uncertain whether to speak or not when I came in, but now I decided to do so. I like Haydock as well as any man I know. He is a splendid fellow in every way. I felt that what I had to tell might be useful to him.

I recited my interviews with Miss Hartnell and Miss Wetherby.

He was silent for a long time after I'd spoken.

"It's quite true, Clement," he said at last. "I've been trying to shield Mrs. Lestrange from any inconvenience that I could. As a matter of fact, she's an old friend. But that's not my only reason. That medical certificate of mine isn't the put-up job you all think it was."

He paused and then said gravely:

"This is between you and me, Clement. Mrs. Lestrange is doomed."

"What?"

"She's a dying woman. I give her a month at longest. Do you wonder that I want to keep her from being badgered and questioned?"

He went on:

"When she turned into this road that evening, it was here she came—to this house."

"You haven't said so before."

"I didn't want to create talk. Six to seven isn't my time for seeing patients, and everyone knows that. But you can take my word for it that she was here."

"She wasn't here when I came for you, though. I mean when we discovered the body."

"No," he seemed perturbed. "She'd left—to keep an appointment."

"In what direction was the appointment? In her own house?"

"I don't know, Clement. On my honour, I don't know."

I believed him, but—

"And supposing an innocent man is hanged?" I said.

He shook his head.

"No," he said. "No one will be hanged for the murder of Colonel Protheroe. You can take my word for that."

But that is just what I could not do. And yet the certainty in his voice was very great.

"No one will be hanged," he repeated.

"This man, Archer—"

He made an impatient movement.

"Hasn't got brains enough to wipe his finger prints off the pistol."

"Perhaps not," I said dubiously.

Then I remembered something, and taking the little brownish crystal I had found in the wood from my pocket I held it out to him and asked him what it was.

"H'm," he hesitated. "Looks like picric acid. Where did you find it?"

"That," I replied, "is Sherlock Holmes' secret."

He smiled.

"What is picric acid?"

"Well, it's an explosive."

"Yes, I know that, but it's got another use, hasn't it?"

He nodded.

"It's used medically—in solution for burns. Wonderful stuff."

I held out my hand and rather reluctantly he handed it back to me.

"It's of no consequence probably," I said. "But I found it in rather an unusual place."

"You won't tell me where?"

Rather childishly, I wouldn't.

He had his secrets. Well, I would have mine.

I was a little hurt that he had not confided in me more fully.

XXVI

I WAS IN a strange mood when I mounted the pulpit that night.

The church was unusually full. I cannot believe that it was the prospect of Hawes preaching which had attracted so many. Hawes' sermons are dull and dogmatic. And if the news had got round that I was preaching instead, that would not have attracted them either. For my sermons are dull and scholarly. Neither, I am afraid, can I attribute it to devotion.

Everybody had come, I concluded, to see who else was there, and possibly to exchange a little gossip in the church porch afterwards.

Haydock was in church, which is unusual, and also Lawrence Redding. And, to my surprise, beside Lawrence I saw the white strained face of Hawes. Anne Protheroe was there, but she usually attends Evensong on Sundays, though I had hardly thought she would today. I was far more surprised to see Lettice. Churchgoing was compulsory on Sunday morning—Colonel Protheroe was adamant on that point—but I had never seen Lettice at evening service before.

Gladys Cram was there, looking rather blatantly young and healthy against a background of wizened spinsters, and I fancied that a dim figure at the end of the church, who had slipped in late, was Mrs. Lestrange.

I need hardly say that Mrs. Price Ridley, Miss Hartnell, Miss Wetherby and Miss Marple were there in full force. All the village people were there, with hardly a single exception. I don't know when we have had such a crowded congregation.

Crowds are queer things. There was a magnetic atmosphere that night, and the first person to feel its influence was myself.

As a rule, I prepare my sermons beforehand. I am careful and conscientious over them, but no one is better aware than myself of their deficiencies.

Tonight I was of necessity preaching *ex tempore,* and as I looked down on the sea of upturned faces, a sudden madness entered my brain. I ceased to be in any sense a minister of God. I became an actor. I had an audience before me and I wanted to move that audience—and more, I felt the power to move it.

I am not proud of what I did that night. I am an utter disbeliever in the emotional revivalist spirit. Yet that night I acted the part of a raving, ranting evangelist.

I gave out my text slowly.

I am come to call not the righteous but the sinners to repentance.

I repeated it twice, and I heard my own voice, a resonant, ringing voice unlike the voice of the everyday Leonard Clement.

I saw Griselda from her front pew look up in surprise, and Dennis follow her example.

I held my breath for a moment or two, and then I let myself rip.

The congregation in that church were in a state of pent-up emotion, ripe to be played upon. I played upon them. I exhorted sinners to repentance. I lashed myself into a kind of emotional frenzy. Again and again I threw out a denouncing hand and reiterated the phrase:

"I am speaking to *you.*"

And each time, from different parts of the church, a kind of sighing gasp went up.

Mass-emotion is a strange and terrible thing.

I finished up with those beautiful and poignant words—perhaps the most poignant words in the whole Bible:

"This very night shall thy soul be required of thee . . ."

It was a strange brief possession. When I got back to the Vicarage I was my usual faded, indeterminate self. I found Griselda rather pale. She slipped her arm through mine.

"Len," she said. "You were rather terrible tonight. I—I didn't like it. I've never heard you preach like that before."

"I don't suppose you ever will again," I said, sinking down wearily on the sofa. I was tired.

"What made you do it?"

"A sudden madness came over me."

"Oh! it—it wasn't something special?"

"What do you mean—something special?"

"I wondered—that was all. You're very unexpected, Len. I never feel I really know you."

We sat down to cold supper, Mary being out.

"There's a note for you in the hall," said Griselda. "Get it, will you, Dennis?"

Dennis, who had been very silent, obeyed.

I took it and groaned. Across the top left-hand corner was written, *By hand—Urgent.*

"This," I said, "must be from Miss Marple. There's no one else left."

I had been perfectly correct in my assumption.

Dear Mr. Clement,

I should so much like to have a little chat with you about one or two things that have occurred to me. I feel we should all try and help in elucidating this sad mystery. I will come over about half past nine, if I may, and tap on your study window. Perhaps dear Griselda would be so very kind as to run over here and cheer up my nephew. And Mr. Dennis too, of course, if he cares to come. If I do not hear, I will expect them and will come over myself at the time I have stated.

Yours very sincerely,

Jane Marple.

I handed the note to Griselda.

"Oh! we'll go," she said cheerfully. "A glass or two of home-made liqueur is just what one needs on Sunday evening. I think it's Mary's blanc mange that is so frightfully depressing. It's like something out of a mortuary."

Dennis seemed less charmed at the prospect.

"It's all very well for you," he grumbled. "You can talk all this high brow stuff about art and books. I always feel a perfect fool sitting and listening to you."

"That's good for you," said Griselda serenely. "It puts you in your place. Anyway I don't think Mr. Raymond West is so frightfully clever as he pretends to be."

"Very few of us are," I said.

I wondered very much what exactly it was that Miss Marple wished to talk over. Of all the ladies in my congregation, I consider her by far the shrewdest. Not only does she see and hear practically everything that goes on, but she draws amazingly neat and apposite deductions from the facts that come under her notice.

If I were at any time to set out on a career of deceit, it would be of Miss Marple that I should be afraid.

What Griselda called the Nephew Amusing Party started off at a little after nine, and while I was waiting for Miss Marple to arrive I amused myself by drawing up a kind of schedule of the facts connected with the crime. I arranged them so far as possible in chronological order. I am not a punctual person, but I am a neat one, and I like things jotted down in a methodical fashion.

At half past nine punctually, there was a little tap on the window and I rose and admitted Miss Marple.

She had a very fine Shetland shawl thrown over her head and shoulders, and was looking rather old and frail. She came in full of little fluttering remarks.

"So good of you to let me come—and so good of dear Griselda—Raymond admires her so much—the perfect Greuze he always calls her. Shall I sit here? I am not taking your chair? Oh! thank you. No, I won't have a footstool."

I deposited the Shetland shawl on a chair and returned to take a chair facing my guest. We looked at each other, and a little deprecating smile broke out on her face.

"I feel that you must be wondering why—why I am so interested in all this. You may possibly think it's very unwomanly. No—please—I should like to explain if I may."

She paused a moment, a pink colour suffusing her cheeks.

"You see," she began at last, "living alone as I do, in a rather out of the way part of the world, one has to have a hobby. There is, of course, woolwork, and Guides, and Welfare, and sketching, but my hobby is—and always has been—Human Nature. So varied—and so very fascinating. And, of course, in a small village, with nothing to distract one, one has such ample opportunity for becoming what I might call proficient in one's study. One begins to class people, quite definitely, just as though they were birds or flowers, group so and so, genus this, species that. Sometimes, of course, one makes mistakes, but less and less as time goes on. And then, too, one tests oneself. One takes a little problem—for instance the gill of picked shrimps that amused dear Griselda so much—a quite unimportant mystery, but absolutely incomprehensible unless one solves it right. And then there was that matter of the changed cough drops, and the butcher's wife's umbrella—the last absolutely meaningless, unless on the assumption that the greengrocer was not behaving at all nicely with the chemist's wife—which, of course, turned out to be the case. It is so fascinating, you know, to apply one's judgment and find that one is right."

"You usually are, I believe," I said smiling.

"That, I am afraid, is what has made me a little conceited," confessed Miss Marple. "But I have always wondered whether, if some day a really big mystery came along, I should be able to do the same thing. I mean—just solve it correctly. Logically, it ought to be exactly the same thing. After all, a tiny working model of a torpedo is just the same as a real torpedo."

"You mean it's all a question of relativity," I said slowly. "It should be—logically, I admit. But I don't know whether it really is."

"Surely it must be the same," said Miss Marple. "The—what one used to call the factors at school—are the same. There's money, and mutual attraction between people of an—er—opposite sex—and there's queerness, of course—so many people are a little queer, aren't they?—in fact, most people are when you know them well. And normal people do such astonishing things sometimes, and abnormal people are sometimes so very sane and ordinary. In fact, the only way is to compare people with other people you have known or come across. You'd be surprised if you knew how very few distinct types there are in all."

"You frighten me," I said. "I feel I'm being put under the microscope."

"Of course, I wouldn't dream of saying any of this to Colonel Melchett—such an autocratic man, isn't he?—and poor Inspector Slack—well, he's exactly like the young lady in the boot shop who wants to sell you patent leather because she's got it in your size, and doesn't take any notice of the fact that you want brown calf."

That really is a very good description of Slack.

"But you, Mr. Clement, know, I'm sure, quite as much about the crime as Inspector Slack. I thought, if we could work together—"

"I wonder," I said. "I think each one of us in his secret heart fancies himself as Sherlock Holmes."

Then I told her of the three summons I had received that afternoon. I told her of Anne's discovery of the picture with the slashed face. I also told her of Miss Cram's attitude at the police station, and I described Haydock's identification of the crystal I had picked up.

"Having found that myself," I finished up, "I should like it to be important. But it's probably got nothing to do with the case."

"I have been reading a lot of American detective stories from the library lately," said Miss Marple, "hoping to find them helpful."

"Was there anything in them about picric acid?"

"I'm afraid not. I do remember reading a story once, though, in which a man was poisoned by picric acid and lanoline being rubbed on him as an ointment."

"But as nobody has been poisoned here, that doesn't seem to enter into the question," I said.

Then I took up my schedule and handed it to her.

"I've tried," I said, "to recapitulate the facts of the case as clearly as possible."

MY SCHEDULE

THURSDAY 21st. inst.

12.30 a.m. *Colonel Protheroe alters his appointment from six to six fifteen. Overheard by half village very probably.*

12.45. *Pistol last seen in its proper place. (But this is doubtful as Mrs. Archer had previously said she could not remember.)*

5.30 (*approx.*). *Colonel and Mrs. Protheroe leave Old Hall for village in car.*

5.30. *Fake call put through to me from the East Lodge, Old Hall.*

6.15 (*or a minute or two earlier*). *Colonel Protheroe arrives at Vicarage. Is shown into study by Mary.*

6.20. *Mrs. Protheroe comes along back lane and across garden to study window. Colonel Protheroe not visible.*

6.29. *Call from Lawrence Redding's cottage put through to Mrs. Price Ridley (according to exchange).*

6.30–6.35. *Shot heard (accepting telephone call time as correct). Lawrence Redding, Anne Protheroe, and Dr. Stone's evidence seem to point to its being earlier, but Mrs. P. R. probably right.*

6.45. *Lawrence Redding arrives Vicarage and finds the body.*

6.48. *I meet Lawrence Redding.*

6.49. *Body discovered by me.*

6.55. *Haydock examines body.*

Note. The only two people who have no kind of alibi for 6.30–6.35 are Miss Cram and Mrs. Lestrange. Miss Cram says she was at the barrow, but no confirmation. It seems reasonable, however, to dismiss her from case, as there seems nothing to connect her with it. Mrs. Lestrange left Dr. Haydock's house some time after six to keep an appointment. Where was the appointment, and with whom? It could hardly have been with Colonel Protheroe, as he expected to be engaged with me. It is true that Mrs. Lestrange was near the spot at the time the crime was committed, but it seems doubtful what motive she could have had for murdering him. She did not gain by his death, and the Inspector's theory of blackmail I cannot accept. Mrs. Lestrange is not that kind of woman. Also, it seems unlikely that she should have got hold of Lawrence Redding's pistol.

"Very clear," said Miss Marple nodding her head in approval. "Very clear, indeed. Gentlemen always make such excellent memoranda."

"You agree with what I have written?" I asked.

"Oh! yes—you have put it all beautifully."

I asked her the question then that I had been meaning to put all along.

"Miss Marple," I said. "Whom do you suspect? You once said that there were seven people."

"Quite that, I should think," said Miss Marple absently. "I expect everyone of us suspects someone different. In fact, one can see they do."

She didn't ask me whom I suspected.

"The point is," she said, "that one must provide an explanation for everything. Each thing has got to be explained away satisfactorily. If you have a theory that fits every fact—well, then it must be the right one. But that's extremely difficult. If it wasn't for that note—"

"The note?" I said surprised.

"Yes, you remember, I told you. That note has worried me all along. It's wrong, somehow."

"Surely," I said, "that is explained now. It was written at six thirty-five, and another hand—the murderer's—put the misleading 6.20 at the top. I think that is clearly established."

"But even then," said Miss Marple, "it's all wrong."

"But why?"

"Listen—" Miss Marple leant forward eagerly. "Mrs. Protheroe passed my garden, as I told you, and she went as far as the study window and she looked in and she didn't see Colonel Protheroe."

"Because he was writing at the desk," I said.

"And that's what's all wrong. That was at twenty past six. We agreed that he wouldn't sit down to say he couldn't wait any longer until after half past six—so, why was he sitting at the writing table then?"

"I never thought of that," I said slowly.

"Let us, dear Mr. Clement, just go over it again. Mrs. Protheroe comes to the window and she thinks the room is empty—she must have thought so, because otherwise she would never have gone down to the studio to meet Mr. Redding. It wouldn't have been safe. The room must have been absolutely silent if she thought it was empty. And that leaves us three alternatives, doesn't it?"

"You mean—"

"Well, the first alternative would be that Colonel Protheroe was dead already—but I don't think that's the most likely one. To begin with, he'd only been there about five minutes, and she or I would have heard the shot; and, secondly, the same difficulty remains about his being at the writing table. The second alternative is, of course, that he was sitting at the writing table writing a note, but in that case it must have been a different note altogether. It can't have been to say he couldn't wait. And the third—"

"Yes?" I said.

"Well, the third is, of course, that Mrs. Protheroe was right, and that the room was actually empty."

"You mean that, after he had been shown in, he went out again and came back later?"

"Yes."

"But why should he have done that?"

Miss Marple spread out her hands in a little gesture of bewilderment.

"That would mean looking at the case from an entirely different angle," I said.

"One so often has to do that—about everything. Don't you think so?"

I did not reply. I was going over carefully in my mind the three alternatives that Miss Marple had suggested.

With a slight sigh, the old lady rose to her feet.

"I must be getting back. I am very glad to have had this little chat—though we haven't got very far, have we?"

"To tell you the truth," I said, as I fetched her shawl, "the whole thing seems to me a bewildering maze."

"Oh! I wouldn't say that. I think, on the whole, one theory fits nearly everything. That is, if you admit one coincidence—and I think one coincidence is allowable. More than one, of course, is unlikely."

"Do you really think that? About the theory, I mean?" I asked looking at her.

"I admit that there is one flaw in my theory—one fact that I can't get over. Oh! if only that note had been something quite different—"

She sighed and shook her head. She moved towards the window and absent-mindedly reached up her hand and felt the rather depressed looking plant that stood in a stand.

"You know, dear Mr. Clement, this should be watered oftener. Poor thing, it needs it badly. Your maid should water it every day. I suppose it is she who attends to it?"

"As much," I said, "as she attends to anything."

"A little raw at present," suggested Miss Marple.

"Yes," I said. "And Griselda steadily refuses to attempt to cook her. Her idea is that only a thoroughly undesirable maid will remain with us. However, Mary herself gave us notice the other day."

"Indeed. I always imagined she was very fond of you both."

"I haven't noticed it," I said. "But as a matter of fact, it was Lettice Protheroe who upset her. Mary came back from the inquest in rather a temperamental state and found Lettice here and—well, they had words."

"Oh!" said Miss Marple. She was just about to step through the window when she stopped suddenly, and a bewildering series of changes passed over her face.

"Oh! dear," she muttered to herself. "I have been stupid. So that was it! Perfectly possible all the time."

"I beg your pardon?"

She turned a worried face upon me.

"Nothing. An idea that has just occurred to me. I must go home and think things out thoroughly. Do you know, I believe I have been extremely stupid—almost incredibly so."

"I find that hard to believe," I said gallantly.

I escorted her through the window and across the lawn.

"Can you tell me what it is that has occurred to you so suddenly?" I asked.

"I would rather not—just at present. You see, there is still a possibility that I may be mistaken. But I do not think so. Here we are at my garden gate. Thank you so much. Please do not come any farther."

"Is the note still a stumbling block?" I asked as she passed through the gate and latched it behind her.

She looked at me abstractedly.

"The note? Oh! of course that wasn't the real note. I never thought it was. Good night, Mr. Clement."

She went rapidly up the path to the house, leaving me staring after her.

I didn't know what to think.

XXVII

GRISELDA AND DENNIS had not yet returned. I realized that the most natural thing would have been for me to go up to the house with Miss Marple and fetch them home. Both she and I had been so entirely taken up with our preoccupation over the mystery that we had forgotten anybody existed in the world except ourselves.

I was just standing in the hall, wondering whether I would not even now go over and join them, when the door bell rang.

I crossed over to it. I saw there was a letter in the box and, presuming that this was the cause of the ring, I took it out.

As I did so, however, the bell rang again, and I shoved the letter hastily into my pocket and opened the front door.

It was Colonel Melchett.

"Hullo, Clement. I'm on my way home from town in the car. Thought I'd just look in and see if you could give me a drink."

"Delighted," I said. "Come into the study."

He pulled off the leather coat that he was wearing and followed me into the study. I fetched the whisky and soda and two glasses. Melchett was standing in front of the fireplace, legs wide apart, stroking his closely clipped moustache.

"I've got one bit of news for you, Clement. Most astounding thing you've ever heard. But let that go for the minute. How are things going down here? Any more old ladies hot on the scent?"

"They're not doing so badly," I said. "One of them, at all events, thinks she's got there."

"Our friend, Miss Marple, eh?"

"Our friend Miss Marple."

"Women like that always think they know everything," said Colonel Melchett.

He sipped his whisky and soda appreciatively.

"It's probably unnecessary interference on my part asking," I said, "but I suppose somebody has questioned the fish boy. I mean, if the murderer left by the front door, there's a chance the boy may have seen him."

"Slack questioned him right enough," said Melchett, "but the boy says he didn't meet anybody. Hardly likely he would. The murderer wouldn't be exactly courting observation. Lots of cover by your front gate. He would have taken a look to see if the road was clear. The boy had to call at the Vicarage, at Haydock's and at Mrs. Price Ridley's. Easy enough to dodge him."

"Yes," I said. "I suppose it would be."

"On the other hand," went on Melchett, "if by any chance that rascal Archer did the job, and young Fred Jackson saw him about the place, I doubt very much whether he'd let on. Archer is a cousin of his."

"Do you seriously suspect Archer?"

"Well, you know, old Protheroe had his knife into Archer pretty badly. Lots of bad blood between them. Leniency wasn't Protheroe's strong point."

"No," I said. "He was a very ruthless man."

"What I say is," said Melchett, "live and let live. Of course, the law's the law, but it never hurts to give a man the benefit of the doubt. That's what Protheroe never did."

"He prided himself on it," I said.

There was a pause and then I asked:

"What is this 'astounding bit of news' you promised me?"

"Well, it is astounding. You know that unfinished letter that Protheroe was writing when he was killed?"

"Yes."

"We got an expert on it—to say whether the 6.20 was added by a different hand. Naturally we sent up samples of Protheroe's handwriting. And do you know the verdict? That letter was never written by Protheroe at all."

"You mean a forgery?"

"It's a forgery. The 6.20 they think is written in a different hand again —but they're not sure about that. The heading is in a different ink, but the letter itself is a forgery. Protheroe never wrote it."

"Are they certain?"

"Well, they're as certain as experts ever are. You know what an expert is! Oh! but they're sure enough."

"Amazing," I said.

Then a memory assailed me.

"Why," I said, "I remember at the time Mrs. Protheroe said it wasn't like her husband's handwriting at all, and I took no notice."

"Really?"

"I thought it one of those silly remarks women will make. If there seemed one thing sure on earth it was that Protheroe had written that note."

We looked at each other.

"It's curious," I said slowly. "Miss Marple was saying this evening that that note was all wrong."

"Confound the woman, she couldn't know more about it if she had committed the murder herself."

At that moment the telephone bell rang. There is a queer kind of psychology about a telephone bell. It rang now persistently and with a kind of sinister significance.

I went over and took up the receiver.

"This is the Vicarage," I said. "Who's speaking?"

A strange high-pitched hysterical voice came over the wire.

"I want to confess," it said. *"My God, I want to confess."*

"Hullo," I said. "Hullo. Look here, you've cut me off. What number was that?"

A languid voice said it didn't know. It added that it was sorry I had been troubled.

I put down the receiver, and turned to Melchett.

"You once said," I remarked, "that you would go mad if anyone else accused themselves of the crime."

"What about it?"

"That was someone who wanted to confess . . . and the exchange has cut us off."

Melchett dashed over and took up the receiver.

"I'll speak to them."

"Do," I said. "You may have some effect. I'll leave you to it. I'm going out. I've a fancy I recognized that voice."

XXVIII

I HURRIED DOWN the village street. It was eleven o'clock, and at eleven o'clock on a Sunday night the whole village of St. Mary Mead might be dead. I saw, however, a light in a first floor window as I passed, and, realizing that Hawes was still up, I stopped and rang the door bell.

After what seemed a long time, Hawes' landlady, Mrs. Sadler, laboriously unfastened two bolts, a chain, and turned a key, and peered out at me suspiciously.

"Why, it's Vicar!" she exclaimed.

"Good evening," I said. "I want to see Mr. Hawes. I see there's a light in the window, so he's up still."

"That may be. I've not seen him since I took up his supper. He's had a quiet evening—no one to see him, and he's not been out."

I nodded, and, passing her, went quickly up the stairs. Hawes has a bedroom and sitting room on the first floor.

I passed into the latter. Hawes was lying back in a long chair asleep. My entrance did not wake him. An empty cachet box and a glass of water, half full, stood beside him.

On the floor, by his left foot, was a crumpled sheet of paper with writing on it. I picked it up and straightened it out.

It began: *"My dear Clement—"*

I read it through, uttered an exclamation and shoved it into my pocket. Then I bent over Hawes and studied him attentively.

Next, reaching for the telephone which stood by his elbow, I gave the number of the Vicarage. Melchett must have been still trying to trace the call, for I was told that the number was engaged. Asking them to call me, I put the instrument down again.

I put my hand into my pocket to look at the paper I had picked up once more. With it, I drew out the note that I had found in the letter box, and which was still unopened.

Its appearance was horribly familiar. It was the same handwriting as the anonymous letter that had come that afternoon.

I tore it open.

I read it once—twice—unable to realize its contents.

I was beginning to read it a third time when the telephone rang. Like a man in a dream I picked up the receiver and spoke.

"Hullo?"

"Hullo."

"Is that you, Melchett?"

"Yes, where are you? I've traced that call. The number is—"

"I know the number."

"Oh! good. Is that where you are speaking from?"

"Yes."

"What about that confession?"

"I've got the confession all right."

"You mean you've got the murderer?"

I had then the strongest temptation of my life. I looked at Hawes. I looked at the crumpled letter. I looked at the anonymous scrawl. I looked at the empty cachet box with the name of Cherubim on it. I remembered a certain casual conversation.

I made an immense effort.

"I—don't know," I said. "You'd better come round."

And I gave him the address.

Then I sat down in the chair opposite Hawes to think.

I had two clear minutes in which to do so.

In two minutes time, Melchett would have arrived.

I took up the anonymous letter and read it through again for the third time.

Then I closed my eyes and thought. . . .

XXIX

I DON'T KNOW how long I sat there—only a few minutes in reality, I suppose. Yet it seemed as though an eternity had passed when I heard the door open and, turning my head, looked up to see Melchett entering the room.

He stared at Hawes asleep in his chair, then turned to me.

"What's this, Clement? What does it all mean?"

Of the two letters in my hand I selected one and passed it to him. He read it aloud in a low voice.

MY DEAR CLEMENT:

It is a peculiarly unpleasant thing that I have to say. After all, I think I prefer writing it. We can discuss it at a later date. It concerns the recent peculations. I am sorry to say that I have satisfied myself beyond any possible doubt as to the identity of the culprit. Painful as it is for me to have to accuse an ordained priest of the church, my duty is only too painfully clear. An example must be made and—

He looked at me questioningly. At this point the writing tailed off in an undistinguishable scrawl where death had overtaken the writer's hand.

Melchett drew a deep breath, then looked at Hawes.

"So that's the solution! The one man we never even considered. And remorse drove him to confess!"

"He's been very queer lately," I said.

Suddenly Melchett strode across to the sleeping man with a sharp exclamation. He seized him by the shoulder and shook him, at first gently, then with increasing violence.

"He's not asleep! He's drugged! What's the meaning of this?"

His eye went to the empty cachet box. He picked it up.

"Has he—?"

"I think so," I said. "He showed me these the other day. Told me he'd been warned against an overdose. It's his way out, poor chap. Perhaps the best way. It's not for us to judge him."

But Melchett was Chief Constable of the County before anything else. The arguments that appealed to me had no weight with him. He had caught a murderer and he wanted his murderer hanged.

In one second he was at the telephone, jerking the receiver up and down impatiently until he got a reply. He asked for Haydock's number. Then there was a further pause during which he stood, his ear to the telephone and his eyes on the limp figure in the chair.

"Hullo—Hullo—Hullo—is that Dr. Haydock's? Will the doctor come around at once to High Street? Mr. Hawes'. It's urgent—what's that? Well, what number is it, then? Oh! sorry."

He rang off, fuming.

"Wrong number, wrong number—always wrong numbers! And a man's life hanging on it. HULLO—you gave me the wrong number—yes—don't waste time—give me three nine—*nine,* not five."

Another period of impatience—shorter this time.

"Hullo—is that you, Haydock? Melchett speaking. Come to 19 High Street at once, will you? Hawes has taken some kind of overdose. At once, man, it's vital."

He rang off, strode impatiently up and down the room.

"Why on earth you didn't get hold of the doctor at once, Clement, I cannot think. Your wits must have all gone wool gathering."

Fortunately it never occurs to Melchett that anyone can possibly have any different ideas on conduct from those he holds himself. I said nothing and he went on:

"Where did you find this letter?"

"Crumpled on the floor—where it had fallen from his hand."

"Extraordinary business—that old maid was right about its being the wrong note we found. Wonder how she tumbled to that. But what an ass the fellow was not to destroy this one. Fancy keeping it—the most damaging evidence you can imagine!"

"Human nature is full of inconsistencies."

"If it weren't, I doubt if we should ever catch a murderer! Sooner or later they always do some fool things. You're looking very under the weather, Clement. I suppose this has been the most awful shock to you?"

"It has. As I say, Hawes has been queer in his manner for some time, but I never dreamed—"

"Who would? Hullo, that sounds like a car." He went across to the window, pushing up the sash and leaning out. "Yes, it's Haydock all right."

A moment later the doctor entered the room.

In a few succinct words, Melchett explained the situation.

Haydock is not a man who ever shows his feelings. He merely raised his eyebrows, nodded, and strode across to his patient. He felt his pulse, raised the eyelid and looked intently at the eye.

Then he turned to Melchett.

"Want me to save him for the gallows?" he asked. "He's pretty far gone, you know. It will be touch and go anyway. I doubt if I can bring him round."

"Do everything possible."

"Right."

He busied himself with the case he had brought with him, preparing a hypodermic injection which he injected into Hawes' arm. Then he stood up.

"Best thing is to run him into Much Benham—to the Hospital there. Give me a hand to get him down to the car."

We both lent our assistance. As Haydock climbed into the driving seat, he threw a parting remark over his shoulder.

"You won't be able to hang him, you know, Melchett."

"You mean he won't recover?"

"May or may not. I didn't mean that. I mean that even if he does recover—well, the poor devil wasn't responsible for his actions. I shall give evidence to that effect."

"What did he mean by that?" asked Melchett as we went upstairs again.

I explained that Hawes had been a victim of *encephalitis lethargica*.

"Sleeping sickness, eh? Always some good reason nowadays for every dirty action that's done. Don't you agree?"

"Science is teaching us a lot."

"Science be damned—I beg your pardon, Clement—but all this namby pambyism annoys me. I'm a plain man. Well, I suppose we'd better have a look round here."

But at this moment there was an interruption—and a most amazing one. The door opened and Miss Marple walked into the room.

She was pink and somewhat flustered, and seemed to realize our condition of bewilderment.

"So sorry—so very sorry—to intrude—good evening, Colonel Melchett. As I say, I am so sorry, but hearing that Mr. Hawes was taken ill, I felt I must come round and see if I couldn't do something."

She paused. Colonel Melchett was regarding her in a somewhat disgusted fashion.

"Very kind of you, Miss Marple," he said drily. "But no need to trouble. How did you know, by the way?"

It was the question I had been yearning to ask!

"The telephone," explained Miss Marple. "So careless with their wrong numbers, aren't they? You spoke to me first, thinking I was Dr. Haydock. My number is three five."

"So that was it!" I exclaimed.

"There is always some perfectly good and reasonable explanation for Miss Marple's omniscience.

"And so," she continued, "I just came round to see if I could be of any use."

"Very kind of you," said Melchett again, even more drily this time. "But nothing to be done. Haydock's taken him off to hospital."

"Actually to hospital? Oh, that's a great relief! I am so very glad to hear it. He'll be quite safe there. When you say 'nothing to be done,' you don't mean that there's nothing to be done for him, do you? You don't mean that he won't recover?"

"It's very doubtful," I said.

Miss Marple's eyes had gone to the cachet box.

"I suppose he took an overdose?" she said.

Melchett, I think, was in favour of being reticent. Perhaps I might have been under other circumstances. But my discussion of the case with Miss Marple was too fresh in my mind for me to have the same view, though I must admit that her rapid appearance on the scene and eager curiosity repelled me slightly.

"You had better look at this," I said, and handed her Protheroe's unfinished letter.

She took it and read it without any appearance of surprise.

"You had already deduced something of the kind, had you not?" I asked.

"Yes—yes, indeed. May I ask you, Mr. Clement, what made you come here this evening? That is a point which puzzles me. You and Colonel Melchett—not at all what I should have expected."

I explained the telephone call, and that I believed I had recognized Hawes' voice. Miss Marple nodded thoughtfully.

"Very interesting. Very Providential—if I may use the term. Yes, it brought you here in the nick of time."

"In the nick of time for what?" I said bitterly.

Miss Marple looked surprised.

"To save Mr. Hawes' life, of course."

"Don't you think," I said, "that it might be better if Hawes didn't recover? Better for him—better for everyone. We know the truth now and—"

I stopped—for Miss Marple was nodding her head with such a peculiar vehemence that it made me lose the thread of what I was saying.

"Of course," she said. "Of course! That's what he wants you to think! That you know the truth—and that it's best for everyone as it is. Oh, yes, it all fits in—the letter, and the overdose, and poor Mr. Hawes' state of mind and his confession. It all fits in—but it's wrong."

We stared at her.

"That's why I am so glad Mr. Hawes is safe—in the hospital—where no one can get at him. If he recovers, he'll tell you the truth."

"The truth?"

"Yes—that he never touched a hair of Colonel Protheroe's head."

"But the telephone call," I said. "The letter—the overdose. It's all so clear."

"That's what he wants you to think. Oh, he's very clever! Keeping the letter and using it this way was very clever indeed."

"Who do you mean," I said, "by 'he'?"

"I mean the murderer," said Miss Marple.

She added very quietly:

"I mean Mr. Lawrence Redding."

XXX

We stared at her. I really think that for a moment or two we really believed she was out of her mind. The accusation seemed so utterly preposterous.

Colonel Melchett was the first to speak. He spoke kindly and with a kind of pitying tolerance.

"That is absurd, Miss Marple," he said. "Young Redding has been completely cleared."

"Naturally," said Miss Marple. "He saw to that."

"On the contrary," said Colonel Melchett drily, "he did his best to get himself accused of the murder."

"Yes," said Miss Marple. "He took us all in that way—myself as much as anyone else. You will remember, dear Mr. Clement, that I was quite taken aback when I heard Mr. Redding had confessed to the crime. It upset all my ideas and made me think him innocent—when up to then I had felt convinced that he was guilty."

"Then it was Lawrence Redding you suspected?"

"I know that in books it is always the most unlikely person. But I never find that rule applies in real life. There it is so often the obvious that is true. Much as I have always liked Mrs. Protheroe, I could not avoid coming to the conclusion that she was completely under Mr. Redding's thumb and would do anything he told her, and of course he is not the kind of young man who would dream of running away with a penniless woman. From his point of view it was necessary that Colonel Protheroe should be removed—and so he removed him. One of those charming young men who have *no* moral sense."

Colonel Melchett had been snorting impatiently for some time. Now he broke out:

"Absolute nonsense—the whole thing! Redding's time is fully accounted for up to 6.45, and Haydock says positively Protheroe couldn't have been shot then. I suppose you think you know better than a doctor. Or do you suggest that Haydock is deliberately lying—the Lord knows why?"

"I think Dr. Haydock's evidence was absolutely truthful. He is a very upright man. And of course it was Mrs. Protheroe who actually shot Colonel Protheroe—not Mr. Redding."

Again we stared at her. Miss Marple arranged her lace fichu, pushed back the fleecy shawl that draped her shoulders, and began to deliver a gentle, old maidish lecture comprising the most astounding statements in the most natural way in the world.

"I have not thought it right to speak until now. One's own belief—even so strong as to amount to knowledge—is not the same as proof. And unless one has an explanation that will fit all the facts (as I was saying to dear Mr. Clement this evening) one cannot advance it with any real conviction. And my own explanation was not quite complete—it lacked just one thing—but suddenly, just as I was leaving Mr. Clement's study, I noticed the palm in the pot by the window—and—well—there the whole thing was: Clear as daylight!"

"Mad—quite mad," murmured Melchett to me.

But Miss Marple beamed on us serenely and went on in her gentle lady-like voice.

"I was very sorry to believe what I did—very sorry. Because I liked them both. But you know what human nature is. And to begin with, when first he and then she both confessed in the most foolish way—well, I was more relieved than I could say. I had been wrong. And I began to think of other people who had a possible motive for wishing Colonel Protheroe out of the way."

"The seven suspects!" I murmured.

She smiled at me.

"Yes, indeed. There was that man Archer—not likely, but primed with drink (so inflaming) you never know. And of course there was your Mary. She's been walking out with Archer a long time, and she's a queer tempered girl. Motive and opportunity—why, she was alone in the house! Old Mrs. Archer could easily have got the pistol from Mr. Redding's house for either of those two. And then, of course, there was Lettice—wanting freedom and money to do as she liked. I've known many cases where the most beautiful and ethereal girls have shown next to no moral scruple—though, of course, gentlemen never wish to believe it of them."

I winced.

"And then there was the tennis racquet," continued Miss Marple.

"The tennis racquet?"

"Yes, the one Mrs. Price Ridley's Clara saw lying on the grass by the Vicarage gate. That looked as though Mr. Dennis had got back earlier from his tennis party than he said. Boys of sixteen are so very susceptible and so very unbalanced. Whatever the motive—for Lettice's sake or for yours—it was a possibility. And then, of course, there was poor Mr. Hawes and you—not both of you naturally, but alternatively, as the lawyers say."

"Me?" I exclaimed in lively astonishment.

"Well, yes. I do apologize—and indeed I never really thought—but there was the question of these disappearing sums of money. Either you or Mr. Hawes must be guilty, and Mrs. Price Ridley was going about everywhere hinting that you were the person in fault—principally because you objected so vigorously to any kind of inquiry into the matter. Of course, I myself was always convinced it was Mr. Hawes—he reminded me so much of that unfortunate organist I mentioned—but all the same one couldn't be absolutely sure—"

"Human nature being what it is," I ended grimly.

"Exactly. And then of course there was dear Griselda."

"But Mrs. Clement was completely out of it," interrupted Melchett. "She returned by the 6.50 train."

"That's what she said," retorted Miss Marple. "One should never go by what people say. The 6.50 was half an hour late that night. But at a quarter past seven I saw her with my own eyes starting for Old Hall. So it followed that she must have come by the earlier train. Indeed she was seen—but perhaps you know that?"

She looked at me inquiringly.

Some magnetism in her glance impelled me to hold out the last anonymous letter, the one I had opened so short a time ago. It set out in detail that Griselda had been seen leaving Lawrence Redding's cottage by the back window at half past six on the fatal day.

I said nothing then or at any time of the dreadful suspicion that had for one moment assailed my mind. I had seen it in nightmare terms—past intrigue between Lawrence and Griselda, the knowledge of it coming to Protheroe's ears, his decision to make me acquainted with the facts—and Griselda, desperate, stealing the pistol and silencing Protheroe. As I say—

a nightmare only—but invested for a few long minutes with a dreadful appearance of reality.

I don't know whether Miss Marple had any inkling of all this. Very probably she had. Few things are hidden from her.

She handed me back the note with a little nod.

"That's been all over the village," she said. "And it did look rather suspicious, didn't it? Especially with Mrs. Archer swearing at the inquest that the pistol was still in the cottage when she left at midday."

She paused a minute and then went on.

"But I'm wandering terribly from the point. What I want to say—and I believe it my duty—is to put my own explanation of the mystery before you. If you don't believe it—well, I shall have done my best. Even as it is, my wish to be quite sure before I spoke may have cost poor Mr. Hawes his life."

Again she paused, and when she resumed, her voice held a different note. It was less apologetic, more decided.

"This is my own explanation of the facts. By Thursday afternoon the crime had been fully planned down to the smallest detail. Lawrence Redding first called on the Vicar, knowing him to be out. He had with him the pistol which he concealed in that pot in the stand by the window. When the Vicar came in, Lawrence explained his visit by a statement that he had made up his mind to go away. At five-thirty, Lawrence Redding telephoned from the North Lodge to the Vicar, adopting a woman's voice (you remember what a good amateur actor he was).

"Mrs. Protheroe and her husband had just started for the village. And —a very curious thing (though no one happened to think of it that way) —Mrs. Protheroe took no handbag with her. Really a most unusual thing for a woman to do. Just before twenty past six she passes my garden and stops and speaks, so as to give me every opportunity of noticing that she has no weapon with her, and also that she is quite her normal self. They realized, you see, that I am a noticing kind of person. She disappears round the corner of the house to the study window. The poor Colonel is sitting at the desk writing his letter to you. He is deaf, as we all know. She takes the pistol from the bowl, where it is waiting for her, comes up behind him and shoots him through the head, throws down the pistol and is out again like a flash, and going down the garden to the studio. Nearly anyone would swear that there couldn't have been time!"

"But the shot?" objected the Colonel. "You didn't hear the shot?"

"There is, I believe, an invention called a Maxim silencer. So I gather from detective stories. I wonder if, possibly, the sneeze that the maid Clara heard might have actually been the shot? But no matter. Mrs. Protheroe is met at the studio by Mr. Redding. They go in together—and—human nature being what it is—I'm afraid they realize that I shan't leave the garden till they come out again!"

I had never liked Miss Marple better than at this moment, with her humorous perception of her own weakness.

"When they do come out, their demeanour is gay and natural. And there, in reality, they make a mistake. Because if they had really said good-bye to each other, as they pretended, they would have looked very different. But you see, that was their weak point. They simply dare not appear upset in any way. For the next ten minutes they are careful to provide themselves with what is called an alibi, I believe. Finally Mr. Redding goes to the Vicarage, leaving it as late as he dares. He probably saw you on the footpath from far away and was able to time matters nicely. He picks up the pistol and the silencer, leaves the forged letter with the time on it written in a different ink and apparently in a different handwriting. When the forgery is discovered it will look like a clumsy attempt to incriminate Anne Protheroe.

"But when he leaves the letter, he finds the one actually written by Colonel Protheroe—something quite unexpected. And, being a very intelligent young man, and seeing that this letter may come in very useful to him, he takes it away with him. He alters the hands of the clock to the same time as the letter—knowing that it is always kept a quarter of an hour fast. The same idea—attempt to throw suspicion on Mrs. Protheroe. Then he leaves, meeting you outside the gate, and acting the part of someone nearly distraught. As I say, he is really most intelligent. What would a murderer who had committed a crime try to do? Behave naturally, of course. So that is just what Mr. Redding does not do. He gets rid of the silencer, but marches into the police station with the pistol and makes a perfectly ridiculous self-accusation which takes everybody in."

There was something fascinating in Miss Marple's *résumé* of the case. She spoke with such certainty that we both felt that in this way and in no other could the crime have been committed.

"What about the shot heard in the wood?" I asked. "Was that the coincidence to which you were referring earlier this evening?"

"Oh! dear, no." Miss Marple shook her head briskly. "That wasn't a coincidence—very far from it. It was absolutely necessary that a shot should be heard—otherwise suspicion of Mrs. Protheroe might have continued. How Mr. Redding arranged it, I don't quite know. But I understand that picric acid explodes if you drop a weight on it, and you will remember, dear Vicar, that you met Mr. Redding carrying a large stone just in the part of the wood where you picked up that crystal later. Gentlemen are so clever at arranging things—the stone suspended above the crystals and then a time fuse—or do I mean a slow match? Something that would take about twenty minutes to burn through—so that the explosion would come about 6.30 when he and Mrs. Protheroe had come out of the studio and were in full view. A very safe device because what would there be to find afterwards—only a big stone! But even that he tried to remove—when you came upon him."

"I believe you are right," I exclaimed, remembering the start of surprise Lawrence had given on seeing me that day. It had seemed natural enough at the time, but now—

Miss Marple seemed to read my thoughts, for she nodded her head shrewdly.

"Yes," she said, "it must have been a very nasty shock for him to come across you just then. But he turned it off very well—pretending he was bringing it to me for my rock gardens. Only—" Miss Marple became suddenly very emphatic. *"It was the wrong sort of stone for my rock gardens!* And that put me on the right track!"

All this time Colonel Melchett had sat like a man in a trance. Now he showed signs of coming to. He snorted once or twice, blew his nose in a bewildered fashion, and said:

"Upon my word! Well, upon my word!"

Beyond that, he did not commit himself. I think that he, like myself, was impressed with the logical certainty of Miss Marple's conclusions. But for the moment he was not willing to admit it.

Instead, he stretched out a hand, picked up the crumpled letter and barked out:

"All very well. But how do you account for this fellow Hawes? Why, he actually rang up and confessed."

"Yes—that was what was so Providential. The Vicar's sermon, doubtless. You know, dear Mr. Clement, you really preached a most remarkable sermon. It must have affected Mr. Hawes deeply. He could bear it no longer, and felt he must confess—about the misappropriations of the Church funds."

"What?"

"Yes—and that, under Providence, is what has saved his life. (For I hope and trust it *is* saved. Dr. Haydock is so clever.) As I see the matter, Mr. Redding kept this letter (a risky thing to do, but I expect he hid it in some safe place) and waited till he found out for certain to whom it referred. He soon made quite sure that it was Mr. Hawes. I understand he came back here with Mr. Hawes last night and spent a long time with him. I suspect that he then substituted a cachet of his own for one of Mr. Hawes', and slipped this letter in the pocket of Mr. Hawes' dressing gown. The poor young man would swallow the fatal cachet in all innocence—after his death his things would be gone through and the letter found and everyone would jump to the conclusion that he had shot Colonel Protheroe and taken his own life out of remorse. I rather fancy Mr. Hawes must have found that letter tonight just after taking the fatal cachet. In his disordered state, it must have seemed like something supernatural, and, coming on top of the Vicar's sermon, it must have impelled him to confess the whole thing."

"Upon my word," said Colonel Melchett. "Upon my word! Most extraordinary! I—I—don't believe a word of it."

He had never made a statement that sounded more unconvincing. It must have sounded so in his own ears for he went on:

"And can you explain the other telephone call—the one from Mr. Redding's cottage to Mrs. Price Ridley?"

"Ah!" said Miss Marple. "That is what I call the coincidence. Dear Griselda sent that call—she and Mr. Dennis between them, I fancy. They had heard the rumours Mrs. Price Ridley was circulating about the Vicar, and they thought of this (perhaps rather childish) way of silencing her. The coincidence lies in the fact that the call should have been put through at exactly the same time as the fake shot from the wood. It led one to believe that the two must be connected."

I suddenly remembered how everyone who spoke of that shot had described it as "different" from the usual shot. They had been right. Yet how hard to explain just in what way the "difference" of the shot consisted.

Colonel Melchett cleared his throat.

"Your solution is a very plausible one, Miss Marple," he said. "But you will allow me to point out that there is not a shadow of proof."

"I know," said Miss Marple. "But you believe it to be true, don't you?"

There was a pause, then the Colonel said almost reluctantly:

"Yes, I do. Dash it all, it's the only way the thing could have happened. But there's no proof—not an atom."

Miss Marple coughed.

"That is why I thought perhaps—under the circumstances—"

"Yes?"

"A little trap might be permissible."

XXXI

Colonel Melchett and I both stared at her.

"A trap? What kind of a trap?"

Miss Marple was a little diffident, but it was clear that she had a plan fully outlined.

"Supposing Mr. Redding were to be rung up on the telephone and warned."

Colonel Melchett smiled.

"'All is discovered. Fly!' That's an old wheeze, Miss Marple. Not that it isn't often successful! But I think in this case young Redding is too downy a bird to be caught that way."

"It would have to be something specific. I quite realize that," said Miss Marple. "I would suggest—this is just a mere suggestion—that the warning should come from somebody who is known to have rather unusual views on these matters. Dr. Haydock's conversation would lead anyone to suppose that he might view such a thing as murder from an unusual angle. If he were to hint that somebody—Mrs. Sadler—or one of her children—had actually happened to see the transposing of the cachets—well—of course if Mr. Redding is an innocent man, that statement will mean nothing to him, but if he isn't—"

"If he isn't?"

"Well—he might just possibly do something foolish."

"And deliver himself into our hands. It's possible. Very ingenious, Miss Marple. But will Haydock stand for it? As you say his views—"

Miss Marple interrupted him brightly.

"Oh! but that's theory! So very different from practice, isn't it. But anyway here he is, so we can ask him."

Haydock was, I think, rather astonished to find Miss Marple with us. He looked tired and haggard.

"It's been a near thing," he said. "A very near thing. But he's going to pull through. It's a doctor's business to save his patient, and I've saved him, but I'd have been just as glad if I hadn't pulled it off."

"You may think differently," said Melchett, "when you have heard what we have to tell you."

And briefly and succinctly, he put Miss Marple's theory of the crime before the doctor, ending up with her final suggestion.

We were then privileged to see exactly what Miss Marple meant by the difference between theory and practice.

Haydock's views appeared to have undergone complete transformation. He would, I think, have liked Lawrence Redding's head on a charger. It was not, I imagine, the murder of Colonel Protheroe that so stirred his rancour. It was the assault on the unlucky Hawes.

"The damned scoundrel," said Haydock. "The damned scoundrel! That poor devil Hawes. He's got a mother and a sister too. The stigma of being the mother and sister of a murderer would have rested on them for life, and think of their mental anguish. Of all the cowardly dastardly tricks!"

For sheer primitive rage, commend me to a thoroughgoing humanitarian when you get him well roused.

"If this thing's true," he said, "you can count on me. The fellow's not fit to live. A defenceless chap like Hawes."

A lame dog of any kind can always count on Haydock's sympathy.

He was eagerly arranging details with Melchett when Miss Marple rose and I insisted on seeing her home.

"It is most kind of you, Mr. Clement," said Miss Marple as we walked down the deserted street. "Dear me, past twelve o'clock. I hope Raymond has gone to bed and not waited up."

"He should have accompanied you," I said.

"I didn't let him know I was going," said Miss Marple.

I smiled suddenly as I remembered Raymond West's subtle psychological analysis of the crime.

"If your theory turns out to be the truth—which I for one do not doubt for a minute," I said, "you will have a very good score over your nephew."

Miss Marple smiled also—an indulgent smile.

"I remember a saying of my Great Aunt Fanny's. I was sixteen at the time and thought it particularly foolish."

"Yes?" I inquired.

"She used to say, 'The young people think the old people are fools—but the old people know the young people are fools!'"

XXXII

There is little more to be told. Miss Marple's plan succeeded. Lawrence Redding was not an innocent man, and the hint of a witness of the change of capsule did indeed cause him to do "something foolish." Such is the power of an evil conscience.

He was, of course, peculiarly placed. His first impulse, I imagine, must have been to cut and run. But there was his accomplice to consider. He could not leave without getting word to her, and he dared not wait till morning. So he went up to Old Hall that night—and two of Colonel Melchett's most efficient officers followed him. He threw gravel at Anne Protheroe's window, aroused her, and an urgent whisper brought her down to speak with him. Doubtless they felt safer outside than in—with the possibility of Lettice waking. But as it happened, the two police officers were able to overhear their conversation in full. It left the matter in no doubt. Miss Marple had been right on every count.

The trial of Lawrence Redding and Anne Protheroe is a matter of public knowledge. I do not propose to go into it. I will only mention that great credit was reflected upon Inspector Slack, whose zeal and intelligence had resulted in the criminals being brought to justice. Naturally, nothing was said of Miss Marple's share in the business. She herself would have been horrified at the thought of such a thing.

Lettice came to see me just before the trial took place. She drifted through my study window, wraithlike as ever. She told me then that she had all along been convinced of her stepmother's complicity. The loss of the yellow beret had been a mere excuse for searching the study. She hoped against hope that she might find something the police had overlooked.

"You see," she said in her dreamy voice, "they didn't hate her like I did. And hate makes things easier for you."

Disappointed in the result of her search, she had deliberately dropped Anne's earring by the desk.

"Since I knew she had done it, what did it matter? One way was as good as another. She had killed him."

I sighed a little. There are always some things that Lettice will never see. In some respects she is morally colour blind.

"What are you going to do, Lettice?" I asked.

"When—when it's all over, I am going abroad." She hesitated and then went on. "I am going abroad with my mother."

I looked up, startled.

She nodded.

"Didn't you ever guess? Mrs. Lestrange is my mother. She is—is dying, you know. She wanted to see me, and so she came down here under an assumed name. Dr. Haydock helped her. He's a very old friend of hers—he was keen about her once—you can see that! In a way, he still is. Men always went batty about Mother, I believe. She's awfully attractive, even now. Anyway, Dr. Haydock did everything he could to help her. She didn't come down here under her own name, because of the disgusting way people talk and gossip. She went to see Father that night, and told him she was dying and had a great longing to see something of me. Father was a beast. He said she'd forfeited all claim, and that I thought she was dead—as though I had ever swallowed that story! Men like Father never see an inch before their noses!"

"But Mother is not the sort to give in. She thought it only decent to go to Father first, but when he turned her down so brutally she sent a note to me, and I arranged to leave the tennis party early and meet her at the end of the footpath at a quarter past six. We just had a hurried meeting and arranged when to meet again. We left each other before half past six. Afterwards, I was terrified that she would be suspected of having killed Father. After all, she had got a grudge against him. That's why I got hold of that old picture of her up in the attic and slashed it about. I was afraid the police might go nosing about and get hold of it and recognize it. Dr. Haydock was frightened too. Sometimes, I believe, he really thought she had done it! Mother is rather a—desperate kind of person. She doesn't count consequences."

She paused.

"It's queer. She and I belong to each other. Father and I didn't. But Mother—well, anyway, I'm going abroad with her. I shall be with her till—till the end."

She got up and I took her hand.

"God bless you both," I said. "Some day, I hope, there is a lot of happiness coming to you, Lettice."

"There should be," she said, with an attempt at a laugh. "There hasn't been much so far—has there? Oh, well, I don't suppose it matters. Good-bye, Mr. Clement. You've been frightfully decent to me always—you and Griselda."

Griselda!

I had to own to her how terribly the anonymous letter had upset me, and first she laughed, and then solemnly read me a lecture.

"However," she added, "I'm going to be very sober and godfearing in future—quite like the Pilgrim Fathers."

I did not see Griselda in the rôle of a Pilgrim Father.

She went on:

"You see, Len, I have a steadying influence coming into my life. It's coming into your life, too, but in your case it will be a kind of—of rejuvenating one—at least, I hope so! You can't call me a dear child half so much when we have a real child of our own. And, Len, I've decided that, now I'm going to be a real 'wife and mother' (as they say in books), I must be a housekeeper too. I've bought two books on Household Management and one on Mother Love and if that doesn't turn me out a pattern I don't know what will! They are all simply screamingly funny—not intentionally, you know. Especially the one about bringing up children."

"You haven't bought a book on How To Treat a Husband, have you?" I asked with sudden apprehension as I drew her to me.

"I don't need to," said Griselda. "I'm a very good wife. I love you dearly. What more do you want?"

"Nothing," I said.

"Could you say, just for once, that you love me madly?"

"Griselda," I said, "I adore you! I worship you! I am wildly, hopeless and quite unclerically crazy about you!"

My wife gave a deep and contented sigh.

Then she drew away suddenly.

"Bother! Here's Miss Marple coming. Don't let her suspect, will you? I don't want everyone offering me cushions and urging me to put my feet up. Tell her I've gone down to the golf links. That will put her off the scent—and it's quite true because I left my yellow pullover there, and I want it."

Miss Marple came to the window, halted apologetically and asked for Griselda.

"Griselda," I said, "has gone to the golf links."

An expression of concern leaped into Miss Marple's eyes.

"Oh! but surely," she said, "that is most unwise—just now."

And then in a nice, old-fashioned, ladylike, maiden-lady way, she blushed.

And to cover the moment's confusion, we talked hurriedly of the Protheroe case, and of "Dr. Stone," who had turned out to be a well-known cracksman with several different aliases. Miss Cram, by the way, had been cleared of all complicity. She had at last admitted taking the suitcase to the wood, but had done so in all good faith, Dr. Stone having told her that he feared the rivalry of other archæologists who would not stick at burglary to gain their object of discrediting his theories. The girl apparently swallowed this not very plausible story. She is now, according to the village, looking out for a more genuine article in the line of an elderly bachelor requiring a secretary.

As we talked, I wondered very much how Miss Marple had discovered our latest secret. But presently, in a discreet fashion, Miss Marple herself supplied me with a clue.

"I hope dear Griselda is not overdoing it," she murmured, and added after a discreet pause. "I was in the bookshop in Much Benham yesterday—"

Poor Griselda—that book on Mother Love has been her undoing!

"I wonder, Miss Marple," I said suddenly, "if you were to commit a murder whether you would ever be found out."

"What a terrible idea," said Miss Marple, shocked. "I hope I could never do such a wicked thing."

"But human nature being what it is," I murmured.

Miss Marple acknowledged the hit with a pretty old-ladyish laugh.

"How naughty of you, Mr. Clement." She rose. "But naturally you are in good spirits."

She paused by the window.

"My love to dear Griselda—and tell her—that any little secret is quite safe with me."

Really Miss Marple is rather a dear. . . .

The Moving Finger

I

I HAVE OFTEN recalled the morning when the first of the anonymous letters came.

It arrived at breakfast and I turned it over in the idle way one does when time goes slowly and every event must be spun out to its full extent. It was, I saw, a local letter with a typewritten address. I opened it before the two with London postmarks, since one of them was clearly a bill, and on the other I recognized the handwriting of one of my more tiresome cousins.

It seems odd, now, to remember that Joanna and I were more amused by the letter than anything else. We hadn't, then, the faintest inkling of what was to come—the trail of blood and violence and suspicion and fear.

One simply didn't associate that sort of thing with Lymstock.

I see that I have begun badly. I haven't explained Lymstock.

When I took a bad crash flying, I was afraid for a long time, in spite of soothing words from doctors and nurses, that I was going to be condemned to lie on my back all my life. Then at last they took me out of the plaster and I learned cautiously to use my limbs, and finally Marcus Kent, my doctor, clapped me on my back and told me that everything was going to be all right, but that I'd got to go and live in the country and lead the life of a vegetable for at least six months.

"Go to some part of the world where you haven't any friends. Get right away from things. Take an interest in local politics, get excited about village gossip, absorb all the local scandal. Small beer—that's the prescription for you. Absolute rest and quiet."

Rest and quiet! It seems funny to think of that now.

And so Lymstock—and Little Furze.

Lymstock had been a place of importance at the time of the Norman Conquest. In the twentieth century it was a place of no importance whatsoever. It was three miles from a main road—a little provincial market town with a sweep of moorland rising above it. Little Furze was situated on the road leading up to the moors. It was a prim, low, white house with a sloping Victorian veranda painted a faded green.

My sister Joanna, as soon as she saw it, decided that it was the ideal spot for a convalescent. Its owner matched the house, a charming little old lady, quite incredibly Victorian, who explained to Joanna that she would never have dreamed of letting her house if "things had not been so different nowadays—this terrible taxation."

So everything was settled, and the agreement signed, and in due course Joanna and I arrived and settled in, while Miss Emily Barton went into rooms in Lymstock kept by a former parlormaid ("my faithful Florence") and we were looked after by Miss Barton's present maid, Partridge, a grim but efficient personage who was assisted by a daily "girl."

As soon as we had been given a few days to settle down, Lymstock came solemnly to call. Everybody in Lymstock had a label—"rather like happy families" as Joanna said. There was Mr. Symmington the lawyer, thin and dry, with his querulous bridge-playing wife. Dr. Griffith—the dark, melancholy doctor—and his sister who was big and hearty. The vicar, a scholarly absent-minded elderly man and his erratic eager-faced wife. Rich dilettante Mr. Pye of Prior's End, and finally Miss Emily Barton herself, the perfect spinster of village tradition.

Joanna fingered the cards with something like awe. "I didn't know," she said in an awestruck voice, "that people really called—with cards!"

"That," I told her, "is because you know nothing about the country."

Joanna is very pretty and very gay, and she likes dancing and cocktails and love affairs and rushing about in high-powered cars. She is definitely and entirely urban.

"At any rate," said Joanna, "I look all right."

I studied her critically and was not able to agree.

Joanna was dressed (by Mirotin) for le sport. The effect was quite charming, but a bit startling for Lymstock.

"No," I said. "You're all wrong. You ought to be wearing an old faded tweed skirt with a nice cashmere jumper matching it and perhaps a rather baggy cardigan coat, and you'd wear a felt hat and thick stockings and old well-worn brogues. Your face is all wrong, too," I added.

"What's wrong with that? I've got on my Country Tan Make-Up No. 2."

"Exactly," I said. "If you lived here, you would have just a little powder to take the shine off the nose and you would almost certainly be wearing all your eyebrows instead of only a quarter of them."

Joanna laughed, and said that coming to the country was a new experience and she was going to enjoy it.

"I'm afraid you'll be terribly bored," I said remorsefully.

"No, I shan't. I really was fed up with all my crowd, and though you won't be sympathetic I really was very cut up about Paul. It will take me a long time to get over it."

I was skeptical over this. Joanna's love affairs always run the same course. She has a mad infatuation for some completely spineless young man who is a misunderstood genius. She listens to his endless complaints and works to get him recognition. Then, when he is ungrateful, she is deeply wounded and says her heart is broken—until the next gloomy young man comes along, which is usually about three weeks later.

I did not take Joanna's broken heart very seriously, but I did see that living in the country was like a new game to my attractive sister. She entered with zest into the pastime of returning calls. We duly received invitations to tea and to bridge, which we accepted, and issued invitations in our turn.

To us, it was all novel and entertaining—a new game.

And, as I say, when the anonymous letter came, it struck me, at first, as amusing too.

For a minute or two after opening the letter, I stared at it uncomprehendingly. Printed words had been cut out and pasted on a sheet of paper.

The letter, using terms of the coarsest character, expressed the writer's opinion that Joanna and I were not brother and sister.

"Hullo," said Joanna. "What is it?"

"It's a particularly foul anonymous letter," I said.

I was still suffering from shock. Somehow one didn't expect that kind of thing in the placid backwater of Lymstock.

Joanna at once displayed lively interest. "No? What does it say?"

In novels, I have noticed, anonymous letters of a foul and disgusting character are never shown, if possible, to women. It is implied that women must at all cost be shielded from the shock it might give their delicate nervous systems.

I am sorry to say it never occurred to me not to show the letter to Joanna. I handed it to her at once.

She vindicated my belief in her toughness by displaying no emotion but that of amusement. "What an awful bit of dirt! I've always heard about anonymous letters, but I've never seen one before. Are they always like this?"

"I can't tell you," I said. "It's my first experience, too."

Joanna began to giggle. "You must have been right about my make-up, Jerry. I suppose they think I just must be an abandoned female!"

"That," I said, "coupled with the fact that our father was a tall, dark, lantern-jawed man and our mother a fair-haired blue-eyed little creature, and that I take after him and you take after her."

Joanna nodded thoughtfully. "Yes, we're not a bit alike. Nobody would take us for brother and sister."

"Somebody certainly hasn't," I said with feeling.

Joanna said she thought it was frightfully funny. She dangled the letter thoughtfully by one corner and asked what we were to do with it.

"The correct procedure, I believe," I said, "is to drop it into the fire with a sharp exclamation of disgust."

I suited the action to the word, and Joanna applauded. "You did that beautifully," she said. "You ought to have been on the stage. It's lucky we still have fires, isn't it?"

"The waste-paper basket would have been much less dramatic," I agreed. "I could, of course, have set light to it with a match and slowly watched it burn—or watched it slowly burn."

"Things never burn when you want them to," said Joanna. "They go out. You'd probably have had to strike match after match."

She got up and went toward the window. Then, standing there, she turned her head sharply. "I wonder," she said, "who wrote it?"

"We're never likely to know," I said.

"No—I suppose not." She was silent a moment, and then said: "I don't know when I come to think of it that it is so funny after all. You know, I thought they—they liked us down here."

"So they do," I said. "This is just some half-crazy brain on the borderline."

"I suppose so. Ugh—nasty!"

As she went out into the sunshine I thought to myself as I smoked my after-breakfast cigarette that she was quite right. It was nasty. Someone resented our coming here—someone resented Joanna's bright young sophisticated beauty—someone wanted to hurt. To take it with a laugh was perhaps the best way—but deep down it wasn't funny.

Dr. Griffith came that morning. I had fixed up for him to give me a weekly overhaul. I liked Owen Griffith. He was dark, ungainly, with awkward ways of moving and deft very gentle hands. He had a jerky way of talking and was rather shy.

He reported progress to be encouraging. Then he added, "You're feeling all right, aren't you? Is it my fancy, or are you a bit under the weather this morning?"

"Not really," I said. "A particularly scurrilous anonymous letter arrived with the morning coffee, and it's left rather a nasty taste in the mouth."

He dropped his bag on the floor. His thin dark face was excited. "Do you mean to say that you've had one of them?"

I was interested. "They've been going about, then?"

"Yes. For some time."

"Oh," I said. "I see. I was under the impression that our presence as strangers was resented here."

"No, no, it's nothing to do with that. It's just—" He paused and then asked, "What did it say? At least"—he turned suddenly red and embarrassed—"perhaps I oughtn't to ask?"

"I'll tell you with pleasure," I said. "It just said that the fancy tart I'd brought down with me wasn't my sister—not 'alf! And that, I may say, is a shortened version."

His dark face flushed angrily. "How damnable! Your sister didn't—she's not upset, I hope?"

"Joanna," I said, "looks a little like the angel off the top of the Christmas tree, but she's eminently modern and quite tough. She found it highly entertaining. Such things haven't come her way before."

"I should hope not, indeed," said Griffith warmly.

"And anyway," I said firmly, "that's the best way to take it, I think. As something utterly ridiculous."

"Yes," said Owen Griffith, "only—"

He stopped, and I chimed in quickly. "Quite so," I said. "Only is the word!"

"The trouble is," he said, "that this sort of thing, once it starts, grows."

"So I should imagine."

"It's pathological, of course."

I nodded. "Any idea who's behind it?" I asked.

"No, I wish I had. You see, the anonymous letter pest arises from one of two causes. Either it's particular—directed at one person or set of people, that is to say it's motivated, it's someone who's got a definite grudge (or thinks he has) and who chooses a particularly nasty and underhand way of working it off. It's mean and disgusting but it's not necessarily crazy, and it's usually fairly easy to trace the writer—a discharged servant, a jealous woman, and so on. But if it's general, and not particular, then it's more serious.

"The letters are sent indiscriminately and serve the purpose of working off some frustration in the writer's mind. As I say, it's definitely pathological. And the craze grows. In the end, of course, you track down the person in question—(it's often someone extremely unlikely) and that's that. There was a bad outburst of the kind over the other side of the county last year—turned out to be the head of the millinery department in a big draper's establishment. Quiet, refined woman—had been there for years.

"I remember something of the same kind in my last practice up north. But that turned out to be purely personal spite. Still, as I say, I've seen something of this kind of thing, and, quite frankly, it frightens me!"

"Has it been going on long?" I asked.

"I don't think so. Hard to say, of course, because people who get these letters don't go round advertising the fact. They put them in the fire."

He paused.

"I've had one myself. Symmington, the solicitor, he's had one. And one or two of my poorer patients have told me about them."

"All much the same sort of thing?"

"Oh, yes. A definite harping on the sex theme. That's always a feature." He grinned. "Symmington was accused of illicit relations with his lady clerk—poor old Miss Ginch, who's forty at least, with pince-nez and teeth like a rabbit. Symmington took it straight to the police. My letters accused me of violating professional decorum with my lady patients, stressing the details. They're all quite childish and absurd, but horribly venomous." His face changed, grew grave. "But all the same, I'm afraid. These things can be dangerous, you know."

"I suppose they can."

"You see," he said, "crude, childish spite though it is, sooner or later one of these letters will hit the mark. And then, God knows what may happen! I'm afraid, too, of the effect upon the slow, suspicious, uneducated mind. If they see a thing written, they believe it's true. All sorts of complications may arise."

"It was an illiterate sort of letter," I said thoughtfully, "written by somebody practically illiterate, I should say."

"Was it?" said Owen and went away.

Thinking it over afterward, I found that "Was it?" rather disturbing.

I am not going to pretend that the arrival of our anonymous letter did not leave a nasty taste in the mouth. It did. At the same time, it soon passed out of my mind. I did not, you see, at that point, take it seriously. I think I remember saying to myself that these things probably happen fairly often in out-of-the-way villages. Some hysterical woman with a taste for dramatizing herself was probably at the bottom of it. Anyway, if the letters were as childish and silly as the one we had got, they couldn't do much harm.

The next incident, if I may put it so, occurred about a week later, when

Partridge, her lips set tightly together, informed me that Beatrice, the daily help, would not be coming today.

"I gather, sir," said Partridge, "that the girl has been upset."

I was not very sure what Partridge was implying, but I diagnosed (wrongly) some stomach trouble to which Partridge was too delicate to allude more directly. I said I was sorry and hoped she would soon be better.

"The girl is perfectly well, sir," said Partridge. "She is upset in her feelings."

"Oh," I said rather doubtfully.

"Owing," went on Partridge, "to a letter she has received. Making, I understand, insinuations."

The grimness of Partridge's eye made me apprehensive that the insinuations were concerned with me. Since I could hardly have recognized Beatrice by sight if I had met her in the town, so unaware of her had I been, I felt a not unnatural annoyance. An invalid hobbling about on two sticks is hardly cast for the role of deceiver of village girls.

I said irritably, "What nonsense!"

"My very words, sir, to the girl's mother," said Partridge. "'Goings-on in this house,' I said to her, 'there never have been and never will be while I am in charge. As to Beatrice,' I said, 'girls are different nowadays, and as to goings-on elsewhere I can say nothing.' But the truth is, sir, that Beatrice's friend from the garage as she walks out with got one of them nasty letters, too, and he isn't acting reasonable at all."

"I have never heard anything so preposterous in my life," I said angrily.

"It's my opinion, sir," said Partridge, "that we're well rid of the girl. What I say is, she wouldn't take on so if there wasn't something she didn't want found out. No smoke without fire, that's what I say."

I had no idea how horribly tired I was going to get of that particular phrase.

That morning, by way of adventure, I was to walk down to the village. The sun was shining, the air was cool and crisp with the sweetness of spring in it. I assembled my sticks and started off, firmly refusing to permit Joanna to accompany me.

It was arranged that she should pick me up with the car and drive me back up the hill in time for lunch.

"That ought to give you time to pass the time of day with everyone in Lymstock."

"I have no doubt," I said, "that I shall have seen anybody who is anybody by then."

For morning in the High Street was a kind of rendezvous for shoppers, when news was exchanged.

I did not, after all, walk down to the town unaccompanied. I had gone about two hundred yards, when I heard a bicycle bell behind me, then a scrunching of brakes, and then Megan Hunter more or less fell off her machine at my feet.

"Hullo," she said breathlessly as she rose and dusted herself off.

I rather liked Megan and always felt oddly sorry for her.

She was Symmington the lawyer's stepdaughter, Mrs. Symmington's daughter by a first marriage. Nobody talked much about Mr. (or Captain) Hunter, and I gathered that he was considered best forgotten. He was reported to have treated Mrs. Symmington very badly. She had divorced him a year or two after the marriage. She was a woman with means of her own and had settled down with her little daughter in Lymstock "to forget," and had eventually married the only eligible bachelor in the place, Richard Symmington.

There were two boys of the second marriage to whom their parents were devoted, and I fancied that Megan sometimes felt odd-man in the establishment. She certainly did not resemble her mother, who was a small anemic woman, fadedly pretty, who talked in a thin melancholy voice of servant difficulties and her health.

Megan was a tall awkward girl, and although she was actually twenty, she looked more like a schoolgirlish sixteen. She had a shock of untidy brown hair, hazel green eyes, a thin bony face, and an unexpectedly charming one-sided smile. Her clothes were drab and unattractive and she usually had on lisle-thread stockings with holes in them.

She looked, I decided this morning, much more like a horse than a human being. In fact, she would have been a very nice horse with a little grooming.

She spoke, as usual, in a kind of breathless rush:

"I've been up to the farm—you know, Lasher's—to see if they'd got any duck eggs. They've got an awfully nice lot of little pigs. Sweet! Do you like pigs? I do. I even like the smell."

"Well-kept pigs shouldn't smell," I said.

"Shouldn't they? They all do around here. Are you walking down to the town? I saw you were alone, so I thought I'd stop and walk with you, only I stopped rather suddenly."

"You've torn your stocking," I said.

Megan looked rather ruefully at her right leg. "So I have. But it's got two holes already, so it doesn't matter very much, does it?"

"Don't you ever mend your stockings, Megan?"

"Rather. When Mummie catches me. But she doesn't notice awfully what I do—so it's lucky in a way, isn't it?"

"You don't seem to realize you're grown up," I said.

"You mean I ought to be more like your sister? All dolled up?"

I rather resented this description of Joanna. "She looks clean and tidy and pleasing to the eye," I said.

"She's awfully pretty," said Megan. "She isn't a bit like you, is she? Why not?"

"Brothers and sisters aren't always alike."

"No. Of course I'm not very like Brian or Colin. And Brian and Colin aren't like each other." She paused and said, "It's very rum, isn't it?"

"What is?"

Megan replied briefly:

"Families."

I said thoughtfully, "I suppose they are."

I wondered just what was passing in her mind. We walked on in silence for a moment or two, then Megan said in a rather shy voice, "You fly, don't you?"

"Yes."

"That's how you got hurt?"

"Yes, I crashed."

Megan said, "Nobody down here flies."

"No," I said, "I suppose not. Would you like to fly, Megan?"

"Me?" Megan seemed surprised. "Goodness, no. I should be sick. I'm sick in a train even."

She paused and then asked with that directness which only a child usually displays: "Will you get all right and be able to fly again, or will you always be a bit of a crock?"

"My doctor says I shall be quite all right."

"Yes, but is he the kind of man who tells lies?"

"I don't think so," I replied. "In fact, I'm quite sure of it. I trust him."

"That's all right then. But a lot of people do tell lies."

I accepted this undeniable statement of fact in silence.

Megan said in a detached judicial kind of way, "I'm glad. I was afraid you looked bad-tempered because you were crocked up for life—but if it's just natural, it's different."

"I'm not bad-tempered," I said coldly.

"Well, irritable, then."

"I'm irritable because I'm in a hurry to get fit again—and these things can't be hurried."

"Then why fuss?"

I began to laugh. "My dear girl, aren't you ever in a hurry for things to happen?"

Megan considered the question. She said, "No. Why should I be? There's nothing to be in a hurry about. Nothing ever happens."

I was struck by something forlorn in the words. I said gently, "What do you do with yourself down here?"

She shrugged her shoulders. "What is there to do?"

"Haven't you any hobbies? Don't you play games? Haven't you got friends around about?"

"I'm stupid at games. There aren't many girls around here, and the ones there are I don't like. They think I'm awful."

"Nonsense. Why should they?"

Megan shook her head.

We were now entering the High Street. Megan said sharply:

"Here's Miss Griffith coming. Hateful woman. She's always at me to join her foul Guides. I hate Guides. Why dress up and go about in clumps and put badges on yourself for something you haven't really learned to do properly. I think it's all rot."

On the whole I rather agreed with Megan. But Miss Griffith had descended upon us before I could voice my assent.

The doctor's sister, who rejoiced in the singularly inappropriate name of Aimée, had all the positive assurance her brother lacked. She was a handsome woman in a masculine weather-beaten way, with a deep voice.

"Hullo, you two," she bayed at us. "Gorgeous morning, isn't it? Megan, you're just the person I want to see. I want some help. Addressing envelopes for the Conservative Association."

Megan muttered something elusive, propped up her bicycle against the curb and dived in a purposeful way into the International Stores.

"Extraordinary child," said Miss Griffith, looking after her. "Bone lazy. Spends her time mooning about. Must be a great trial to poor Mrs. Symmington. I know her mother's tried more than once to get her to take up something—shorthand-typing, you know, or cookery, or keeping Angora rabbits. She needs an interest in life."

I thought that was probably true, but felt that in Megan's place I should have withstood firmly any of Aimée Griffith's suggestions for the simple reason that her aggressive personality would have put my back up.

"I don't believe in idleness," went on Miss Griffith. "And certainly not for young people. It's not as though Megan was pretty or attractive or anything like that. Sometimes I think the girl's half-witted. A great disappointment to her mother. The father, you know," she lowered her voice slightly, "was definitely a wrong 'un. Afraid the child takes after him. Painful for her mother. Oh, well, it takes all sorts to make a world, that's what I say."

"Fortunately," I responded.

Aimée Griffith gave a "jolly" laugh.

"Yes, it wouldn't do if we were all made to one pattern. But I don't like to see anyone not getting all he can out of life. I enjoy life myself and I want everyone to enjoy it too. People say to me you must be bored to death living down there in the country all the year around. Not a bit of it, I say. I'm always busy, always happy! There's always something going on in the country. My time's taken up, what with my Guides, and the Institute and various committees—to say nothing of looking after Owen."

At this minute, Miss Griffith saw an acquaintance on the other side of the street, and uttering a bay of recognition she leaped across the road, leaving me free to pursue my course to the bank.

I always found Miss Griffith rather overwhelming.

My business at the bank transacted satisfactorily, I went on to the offices of Messrs. Galbraith, Galbraith and Symmington. I don't know if there were any Galbraiths extant. I never saw any. I was shown into Richard Symmington's inner office which had the agreeable mustiness of a long-established legal firm.

Vast numbers of deed boxes labeled Lady Hope, Sir Everard Carr, William Yatesby-Hoares Esq., Deceased, etc., gave the required atmosphere of decorous county families and legitimate, long-established business.

Studying Mr. Symmington as he bent over the documents I had brought, it occurred to me that if Mrs. Symmington had encountered disaster in her first marriage, she had certainly played safe in her second. Richard Symmington was the acme of calm respectability, the sort of man who would never give his wife a moment's anxiety. A long neck with a pronounced Adam's apple, a slightly cadaverous face and a long thin nose. A kindly man, no doubt, a good husband and father, but not one to set the pulses madly racing.

Presently Mr. Symmington began to speak. He spoke clearly and slowly, delivering himself of much good sense and shrewd acumen. We settled the matter in hand and I rose to go, remarking as I did so, "I walked down the hill with your stepdaughter."

For a moment Mr. Symmington looked as though he did not know who his stepdaughter was, then he smiled.

"Oh, yes, of course—Megan. She—er—has been back from school some time. We're thinking about finding her something to do—yes, to do. But, of course, she's very young still. And backward for her age, so they say. Yes, so they tell me."

I went out. In the outer office was a very old man on a stool writing slowly and laboriously, a small, cheeky-looking boy and a middle-aged woman with frizzy hair and pince-nez who was typing with some speed and dash.

If this was Miss Ginch I agreed with Owen Griffith that tender passages between her and her employer were exceedingly unlikely.

I went into the baker's and said my piece about the currant loaf. It was received with the exclamations and incredulity proper to the occasion, and a new currant loaf was thrust upon me in replacement—"fresh from the oven this minute"—as its indecent heat pressed against my chest proclaimed to be no less than truth.

I came out of the shop and looked up and down the street, hoping to see Joanna with the car. The walk had tired me a good deal and it was awkward getting along with my sticks and the currant loaf.

But there was no sign of Joanna as yet.

Suddenly my eyes were held in glad and incredulous surprise. Along the pavement toward me there came floating a goddess. There is really no other word for it. The perfect features, the crisply curling golden hair, the tall exquisitely shaped body. And she walked like a goddess, without effort, seeming to swim nearer and near. A glorious, an incredible, a breath-taking girl!

In my intense excitement something had to go. What went was the currant loaf. It slipped from my clutches. I made a dive after it and lost my stick, which clattered to the pavement, and I slipped and nearly fell myself.

It was the strong arm of the goddess that caught and held me.

I began to stammer: "Th-thanks awfully, I'm f-f-frightfully sorry."

She had retrieved the currant loaf and handed it to me together with the stick. And then she smiled kindly and said cheerfully, "Don't mention it. No trouble, I assure you," and the magic died completely before the flat, competent voice.

A nice, healthy-looking, well set-up girl; no more.

I fell to reflecting what would have happened if the gods had given Helen of Troy exactly those flat accents. How strange that a girl could trouble your inmost soul so long as she kept her mouth shut, and that the moment she spoke the glamor could vanish as though it had never been.

I had known the reverse happen, though. I had seen a little sad monkey-faced woman whom no one would turn to look at twice. Then she had opened her mouth and suddenly enchantment had lived and bloomed and Cleopatra had cast her spell anew.

Joanna had drawn up at the curb beside me without my noticing her arrival. She asked if there was anything the matter.

"Nothing," I said, pulling myself together. "I was reflecting on Helen of Troy and others."

"What a funny place to do it," said Joanna. "You looked most odd, standing there clasping currant bread to your breast with your mouth wide open."

"I've had a shock," I said. "I had been transplanted to Ilium and back again."

I added, indicating a retreating back that was swimming gracefully away, "Do you know who that is?"

Peering after the girl Joanna said that it was Elsie Holland, the Symmington's nursery governess.

"Is that what struck you all of a heap?" she asked. "She's good-looking, but a bit of a wet fish."

"I know," I said. "Just a nice kind girl. And I'd been thinking her Aphrodite."

Joanna opened the door of the car and I got in.

"It's funny, isn't it?" she said. "Some people have lots of looks and absolutely no S. A. That girl hasn't. It seems such a pity."

I said that if she was a nursery governess it was probably just as well.

That afternoon we went to tea with Mr. Pye.

Mr. Pye was an extremely ladylike plump little man, devoted to his petit point chairs, his Dresden shepherdesses and his collection of period furniture. He lived at Prior's Lodge in the grounds of which were the ruins of the old Priory dissolved at the Reformation.

It was hardly a man's house. The curtains and cushions were of pastel shades in the most expensive silks.

Mr. Pye's small plump hands quivered with excitement as he described and exhibited his treasures, and his voice rose to a falsetto squeak as he narrated the exciting circumstances in which he had brought his Italian bedstead home from Verona.

Joanna and I, both being fond of antiques, met with approval.

"It is really a pleasure, a great pleasure, to have such an acquisition to our little community. The dear good people down here, you know, so painfully bucolic—not to say provincial. Vandals—absolute vandals! And the insides of their houses—it would make you weep, dear lady, I assure you it would make you weep. Perhaps it has done so?"

Joanna said she hadn't gone quite as far as that.

"The house you have taken," went on Mr. Pye, "Miss Emily Barton's house. Now that is charming, and she has some quite nice pieces. Quite nice. One or two of them are really first-class. And she has taste, too—although I'm not quite so sure of that as I was. Sometimes, I am afraid, I think it's really sentiment. She likes to keep things as they were—but not for *le bon motif*—not because of the resultant harmony—but because it is the way her mother had them."

He transferred his attention to me, and his voice changed. It altered from that of the rapt artist to that of the born gossip:

"You didn't know the family at all? No, quite so—yes, through house agents. But, my dears, you ought to have known that family! When I came here the old mother was still alive. An incredible person—quite incredible! A monster, if you know what I mean. Positively a monster. The old-fashioned Victorian monster, devouring her young. Yes, that's what it amounted to. She was monumental, you know, must have weighed seventeen stone, and all the five daughters revolved around her. 'The girls!' That's how she always spoke of them. The girls! And the eldest was well over sixty then.

"'Those stupid girls!' she used to call them sometimes. Black slaves, that's all they were, fetching and carrying and agreeing with her. Ten o'clock they had to go to bed and they weren't allowed a fire in their bedroom, and as for asking their own friends to the house, that would have been unheard of. She despised them, you know, for not getting married, and yet so arranged their lives that it was practically impossible for them to meet anybody. I believe Emily, or perhaps it was Agnes, did have some kind of affair with a curate. But his family wasn't good enough and Mamma soon put a stop to that!"

"It sounds like a novel," said Joanna.

"Oh, my dear, it was. And then the dreadful old woman died, but of course, it was far too late then. They just went on living there and talking in hushed voices about what poor Mamma would have wished. Even repapering her bedroom they felt to be quite sacrilegious. Still they did enjoy themselves in the parish in a quiet way. . . . But none of them had much stamina, and they just died off one by one. Influenza took off

Edith, and Minnie had an operation and didn't recover and poor Mable had a stroke—Emily looked after her in the most devoted manner. Really that poor woman has done nothing but nursing for the last ten years. A charming creature, don't you think? Like a piece of Dresden. So sad for her having financial anxieties—but of course, all investments have depreciated."

"We feel rather awful being in her house," said Joanna.

"No, no, my dear young lady. You mustn't feel that way. Her dear good Florence is devoted to her and she told me herself how happy she was to have got such nice tenants." Here Mr. Pye made a little bow. "She told me she thought she had been most fortunate."

"The house," I said, "has a very soothing atmosphere."

Mr. Pye darted a quick glance at me.

"Really? You feel that? Now, that's very interesting. I wondered, you know. Yes, I wondered."

"What do you mean, Mr. Pye?" asked Joanna.

Mr. Pye spread out his plump hands. "Nothing, nothing. One wondered, that is all. I do believe in atmosphere, you know. People's thoughts and feelings. They give their impression to the walls and the furniture."

I did not speak for a moment or two. I was looking around me and wondering how I would describe the atmosphere of Prior's Lodge. It seemed to me that the curious thing was that it hadn't any atmosphere! That was really very remarkable.

I reflected on this point so long that I heard nothing of the conversation going on between Joanna and her host. I was recalled to myself, however, by hearing Joanna uttering farewell preliminaries. I came out of my dream and added my quota.

We all went out into the hall. As we came toward the front door a letter came through the box and fell on the mat.

"Afternoon post," murmured Mr. Pye as he picked it up. "Now, my dear young people, you will come again, won't you? Such a pleasure to meet some broader minds, if you understand me, in this peaceful backwater where nothing ever happens."

Shaking hands with us twice over, he helped me with exaggerated care into the car. Joanna took the wheel, she negotiated with some care the circular sweep around a plot of unblemished grass, then with a straight drive ahead, she raised a hand to wave goodby to our host where he stood on the steps of the house. I leaned forward to do the same.

But our gesture of farewell went unheeded. Mr. Pye had opened his mail. He was standing staring down at the open sheet in his hand.

Joanna had described him once as a plump pink cherub. He was still plump, but he was not looking like a cherub now. His face was a dark congested purple, contorted with rage and surprise. Yes, and fear, too.

And at that moment I realized that there had been something familiar about the look of that envelope. I had not realized it at the time—indeed, it had been one of those things that you note unconsciously without knowing that you do note them.

"Goodness," said Joanna, "what's bitten the poor pet?"

"I rather fancy," I said, "that it's the Hidden Hand again."

She turned an astonished face toward me and the car swerved.

"Careful, wench," I said.

Joanna refixed her attention on the road. She was frowning. "You mean a letter like the one you got."

"That's my guess."

"What is this place?" asked Joanna. "It looks the most innocent, sleepy, harmless little bit of England you can imagine."

"Where, to quote Mr. Pye, nothing ever happens," I cut in. "He chose the wrong minute to say that. Something has happened."

"Jerry," said Joanna. "I—I don't think I like this." For the first time, there was a note of fear in her voice.

I did not answer, for I, too, did not like it. . . .

Such a peaceful smiling happy countryside—and down underneath something evil. . . .

It was as though at that moment I had a premonition of all that was to come. . . .

The days passed. We went and played bridge at the Symmingtons' and Mrs. Symmington annoyed me a good deal by the way she referred to Megan.

"The poor child's so awkward. They are at that age, when they've left school and before they are properly grown up."

Joanna said sweetly, "But Megan's twenty, isn't she?"

"Oh, yes, yes. But of course, she's very young for her age. Quite a child still. It's so nice, I think, when girls don't grow up too quickly." She laughed. "I expect all mothers want their children to remain babies."

"I can't think why," said Joanna. "After all, it would be a bit awkward if one had a child who remained mentally six while his body grew up."

Mrs. Symmington looked annoyed and said Miss Burton mustn't take things so literally.

I was pleased with Joanna, and it occurred to me that I did not really much care for Mrs. Symmington. That anemic middle-aged prettiness concealed, I thought, a selfish, grasping nature.

Joanna asked maliciously if Mrs. Symmington were going to give a dance for Megan.

"A dance?" Mrs. Symmington seemed surprised and amused. "Oh, no, we don't do things like that down here."

"I see. Just tennis parties and things like that."

"Our tennis court has not been played on for years. Neither Richard nor I play. I suppose, later, when the boys grow up—oh, Megan will find plenty to do. She's quite happy just pottering about, you know. Let me see, did I deal? Two no trumps."

As we drove home, Joanna said with a vicious pressure on the accelerator pedal that made the car leap forward, "I feel awfully sorry for that girl."

"Megan?"

"Yes. Her mother doesn't like her."

"Oh, come now, Joanna, it's not as bad as that."

"Yes, it is. Lots of mothers don't like their children. Megan, I should imagine, is an awkward sort of creature to have about the house. She disturbs the pattern—the Symmington pattern. It's a complete unit without her—and that's a most unhappy feeling for a sensitive creature to have—and she is sensitive."

"Yes," I said, "I think she is."

I was silent a moment.

Joanna suddenly laughed mischievously. "Bad luck for you about the governess."

"I don't know what you mean," I said with dignity.

"Nonsense. Masculine chagrin was written on your face every time you looked at her. I agree with you, it is a waste. And I don't see who else there is here for you. You'll have to fall back upon Aimée Griffith."

"God forbid," I said with a shudder. "And anyway," I added, "why all this concern about my love life? What about you, my girl? You'll need a little distraction down here, if I know you. No unappreciated genius, knocking about here. You'll have to fall back on Owen Griffith. He's the only unattached male in the place."

Joanna tossed her head. "Dr. Griffith doesn't like me."

"He's not seen much of you."

"He's seen enough apparently to make him cross over if he sees me coming along the High Street!"

"A most unusual reaction," I said sympathetically. "And one you're not used to."

Joanna drove in silence through the gate of Little Furze and around to the garage. Then she said, "There may be something in that idea of yours. I don't see why any man should deliberately cross the street to avoid me. It's rude apart from everything else."

"I see," I said. "You're going to hunt the man down in cold blood."

"Well, I don't like being avoided."

I got slowly and carefully out of the car and balanced my sticks. Then I offered my sister a piece of advice:

"Let me tell you this, girl. Owen Griffith isn't any of your tame, whining, artistic young men. Unless you're careful, you'll stir up a hornets' nest about your ears. That man could be dangerous."

"Oh, do you think so?" demanded Joanna with every symptom of pleasure at the prospect.

"Leave the poor devil alone," I said sternly.

"How dare he cross the street when he saw me coming?"

"All you women are alike. You harp on one theme. You'll have sister Aimée gunning for you, too, if I'm not mistaken."

"She dislikes me already," said Joanna. She spoke meditatively, but with a certain satisfaction.

"We have come down here," I said sternly, "for peace and quiet, and I mean to see we get it."

But peace and quiet were the last things we were to have.

II

It was about a week later that I came back to the house to find Megan sitting on the veranda steps, her chin resting on her knees.

She greeted me with her usual lack of ceremony. "Hullo," she said. "Do you think I could come to lunch?"

"Certainly," I said.

"If it's chops, or anything difficult like that and they won't go around, just tell me," shouted Megan as I went around to apprise Partridge of the fact that there would be three to lunch.

I fancy that Partridge sniffed. She certainly managed to convey without saying a word of any kind, that she didn't think much of that Miss Megan.

I went back to the veranda.

"Is it all right?" asked Megan anxiously.

"Quite all right," I said. "Irish stew."

"Oh, well, that's rather like dogs' dinner anyway, isn't it? I mean it's mostly potato and flavor."

"Quite," I said.

We were silent while I smoked my pipe. It was quite a companionable silence.

Megan broke it by saying suddenly and violently, "I suppose you think I'm awful like everyone else."

I was so startled that my pipe fell out of my mouth. It was a meerschaum, just coloring nicely, and it broke. I said angrily to Megan, "Now see what you've done."

That most unaccountable of children, instead of being upset, merely grinned broadly. "I do like you," she said.

It was a most warming remark. It is the remark that one fancies perhaps erroneously that one's dog would say if he could talk. It occurred to me that Megan, for all she looked like a horse had the disposition of a dog. She was certainly not quite human.

"What did you say before the catastrophe?" I asked, carefully picking up the fragments of my cherished pipe.

"I said I supposed you thought me awful," said Megan but not at all in the same tone she had said it before.

"Why should I?"

Megan said gravely, "Because I am."

I said sharply, "Don't be stupid."

Megan shook her head. "That's just it. I'm not really stupid. People think I am. They don't know that inside I know just what they're like, and that all the time I'm hating them."

"Hating them?"

"Yes," said Megan.

Her eyes, those melancholy, unchildlike eyes stared straight into mine, without blinking. It was a long, mournful gaze.

"You would hate people if you were like me," she said. "If you weren't wanted."

"Don't you think you're being rather morbid?" I asked.

"Yes," said Megan. "That's what people always say when you're saying the truth. And it is true. I'm not wanted and I can quite see why. Mummie doesn't like me a bit. I remind her, I think, of my father, who was cruel to her and pretty dreadful from all I can hear. Only mothers can't say they don't want their children and just go away. Or eat them. Cats eat the kittens they don't like. Awfully sensible, I think. No waste or mess. But human mothers have to keep their children, and look after them. It hasn't been so bad while I could be sent away to school—but you see what Mummie would really like is to be just herself and my stepfather and the boys."

I said slowly, "I still think you're morbid, Megan, but accepting some of what you say as true, why don't you go away and have a life of your own?"

She gave me an odd unchildlike smile. "You mean take up a career. Earn my living?"

"Yes."

"What at?"

"You could train for something, I suppose. Shorthand, typing, bookkeeping."

"I don't believe I could. I am stupid about doing things. And besides—"

"Well?"

She had turned her head away, now she turned it slowly back again. It was crimson and there were tears in her eyes. She spoke now with all the childishness back in her voice:

"Why should I go away? And be made to go away? They don't want me, but I'll stay. I'll stay and make everyone sorry. I'll make them all sorry. Hateful pigs! I hate everyone here in Lymstock. They all think I'm stupid and ugly. I'll show them! I'll show them! I'll—"

It was a childish, oddly pathetic rage.

I heard a step on the gravel around the corner of the house.

"Get up," I said savagely. "Go into the house through the drawing room. Go up to the bathroom. Wash your face. Quick."

She sprang awkwardly to her feet and darted through the window as Joanna came around the corner of the house.

I told her Megan had come to lunch.

"Good," said Joanna. "I like Megan, though I rather think she's a changeling. Something left on a doorstep by the fairies. But she's interesting."

I see that so far I have made little mention of the Reverend and Mrs. Calthrop.

And yet both the vicar and his wife were distinct personalities. Dane Calthrop himself was perhaps a being more remote from everyday life than anyone I have ever met. His existence was in his books and in his study. Mrs. Dane Calthrop, on the other hand, was quite terrifyingly on the spot. Though she seldom gave advice and never interfered, yet she represented to the uneasy consciences of the village the Deity personified.

She stopped me in the High Street the day after Megan had come to lunch. I had the usual feeling of surprise, because Mrs. Dane Calthrop's progress resembled coursing more than walking, thus according with her startling resemblance to a greyhound, and as her eyes were always fixed on the distant horizon you felt sure that her real objective was about a mile and a half away.

"Oh!" she said. "Mr. Burton!"

She said it rather triumphantly, as someone might who had solved a particularly clever puzzle. I admitted that I was Mr. Burton and Mrs. Dane Calthrop stopped focusing on the horizon and seemed to be trying to focus on me instead.

"Now what," she said, "did I want to see you about?"

I could not help her there. She stood frowning, deeply perplexed. "Something rather nasty," she said.

"I'm sorry about that," I said startled.

"Ah," cried Mrs. Dane Calthrop. "Anonymous letters! What's this story you've brought down here about anonymous letters?"

"I didn't bring it," I said, "it was here already."

"Nobody got any until you came, though," said Mrs. Dane Calthrop accusingly.

"But they did, Mrs. Dane Calthrop. The trouble had already started."

"Oh, dear," said Mrs. Dane Calthrop. "I don't like that."

She stood there, her eyes absent and far away again. She said:

"I can't help feeling it's all wrong. We're not like that here. Envy, of course, and malice, and all the mean spiteful little sins—but I didn't think there was anyone who would do that. No, I really didn't. And it distresses me, you see, because I ought to know."

Her fine eyes came back from the horizon and met mine. They were worried, and seemed to hold the honest bewilderment of a child's.

"Why ought you to know?" I said.

"I usually do. I've always felt that's my function. Caleb preaches good sound doctrine and administers the sacraments. That's a priest's duty, but if you admit marriage at all for a priest, then I think his wife's duty is to know what people are feeling and thinking, even if she can't do anything about it. And I haven't the least idea whose mind is—"

She broke off, adding absently, "They are such silly letters, too."

"Have you—er—had any yourself?"

I was a little diffident of asking, but Mrs. Dane Calthrop replied perfectly naturally, her eyes opening a little wider:

"Oh, yes, two—no, three. I forget exactly what they said. Something very silly about Caleb and the schoolmistress, I think. Quite absurd, because Caleb has absolutely no taste for flirtation. He never has had. So lucky being a clergyman."

"Quite," I said, "oh, quite."

"Caleb would have been a saint," said Mrs. Dane Calthrop, "if he hadn't been just a little too intellectual."

I did not feel qualified to answer this criticism, and anyway Mrs. Dane Calthrop went on, leaping back from her husband to the letters in rather a puzzling way.

"There are so many things the letters might say, but don't. That's what is so curious."

"I should hardly have thought they erred on the side of restraint," I said bitterly.

"But they don't seem to know anything. None of the real things."

"You mean?"

Those fine vague eyes met mine.

"Well, of course. There's plenty of wrongdoing here—any amount of shameful secrets. Why doesn't the writer use those?" She paused and then asked abruptly, "What did they say in your letter?"

"They suggested that my sister wasn't my sister."

"And she is?"

Mrs. Dane Calthrop asked the question with unembarrassed friendly interest.

"Certainly Joanna is my sister."

Mrs. Dane Calthrop nodded her head. "That just shows you what I mean. I daresay there are other things—"

Her clear uninterested eyes looked at me thoughtfully, and I suddenly understood why Lymstock was afraid of Mrs. Dane Calthrop.

In everybody's life there are hidden chapters which they hope may never be known. I felt that Mrs. Dane Calthrop knew them.

For once in my life, I was positively delighted when Aimée Griffith's hearty voice boomed out:

"Hullo, Maud. Glad I've just caught you. I want to suggest an alteration of date for the Sale of Work. Morning, Mr. Burton."

She went on:

"I must just pop into the grocer's and leave my order, then I'll come along to the Institute if that suits you?"

"Yes, yes, that will do quite well," said Mrs. Dane Calthrop.

Aimée Griffith went into the International Stores.

Mrs. Dane Calthrop said, "Poor thing."

I was puzzled. Surely she could not be pitying Aimée?

She went on, however: "You know, Mr. Burton, I'm rather afraid—"

"About this letter business?"

"Yes, you see it means—it must mean—" She paused, lost in thought, her eyes screwed up. Then she said slowly, as one who solves a problem, "Blind hatred . . . yes, blind hatred. But even a blind man might stab to the heart by pure chance. . . . And what would happen then, Mr. Burton?"

We were to know that before another day had passed.

Partridge, who enjoys calamity, came into Joanna's room at an early hour the following morning, and told her with considerable relish that Mrs. Symmington had committed suicide on the preceding afternoon.

Joanna, who had been lost in the mists of sleep, sat up in bed shocked wide awake.

"Oh, Partridge, how awful."

"Awful it is, Miss. It's wickedness taking your own life. Not but what she was drove to it, poor soul."

Joanna had an inkling of the truth then. She felt rather sick.

"Not—?" Her eyes questioned Partridge and Partridge nodded.

"That's right, Miss. One of them nasty letters."

"How beastly," said Joanna. "How absolutely beastly! All the same, I don't see why she should kill herself for a letter like that."

"Looks as though what was in the letter was true, Miss."

"What was in it?"

But that, Partridge couldn't or wouldn't say. Joanna came in to me, looking white and shocked. It seemed worse, somehow, that Mrs. Symmington was not the kind of person you associated with tragedy.

Joanna suggested that we might ask Megan to come to us for a day or two. Elsie Holland, she said, would be all right with the children, but was the kind of person who would, almost certainly, drive Megan half mad.

I agreed. I could imagine Elsie Holland uttering platitude after platitude and suggesting innumerable cups of tea. A kindly creature but not the right person for Megan.

We drove down to the Symmingtons' house after breakfast. We were both of us a little nervous. Our arrival might look like sheer ghoulish curiosity. Luckily we met Owen Griffith just coming out. He greeted me with some warmth, his worried face lighting up.

"Oh, hullo, Burton, I'm glad to see you. What I was afraid would happen sooner or later has happened. A damnable business!"

"Good morning, Dr. Griffith," said Joanna, using the voice she keeps for one of our deafer aunts.

Griffith started and flushed. "Oh—oh, good morning, Miss Burton."

"I thought perhaps," said Joanna, "that you didn't see me."

Owen Griffith got redder still. His shyness enveloped him like a mantle. "I'm—I'm so sorry—preoccupied—I didn't."

Joanna went on mercilessly.

"After all, I am life-size."

"Merely kit-kat," I said in a stern aside to her. Then I went on:

"My sister and I, Griffith, wondered whether it would be a good thing if the girl came and stopped with us for a day or two? What do you think? I don't want to butt in—but it must be rather grim for the poor child. What would Symmington feel about it, do you think?"

Griffith turned the idea over in his mind for a moment or two.

"I think it would be an excellent thing," he said at last. "She's a queer, nervous sort of girl, and it would be good for her to get away from the whole thing. Miss Holland is doing wonders—she's an excellent head on her shoulders, but she really has quite enough to do with the two children and Symmington himself. He's quite broken up—bewildered."

"It was"—I hesitated—"suicide?"

Griffith nodded.

"Oh, yes. No question of accident. She wrote, 'I can't go on,' on a scrap of paper. The letter must have come by yesterday afternoon's post. The envelope was down on the floor by her chair and the letter itself was screwed up into a ball and thrown into the fireplace."

"What did—"

I stopped, rather horrified at myself.

"I beg your pardon," I said.

Griffith gave a quick, unhappy smile.

"You needn't mind asking. That letter will have to be read at the inquest. No getting out of it, more's the pity. It was the usual kind of thing—couched in the same foul style. The specific accusation was that the second boy, Colin, was not Symmington's child."

"Do you think that was true?" I exclaimed incredulously.

Griffith shrugged his shoulders.

"I've no means of forming a judgment. I've only been here five years. As far as I've ever seen, the Symmingtons were a placid, happy couple devoted to each other and their children. It's true that the boy doesn't particularly resemble his parents—he's got bright red hair, for one thing—but a child often throws back in appearance to a grandfather or grandmother."

"That lack of resemblance might have been what prompted the particular accusation. A foul and quite uncalled-for blow at a venture."

"But it happened to hit the bull's-eye," said Joanna. "After all, she wouldn't have killed herself otherwise, would she?"

Griffith said doubtfully:

"I'm not quite sure. She's been ailing in health for sometime—neurotic, hysterical. I've been treating her for a nervous condition. It's possible, I think, that the shock of receiving such a letter, couched in those terms, may have induced such a state of panic and despondency that she may have decided to take her life. She may have worked herself up to feel that her husband might not believe her if she denied the story, and the general shame and disgust might have worked upon her so powerfully as to unbalance her judgment temporarily."

"Suicide while of unsound mind," said Joanna.

"Exactly. I shall be quite justified, I think, in putting forward that point of view at the inquest."

Joanna and I went on into the house.

The front door was open and it seemed easier than ringing the bell, especially as we heard Elsie Holland's voice inside.

She was talking to Mr. Symmington who, huddled in a chair, was looking completely dazed.

"No, but really, Mr. Symmington, you must take something. You haven't had any breakfast, not what I call a proper breakfast, and nothing to eat last night, and what with the shock and all, you'll be getting ill yourself, and you'll need all your strength. The doctor said so before he left."

Symmington said in a toneless voice, "You're very kind, Miss Holland, but—"

"A nice cup of hot tea," said Elsie Holland, thrusting the beverage on him firmly.

Personally I should have given the poor devil a stiff whisky-and-soda. He looked as though he needed it. However he accepted the tea, and looking up at Elsie Holland:

"I can't thank you for all you've done and are doing, Miss Holland. You've been perfectly splendid."

The girl flushed and looked pleased.

"It's nice of you to say that, Mr. Symmington. You must let me do all I can to help. Don't worry about the children—I'll see to them, and I've got the servants calmed down, and if there's anything I can do, letter-writing or telephoning, don't hesitate to ask me."

"You're very kind," Symmington said again.

Elsie Holland, turning, caught sight of us and came hurrying out into the hall.

"Isn't it terrible?" she said in a hushed whisper.

I thought, as I looked at her, that she was really a very nice girl. Kind, competent, practical in an emergency. Her magnificent blue eyes were just faintly rimmed with pink, showing that she had been soft-hearted enough to shed tears for her employer's death.

"Can we speak to you a minute?" asked Joanna. "We don't want to disturb Mr. Symmington."

Elsie Holland nodded comprehendingly and led the way into the dining room on the other side of the hall.

"It's been awful for him," she said. "Such a shock. Who ever would have thought a thing like this could happen? But of course, I do realize now that she had been queer for some time. Awfully nervous and weepy. I thought it was her health, though Dr. Griffith always said there was nothing really wrong with her. But she was snappy and irritable and some days you wouldn't know just how to take her."

"What we really came for," said Joanna, "was to know whether we could have Megan for a few days—that is, if she'd like to come."

Elsie Holland looked rather surprised.

"Megan?" she said doubtfully. "I don't know, I'm sure. I mean, it's ever so kind of you, but she's such a queer girl. One never knows what she's going to say or feel about things."

Joanna said rather vaguely, "We thought it might be a help, perhaps."

"Oh, well, as far as that goes, it would. I mean, I've got the boys to look after (they're with cook just now) and poor Mr. Symmington—he really needs looking after as much as anyone, and such a lot to do and see to. I really haven't had time to say much to Megan. I think she's upstairs in the old nursery at the top of the house. She seems to want to get away from everyone. I don't know if—"

Joanna gave me the faintest of looks. I slipped quickly out of the room and upstairs.

The old nursery was at the top of the house. I opened the door and went in. The room downstairs had given on to the garden behind and the blinds had not been down there. But in this room which faced the road they were decorously drawn down.

Through a dim gray gloom I saw Megan. She was crouching on a divan set against the far wall, and I was reminded at once of some terrified animal, hiding. She looked petrified with fear.

"Megan," I said.

I came forward, and unconsciously I adopted the tone one does adopt when you want to reassure a frightened animal. I'm really surprised I didn't hold out a carrot or a piece of sugar. I felt like that.

She stared at me, but she did not move, and her expression did not alter.

"Megan," I said again. "Joanna and I have come to ask you if you would like to come and stay with us for a little."

Her voice came hollowly out of the dim twilight:

"Stay with you? In your house?"

"Yes."

"You mean, you'll take me away from here?"

"Yes, my dear."

Suddenly she began to shake all over. It was frightening and very moving.

"Oh, do take me away! Please do. It's so awful, being here, and feeling so wicked."

I came over to her and her hands fastened on my coat sleeve.

"I'm an awful coward. I didn't know what a coward I was."

"It's all right, funnyface," I said. "These things are a bit shattering. Come along."

"Can we go at once? Without waiting a minute?"

"Well, you'll have to put a few things together, I suppose."

"What sort of things? Why?"

"My dear girl," I said. "We can provide you with a bed and a bath and the rest of it, but I'm darned if I lend you my toothbrush."

She gave a very faint weak little laugh.

"I see. I think I'm stupid today. You mustn't mind. I'll go and pack some things. You—you won't go away? You'll wait for me?"

"I'll be on the mat."

"Thank you. Thank you very much. I'm sorry I'm so stupid. But you see it's rather dreadful when your mother dies."

"I know," I said.

I gave her a friendly pat on the back and she flashed me a grateful look and disappeared into a bedroom. I went on downstairs.

"I found Megan," I said. "She's coming."

"Oh, now, that is a good thing," exclaimed Elsie Holland. "It will take her out of herself. She's rather a nervy girl, you know. Difficult. It will be a great relief to feel I haven't got her on my mind as well as everything else. It's very kind of you, Miss Burton. I hope she won't be a nuisance. Oh, dear, there's the telephone. I must go and answer it. Mr. Symmington isn't fit."

She hurried out of the room.

Joanna said, "Quite the ministering angel!"

"You said that rather nastily," I observed. "She's a nice, kind girl, and obviously most capable."

"Most. And she knows it."

"This is unworthy of you, Joanna," I said.

"Meaning why shouldn't the girl do her stuff?"

"Exactly."

"I never can stand seeing people pleased with themselves," said Joanna. "It arouses all my worst instincts. How did you find Megan?"

"Crouching in a darkened room looking rather like a stricken gazelle."

"Poor kid. She was quite willing to come?"

"She leaped at it."

A series of thuds out in the hall announced the descent of Megan and her suitcase. I went out and took it from her.

Joanna, behind me, said urgently, "Come on. I've already refused some nice hot tea twice."

We went out to the car. It annoyed me that Joanna had to sling the suitcase in. I could get along with one stick now, but I couldn't do any athletic feats.

"Get in," I said to Megan.

She got in, I followed her. Joanna started the car and we drove off.

We got to Little Furze and went into the drawing room.

Megan dropped into a chair and burst into tears. She cried with the hearty fervor of a child—bawled, I think, is the right word. I left the room in search of a remedy. Joanna stood by feeling rather helpless, I think.

Presently I heard Megan say in a thick choked voice, "I'm sorry for doing this. It seems idiotic."

Joanna said kindly, "Not at all. Have another handkerchief."

I gather she supplied the necessary article. I re-entered the room and handed Megan a brimming glass.

"What is it?"

"A cocktail," I said.

"Is it? Is it really?" Megan's tears were instantly dried. "I've never drunk a cocktail."

"Everything has to have a beginning," I said.

Megan sipped her drink gingerly, then a beaming smile spread over her face, she tilted her head back and gulped it down at a draught.

"It's lovely," she said. "Can I have another?"

"No," I said.

"Why not?"

"In about ten minutes you'll probably know."

"Oh!"

Megan transferred her attention to Joanna.

"I really am awfully sorry for having made such a nuisance of myself howling away like that. I can't think why. It seems awfully silly when I'm so glad to be here."

"That's all right," said Joanna. "We're very pleased to have you."

"You can't be really. It's just kindness on your part. But I am grateful."

"Please don't be grateful," said Joanna, "it will embarrass me. You're our friend and we're glad to have you here. That's all there is to it. . . ."

She took Megan upstairs to unpack.

Partridge came in, looking sour, and said she had made two cup custards for lunch and what should she do about it?

The inquest was held three days later.

The time of Mrs. Symmington's death was put at between three and four o'clock. She was alone in the house, Symmington was at his office, the maids were having their day out, Elsie Holland and the children were out walking and Megan had gone for a bicycle ride.

The letter must have come by the afternoon post. Mrs. Symmington must have taken it out of the box, read it—and then in a state of agitation she had gone to the potting shed, fetched some of the cyanide kept there for taking wasps' nests, dissolved it in water and drunk it after writing those last agitated words, "I can't go on . . ."

Owen Griffith gave medical evidence and stressed the view he had outlined to us of Mrs. Symmington's nervous condition and poor stamina. The coroner was suave and discreet. He spoke with bitter condemnation of people who write those despicable things, anonymous letters. Whoever had written that wicked and lying letter was morally guilty of murder, he said. He hoped the police would soon discover the culprit and take action against him or her. Such a dastardly and malicious piece of spite deserved to be punished with the utmost rigor of the law. Directed by him, the jury brought in the inevitable verdict: Suicide while temporarily insane.

The coroner had done his best—Owen Griffith also, but afterward, jammed in the crowd of eager village women, I heard the same hateful sibilant whisper I had begun to know so well: "No smoke without fire, that's what I say!" "Must 'a been something in it for certain sure. She wouldn't never have done it otherwise . . ."

Just for a moment I hated Lymstock and its narrow boundaries, and its gossiping whispering women.

Outside, Aimée Griffith said with a sigh:

"Well, that's over. Bad luck on Dick Symmington, its all having to come out. I wonder whether he'd ever had any suspicion."

I was startled.

"But surely you heard him say most emphatically that there wasn't a word of truth in that lying letter?"

"Of course he said so. Quite right. A man's got to stick up for his wife. Dick would." She paused and then explained: "You see, I've known Dick Symmington a long time."

"Really?" I said surprised. "I understood from your brother that he only bought this practice a few years ago."

"Yes, but Dick Symmington used to come and stay in our part of the world up north. I've known him for years."

I looked at Aimée curiously. She went on, still in that softened tone, "I know Dick very well . . . He's a proud man and very reserved. But he's the sort of man who could be very jealous."

"That would explain," I said deliberately, "why Mrs. Symmington was afraid to show him or tell him about the letter. She was afraid that, being a jealous man, he might not believe her denials."

Miss Griffith looked at me angrily and scornfully. "Good Lord," she said. "Do you think any woman would go and swallow a lot of cyanide of potassium for an accusation that wasn't true?"

"The coroner seemed to think it was possible. Your brother, too—"

Aimée interrupted me:

"Men are all alike. All for preserving the decencies. But you don't catch me believing that stuff. If an innocent woman gets some foul anonymous letter, she laughs and chucks it away. That's what I—" she paused suddenly, and then finished—"would do."

But I had noticed the pause. I was almost sure that what she had been about to say was "That's what I did."

I decided to take the war into the enemy's country.

"I see," I said pleasantly. "So you've had one, too?"

Aimée Griffith was the type of woman who scorns to lie. She paused a minute—flushed, then said, "Well, yes. But I didn't let it worry me!"

"Nasty?" I inquired sympathetically, as a fellow sufferer.

"Naturally. These things always are. The ravings of a lunatic! I read a few words of it, realized what it was and chucked it straight into the wastepaper basket."

"You didn't think of taking it to the police?"

"Not then. Least said soonest mended—that's what I felt."

An urge came over me to say solemnly, "No smoke without fire!" but I restrained myself.

I asked her if she had any idea how her mother's death would affect Megan financially. Would it be necessary for the girl to earn her own living?

"I believe she has a small income left her by her grandmother and of course Dick would always give her a home. But it would be much better for her to do something—not just slack about the way she does."

"I should have said Megan is at the age when a girl wants to enjoy herself—not to work."

Aimée flushed and said sharply, "You're like all men—you dislike the idea of women competing. It is incredible to you that women should want a career. It was incredible to my parents. I was anxious to study for a doctor. They would not hear of paying the fees. But they paid them readily for Owen. Yet I should have made a better doctor than my brother."

"I'm sorry about that," I said. "It was tough on you. If one wants to do a thing—"

She went on quickly.

"Oh, I've got over it now. I've plenty of will power. My life is busy and active. I'm one of the happiest people in Lymstock. Plenty to do. But I go up in arms against the silly old-fashioned prejudice that woman's place is always the home."

"I'm sorry if I offended you," I said. I had had no idea that Aimée Griffith could be so vehement.

III

I MET SYMMINGTON in the town later in the day.

"Is it quite all right for Megan to stay on with us for a bit?" I asked. "It's company for Joanna—she's rather lonely sometimes with none of her own friends."

"Oh—er—Megan? Oh, yes, very good of you."

I took a dislike to Symmington then which I never quite overcame. He had so obviously forgotten all about Megan. I wouldn't have minded if he had actively disliked the girl—a man may sometimes be jealous of a first husband's child—but he didn't dislike her, he just hardly noticed her. He felt toward her much as a man who doesn't care much for dogs would feel about a dog in the house. You notice it when you fall over it and swear at it, and you give it a vague pat sometimes when it presents itself to be patted. Symmington's complete indifference to his stepdaughter annoyed me very much.

I said, "What are you planning to do with her?"

"With Megan?" He seemed rather startled. "Well, she'll go on living at home. I mean, naturally, it is her home."

My grandmother, of whom I had been very fond, used to sing old-fashioned songs to her guitar. One of them, I remember, ended thus:

"Oh, maid most dear, I am not here,
I have no place, no part,
No dwelling more, by sea nor shore,
But only in your heart."

I went home humming it.

Emily Barton came just after tea had been cleared away.

She wanted to talk about the garden.

We talked garden for about half an hour. Then we turned back toward the house.

It was then that lowering her voice, she murmured, "I do hope that that child—that she hasn't been too much upset by all this dreadful business?"

"Her mother's death, you mean?"

"That, of course. But I really meant, the—the unpleasantness behind it."

I was curious. I wanted Miss Barton's reaction.

"What do you think about that? Was it true?"

"Oh, no, no, surely not. I'm quite sure that Mrs. Symmington never—that he wasn't—" little Emily Barton was pink and confused—"I mean it's quite untrue—although of course it may have been a judgment."

"A judgment?" I said, staring.

Emily Barton was very pink, very Dresden china shepherdesslike.

"I cannot help feeling that all these dreadful letters, all the sorrow and pain they have caused, may have been sent for a purpose."

"They were sent for a purpose, certainly," I said grimly.

"No, no, Mr. Burton, you misunderstand me. I'm not talking of the misguided creature who wrote them—someone quite abandoned that must be. I mean that they have been permitted—by Providence! To awaken us to a sense of our shortcomings."

"Surely," I said, "the Almighty could choose a less unsavory weapon."

Miss Emily murmured that God moved in a mysterious way.

"No," I said. "There's too much tendency to attribute to God the evils that man does of his own free will. I might concede you the Devil. God doesn't really need to punish us, Miss Barton. We're so very busy punishing ourselves."

"What I can't make out is why should anyone want to do such a thing?"

I shrugged my shoulders. "A warped mentality."

"It seems very sad."

"It doesn't seem to me sad. It seems to me just damnable. And I don't apologize for the word. I mean just that."

The pink had gone out of Miss Barton's cheeks. They were very white.

"But why, Mr. Burton, why? What pleasure can anyone get out of it?"

"Nothing you and I can understand, thank goodness."

Emily Barton lowered her voice: "Nothing of this kind has ever happened before—never in my memory. It has been such a happy little community. What would my dear mother have said? Well, one must be thankful that she has been spared."

I thought from all I had heard that old Mrs. Barton had been sufficiently tough to have taken anything, and would probably have enjoyed this sensation.

Emily went on, "It distresses me deeply."

"You've not—er—had anything yourself?"

She flushed crimson. "Oh, no—oh, no, indeed. Oh! that would be dreadful."

I apologized hastily, but she went away looking rather upset.

I went into the house. Joanna was standing by the drawing-room fire which she had just lit, for the evenings were still chilly. She had an open letter in her hand.

She turned her head quickly as I entered.

"Jerry! I found this in the letter box—dropped in by hand. It begins: 'You painted trollop . . .' "

"What else does it say?"

Joanna gave a wide grimace. "Same old muck."

She dropped it on to the fire. With a quick gesture that hurt my back I jerked it off again just before it caught.

"Don't," I said. "We may need it."

"Need it?"

"For the police."

Superintendent Nash came to see me the following morning. From the first moment I saw him I took a great liking to him. He was the best type of C.I.D. County Superintendent. Tall, soldierly, with quiet, reflective eyes and a straightforward, unassuming manner.

"Good morning, Mr. Burton," he said. "I expect you can guess what I've come to see you about."

"Yes, I think so. This letter business."

He nodded.

"I understand you had one of them?"

"Yes, soon after we got here."

"What did it say exactly?"

I thought a minute, then conscientiously repeated the wording of the letter as closely as possible.

The superintendent listened with an immovable face, showing no signs of any kind of emotion.

When I had finished, he said, "I see. You didn't keep the letter, Mr. Burton?"

"I'm sorry. I didn't. You see, I thought it was just an isolated instance of spite against newcomers to the place."

The superintendent inclined his head comprehendingly.

"A pity," he said briefly.

"However," I said, "my sister got one yesterday. I just stopped her putting it in the fire."

"Thank you, Mr. Burton, that was thoughtful of you."

I went across to my desk and unlocked the drawer in which I had put it. It was not, I thought, very suitable for Partridge's eyes. I gave it to Nash.

He read it through. Then he looked up and asked:

"Is this the same in appearance as the last one?"

"I think so—as far as I can remember."

"The same difference between the envelope and the text?"

"Yes," I said. "The envelope was typed. The letter itself had printed words pasted on to a sheet of paper."

Nash nodded and put it in his pocket. Then he said:

"I wonder, Mr. Burton, if you would mind coming down to the station with me? We could have a conference there and it would save a good deal of time and overlapping."

"Certainly," I said. "You would like me to come now?"

"If you don't mind."

There was a police car at the door. We drove down in it.

I said, "Do you think you'll be able to get to the bottom of this?"

Nash nodded with easy confidence. "Oh, yes, we'll get to the bottom of it all right. It's a question of time and routine. They're slow, these cases, but they're pretty sure. It's a matter of narrowing things down."

"Elimination?" I said.

"Yes. And general routine."

"Watching post boxes, examining typewriters, fingerprints, all that?"

He smiled. "As you say."

At the police station I found Symmington and Griffith were already there. I was introduced to a tall, lantern-jawed man in plain clothes, Inspector Graves.

"Inspector Graves," explained Nash, "has come down from London to help us. He's an expert on anonymous letter cases."

Inspector Graves smiled mournfully. I reflected that a life spent in the pursuit of anonymous letter writers must be singularly depressing. Inspector Graves, however, showed a kind of melancholy enthusiasm.

"They're all the same, these cases," he said in a deep lugubrious voice like a depressed bloodhound. "You'd be surprised. The wording of the letters and the things they say."

"We had a case just on two years ago," said Nash. "Inspector Graves helped us then."

Some of the letters, I saw, were spread out on the table in front of Graves. He had evidently been examining them.

"Difficulty is," said Nash, "to get hold of the letters. Either people put them in the fire, or they won't admit to having received anything of the kind. Stupid, you see, and afraid of being mixed up with the police. They're a backward lot here."

"Still we've got a fair amount to get on with," said Graves. Nash took the letter I had given him from his pocket and tossed it over to Graves.

The latter glanced through it, laid it with the others and observed approvingly, "Very nice—very nice indeed."

It was not the way I should have chosen to describe the epistle in question, but experts, I suppose, have their own point of view. I was glad that that screed of vituperative and obscene abuse gave somebody pleasure.

"We've got enough, I think, to go on with," said Inspector Graves, "and I'll ask all you gentlemen, if you should get any more, to bring them along at once. Also, if you hear of someone else getting one (you, in particular, doctor, among your patients) do your best to get them to come along here with them. I've got"—he sorted with deft fingers among his exhibits—"one to Mr. Symmington, received as far back as two months ago, one to Dr. Griffith, one to Miss Ginch, one written to Mrs. Mudge, the butcher's wife, one to Jennifer Clark, barmaid at the Three Crowns, the one received by Mrs. Symmington, this one now to Miss Burton—oh, yes, and one to the bank manager."

"Quite a representative collection," I remarked.

"And not one I couldn't match from other cases! This one here is as near as nothing to one written by that milliner woman. This one is the dead spit of an outbreak we had up in Northumberland—written by a schoolgirl, they were. I can tell you, gentlemen, I'd like to see something new sometimes, instead of the same old treadmill."

"There is nothing new under the sun," I murmured.

"Quite so, sir. You'd know that if you were in our profession."

Nash sighed and said, "Yes, indeed."

Symmington asked, "Have you come to any definite opinion as to the writer?"

Graves cleared his throat and delivered a small lecture:

"There are certain similarities shared by all these letters. I shall enumerate them, gentlemen, in case they suggest anything to your minds. The text of the letters is composed of words made up from individual letters cut out of a printed book. It's an old book, printed, I should say, about the year 1830. This has obviously been done to avoid the risk of recognition through handwriting which is, as most people know nowadays, a fairly easy matter . . . the so-called disguising of a hand not amounting to much when faced with expert tests. There are no fingerprints on the letters and envelopes of a distinctive character. That is to say, they have been handled by the postal authorities, the recipient, and there are other stray fingerprints, but no set common to all, showing therefore that the person who put them together was careful to wear gloves.

"The envelopes are typewritten by a Windsor 7 machine, well worn, with the a and the t out of alignment. Most of them have been posted locally, or put in the box of a house by hand. It is therefore evident that they are of local provenance. They were written by a woman, and in my opinion a woman of middle age or over, and probably, though not certainly, unmarried."

We maintained a respectful silence for a minute or two. Then I said, "The typewriter's your best bet, isn't it? That oughtn't to be difficult in a little place like this."

Inspector Graves shook his head sadly and said, "That's where you're wrong, sir."

"The typewriter," said Superintendent Nash, "is unfortunately too easy. It is an old one from Mr. Symmington's office, given by him to the Women's Institute where, I may say, it's fairly easy of access. The ladies here all often go into the Institute."

"Can't you tell something definite from the—er—the touch, don't you call it?"

Again Graves nodded. "Yes, that can be done—but these envelopes have all been typed by someone using one finger."

"Someone, then, unused to the typewriter?"

"No, I wouldn't say that. Someone, perhaps, who can type but doesn't want us to know the fact."

"Whoever writes these things has been very cunning," I said slowly.

"She is, sir, she is," said Graves. "Up to every trick of the trade."

"I shouldn't have thought one of these bucolic women down here would have had the brains," I said.

Graves coughed. "I haven't made myself plain, I'm afraid. Those letters were written by an educated woman."

"What, by a lady?"

The word slipped out involuntarily. I hadn't used the term "lady" for years. But now it came automatically to my lips, re-echoed from days long ago, and my grandmother's faint unconsciously arrogant voice saying, "Of course, she isn't a lady, dear."

Nash understood at once. The word lady still meant something to him.

"Not necessarily a lady," he said. "But certainly not a village woman. They're mostly pretty illiterate down here, can't spell, and certainly can't express themselves with fluency."

I was silent, for I had had a shock. The community was so small. Unconsciously I had visualized the writer of the letters as a Mrs. Cleat or her like, some spiteful, cunning half-wit.

Symmington put my thoughts into words. He said sharply, "But that narrows it down to about half a dozen to a dozen people in the whole place! I can't believe it."

Then, with a slight effort, and looking straight in front of him as though the mere sound of his own words was distasteful, he said:

"You have heard what I stated at the inquest. In case you may have thought that that statement was actuated by a desire to protect my wife's memory, I should like to repeat now that I am firmly convinced that the subject matter of the letter my wife received was absolutely false. I know it was false. My wife was a very sensitive woman, and—er—well, you might call it prudish in some respects. Such a letter would have been a great shock to her, and she was in poor health."

Graves responded instantly:

"That's quite likely to be right, sir. None of these letters show any signs of intimate knowledge. They're just blind accusations. There's been no attempt to blackmail. And there doesn't seem to be any religious bias—such as we sometimes get. It's just sex and spite! And that's going to give us quite a good pointer toward the writer."

Symmington got up. Dry and unemotional as the man was, his lips were trembling.

"I hope you find the devil who writes these soon. She murdered my wife as surely as if she'd put a knife into her." He paused. "How does she feel now, I wonder?"

He went out, leaving that question unanswered.

"How does she feel, Griffith?" I asked. It seemed to me the answer was in his province.

"God knows. Remorseful, perhaps. On the other hand, it may be that she's enjoying her power. Mrs. Symmington's death may have fed her mania."

"I hope not," I said, with a slight shiver. "Because if so, she'll—"

I hesitated and Nash finished the sentence for me:

"She'll try it again? That, Mr. Burton, would be the best thing that could happen, for us. The pitcher goes to the well once too often, remember."

"She'd be mad to go on with it," I exclaimed.

"She'll go on," said Graves. "They always do. It's a vice, you know, they can't let it alone."

I shook my head with a shudder. I asked if they needed me any longer, I wanted to get out into the air. The atmosphere seemed tinged with evil.

"There's nothing more, Mr. Burton," said Nash. "Only keep your eyes open, and do as much propaganda as you can—that is to say, urge on everyone that they've got to report any letter they receive."

I nodded.

"I should think everyone in the place has had one of the foul things by now," I said.

"I wonder," said Graves. He put his sad head a little on one side and asked, "You don't know, definitely, of anyone who hasn't had a letter?"

"What an extraordinary question! The population at large isn't likely to take me into their confidence."

"No, no, Mr. Burton, I didn't mean that. I just wondered if you knew of any one person who quite definitely, to your certain knowledge, has not received an anonymous letter."

"Well, as a matter of fact," I hesitated, "I do, in a way."

And I repeated my conversation with Emily Barton and what she had said.

Graves received the information with a wooden face and said, "Well, that may come in useful. I'll note it down."

I went out into the afternoon sunshine with Owen Griffith. Once in the street, I swore aloud.

"What kind of place is this for a man to come to to lie in the sun and heal his wounds? It's full of festering poison, this place, and it looks as peaceful and as innocent as the Garden of Eden."

"Even there," said Owen drily, "there was one serpent."

"Look here, Griffith, do they know anything? Have they got any idea?"

"I don't know. They've got a wonderful technique, the police. They're seemingly so frank, and they tell you nothing."

"Yes. Nash is a nice fellow."

"And a very capable one."

"If anyone's batty in this place, you ought to know it," I said accusingly.

Griffith shook his head. He looked discouraged. But he looked more than that—he looked worried. I wondered if he had an inkling of some kind.

We had been walking along the High Street. I stopped at the door of the house agents.

"I believe my second installment of rent is due—in advance. I've got a good mind to pay it and clear out with Joanna right away. Forfeit the rest of the tenancy."

"Don't go," said Owen.

"Why not?"

He didn't answer. He said slowly after a minute or two, "After all—I dare say you're right. Lymstock isn't healthy just now. It might—it might harm you or—or your sister."

"Nothing harms Joanna," I said. "She's tough. I'm the weakly one. Somehow this business makes me sick."

"It makes me sick," said Owen.

I pushed the door of the house agents' place half open.

"But I shan't go," I said. "Vulgar curiosity is stronger than pusillanimity. I want to know the solution."

I went in.

A woman who was typing got up and came toward me. She had frizzy hair and simpered, but I found her more intelligent than the spectacled youth who had previously held sway in the outer office.

A minute or two later something familiar about her penetrated through to my consciousness. It was Miss Ginch, lately Symmington's lady clerk.

I commented on the fact.

"You used to be with Galbraith, Galbraith and Symmington, weren't you?" I said.

"Yes. Yes, indeed. But I thought it was better to leave. This is quite a good post, though not quite so well paid. But there are things that are more valuable than money, don't you think so?"

"Undoubtedly," I said.

"Those awful letters," breathed Miss Ginch in a sibilant whisper. "I got a dreadful one. About me and Mr. Symmington—oh, terrible it was, saying the most awful things! I knew my duty and I took it to the police, though of course it wasn't exactly pleasant for me, was it?"

"No, no, most unpleasant."

"But they thanked me and said I had done quite right. But I felt that, after that, if people were talking—and evidently they must have been, or where did the writer get the idea from?—then I must avoid even the appearance of evil, though there has never been anything at all wrong between me and Mr. Symmington."

I felt rather embarrassed.

"No, no, of course not."

"But people have such evil minds. Yes, alas, such evil minds!"

Nervously trying to avoid it, I nevertheless met her eye, and I made a most unpleasant discovery.

Miss Ginch was thoroughly enjoying herself.

Already once today I had come across someone who reacted pleasurably to anonymous letters. Inspector Graves' enthusiasm was professional. Miss Ginch's enjoyment I found merely suggestive and disgusting.

An idea flashed across my startled mind.

Had Miss Ginch written these letters herself?

When I got home I found Mrs. Dane Calthrop sitting talking to Joanna. She looked, I thought, gray and ill.

This has been a terrible shock to me, Mr. Burton," she said. "Poor thing, poor thing."

"Yes," I said. "It's awful to think of someone being driven to the stage of taking their own life."

"Oh, you mean Mrs. Symmington?"

"Didn't you?"

Mrs. Dane Calthrop shook her head. "Of course one is sorry for her, but it would have been bound to happen anyway, wouldn't it?"

"Would it?" said Joanna drily.

Mrs. Dane Calthrop turned to her.

"Oh, I think so, dear. If suicide is your idea of escape from trouble then it doesn't very much matter what the trouble is. Whenever some very unpleasant shock had to be faced, she'd have done the same thing. What it really comes down to is that she was that kind of woman. Not that one would have guessed it. She always seemed to me a selfish rather stupid woman, with a good firm hold on life. Not the kind to panic, you would think—but I'm beginning to realize how little I really know about anyone."

"I'm still curious as to whom you meant when you said 'Poor thing,'" I remarked.

She stared at me. "The woman who wrote the letters, of course."

"I don't think," I said drily, "I shall waste sympathy on her."

Mrs. Dane Calthrop leaned forward. She laid a hand on my knee.

"But don't you realize—can't you feel? Use your imagination. Think how desperately, violently unhappy anyone must be to sit down and write these things. How lonely, how cut off from human kind. Poisoned through and through, with a dark stream of poison that finds its outlet in this way. That's why I feel so self-reproachful. Somebody in this town has been racked with that terrible unhappiness, and I've had no idea of it. I should have had. You can't interfere with actions—I never do. But that black inward unhappiness—like a septic arm physically, all black and swollen. If you could cut it and let the poison out it would flow away harmlessly. Yes, poor soul, poor soul."

She got up to go.

I did not feel like agreeing with her. I had no sympathy for our anonymous letter writer whatsoever. But I did ask curiously:

"Have you any idea at all, Mrs. Calthrop, who this woman is?"

She turned her fine perplexed eyes on me. "Well, I can guess," she said. "But then I might be wrong, mightn't I?"

She went swiftly out through the door, popping her head back to ask: "Do tell me, why have you never married, Mr. Burton?"

In anyone else it would have been impertinence, but with Mrs. Dane Calthrop you felt that the idea had suddenly come into her head and she had really wanted to know.

"Shall we say," I said, rallying, "that I have never met the right woman?"

"We can say so," said Mrs. Dane Calthrop, "but it wouldn't be a very good answer, because so many men have obviously married the wrong woman."

This time she really departed.

Joanna said, "You know I really do think she's mad. But I like her. The people in the village here are afraid of her."

"So am I, a little."

"Because you never know what's coming next?"

"Yes. And there's a careless brilliancy about her guesses."

Joanna said slowly, "Do you really think whoever wrote these letters is very unhappy?"

"I don't know what the damned hag is thinking or feeling! And I don't care. It's her victims I'm sorry for."

It seems odd to me now that in our speculations about Poison Pen's frame of mind, we missed the most obvious one. Griffith had pictured her as possibly exultant. I had envisaged her as remorseful—appalled by the result of her handiwork. Mrs. Dane Calthrop had seen her as suffering.

Yet the obvious, the inevitable reaction we did not consider—or perhaps I should say, I did not consider. That reaction was Fear.

For with the death of Mrs. Symmington, the letters had passed out of one category into another. I don't know what the legal position was—Symmington knew, I suppose, but it was clear that with a death resulting, the position of the writer of the letters was much more serious. There could now be no question of passing it off as a joke if the identity of the writer was discovered. The police were active, a Scotland Yard expert was called in. It was vital now for the anonymous author to remain anonymous.

And granted that Fear was the principal reaction, other things followed. Those possibilities also I was blind to. Yet surely they should have been obvious.

Joanna and I came down rather late to breakfast the next morning. That is to say, late by the standards of Lymstock. It was nine-thirty, an hour at which, in London, Joanna was just unclosing an eyelid, and mine would probably be still tight shut.

However when Partridge had said, "Breakfast at half past eight, or nine o'clock?" neither Joanna nor I had had the nerve to suggest a later hour.

To my annoyance, Aimée Griffith was standing on the doorstep talking to Megan.

She gave tongue with her usual heartiness at the sight of us:

"Hullo, there, slackers! I've been up for hours."

That, of course, was her own business. A doctor, no doubt, has to have early breakfast, and a dutiful sister is there to pour out his tea or coffee. But it is no excuse for coming and butting in on one's more somnolent neighbors. Nine-thirty is not the time for a morning call.

Megan slipped back into the house and into the dining room, where I gathered she had been interrupted in her breakfast.

"I said I wouldn't come in," said Aimée Griffith—"though why it is more of a merit to force people to come and speak to you on the doorstep, than to talk to them inside the house I do not know. Just wanted to ask Miss Burton if she'd any vegetables to spare for our Red Cross stall on the main road. If so, I'd get Owen to call for them in the car."

"You're out and about very early," I said.

"The early bird catches the worm," said Aimée. "You have a better chance of finding people in this time of day. I'm off to Mr. Pye's next. Got to go over to Brenton this afternoon. Guides."

"Your energy makes me quite tired," I said, and at that moment the telephone rang and I retired to the back of the hall to answer it, leaving Joanna murmuring rather doubtfully something about rhubarb and French beans and exposing her ignorance of the vegetable garden.

"Yes?" I said into the telephone mouthpiece.

A confused noise of deep breathing came from the other end of the wire and a doubtful female voice said, "Oh!"

"Yes?" I said again encouragingly.

"Oh," said the voice again, and then it inquired adenoidally, "Is that—what I mean—is that Little Furze?"

"This is Little Furze."

"Oh!" This clearly a stock beginning to every sentence. The voice inquired cautiously: "Could I speak to Miss Partridge just a minute?"

"Certainly," I said. "Who shall I say?"

"Oh. Tell her it's Agnes, would you? Agnes Waddle."

"Agnes Waddle?"

"That's right."

Resisting the temptation to say "Donald Duck to you," I put down the telephone receiver and called up the stairs to where I could hear the sound of Partridge's activities overhead.

"Partridge! Partridge!"

Partridge appeared at the head of the stairs, a long mop in one hand, and a look of "What is it now?" clearly discernible behind her invariably respectful manner.

"Yes, sir?"

"Agnes Waddle wants to speak to you on the telephone."

"I beg your pardon, sir?"

I raised my voice: "Agnes Waddle."

I have spelled the name as it presented itself to my mind. But I will now spell it as it was actually written:

"Agnes Woddell—whatever can she want now?"

Very much put out of countenance Partridge relinquished her mop and rustled down the stairs, her print dress crackling with agitation.

I beat an unobtrusive retreat into the dining room where Megan was wolfing down kidneys and bacon. Megan, unlike Aimée Griffith, was displaying no "glorious morning face." In fact she replied very gruffly to my morning salutations and continued to eat in silence.

I opened the morning paper and a minute or two later Joanna entered looking somewhat shattered.

"Whew!" she said. "I'm so tired. And I think I've exposed my utter ignorance of what grows when. Aren't there runner beans this time of year?"

"August," said Megan.

"Well, one has them any time in London," said Joanna defensively.

"Tins, sweet fool," I said. "And cold storage on ships from the far-flung limits of Empire."

"Like ivory, apes and peacocks?" asked Joanna.

"Exactly."

"I'd rather have peacocks," said Joanna thoughtfully.

"I'd like a monkey of my own as a pet," said Megan.

Meditatively peeling an orange, Joanna said:

"I wonder what it would feel like to be Aimée Griffith, all bursting with health and vigor and enjoyment of life. Do you think she's ever tired, or depressed, or—or wistful?"

I said I was quite certain Aimée Griffith was never wistful, and followed Megan out of the open French window onto the veranda.

Standing there, filling my pipe, I heard Partridge enter the dining room from the hall and heard her voice say grimly, "Can I speak to you a minute, Miss?"

"Dear me," I thought. "I hope Partridge isn't going to give notice. Emily Barton would be very annoyed with us if so."

Partridge went on:

"I must apologize, Miss, for being rung up on the telephone. That is to say, the young person who did so should have known better. I have never been in the habit of using the telephone or of permitting my friends to ring me up on it, and I'm very sorry indeed that it should have occurred, and the master taking the call and everything."

"Why, that's quite all right, Partridge," said Joanna soothingly, "why shouldn't your friends use the phone if they want to speak to you?"

Partridge's face, I could feel, though I could not see it, was more dour than ever as she replied coldly:

"It is not the kind of thing that has ever been done in this house. Miss Emily would never permit it. As I say, I am sorry it occurred, but Agnes Woddell, the girl who did it, was upset and she's young too, and doesn't know what's fitting in a gentleman's house."

"That's one for you, Joanna," I thought gleefully.

"This Agnes who rung me up, Miss," went on Partridge, "she used to be in service here under me. Sixteen she was, then, and come straight from the orphanage. And you see, not having a home, or a mother or any relations to advise her, she's been in the habit of coming to me. I can tell her what's what, you see."

"Yes?" said Joanna and waited. Clearly there was more to follow.

"So I am taking the liberty of asking you, Miss, if you would allow Agnes to come here to tea this afternoon in the kitchen. It's her day out, you see, and she's got something on her mind she wants to consult me about. I wouldn't dream of suggesting such a thing in the usual way."

Joanna said bewildered, "But why shouldn't you have anyone to tea with you?"

Partridge drew herself up at this, so Joanna said afterward and really looked most formidable, as she replied:

"It has never been the custom of this house, Miss. Old Mrs. Barton never allowed visitors in the kitchen, excepting as it should be our own day out, in which case we were allowed to entertain friends here instead of going out, but otherwise, on ordinary days, no. And Miss Emily keeps to the old ways."

Joanna is very nice to servants and most of them like her but she has never cut any ice with Partridge.

"It's no good, my girl," I said when Partridge had gone and Joanna had joined me outside. "Your sympathy and leniency are not appreciated. The good old overbearing ways for Partridge and things done the way they should be done in a gentleman's house."

"I never heard of such tyranny as not allowing them to have their friends to see them," said Joanna. "It's all very well, Jerry, but they can't like being treated like black slaves."

"Evidently they do," I said. "At least the Partridges of this world do."

"I can't imagine why she doesn't like me. Most people do."

"She probably despises you as an inadequate housekeeper. You never draw your hand across a shelf and examine it for traces of dust. You don't look under the mats. You don't ask what happened to the remains of the chocolate soufflé, and you never order a nice bread pudding."

"Ugh!" said Joanna.

She went on sadly: "I'm a failure all around today. Despised by our Aimée for ignorance of the vegetable kingdom. Snubbed by Partridge for being a human being. I shall now go out into the garden and eat worms."

"Megan's there already," I said.

For Megan had wandered away a few minutes previously and was now standing aimlessly in the middle of a patch of lawn looking not unlike a meditative bird waiting for nourishment.

She came back however toward us and said abruptly, "I say, I must go home today."

"What?" I was dismayed.

She went on, flushing, but speaking with nervous determination:

"It's been awfully good of you having me and I expect I've been a fearful nuisance, but I have enjoyed it awfully, only now I must go back, because after all, well, it's my home and one can't stay away for ever, so I think I'll go this morning."

Both Joanna and I tried to make her change her mind, but she was quite adamant, and finally Joanna got out the car and Megan went upstairs and came down a few minutes later with her belongings packed up again.

The only person pleased seemed to be Partridge, who had almost a smile on her grim face. She had never liked Megan much.

I was standing in the middle of the lawn when Joanna returned.

She asked me if I thought I was a sundial.

"Why?"

"Standing there like a garden ornament. Only one couldn't put on you the motto of only marking the sunny hours. You looked like thunder!"

"I'm out of humor. First Aimée Griffith—'Gracious!' murmured Joanna in parenthesis, 'I must speak about those vegetables!' and then Megan beetling off. I'd thought of taking her for a walk up to Legge Tor."

"With a collar and lead, I suppose," said Joanna.

"What?"

Joanna repeated loudly and clearly as she moved off around the corner of the house to the kitchen garden:

"I said 'With a collar and lead, I suppose?' Master's lost his dog, that's what's the matter with you!"

IV

I WAS ANNOYED, I must confess, at the abrupt way in which Megan had left us. Perhaps she had suddenly got bored with us.

After all, it wasn't a very amusing life for a girl. At home she had the kids and Elsie Holland.

I heard Joanna returning and hastily moved in case she should make more rude remarks about sundials.

Owen Griffith called in his car just before lunch time, and the gardener was waiting for him with the necessary garden produce.

While Old Adams was stowing it in the car I brought Owen indoors for a drink. He wouldn't stay to lunch.

When I came in with the sherry I found Joanna had begun doing her stuff.

No signs of animosity now. She was curled up in the corner of the sofa and was positively purring, asking Owen questions about his work, if he liked being a G.P., if he wouldn't rather have specialized? She thought doctoring was one of the most fascinating things in the world.

Say what you will of her, Joanna is a lovely, a heaven-born listener. And after listening to so many would-be geniuses telling her how they had been unappreciated, listening to Owen Griffith was easy money. By the time we had got to the third glass of sherry, Griffith was telling her about some obscure reaction or lesion in such scientific terms that nobody could have understood a word of it except a fellow medico.

Joanna was looking intelligent and deeply interested.

I felt a moment's qualm. It was really too bad of Joanna. Griffith was too good a chap to be played fast and loose with. Women really were devils.

Then I caught a sideways view of Griffith, his long, purposeful chin and the grim set of his lips, and I was not so sure that Joanna was going to have it her own way after all. And anyway a man has no business to let himself be made a fool of by a woman. It's his own lookout if he does.

Then Joanna said:

"Do change your mind and stay to lunch with us, Dr. Griffith," and Griffith flushed a little and said he would, only his sister would be expecting him back—

"We'll ring her up and explain," said Joanna quickly and went out into the hall and did so.

I thought Griffith looked a little uneasy, and it crossed my mind that he was probably a little afraid of his sister.

Joanna came back smiling and said that that was all right.

And Owen Griffith stayed to lunch and seemed to enjoy himself. We talked about books and plays and world politics, and about music and painting and modern architecture.

We didn't talk about Lymstock at all, or about anonymous letters, or Mrs. Symmington's suicide.

We got right away from everything, and I think Owen Griffith was happy. His dark sad face lighted up, and he revealed an interesting mind.

When he had gone I said to Joanna, "That fellow's too good for your tricks."

"That's what you say!" Joanna said. "You men all stick together!"

"Why are you out after his hide, Joanna? Wounded vanity?"

"Perhaps," said my sister.

That afternoon we were to go to tea with Miss Emily Barton at her rooms in the village.

We strolled down there on foot, for I felt strong enough now to manage the hill back again.

We must actually have allowed too much time and got there early, for the door was opened to us by a tall, raw-boned, fierce-looking woman who told us that Miss Barton wasn't in yet.

"But she's expecting you, I know, so if you'll come up and wait, please."

This was evidently faithful Florence.

We followed her up the stairs and she threw open a door and showed us into what was quite a comfortable sitting room, though perhaps a little over-furnished. Some of the things, I suspected, had come from Little Furze.

The woman was clearly proud of her room.

"It's nice, isn't it?" she demanded.

"Very nice," said Joanna warmly.

"I make her as comfortable as I can. Not that I can do for her as I'd like to and in the way she ought to have. She ought to be in her own house, properly, not turned out into rooms."

Florence, who was clearly a dragon, looked from one to the other of us reproachfully. It was not, I felt, our lucky day. Joanna had been ticked off by Aimée Griffith and Partridge and now we were both being ticked off by the dragon Florence.

"Parlormaid I was for nine years there," she added.

Joanna, goaded by injustice, said, "Well, Miss Barton wanted to let the house. She put it down at the house agents."

"Forced to it," said Florence. "And she living so frugal and careful. But even then, the government can't leave her alone! Has to have its pound of flesh just the same."

I shook my head sadly.

"Plenty of money there was in the old lady's time," said Florence. "And then they all died off one after another, poor dears. Miss Emily nursing of them one after the other. Wore herself out she did, and always so patient and uncomplaining. But it told on her, and then to have worry about money on top of it all! Shares not bringing in what they used to, so she says, and why not, I should like to know? They ought to be ashamed of themselves. Doing down a lady like her who's got no head for figures and can't be up to their tricks."

"Practically everyone has been hit that way," I said, but Florence remained unsoftened.

"It's all right for some as can look after themselves, but not for her. She needs looking after, and as long as she's with me I'm going to see no one imposes on her or upsets her in any way. I'd do anything for Miss Emily."

And glaring at us for some moments in order to drive that point thoroughly home, the indomitable Florence left the room, carefully shutting the door behind her.

"Do you feel like a bloodsucker, Jerry?" inquired Joanna. "Because I do. What's the matter with us?"

"We don't seem to be going down very well," I said. "Megan gets tired of us, Partridge disapproves of you, faithful Florence disapproves of both of us."

Joanna murmured, "I wonder why Megan did leave?"

"She got bored."

"I don't think she did at all. I wonder—do you think, Jerry, it could have been something that Aimée Griffith said?"

"You mean this morning, when they were talking on the doorstep?"

"Yes. There wasn't much time, of course, but—"

I finished the sentence: "But that woman's got the tread of a cow elephant! She might have—"

The door opened and Miss Emily came in. She was pink and a little out of breath and seemed excited. Her eyes were very blue and shining. She chirruped at us in quite a distracted manner:

"Oh, dear, I'm so sorry I'm late. Just doing a little shopping in the town, and the cakes at the Blue Rose didn't seem to me quite fresh, so I went on to Mrs. Lygon's. I always like to get my cakes the last thing, then one gets the newest batch just out of the oven, and one isn't put off with the day before's. But I am so distressed to have kept you waiting—really unpardonable—"

Joanna cut in:

"It's our fault, Miss Barton. We're early. We walked down and Jerry strides along so fast now that we arrive everywhere too soon."

"Never too soon, dear. Don't say that. One cannot have too much of a good thing, you know."

And the old lady patted Joanna affectionately on the shoulder.

Joanna brightened up. At last, so it seemed, she was being a success. Emily Barton extended her smile to include me, but with a slight timidity in it, rather as one might approach a man-eating tiger guaranteed for the moment harmless.

"It's very good of you to come to such a feminine meal as tea, Mr. Burton."

Emily Barton, I think, has a mental picture of men as interminably consuming whisky-and-sodas and smoking cigars, and in the intervals dropping out to do a few seductions of village maidens, or to conduct a liaison with a married woman.

When I said this to Joanna later, she replied that it was probably wishful thinking, that Emily Barton would have liked to come across such a man, but alas, had never done so.

In the meantime, Miss Emily was fussing around the room, arranging Joanna and myself with little tables, and carefully providing ashtrays, and a minute later the door opened and Florence came in bearing a tray of tea with some fine Crown Derby cups on it, which I gathered Miss Emily had brought with her. The tea was China and delicious and there were plates of sandwiches and thin bread and butter, and a quantity of little cakes.

Florence was beaming now, and looked at Miss Emily with a kind of maternal pleasure, as at a favorite child enjoying a doll's tea party.

Joanna and I ate far more than we wanted to, our hostess pressed us so earnestly. The little lady was clearly enjoying her tea party and I perceived that to Emily Barton, Joanna and I were a big adventure, two people from the mysterious world of London and sophistication.

Naturally, our talk soon dropped into local channels. Miss Barton spoke warmly of Dr. Griffith, his kindness and his cleverness as a doctor. Mr. Symmington, too, was a very clever lawyer, and had helped Miss Barton to get some money back from the Income Tax which she would never have known about. He was so nice to his children, too, devoted to them and to his wife—she caught herself up. "Poor Mrs. Symmington, it's so dreadfully sad, with those young children left motherless. Never, perhaps, a very strong woman—and her health had been bad of late.

"A brain storm, that is what it must have been. I read about such a thing in the paper. People really do not know what they are doing under those circumstances. And she can't have known what she was doing or else she would have remembered Mr. Symmington and the children."

"That anonymous letter must have shaken her up very badly," said Joanna.

Miss Barton flushed. She said, with a tinge of reproof in her voice:

"Not a very nice thing to discuss, do you think, dear? I know there have been—er—letters, but we won't talk about them. Nasty things. I think they are better just ignored."

Well, Miss Barton might be able to ignore them, but for some people it wasn't so easy. However I obediently changed the subject and we discussed Aimée Griffith.

"Wonderful, quite wonderful," said Emily Barton. "Her energy and her organizing powers are really splendid. She's so good with girls too. And she's so practical and up to date in every way. She really runs this place. And absolutely devoted to her brother. It's very nice to see such devotion between brother and sister."

"Doesn't he ever find her a little overwhelming?" asked Joanna.

Emily Barton stared at her in a startled fashion.

"She has sacrificed a great deal for his sake," she said with a touch of reproachful dignity.

I saw a touch of Oh, Yeah? in Joanna's eye and hastened to divert the conversation to Mr. Pye.

Emily Barton was a little dubious about Mr. Pye.

All she could say was, repeated rather doubtfully, that he was very kind—yes, very kind. Very well off, too, and most generous. He had very strange visitors sometimes, but then, of course, he had traveled a lot.

We agreed that travel not only broadened the mind, but occasionally resulted in the forming of strange acquaintances.

"I have often wished, myself, to go on a cruise," said Emily Barton wistfully. "One reads about them in the papers and they sound so attractive."

"Why don't you go?" asked Joanna.

This turning of a dream into a reality seemed to alarm Miss Emily.

"Oh, no, no, that would be quite impossible."

"But why? They're fairly cheap."

"Oh, it's not only the expense. But I shouldn't like to go alone. Traveling alone would look very peculiar, don't you think?"

"No," said Joanna.

Miss Emily looked at her doubtfully.

"And I don't know how I would manage about my luggage—and going ashore at foreign ports—and all the different currencies—"

Innumerable pitfalls seemed to rise up before the little lady's affrighted gaze, and Joanna hastened to calm her by a question about an approaching garden fete and sale of work. This led us quite naturally to Mrs. Dane Calthrop.

A faint spasm showed for a minute on Miss Barton's face. "You know, dear," she said, "she is really a very odd woman. The things she says sometimes."

I asked what things.

"Oh, I don't know. Such very unexpected things. And the way she looks at you, as though you weren't there but somebody else was—I'm expressing it badly but it is so hard to convey the impression I mean. And then she won't—well, interfere at all. There are so many cases where a vicar's wife could advise and—perhaps admonish. Pull people up, you know, and make them mend their ways. Because people would listen to her, I'm sure of that, they're all quite in awe of her. But she insists on being aloof and far away, and has such a curious habit of feeling sorry for the most unworthy people."

"That's interesting," I said, exchanging a quick glance with Joanna.

"Still, she is a very well-bred woman. She was a Miss Farroway of Bellpath, very good family, but these old families sometimes are a little peculiar, I believe. But she is devoted to her husband who is a man of very fine intellect—wasted, I am sometimes afraid, in this country circle. A good man, and most sincere, but I always find his habit of quoting Latin a little confusing."

"Hear, hear," I said fervently.

"Jerry had an expensive public school education, so he doesn't recognize Latin when he hears it," said Joanna.

This led Miss Barton to a new topic.

"The schoolmistress here is a most unpleasant young woman," she said. "Quite Red, I'm afraid." She lowered her voice over the word "Red."

Later, as we walked home up the hill, Joanna said to me:

"She's rather sweet."

At dinner that night Joanna said to Partridge that she hoped her tea party had been a success.

Partridge got rather red in the face and held herself even more stiffly. "Thank you, Miss, but Agnes never turned up after all."

"Oh, I'm sorry."

"It didn't matter to me," said Partridge.

She was so swelling with grievance that she condescended to pour it out to us:

"It wasn't me who thought of asking her! She rang up herself, said she'd something on her mind and could she come here, it being her day off. And I said, yes, subject to your permission which I obtained. And after that, not a sound or sign of her! And no word of apology either, though I should hope I'll get a postcard tomorrow morning. These girls nowadays—don't know their place—no idea of how to behave."

Joanna attempted to soothe Partridge's wounded feelings:

"She mightn't have felt well. You didn't ring up to find out?"

Partridge drew herself up again. "No, I did not, Miss! No, indeed. If Agnes likes to behave rudely that's her lookout, but I shall give her a piece of my mind when we meet."

Partridge went out of the room still stiff with indignation, and Joanna and I laughed.

"Probably a case of 'Advice from Aunt Nancy's Column,' " I said. " 'My boy is very cold in his manner to me, what shall I do about it?' Failing Aunt Nancy, Partridge was to be applied to for advice, but instead there has been a reconciliation and I expect at this minute that Agnes and her boy are one of those speechless couples locked in each other's arms that you come upon suddenly standing by a dark hedge. They embarrass you horribly, but you don't embarrass them."

Joanna laughed and said she expected that was it.

We began talking of the anonymous letters and wondered how Nash and the melancholy Graves were getting on.

"It's a week today exactly," said Joanna, "since Mrs. Symmington's suicide. I should think they must have got on to something by now. Fingerprints, or handwriting, or something."

I answered her absently. Somewhere behind my conscious mind, a queer uneasiness was growing. It was connected in some way with the phrase that Joanna had used, "a week exactly."

I ought, I dare say, to have put two and two together earlier. Perhaps, unconsciously, my mind was already suspicious.

Anyway the leaven was working now. The uneasiness was growing—coming to a head.

Joanna noticed suddenly that I wasn't listening to her spirited account of a village encounter.

"What's the matter, Jerry?"

I did not answer because my mind was busy piecing things together.

Mrs. Symmington's suicide. . . . She was alone in the house that afternoon. . . . Alone in the house because the maids were having their day out. . . . A week ago exactly. . . .

"Jerry, what—"

I interrupted:

"Joanna, maids have days out once a week, don't they?"

"And alternate Sundays," said Joanna. "What on—"

"Never mind Sundays. They go out the same day every week?"

"Yes. That's the usual thing."

Joanna was staring at me curiously. Her mind had not taken the track mine had.

I crossed the room and rang the bell.

Partridge came.

"Tell me," I said, "this Agnes Woddell. She's in service?"

"Yes, sir. At Mrs. Symmington's. At Mr. Symmington's I should say now."

I drew a deep breath. I glanced at the clock. It was half past ten.

"Would she be back now, do you think?"

Partridge was looking disapproving. "Yes, sir. The maids have to be in by ten there. They're old-fashioned."

I said, "I'm going to ring up."

I went out to the hall. Joanna and Partridge followed me. Partridge was clearly furious. Joanna was puzzled. She said as I was trying to get the number, "What are you going to do, Jerry?"

"I'd like to be sure that the girl has come in all right."

Partridge sniffed. Just sniffed, nothing more. But I did not care twopence about Partridge's sniffs.

Elsie Holland answered the telephone from the other end.

"Sorry to ring you up," I said. "This is Jerry Burton speaking. Is—has—your maid Agnes come in?"

It was not until after I had said it that I suddenly felt a bit of a fool. For if the girl had come in and it was all right, how on earth was I going to explain my ringing up and asking. It would have been better if I had let Joanna ask the question, though even that would need a bit of explaining. I foresaw a new trail of gossip started in Lymstock, with myself and the unknown Agnes Woddell as its center.

Elsie Holland sounded, not unnaturally, very much surprised: "Agnes? Oh, she's sure to be in by now."

I felt a fool, but I went on with it: "Do you mind just seeing if she has come in, Miss Holland?"

There is one thing to be said for a nursery governess; she is used to doing things when told. Hers not to reason why! Elsie Holland put down the receiver and went off obediently.

Two minutes later I heard her voice:

"Are you there, Mr. Burton?"

"Yes."

"Agnes isn't in yet, as a matter of fact."

I knew then that my hunch had been right.

I heard a noise of voices vaguely from the other end, then Symmington himself spoke:

"Hullo, Burton, what's the matter?"

"Your maid Agnes isn't back yet."

"No. Miss Holland has just been to see. What's the matter? There's not been an accident, has there?"

"Not an accident," I said.

"Do you mean you have reason to believe something has happened to the girl?"

I said grimly, "I shouldn't be surprised."

I slept badly that night.

I think that, even then, there were pieces of the puzzle floating about in my mind. I believe that if I had given my mind to it, I could have solved the whole thing then and there. Otherwise why did those fragments tag along so persistently?

How much do we know at any time? Much more, or so I believe, than we know we know! But we cannot break through to that subterranean knowledge. It is there, but we cannot reach it.

I lay on my bed, tossing uneasily, and only vague bits of the puzzle came to torture me.

There was a pattern, if only I could get hold of it. I ought to know who wrote those damned letters. There was a trail somewhere if only I could follow it. . . .

As I dropped off to sleep, words danced irritatingly through my drowsy mind:

"No smoke without fire. No fire without smoke. Smoke. . . . Smoke? Smoke screen. . . . No, that was the war—a war phrase. War. Scrap of paper. . . . Only a scrap of paper. Belgium—Germany. . . ."

I fell asleep. I dreamed that I was taking Mrs. Dane Calthrop, who had turned into a greyhound, for a walk with a collar and lead.

It was the ringing of the telephone that roused me. A persistent ringing.

I sat up in bed, glanced at my watch. It was half past seven. I had not yet been called. The telephone was ringing in the hall downstairs.

I jumped out of bed, pulled on a dressing gown, and raced down. I beat Partridge coming through the back door from the kitchen by a short head. I picked up the receiver.

"Hullo?"

"Oh—" It was a sob of relief. "It's you!" Megan's voice. Megan's voice indescribably forlorn and frightened. "Oh, please do come—do come. Oh, please do! Will you?"

"I'm coming at once," I said. "Do you hear? At once."

I took the stairs two at a time and burst in on Joanna.

"Look here, Jo, I'm going off to the Symmingtons'."

Joanna lifted a curly blond head from the pillow and rubbed her eyes like a small child.

"Why—what's happened?"

"I don't know. It was the child—Megan. She sounded all in."

"What do you think it is?"

"The girl Agnes, unless I'm very much mistaken."

As I went out of the door, Joanna called after me, "Wait. I'll get up and drive you down."

"No need. I'll drive myself."

"You can't drive the car."

"Yes, I can."

I did, too. It hurt, but not too much. I'd washed, shaved, dressed, got the car out and driven to the Symmingtons' in half an hour. Not bad going.

Megan must have been watching for me. She came out of the house at a run and clutched me. Her poor little face was white and twitching.

"Oh, you've come—you've come!"

"Hold up, funnyface," I said. "Yes, I've come. Now what is it?"

She began to shake. I put my arm around her.

"I—I found her."

"You found Agnes? Where?"

The trembling grew.

"Under the stairs. There's a cupboard there. It has fishing rods and golf clubs and things. You know."

I nodded. It was the usual cupboard.

Megan went on:

"She was there—all huddled up—and—and cold—horribly cold. She was —she was dead, you know!"

I asked curiously, "What made you look there?"

"I—I don't know. You telephoned last night. And we all began wondering where Agnes was. We waited up some time, but she didn't come in, and at last we went to bed. I didn't sleep very well and I got up early. There was only Rose (the cook, you know) about. She was very cross about Agnes not having come back. She said she'd been before somewhere when a girl did a flit like that. I had some milk and bread and butter in the kitchen—and then suddenly Rose came in looking queer and she said that Agnes' outdoor things were still in her room. Her best ones that she goes out in. And I began to wonder if—if she'd ever left the house, and I started looking around, and I opened the cupboard under the stairs and —and she was there . . ."

"Somebody's rung up the police, I suppose?"

"Yes, they're here now. My stepfather rang them up straightaway. And then I—I felt I couldn't bear it, and I rang you up. You don't mind?"

"No," I said. "I don't mind."

I looked at her curiously.

"Did anybody give you some brandy, or some coffee, or some tea after—after you found her?"

Megan shook her head.

I cursed the whole Symmington ménage. That stuffed shirt, Symmington, thought of nothing but the police. Neither Elsie Holland nor the cook seemed to have thought of the effect on the sensitive child who had made that gruesome discovery.

"Come on, slabface," I said. "We'll go to the kitchen."

We went around the house to the back door and into the kitchen. Rose, a plump pudding-faced woman of forty, was drinking strong tea by the kitchen fire. She greeted us with a flow of talk and her hand to her heart.

She'd come all over queer, she told me, awful the palpitations were! Just think of it, it might have been her, it might have been any of them, murdered in their beds they might have been.

"Dish out a good strong cup of that tea for Miss Megan," I said. "She's had a shock, you know. Remember it was she who found the body."

The mere mention of a body nearly sent Rose off again, but I quelled her with a stern eye and she poured out a cup of inky fluid.

"There you are, young woman," I said to Megan. "You drink that down. You haven't got any brandy, I suppose, Rose?"

Rose said rather doubtfully that there was a drop of cooking brandy left over from the Christmas puddings.

"That'll do," I said, and put a dollop of it into Megan's cup. I saw by Rose's eye that she thought it a good idea.

I told Megan to stay with Rose.

"I can trust you to look after Miss Megan?" I said, and Rose replied in a gratified way, "Oh, yes, sir."

I went through into the house. If I knew Rose and her kind, she would soon find it necessary to keep her strength up with a little food, and that would be good for Megan too. Confound these people, why couldn't they look after the child?

Fuming inwardly I ran into Elsie Holland in the hall. She didn't seem surprised to see me. I suppose that the gruesome excitement of the discovery made one oblivious of who was coming and going. The constable, Bert Rundle, was by the front door.

Elsie Holland gasped out, "Oh, Mr. Burton, isn't it awful? Whoever can have done such a dreadful thing?"

"It was murder, then?"

"Oh, yes. She was struck on the back of the head. It's all blood and hair—oh! it's awful—and bundled into that cupboard. Who can have done such a wicked thing? And why? Poor Agnes, I'm sure she never did anyone any harm."

"No," I said. "Somebody saw to that pretty promptly."

She stared at me. Not, I thought, a quick-witted girl. But she had good nerves. Her color was as usual, slightly heightened by excitement, and I even fancied that in a macabre kind of way, and in spite of a naturally kind heart, she was enjoying the drama.

She said apologetically, "I must go up to the boys. Mr. Symmington is so anxious that they shouldn't get a shock. He wants me to keep them right away."

"Megan found the body, I hear," I said. "I hope somebody is looking after her."

I will say for Elsie Holland that she looked conscience-stricken.

"Oh, dear," she said. "I forgot all about her. I do hope she's all right. I've been so rushed, you know, and the police and everything—but it was remiss of me. Poor girl, she must be feeling bad. I'll go and look for her at once."

I relented.

"She's all right," I said. "Rose is looking after her. You get along to the kids."

She thanked me with a flash of white tombstone teeth and hurried upstairs. After all, the boys were her job, and not Megan—Megan was nobody's job. Elsie was paid to look after Symmington's blinking brats. One could hardly blame her for attending to it.

As she flashed around the corner of the stairs, I caught my breath. For a minute I caught a glimpse of a Winged Victory, deathless and incredibly beautiful, instead of a conscientious nursery governess.

Then a door opened and Superintendent Nash stepped out into the hall with Symmington behind him.

"Oh, Mr. Burton," he said, "I was just going to telephone you. I'm glad you are here."

He didn't ask me—then—why I was here.

He turned his head and said to Symmington, "I'll use this room if I may."

It was a small morning room with a window on the front of the house.

"Certainly, certainly."

Symmington's poise was pretty good, but he looked desperately tired. Superintendent Nash said gently:

"I should have some breakfast if I were you, Mr. Symmington. You and Miss Holland and Miss Megan will feel much better after coffee and eggs and bacon. Murder is a nasty business on an empty stomach."

He spoke in a comfortable family-doctor kind of way.

Symmington gave a faint attempt at a smile and said, "Thank you, Superintendent, I'll take your advice."

I followed Nash into the little morning room and he shut the door.

He said then, "You've got here very quickly. How did you hear?"

I told him that Megan had rung me up. I felt well-disposed toward Superintendent Nash. He, at any rate, had not forgotten that Megan, too, would be in need of breakfast.

"I hear that you telephoned last night, Mr. Burton, asking about this girl? Why was that?"

I suppose it did seem odd. I told him about Agnes' telephone call to Partridge and her nonappearance. He said, "Yes, I see. . . ."

He said it slowly and reflectively, rubbing his chin.

Then he sighed.

"Well," he said. "It's murder now, right enough. Direct physical action. The question is, what did the girl know? Did she say anything to this Partridge? Anything definite?"

"I don't think so. But you can ask her."

"Yes, I shall come up and see her when I've finished here."

"What happened exactly?" I asked. "Or don't you know yet?"

"Near enough. It was the maids' day out—"

"Both of them?"

"Yes, it seems that there used to be two sisters here who liked to go out together, so Mrs. Symmington arranged it that way. Then when these two came, she kept to the same arrangement. They used to have cold supper laid out in the dining room, and Miss Holland used to get tea."

"I see."

"It's pretty clear up to a point. The cook, Rose, comes from Nether Mickford, and in order to get there on her day out she has to catch the half-past-two bus. So Agnes has to finish clearing up lunch always. Rose used to wash up the supper things in the evenings to even things up.

"That's what happened today. Rose went off to catch the bus at two-twenty-five, Symmington left for his office at twenty-five to three. Elsie Holland and the children went out at a quarter to three. Megan Hunter went out on her bicycle about five minutes later. Agnes would then be alone in the house. As far as I can make out, she normally left the house between three o'clock and half past three."

"The house being then left empty?"

"Oh, they don't worry about that down here. There's not much locking up done in these parts. As I say, at ten minutes to three Agnes was alone in the house. That she never left it is clear, for she was in her cap and apron still when we found her body."

"I suppose you can tell roughly the time of death?"

"Doctor Griffith won't commit himself. Between two o'clock and four-thirty is his official medical verdict."

"How was she killed?"

"She was first stunned by a blow on the back of the head. Afterward an ordinary kitchen skewer, sharpened to a fine point, was thrust into the base of the skull, causing instantaneous death."

I lit a cigarette. It was not a nice picture.

"Pretty cold-blooded," I said.

"Oh, yes, yes, that was indicated."

I inhaled deeply.

"Who did it?" I said. "And why?"

"I don't suppose," said Nash slowly, "that we shall ever know exactly why. But we can guess."

"She knew something?"

"She knew something."

"She didn't give anyone here a hint?"

"As far as I can make out, no. She's been upset, so the cook says, ever since Mrs. Symmington's death, and according to this Rose, she's been getting more and more worried, and kept saying she didn't know what she ought to do."

He gave a short exasperated sigh.

"It's always the way. They won't come to us. They've got that deep-seated prejudice against 'being mixed up with the police.' If she'd come along and told us what was worrying her, she'd be alive today."

"Didn't she give the other women any hint?"

"No, or so Rose says, and I'm inclined to believe her. For if she had, Rose would have blurted it out at once with a good many fancy embellishments of her own."

"It's maddening," I said, "not to know."

"We can still guess, Mr. Burton. To begin with, it can't be anything very definite. It's got to be the sort of thing that you think over, and as you think it over, your uneasiness grows. You see what I mean?"

"Yes."

"Actually, I think I know what it was."

I looked at him with respect.

"That's good work, Superintendent."

"Well, you see, Mr. Burton, I know something that you don't. On the afternoon that Mrs. Symmington committed suicide both maids were supposed to be out. It was their day out. But actually Agnes came back to the house."

"You know that?"

"Yes. Agnes has a boy friend—young Rendell from the fish shop. Wednesday is early closing and he comes along to meet Agnes and they go for a walk, or to the pictures if it's wet. That Wednesday they had a row practically as soon as they met. Our letter writer had been active, suggesting that Agnes had other fish to fry, and young Fred Rendell was all worked up. They quarreled violently and Agnes bolted back home and said she wasn't coming out unless Fred said he was sorry."

"Well?"

"Well, Mr. Burton, the kitchen faces the back of the house, but the pantry looks out where we are looking now. There's only one entrance gate. You come through it and either up to the front door, or else along the path at the side of the house to the back door."

He paused.

"Now I'll tell you something: That letter that came to Mrs. Symmington that afternoon didn't come by post. It had a used stamp affixed to it, and the postmark faked quite convincingly in lamp black, so that it would seem to have been delivered by the postman with the afternoon letters. But actually it had not been through the post. You see what that means?"

"It means," I said slowly, "that it was left by hand, pushed through the letter box some time before the afternoon post was delivered, so that it should be among the other letters."

"Exactly. The afternoon post comes around about a quarter to four. My theory is this: The girl was in the pantry looking through the window (it's masked by shrubs but you can see through them quite well) watching out for her young man to turn up and apologize."

I said, "And she saw whoever it was delivered that note?"

"That's my guess, Mr. Burton. I may be wrong, of course."

"I don't think you are. . . . It's simple—and convincing—and it means that Agnes knew who the anonymous letter writer was."

V

"Yes," Nash said. "Agnes knew who wrote those letters."

"But then why didn't she—?" I paused, frowning.

Nash said quickly, "As I see it, the girl didn't realize what she had seen. Not at first. Somebody had left a letter at the house, yes—but that somebody was nobody she would dream of connecting with the anonymous letters. It was somebody, from that point of view, quite above suspicion."

"But the more she thought about it, the more uneasy she grew. Ought she, perhaps, to tell someone about it? In her perplexity she thinks of Miss Barton's Partridge who, I gather, is a somewhat dominant personality and whose judgment Agnes would accept unhesitatingly. She decides to ask Partridge what she ought to do."

"Yes," I said thoughtfully. "It fits well enough. And somehow or other, Poison Pen found out. How did she find out, Superintendent?"

"You're not used to living in the country, Mr. Burton. It's a kind of miracle how things get around. First of all there's the telephone call. Who overheard it on your end?"

I reflected.

"I took the call originally. I called up to Partridge."

"Mentioning the girl's name?"

"Yes—yes, I did."

"Anyone overhear you?"

"My sister or Miss Griffith might have done so."

"Ah, Miss Griffith. What was she doing up there?"

I explained.

"Was she going back to the village?"

"She was going to Mr. Pye first."

Superintendent Nash sighed. "That's two ways it could have gone all over the place."

I was incredulous. "Do you mean that either Miss Griffith or Mr. Pye would bother to repeat a meaningless little bit of information like that?"

"Anything's news in a place like this. You'd be surprised. If the dressmaker's mother has got a bad corn everybody hears about it! And then there is this end. Miss Holland, Rose—they could have heard what Agnes said. And there's Fred Rendell. It may have got around through him that Agnes went back to the house that afternoon."

I gave a slight shiver. I was looking out of the window. In front of me was a neat square of grass and a path and the low prim gate.

Someone had opened the gate, had walked very correctly and quietly up to the house, and had pushed a letter through the letter box. I saw, hazily, in my mind's eye, that vague woman's shape. The face was blank—but it must be a face that I knew . . .

Superintendent Nash was saying:

"All the same, this narrows things down. That's always the way we get 'em in the end. Steady, patient elimination. There aren't so very many people it could be now."

"You mean—?"

"It knocks out any women clerks who were at their work all the afternoon. It knocks out the schoolmistress. She was teaching. And the district nurse. I know where she was yesterday. Not that I ever thought it was any of them, but now we're sure. You see, Mr. Burton, we've got two definite times now on which to concentrate—yesterday afternoon, and the week before. On the day of Mrs. Symmington's death from, say, a quarter past three (the earliest possible time at which Agnes could have been back in the house after her quarrel) and four o'clock when the post must have come (but I can get that fixed more accurately with the postman). And yesterday from ten minutes to three (when Miss Megan Hunter left the house) until half past three or more probably a quarter past three as Agnes hadn't begun to change."

"What do you think happened yesterday?"

Nash made a grimace.

"What do I think? I think a certain lady walked up to the front door and rang the bell, quite calm and smiling, the afternoon caller. . . . Maybe she asked for Miss Holland, or for Miss Megan, or perhaps she had brought a parcel. Anyway Agnes turns around to get a salver for cards, or to take the parcel in, and our ladylike caller bats her on the back of her unsuspecting head."

"What with?"

Nash said, "The ladies around here usually carry large sizes in handbags. No saying what mightn't be inside it."

"And then stabs her through the back of the neck and bundles her into the cupboard? Wouldn't that be a hefty job for a woman?"

Superintendent Nash looked at me with rather a queer expression. "The woman we're after isn't normal—not by a long way—and that type of mental instability goes with surprising strength. Agnes wasn't a big girl!" He paused and then asked, "What made Miss Megan Hunter think of looking in that cupboard?"

"Sheer instinct," I said.

Then I asked, "Why drag her out of the way? What was the point?"

"The longer it was before the body was found, the more difficult it would be to fix the time of death accurately. If Miss Holland, for instance, fell over the body as soon as she came in, a doctor might be able to fix it within ten minutes or so—which might be awkward for our lady friend."

I said, frowning, "But if Agnes was suspicious of this person—"

Nash interrupted me: "She wasn't. Not to this pitch. She just thought it 'queer' shall we say? She was a slow-witted girl, I imagine, and she was only vaguely suspicious with a feeling that something was wrong. She certainly didn't suspect that she was up against a woman who would do murder."

"Did you suspect that?" I asked.

Nash shook his head. He said, with feeling:

"I ought to have known. That suicide business, you see, frightened Poison Pen. She got the wind up. Fear, Mr. Burton, is an incalculable thing."

Yes, fear. That was the thing we ought to have foreseen. Fear—in a lunatic brain. . . .

"You see," said Superintendent Nash, and somehow his words made the whole thing seem absolutely horrible. "We're up against someone who's respected and thought highly of—someone, in fact, of good social position!"

Presently Nash said that he was going to interview Rose once more. I asked him, rather diffidently, if I might come too. Rather to my surprise he assented cordially.

"I'm very glad of your co-operation, Mr. Burton, if I may say so."

"That sounds suspicious," I said. "In books when a detective welcomes someone's assistance, that someone is usually the murderer."

Nash laughed shortly. He said, "You're hardly the type to write anonymous letters, Mr. Burton." He added: "Frankly, you can be useful to us."

"I'm glad, but I don't see how."

"You're a stranger down here, that's why. You've got no preconceived ideas about the people here. But at the same time, you've got the opportunity of getting to know things in what I may call a social way."

"The murderer is a person of good social position," I murmured.

"Exactly."

"I'm to be the spy within the gates?"

"Have you any objection?"

I thought it over. "No," I said, "frankly I haven't. If there's a dangerous lunatic about, driving inoffensive women to suicide and hitting miserable little maidservants on the head, then I'm not averse to doing a bit of dirty work to put that lunatic under restraint."

"That's sensible of you, sir. And let me tell you, the person we're after is dangerous. She's about as dangerous as a rattlesnake and a cobra and a black mamba rolled into one."

I gave a slight shiver. I said, "In fact, we've got to make haste?"

"That's right. Don't think we're inactive in the force. We're not. We're working on several different lines."

He said it grimly.

I had a vision of a fine, far-flung spider's web . . .

Nash wanted to hear Rose's story again, so he explained to me, because she had already told him two different versions, and the more versions he got from her, the more likely it was that a few grains of truth might be incorporated.

We found Rose washing up breakfast, and she stopped at once and rolled her eyes and clutched her heart and explained again how she'd been coming over queer all the morning.

Nash was patient with her but firm. He'd been soothing the first time, so he told me, and peremptory the second, and he now employed a mixture of the two.

Rose enlarged pleasurably on the details of the past week, of how Agnes had gone about in deadly fear, and had shivered and said "Don't ask me" when Rose had urged her to say what was the matter. "It would be death if she told me, that's what she said," finished Rose, rolling her eyes happily.

"Had Agnes given no hint of what was troubling her?"

No, except that she went in fear of her life.

Superintendent Nash sighed and abandoned the theme, contenting himself with extracting an exact account of Rose's own activities the preceding afternoon.

This, put baldly, was that Rose had caught the 2:30 bus and had spent the afternoon and evening with her family, returning by the 8:40 bus from Nether Mickford. The recital was complicated by the extraordinary presentiments of evil that Rose had had all the afternoon and how her sister had commented on it and how she hadn't been able to touch a morsel of seed cake.

From the kitchen we went in search of Elsie Holland, who was superintending the children's lessons.

As always, Elsie Holland was competent and obliging. She rose and said, "Now, Colin, you and Brian will do these three sums and have the answers ready for me when I come back."

She then led us into the night nursery.

"Will this do? I thought it would be better not to talk before the children."

"Thank you, Miss Holland. Just tell me, once more, are you quite sure that Agnes never mentioned to you being worried over anything—since Mrs. Symmington's death, I mean?"

"No, she never said anything. She was a very quiet girl, you know, and didn't talk much."

"A change from the other one, then!"

"Yes, Rose talks much too much. I have to tell her not to be impertinent sometimes."

"Now, will you tell me exactly what happened yesterday afternoon? Everything you can remember."

"Well, we had lunch as usual. One o'clock, and we hurried just a little. I don't let the boys dawdle. Let me see. Mr. Symmington went back to the office, and I helped Agnes by laying the table for supper—the boys ran out in the garden till I was ready to take them."

"Where did you go?"

"Toward Combe Acre, by the field path—the boys wanted to fish. I forgot their bait and had to go back for it."

"What time was that?"

"Let me see, we started about twenty to three—or just after. Megan was coming but changed her mind. She was going out on her bicycle. She's got quite a craze for bicycling."

"I mean what time was it when you went back for the bait? Did you go into the house?"

"No. I'd left it in the conservatory at the back. I don't know what time it was then—about ten minutes to three, perhaps."

"Did you see Megan or Agnes?"

"Megan must have started, I think. No, I didn't see Agnes. I didn't see anyone."

"And after that you went fishing?"

"Yes, we went along by the stream. We didn't catch anything. We hardly ever do, but the boys enjoy it. Brian got rather wet. I had to change his things when we got in."

"You attend to tea on Wednesdays?"

"Yes. It's all ready in the drawing room for Mr. Symmington. I just make the tea when he comes in. The children and I have ours in the schoolroom—and Megan, of course. I have my own tea things and everything in the cupboard up there."

"What time did you get in?"

"At ten minutes to five. I took the boys up and started to lay tea. Then when Mr. Symmington came in at five I went down to make his but he said he would have it with us in the schoolroom. The boys were so pleased. We played Animal Grab afterward. It seems so awful to think of now—with that poor girl in the cupboard all the time."

"Would anybody go to that cupboard normally?"

"Oh, no, it's only used for keeping junk. The hats and coats hang in the little cloakroom to the right of the front door as you come in. No one might have gone to the other cupboard for months."

"I see. And you noticed nothing unusual, nothing abnormal at all when you came back?"

The blue eyes opened very wide. "Oh, no, Inspector, nothing at all. Everything was just the same as usual. That's what was so awful about it."

"And the week before?"

"You mean the day Mrs. Symmington—"

"Yes."

"Oh, that was terrible—terrible!"

"Yes, yes, I know. You were out all that afternoon also?"

"Oh, yes, I always take the boys out in the afternoon—if it's fine enough. We do lessons in the morning. We went up on the moor, I remember—quite a long way. I was afraid I was late back because as I turned in at the gate I saw Mr. Symmington coming from his office at the other end of the road, and I hadn't even put the kettle on, but it was just ten minutes to five."

"You didn't go up to Mrs. Symmington?"

"Oh, no. I never did. She always rested after lunch. She had attacks of neuralgia—and they used to come on after meals. Dr. Griffith had given her some powders to take. She used to lie down and try to sleep."

Nash said in a casual voice, "So no one would take her up the post?"

"The afternoon post? No, I'd look in the letter box and put the letters on the hall table when I came in. But very often Mrs. Symmington used to come down and get it herself. She didn't sleep all the afternoon. She was usually up again by four."

"You didn't think anything was wrong because she wasn't up that afternoon?"

"Oh, no, I never dreamed of such a thing. Mr. Symmington was hanging up his coat in the hall and I said, 'Tea's not quite ready, but the kettle's nearly boiling,' and he nodded and called out, 'Mona, Mona!'—and then as Mrs. Symmington didn't answer he went upstairs to her bedroom, and it must have been the most terrible shock to him. He called me and I came, and he said, 'Keep the children away,' and then he phoned Dr. Griffith and we forgot all about the kettle and it burned the bottom out! Oh, dear, it was dreadful, and she'd been so happy and cheerful at lunch."

Nash said abruptly, "What is your own opinion of that letter she received, Miss Holland?"

Elsie Holland said indignantly, "Oh, I think it was wicked—wicked!"

"Yes, yes, I don't mean that. Did you think it was true?"

Elsie Holland said firmly:

"No, indeed I don't. Mrs. Symmington was very sensitive—very sensitive indeed. She had to take all sorts of things for her nerves. And she was very—well, particular." Elsie flushed. "Anything of that sort—nasty, I mean—would have given her a great shock."

Nash was silent for a moment, then he asked: "Have you had any of these letters, Miss Holland?"

"No. No, I haven't had any."

"Are you sure? Please"—he lifted a hand—"don't answer in a hurry. They're not pleasant things to get, I know. And sometimes people don't like to admit they've had them. But it's very important in this case that we should know. We're quite aware that the statements in them are just a tissue of lies, so you needn't feel embarrassed."

"But I haven't, Superintendent. Really I haven't. Not anything of the kind."

She was indignant, almost tearful, and her denials seemed genuine enough.

When she went back to the children, Nash stood looking out of the window.

"Well," he said, "that's that! She says she hasn't received any of these letters. And she sounds as though she's speaking the truth."

"She did certainly. I'm sure she was."

"H'm," said Nash. "Then what I want to know is, why the devil hasn't she?"

He went on rather impatiently, as I stared at him:

"She's a pretty girl, isn't she?"

"Rather more than pretty."

"Exactly. As a matter of fact, she's uncommonly good-looking. And she's young. In fact she's just the meat an anonymous letter writer would like. Then why has she been left out?"

I shook my head.

"It's interesting, you know. I must mention it to Graves. He asked if we could tell him definitely of anyone who hadn't had one."

"She's the second person," I said. "There's Emily Barton, remember."

Nash gave a faint chuckle. "You shouldn't believe everything you're told, Mr. Burton. Miss Barton had one all right—more than one."

"How do you know?"

"That devoted dragon she's lodging with told me—her late parlormaid or cook. Florence Elford. Very indignant she was about it. Would like to have the writer's blood."

"Why did Miss Emily say she hadn't had any?"

"Delicacy. Their language isn't nice. Little Miss Barton has spent her life avoiding the coarse and unrefined."

"What did the letter say?"

"The usual. Quite ludicrous in her case. And incidentally insinuated that she poisoned off her old mother and most of her sisters!"

I said incredulously, "Do you mean to say there's really this dangerous lunatic going about and we can't spot her right away?"

"We'll spot her," said Nash, and his voice was grim. "She'll write just one letter too many."

"But, my goodness, man, she won't go on writing these things—not now."

He looked at me.

"Oh, yes, she will. You see, she can't stop now. It's a morbid craving. The letters will go on, make no mistake about that."

I went and found Megan before leaving the house. She was in the garden and seemed almost back to her usual self. She greeted me quite cheerfully.

I suggested that she should come back to us again for a while, but after a momentary hesitation she shook her head.

"It's nice of you—but I think I'll stay here. After all, it is—well, I suppose it's my home. And I dare say I can help with the boys a bit."

"Well," I said, "it's as you like."

"Then I think I'll stay. I could—I could—"

"Yes?" I prompted.

"If—if anything awful happened, I could ring you up, couldn't I, and you'd come."

I was touched. "Of course. But what awful thing do you think might happen?"

"Oh, I don't know." She looked vague. "Things seem rather like that just now, don't they?"

"Stop it!" I said. "And don't go nosing out any more bodies! It's not good for you."

She gave me a brief flash of a smile. "No, it isn't. It made me feel awfully sick."

I didn't much like leaving her there, but after all, as she had said, it was her home. And I fancied now that Elsie Holland would feel more responsible for her.

Nash and I went up together to Little Furze. While I gave Joanna an account of the morning's doings, Nash tackled Partridge. He rejoined us, looking discouraged.

"Not much help there. According to this woman, the girl only said she was worried about something and didn't know what to do and that she'd like Miss Partridge's advice."

"Did Partridge mention the fact to anyone?" asked Joanna.

Nash nodded, looking grim.

"Yes, she told Mrs. Emory—your daily woman—on the lines, as far as I can gather, that there were some young women who were willing to take advice from their elders and didn't think they could settle everything for themselves offhand! Agnes mightn't be very bright, but she was a nice respectful girl and knew her manners."

"Partridge preening herself, in fact," murmured Joanna. "And Mrs. Emory could have passed it around the town?"

"That's right, Miss Burton."

"There's one thing rather surprises me," I said. "Why were my sister and I included? We were strangers down here—nobody could have had a grudge against us."

"You're failing to allow for the mentality of a Poison Pen—all is grist that comes to their mill. Their grudge, you might say, is against humanity."

"I suppose," said Joanna thoughtfully, "that that is what Mrs. Dane Calthrop meant."

Nash looked at her inquiringly, but she did not enlighten him.

The Superintendent said:

"I don't know if you happened to look closely at the envelope of the letter you got, Miss Burton. If so, you may have noticed that it was actually addressed to Miss Barton, and the *a* altered to a *u* afterward."

That remark, properly interpreted, ought to have given us a clue to the whole business. As it was, none of us saw any significance in it.

Nash went off, and I was left with Joanna. She actually said: "You don't think that letter can really have been meant for Miss Emily, do you?"

"It would hardly have begun 'You painted trollop,'" I pointed out, and Joanna agreed.

Then she suggested that I should go down to the town. "You ought to hear what everyone is saying. It will be the topic this morning!"

I suggested that she should come too, but rather to my surprise Joanna refused. She said she was going to mess about in the garden.

I paused in the doorway and said, lowering my voice, "I suppose Partridge is all right?"

"Partridge!"

The amazement in Joanna's voice made me feel ashamed of my idea.

I said apologetically, "I just wondered. She's rather 'queer' in some ways—a grim spinster—the sort of person who might have religious mania."

"This isn't religious mania—or so you told me Graves said."

"Well, sex mania. They're very closely tied up together, I understand. She's repressed and respectable, and has been shut up here with a lot of elderly women for years."

"What put the idea into your head?"

"Well," I said slowly, "we've only her word for it, haven't we, as to what the girl Agnes said to her? Suppose Agnes asked Partridge to tell her why

Partridge came and left a note that day—and Partridge said she'd call around that afternoon and explain."

"And then camouflaged it by coming to us and asking if the girl could come here?"

"Yes."

"But she never went out that afternoon."

"You don't know that. We were out ourselves, remember."

"Yes, that's true. It's possible, I suppose." Joanna turned it over in her mind. "But I don't think so, all the same. I don't think Partridge has the mentality to cover her tracks over the letters. To wipe off fingerprints, and all that. It isn't only cunning you want—it's knowledge. I don't think she's got that. I suppose—" Joanna hesitated, then said slowly, "they are sure it is a woman, aren't they?"

"You don't think it's a man?" I exclaimed incredulously.

"Not—not an ordinary man—but a certain kind of man. I'm thinking, really, of Mr. Pye."

"So Pye is your selection?"

"Don't you feel yourself that he's a possibility? He's the sort of person who might be lonely—and unhappy—and spiteful. Everyone, you see, rather laughs at him. Can't you see him secretly hating all the normal happy people, and taking a queer, perverse, artistic pleasure in what he was doing?"

"Graves said a middle-aged spinster."

"Mr. Pye," said Joanna, "is a middle-aged spinster."

"A misfit," I said slowly.

"Very much so. He's rich, but money doesn't help. And I do feel he might be unbalanced. He is, really, rather a frightening little man."

"He got a letter himself, remember."

"We don't know that," Joanna pointed out. "We only thought so. And anyway, he might have been putting on an act."

"For our benefit?"

"Yes. He's clever enough to think of that—and not to overdo it."

"He must be a first-class actor."

"But of course, Jerry, whoever is doing this must be a first-class actor. That's partly where the pleasure comes in."

"For heaven's sake, Joanna, don't speak so understandingly! You make me feel that you—that you understand the mentality."

"I think I do. I can—just—get into the mood. If I wasn't Joanna Burton, if I wasn't young and reasonably attractive and able to have a good time, if I was—how shall I put it?—behind bars, watching other people enjoy life, would a black, evil tide rise in me, making me want to hurt, to torture —even to destroy?"

"Joanna!" I took her by the shoulders and shook her. She gave a little sigh and shiver, and smiled at me.

"I frightened you, didn't I, Jerry? But I have a feeling that that's the right way to solve this problem. You've got to be the person, knowing how they feel and what makes them act, and then—and then perhaps you'll know what they're going to do next."

"Oh, gee!" I said. "And I came down here to be a vegetable and get interested in all the dear little local scandals. Dear little local scandals! Libel, vilification, obscene language and murder!"

Joanna was quite right. The High Street was full of interesting groups. I was determined to get everyone's reactions in turn.

I met Griffith first. He looked terribly ill and tired. So much so that I wondered. Murder is not, certainly, all in the day's work to a doctor, but his profession does equip him to face most things including suffering, the ugly side of human nature, and the fact of death.

"You look all in," I said.

"Do I?" He was vague. "Oh! I've had some worrying cases lately."

"Including our lunatic at large?"

"That, certainly." He looked away from me across the street. I saw a fine nerve twitching in his eyelid.

"You've no suspicions as to—who?"

"No. No. I wish I had."

He asked abruptly after Joanna and said, hesitatingly, that he had some photographs she'd wanted to see.

I offered to take them to her.

"Oh, it doesn't matter. I shall be passing that way actually later in the morning."

I began to be afraid that Griffith had got it badly. Curse Joanna! Griffith was too good a man to be dangled as a scalp.

I let him go, for I saw his sister coming and I wanted, for once, to talk to her.

Aimée Griffith began, as it were, in the middle of conversation. "Absolutely shocking!" she boomed. "I hear you were there—quite early?"

There was a question in the words, and her eyes glinted as she stressed the word "early." I wasn't going to tell her that Megan had rung me up.

I said instead, "You see, I was a bit uneasy last night. The girl was due to tea at our house and didn't turn up."

"And so you feared the worst? Very smart of you!"

"Yes," I said. "I'm quite the human bloodhound."

"It's the first murder we've ever had in Lymstock. Excitement is terrific. Hope the police can handle it all right."

"I shouldn't worry," I said. "They're an efficient body of men."

"Can't even remember what the girl looked like, although I suppose she's opened the door to me dozens of times. Quiet, insignificant little thing. Knocked on the head and then stabbed through the back of the neck, so Owen tells me. Looks like a boy friend to me. What do you think?"

"That's your solution?"

"Seems the most likely one. Had a quarrel, I expect. They're very inbred around here—bad heredity, a lot of them." She paused, and then went on: "I hear Megan Hunter found the body? Must have given her a bit of a shock."

I said shortly, "It did."

"Not too good for her, I should imagine. In my opinion she's not too strong in the head—and a thing like this might send her completely off her onion."

I took a sudden resolution. I had to know something.

"Tell me, Miss Griffith, was it you who persuaded Megan to return home yesterday?"

"Well, I wouldn't say exactly persuaded."

I stuck to my guns. "But you did say something to her?"

Aimée Griffith planted her feet firmly and stared me in the eyes. She was, just slightly, on the defensive. She said:

"It's no good—that young woman shirking her responsibility. She's young and she doesn't know how tongues wag, so I felt it my duty to give her a hint."

"Tongues—?" I broke off because I was too angry to go on.

Aimée Griffith continued with that maddeningly complacent confidence in herself which was her chief characteristic:

"Oh, I dare say you don't hear all the gossip that goes around. I do! I know what people are saying. Mind you, I don't for a minute think there's anything in it—not for a minute! But you know what people are—if they can say something ill-natured, they do! And it's rather hard lines on the girl when she's got her living to earn."

"Her living to earn?" I said, puzzled.

Aimée went on:

"It's a difficult position for her, naturally. And I think she did the right thing. I mean, she couldn't go off at a moment's notice and leave the children with no one to look after them. She's been splendid—absolutely splendid. I say so to everybody! But there it is, it's an invidious position, and people will talk."

"Who are you talking about?" I asked.

"Elsie Holland, of course," said Aimée Griffith impatiently. "In my opinion, she's a thoroughly nice girl and has only been doing her duty."

"And what are people saying?"

Aimée Griffith laughed. It was, I thought, rather an unpleasant laugh.

"They're saying that she's already considering the possibility of becoming Mrs. Symmington No. 2—that she's all out to console the widower and make herself indispensable."

"But," I said, shocked, "Mrs. Symmington's only been dead a week!"

Aimée Griffith shrugged her shoulders.

"Of course. It's absurd! But you know what people are! The Holland girl is young and she's good-looking—that's enough. And mind you, being a nursery governess isn't much of a prospect for a girl. I wouldn't blame her if she wanted a settled home and a husband and was playing her cards accordingly.

"Of course," she went on, "poor Dick Symmington hasn't the least idea of all this! He's still completely knocked out by Mona Symmington's death. But you know what men are! If the girl is always there, making him comfortable, looking after him, being obviously devoted to the children—well, he gets to be dependent on her."

I said quietly, "So you do think that Elsie Holland is a designing hussy?"

Aimée Griffith flushed.

"Not at all. I'm sorry for the girl—with people saying nasty things! That's why I more or less told Megan that she ought to go home. It looks better than having Dick Symmington and the girl alone in the house."

I began to understand things.

Aimée Griffith gave her jolly laugh. "You're shocked, Mr. Burton, at hearing what our gossiping little town thinks. I can tell you this—they always think the worst!"

She laughed and nodded and strode away.

I came upon Mr. Pye by the church. He was talking to Emily Barton, who looked pink and excited.

Mr. Pye greeted me with every evidence of delight:

"Ah, Burton, good morning, good morning! How is your charming sister?"

I told him that Joanna was well.

"But not joining our village Parliament? We are all agog over the news. Murder! Real Sunday newspaper murder in our midst! Not the most interesting of crimes, I fear. Somewhat sordid. The brutal murder of a little serving maid. No finer points about the crime, but still undeniably news."

Miss Barton said tremulously, "It is shocking—quite shocking."

Mr. Pye turned on her: "But you enjoy it, dear lady, you enjoy it. Confess it now. You disapprove, you deplore, but there is the thrill. I insist, there is the thrill!"

"Such a nice girl," said Emily Barton. "She came to me from St. Clotilde's Home. Quite a raw girl. But most teachable. She turned into such a nice little maid. Partridge was very pleased with her."

I said quickly, "She was coming to tea with Partridge yesterday afternoon." I turned to Pye: "I expect Aimée Griffith told you."

My tone was quite casual. Pye responded apparently quite unsuspiciously:

"She did mention it, yes. She said, I remember, that it was something quite new for servants to ring up on their employers' telephones."

"Partridge would never dream of doing such a thing," said Miss Emily, "and I am really surprised at Agnes doing so."

"You are behind the times, dear lady," said Mr. Pye. "My two terrors use the telephone constantly and smoked all over the house until I objected. But one daren't say too much. Prescott is a divine cook, though temperamental, and Mrs. Prescott is an admirable house-parlor maid."

"Yes, indeed, we all think you're very lucky."

I intervened, since I did not want the conversation to become purely domestic.

"The news of the murder has got around very quickly," I said.

"Of course, of course," said Mr. Pye. "The butcher, the baker, the candlestick maker. Enter Rumor, painted full of tongues! Lymstock, alas! is going to the dogs. Anonymous letters, murders, any amount of criminal tendencies."

Emily Barton said nervously, "They don't think—there's no idea—that—that the two are connected."

Mr. Pye pounced on the idea. "An interesting speculation. The girl knew something, therefore she was murdered. Yes, yes, most promising. How clever of you to think of it."

"I—I can't bear it."

Emily Barton spoke abruptly and turned away, walking very fast.

Pye looked after her. Her cherubic face was pursed up quizzically.

He turned back to me and shook his head gently.

"A sensitive soul. A charming creature, don't you think? Absolutely a period piece. She's not, you know, of her own generation, she's of the generation before that. The mother must have been a woman of very strong character. She kept the family time ticking at about 1870, I should say. The whole family preserved under a glass case. I do like to come across that sort of thing."

I did not want to talk about period pieces.

"What do you really think about all this business?" I asked.

"Meaning by that?"

"Anonymous letters, murder . . ."

"Our local crime wave? What do you?"

"I asked you first," I said pleasantly.

Mr. Pye said gently:

"I'm a student, you know, of abnormalities. They interest me. Such apparently unlikely people do the most fantastic things. Take the case of Lizzie Borden. There's not really a reasonable explanation of that. In this case, my advice to the police would be—study character. Leave your fingerprints and your measuring of handwriting and your microscopes. Notice instead what people do with their hands, and their little tricks of manner, and the way they eat their food, and if they laugh sometimes for no apparent reason."

I raised my eyebrows.

"Mad?" I said.

"Quite, quite mad," said Mr. Pye, and added, "but you'd never know it!"

"Who?"

His eyes met mine. He smiled.

"No, no, Burton, that would be slander. We can't add slander to all the rest of it."

He fairly skipped off down the street.

VI

As I STOOD staring after Mr. Pye the church door opened and the Rev. Caleb Dane Calthrop came out.

He smiled vaguely at me. "Good—good morning, Mr.—er—er—"

I helped him.

"Burton."

"Of course, of course, you mustn't think I don't remember you. Your name had just slipped my memory for the moment. A beautiful day."

"Yes," I said rather shortly.

He peered at me.

"But something—something, as, yes, that poor unfortunate child who was in service at the Symmingtons'. I find it hard to believe, I must confess, that we have a murderer in our midst, Mr.—er—Burton."

"It does seem a bit fantastic," I said.

"Something else has just reached my ears." He leaned toward me. "I learn that there have been anonymous letters going about. Have you heard any rumor of such things?"

"I have heard," I said.

"Cowardly and dastardly things." He paused and quoted an enormous stream of Latin. "Those words of Horace are very applicable, don't you think?" he said.

"Absolutely," I said.

There didn't seem anyone more I could profitably talk to, so I went home, dropping in for some tobacco and for a bottle of sherry, so as to get some of the humbler opinions on the crime.

"A narsty tramp," seemed to be the verdict.

"Come to the door, they do, and whine and ask for money, and then if it's a girl alone in the house, they turn narsty. My sister Dora, over to Combe Acre, she had a narsty experience one day—drunk, he was, and selling those little printed poems. . . ."

The story went on, ending with the intrepid Dora courageously banging the door in the man's face and taking refuge and barricading herself in some vague retreat, which I gathered from the delicacy in mentioning it, must be the lavatory. "And there she stayed till her lady came home!"

I reached Little Furze just a few minutes before lunch time. Joanna was standing in the drawing-room window doing nothing at all and looking as though her thoughts were miles away.

"What have you been doing with yourself?" I asked.

"Oh, I don't know. Nothing particular."

I went out on the veranda. Two chairs were drawn up to an iron table and there were two empty sherry glasses. On another chair was an object at which I looked with bewilderment for some time.

"What on earth is this?"

"Oh," said Joanna, "I think it's a photograph of a diseased spleen or something. Dr. Griffith seemed to think I'd be interested to see it."

I looked at the photograph with some interest. Every man has his own ways of courting the female sex. I should not, myself, choose to do it with photographs of spleens, diseased or otherwise. Still no doubt Joanna had asked for it!

"It looks most unpleasant," I said.

Joanna said it did, rather.

"How was Griffith?" I asked.

"He looked tired and very unhappy. I think he's got something on his mind."

"A spleen that won't yield to treatment?"

"Don't be silly. I mean something real."

"I should say the man's got you on his mind. I wish you'd lay off him, Joanna."

"Oh, do shut up. I haven't done anything."

"Women always say that."

Joanna whirled angrily out of the room.

The diseased spleen was beginning to curl up in the sun. I took it by one corner and brought it in to the drawing room. I had no affection for it myself, but I presumed it was one of Griffith's treasures.

I stooped down and pulled out a heavy book from the bottom shelf of the bookcase in order to press the photograph flat between its leaves. It was a ponderous volume of somebody's sermons.

The book came open in my hand in rather a surprising way. In another minute I saw why. From the middle of it a number of pages had been neatly cut out.

I stood staring at it. I looked at the title page. It had been published in 1840.

There could be no doubt at all. I was looking at the book from the pages of which the anonymous letters had been put together. Who had cut them out?

Well, to begin with, it could be Emily Barton herself. She was, perhaps, the obvious person to think of. Or it could have been Partridge.

But there were other possibilities. The pages could have been cut out by anyone who had been alone in this room, any visitor, for instance, who had sat there waiting for Miss Emily. Or even anyone who called on business.

No, that wasn't so likely. I had noticed that when, one day, a clerk from the bank had come to see me, Partridge had shown him into the little study at the back of the house. That was clearly the house routine.

A visitor, then? Someone "of good social position." Mr. Pye? Aimée Griffith? Mrs. Dane Calthrop?

The gong sounded and I went in to lunch. Afterward, in the drawing room I showed Joanna my find.

We discussed it from every aspect. Then I took it down to the police station.

They were elated at the find, and I was patted on the back for what was, after all, the sheerest piece of luck.

Graves was not there, but Nash was, and rang up the other man. They would test the book for fingerprints, though Nash was not hopeful of finding anything. I may say that he did not. There were mine, Partridge's and nobody else's, merely showing that Partridge dusted conscientiously.

Nash walked back with me up the hill. I asked how he was getting on.

"We're narrowing it down, Mr. Burton. We've eliminated the people it couldn't be."

"Ah," I said. "And who remains?"

"Miss Ginch. She was to meet a client at a house yesterday afternoon by appointment. That house was situated not far along the Combe Acre road—that's the road that goes past the Symmingtons'. She would have to pass the house both going and coming . . . the week before, the day the anonymous letter was delivered and Mrs. Symmington committed suicide, was her last day at Symmington's office.

"Mr. Symmington thought at first she had not left the office at all that afternoon. He had Sir Henry Lushington with him all the afternoon and rang several times for Miss Ginch. I find, however, that she did leave the office between three and four. She went out to get some high denomination of stamp of which they had run short. The office boy could have gone, but Miss Ginch elected to go, saying she had a headache and would like the air. She was not gone long."

"But long enough?"

"Yes, long enough to hurry along to the other end of the village, slip the letter in the box and hurry back. I must say, however, that I cannot find anybody who saw her near the Symmingtons' house."

"Would they notice?"

"They might and they might not."

"Who else is in your bag?"

Nash looked very straight ahead of him. "You'll understand that we can't exclude anybody—anybody at all."

"No," I said. "I see that."

He said gravely, "Miss Griffith went to Brenton for a meeting of Girl Guides yesterday. She arrived rather late."

"You don't think—"

"No, I don't think. But I don't know. Miss Griffith seems an eminently sane, healthy-minded woman—but I say, I don't know."

"What about the previous week? Could she have slipped the letter in the box?"

"It's possible. She was shopping in the town that afternoon." He paused. "The same applies to Miss Emily Barton. She was out shopping early yesterday afternoon and she went for a walk to see some friends on the road past the Symmingtons' house the week before."

I shook my head unbelievingly. Finding the cut book in Little Furze was bound, I knew, to direct attention to the owner of that house, but when I remembered Miss Emily coming in yesterday so bright and happy and excited . . .

Damn it all—excited. . . . Yes, excited—pink cheeks—shining eyes—surely not because—not because—

I said thickly, "This business is bad for one! One sees things—one imagines things—"

Nash nodded sympathetically. "Yes, it isn't very pleasant to look upon the fellow creatures one meets as possible criminal lunatics."

He paused for a moment, then went on, "And there's Mr. Pye—"

I said sharply, "So you have considered him?"

Nash smiled. "Oh, yes, we've considered him all right. A very curious character—not, I should say, a very nice character. He has no alibi. He was in his garden, alone, on both occasions."

"So you're not only suspecting women?"

"I don't think a man wrote the letters—in fact, I'm sure of it—and so is Graves—always excepting our Mr. Pye, that is to say, who's got an abnormally female streak in his character. But we've checked up on everybody for yesterday afternoon. That's a murder case, you see. You're all right," he grinned, "and so's your sister, and Mr. Symmington didn't leave his office after he got there and Dr. Griffith was on a round in the other direction, and I've checked up on his visits."

He paused, smiled again, and said, "You see, we are thorough."

I said slowly: "So your case is eliminated down to those three? Mr. Pye, Miss Griffith, little Miss Barton?"

"Oh, no, no, we've got a couple more—besides the vicar's lady."

"You've thought of her?"

"We've thought of everybody, but Mrs. Dane Calthrop is a little too openly mad, if you know what I mean. Still, she could have done it. She was in a wood watching birds yesterday afternoon—and the birds can't speak for her."

He turned sharply as Owen Griffith came into the police station.

"Hullo, Nash. I heard you were around asking for me this morning. Anything important?"

"Inquest on Friday, if that suits you, Dr. Griffith."

"Right. Moresby and I are doing the P. M. tonight."

Nash said, "There's just one other thing, Dr. Griffith. Mrs. Symmington was taking some powders or something, that you prescribed for her—"

He paused.

Owen Griffith said interrogatively, "Yes?"

"Would an overdose of those powders have been fatal?"

"Certainly not," Griffith said drily. "Not unless she'd taken about twenty-five of them!"

"But you once warned her about exceeding the dose, so Miss Holland tells me."

"Oh, that, yes. Mrs. Symmington was the sort of woman who would go and overdo anything she was given—fancy that to take twice as much would do her twice as much good, and you don't want anyone to overdo even phenacetin or aspirin—bad for the heart. And anyway there's absolutely no doubt about the cause of death. It was cyanide."

"Oh, I know that—you don't get my meaning. I only thought that when committing suicide you'd prefer to take an overdose of a soporific rather than to feed yourself prussic acid."

"Oh, quite. On the other hand, prussic acid is more dramatic and is pretty certain to do the trick. With barbiturates, for instance, you can bring the victim around if only a short time has elapsed."

"I see; thank you, Dr. Griffith."

Griffith departed, and I said goodby to Nash. I went slowly up the hill home. Joanna was out—at least there was no sign of her, and there was an enigmatical memorandum scribbled on the telephone block presumably for the guidance of either Partridge or myself:

"If Dr. Griffith rings up, I can't go on Tuesday, but could manage Wednesday or Thursday."

I raised my eyebrows and went into the drawing room. I sat down in the most comfortable armchair—(none of them were very comfortable, they tended to have straight backs and were reminiscent of the late Mrs. Barton)—stretched out my legs and tried to think the whole thing out.

With sudden annoyance I remembered that Owen's arrival had interrupted my conversation with the inspector, and that he had mentioned two other people as being possibilities.

I wondered who they were.

Partridge, perhaps, for one? After all, the cut book had been found in this house. And Agnes could have been struck down quite unsuspectingly by her guide and mentor. No, you couldn't eliminate Partridge.

But who was the other?

Somebody, perhaps, that I didn't know? Mrs. Cleat? The original local suspect?

I closed my eyes. I considered the four people, these strangely unlikely people, in turn: Gentle, frail little Emily Barton? What points were there actually against her? A starved life? Dominated and repressed from early childhood? Too many sacrifices asked of her? Her curious horror of discussing anything "not quite nice"? Was that actually a sign of inner preoccupation with just these themes? Was I getting too horribly Freudian? I remembered a doctor once telling me that the mutterings of gentle maiden ladies when going off under an anesthetic were a revelation. "You wouldn't think they knew such words!"

Aimée Griffith?

Surely nothing repressed or "inhibited" about her. Cheery, mannish, successful. A full, busy life. Yet Mrs. Dane Calthrop had said, "Poor thing!"

And there was something—something—some remembrance . . . Ah! I'd got it. Owen Griffith saying something like, "We had an outbreak of anonymous letters up north where I had a practice."

Had that been Aimée Griffith's work, too? Surely rather a coincidence. Two outbreaks of the same thing.

Stop a minute, they'd tracked down the author of those. Griffith had said so. A schoolgirl.

Cold it was suddenly—must be a draft, from the window. I turned uncomfortably in my chair. Why did I suddenly feel so queer and upset?

Go on thinking . . . Aimée Griffith? Perhaps it was Aimée Griffith, not that other girl? And Aimée had come down here and started her tricks again. And that was why Owen Griffith was looking so unhappy and hag-ridden. He suspected. Yes, he suspected. . . .

Mr. Pye? Not, somehow, a very nice little man. I could imagine him staging the whole business, laughing . . .

That telephone message on the telephone pad in the hall—why did I keep thinking of it? Griffith and Joanna—he was falling for her. No, that wasn't why the message worried me. It was something else. . . .

My senses were swimming, sleep was very near. I repeated idiotically to myself: "No smoke without fire. No smoke without fire. . . . That's it . . . it all links up together. . . ."

And then I was walking down the street with Megan, and Elsie Holland passed. She was dressed as a bride, and people were murmuring, "She's going to marry Dr. Griffith at last. Of course, they've been engaged secretly for years . . ."

There we were, in the church, and Dane Calthrop was reading the service in Latin.

And in the middle of it Mrs. Dane Calthrop jumped up and cried energetically, "It's got to be stopped, I tell you. It's got to be stopped!"

For a minute or two I didn't know whether I was asleep or awake. Then my brain cleared, and I realized I was in the drawing room of Little Furze and that Mrs. Dane Calthrop had just come through the window and was standing in front of me saying with nervous violence:

"It has got to be stopped, I tell you."

I jumped up. "I beg your pardon," I said. "I'm afraid I was asleep. What did you say?"

Mrs. Dane Calthrop beat one fist fiercely on the palm of her other hand. "It's got to be stopped. These letters! Murder! You can't go on having poor innocent children like Agnes Woddell killed!"

"You're quite right," I said. "But how do you propose to set about it?"

Mrs. Dane Calthrop said, "We've got to do something!"

I smiled, perhaps in rather a superior fashion. "And what do you suggest that we should do?"

"Get the whole thing cleared up! I said this wasn't a wicked place. I was wrong. It is."

I felt annoyed. "Yes, my dear woman," I said, not too politely, "but what are you going to do?"

Mrs. Dane Calthrop said, "Put a stop to it all, of course."

"The police are doing their best."

"If Agnes could be killed yesterday, their best isn't good enough."

"So you know better than they do?"

"Not at all. I don't know anything at all. That's why I'm going to call in an expert."

I shook my head. "You can't do that. Scotland Yard will only take over on a demand from the chief constable of the county. Actually they have sent Graves."

"I don't mean that kind of an expert. I don't mean someone who knows about anonymous letters or even about murder. I mean someone who knows people. Don't you see? We want someone who knows a great deal about wickedness!"

It was a queer point of view. But it was, somehow, stimulating.

Before I could say anything more, Mrs. Dane Calthrop nodded her head at me and said in a quick, confident tone:

"I'm going to see about it right away."

And she went out of the window again.

The next week, I think, was one of the queerest times I have ever passed through. It had an odd dream quality. Nothing seemed real.

The inquest on Agnes Woddell was held and the curious of Lymstock attended en masse. No new facts came to light and the only possible verdict was returned: "Murder by person or persons unknown."

So poor little Agnes Woddell, having had her hour of limelight, was duly buried in the quiet old churchyard and life in Lymstock went on as before.

No, that last statement is untrue. Not as before. . . .

There was a half-scared, half-avid gleam in almost everybody's eye. Neighbor looked at neighbor. One thing had been brought out clearly at the inquest—it was most unlikely that any stranger had killed Agnes Woddell. No tramps or unknown men had been noticed or reported in the district. Somewhere, then, in Lymstock, walking down the High Street, shopping, passing the time of day, was a person who had cracked a defenseless girl's skull and driven a sharp skewer home to her brain.

And no one knew who that person was.

As I say, the days went on in a kind of dream. I looked at everyone I met in a new light, the light of a possible murderer. It was not an agreeable sensation!

And in the evenings, with the curtain drawn, Joanna and I sat talking, talking, arguing, going over in turn all the various possibilities that still seemed so fantastic and incredible.

Joanna held firm to her theory of Mr. Pye. I, after wavering a little, had gone back to my original suspect, Miss Ginch. But we went over the possible names again and again:

Mr. Pye?

Miss Ginch?

Mrs. Dane Calthrop?

Aimée Griffith?

Emily Barton?

Partridge?

And all the time, nervously, apprehensively, we waited for something to happen.

But nothing did happen. Nobody, so far as we knew, received any more letters. Nash made periodic appearances in the town but what he was doing and what traps the police were setting, I had no idea. Graves had gone again.

Emily Barton came to tea. Megan came to lunch. Owen Griffith went about his practice. We went and drank sherry with Mr. Pye. And we went to tea at the vicarage.

I was glad to find that Mrs. Dane Calthrop displayed none of the militant ferocity she had shown on the occasion of our last meeting. I think she had forgotten all about it.

She seemed now principally concerned with the destruction of white butterflies so as to preserve cauliflower and cabbage plants.

Our afternoon at the vicarage was really one of the most peaceful we had spent. It was an attractive old house and had a big, shabby, comfortable drawing room with faded rose cretonne. The Dane Calthrops had a guest staying with them, an amiable, elderly lady who was knitting something with white, fleecy wool. We had very good hot scones for tea, the vicar came in, and beamed placidly on us while he pursued his gentle erudite conversation. It was very pleasant.

I don't mean that we got away from the topic of the murder, because we didn't.

Miss Marple, the guest, was naturally thrilled by the subject. As she said apologetically:

"We have so little to talk about in the country!" She had made up her mind that the dead girl must have been just like her Edith.

"Such a nice little maid, and so willing, but sometimes just a little slow to take in things."

Miss Marple also had a cousin whose niece's sister-in-law had had a great deal of annoyance and trouble over some anonymous letters, so that, too, was very interesting to the charming old lady.

"But tell me, dear," she said to Mrs. Dane Calthrop, "what do the village people—I mean the townspeople—say? What do they think?"

"Mrs. Cleat still, I suppose," said Joanna.

"Oh, no," said Mrs. Dane Calthrop. "Not now."

Miss Marple asked who Mrs. Cleat was.

Joanna said she was the village witch.

"That's right, isn't it, Mrs. Dane Calthrop?"

The vicar murmured a long Latin quotation about, I think, the evil power of witches, to which we all listened in respectful and uncomprehending silence.

"She's a very silly woman," said his wife. "Likes to show off. Goes out to gather herbs and things at the full of the moon and takes care that everybody in the place knows about it."

"And silly girls go and consult her, I suppose?" said Miss Marple.

I saw the vicar getting ready to unload more Latin on us and I asked hastily, "But why shouldn't people suspect her of the murder now? They thought the letters were her doing."

Miss Marple said finally:

"Oh! But the girl was killed with a skewer, so I hear. Very unpleasant! Well, naturally, that takes all suspicion away from this Mrs. Cleat. Because, you see, she could ill-wish her, so that the girl would waste away and die from natural causes."

"Strange how those old beliefs linger," said the vicar. "In early Christian times, local superstitions were wisely incorporated with Christian doctrines and their most unpleasant attributes gradually eliminated."

"It isn't superstition we've got to deal with here," said Mrs. Dane Calthrop, "but facts."

"And very unpleasant facts," I said.

"As you say, Mr. Burton," said Miss Marple. "Now you—excuse me if I am being too personal—are a stranger here, and have a knowledge of the world and of various aspects of life. It seems to me that you ought to be able to find a solution to this distasteful problem."

I smiled.

"The best solution I have had was a dream. In my dream it all fitted in and panned out beautifully. Unfortunately when I woke up the whole thing was nonsense!"

"How interesting, though. Do tell me how the nonsense went."

"Oh, it all started with the silly phrase 'No smoke without fire.' People have been saying that *ad nauseam*. And then I got it mixed up with war terms. Smoke screen, scrap of paper, telephone messages—no, that was another dream."

"And what was that dream?"

The old lady was so eager about it, that I felt sure she was a secret reader of Napoleon's Book of Dreams, which had been the great stand-by of my old nurse.

"Oh! Only Elsie Holland—the Symmingtons' nursery governess, you know, was getting married to Dr. Griffith and the vicar here was reading the service in Latin—('Very appropriate, dear,' murmured Mrs. Dane Calthrop to her spouse) and then Mrs. Dane Calthrop got up and forbade the banns and said it had got to be stopped!

"But that part," I added with a smile, "was true. I woke up and found you standing over me saying it."

"And I was quite right," said Mrs. Dane Calthrop—but quite mildly, I was glad to note.

"But where did a telephone message come in?" asked Miss Marple, crinkling her brows.

"I'm afraid I'm being rather stupid. That wasn't in the dream. It was just before it. I came through the hall and noticed Joanna had written down a message to be given to someone if they rang up."

Miss Marple leaned forward. There was a pink spot in each cheek. "Will you think me very inquisitive and very rude if I ask just what that message was?" She cast a glance at Joanna. "I do apologize, my dear."

Joanna, however, was highly entertained.

"Oh, I don't mind," she assured the old lady. "I can't remember anything about it myself, but perhaps Jerry can. It must have been something quite trivial."

Solemnly I repeated the message as best I could remember it, enormously tickled at the old lady's rapt attention.

I was afraid the actual words were going to disappoint her, but perhaps she had some sentimental idea of a romance, for she nodded her head and smiled and seemed pleased.

"I see," she said. "I thought it might be something like that."

Mrs. Dane Calthrop said sharply, "Like what, Jane?"

"Something quite ordinary," said Miss Marple.

She looked at me thoughtfully for a moment or two, then she said unexpectedly, "I can see you are a very clever young man—but with not quite enough confidence in yourself. You ought to have!"

Joanna gave a loud hoot. "For goodness' sake don't encourage him to feel like that. He thinks quite enough of himself as it is."

"Be quiet, Joanna," I said. "Miss Marple understands me."

Miss Marple had resumed her fleecy knitting. "You know," she observed pensively, "to commit a successful murder must be very much like bringing off a conjuring trick."

"The quickness of the hand deceives the eye?"

"Not only that. You've got to make people look at the wrong thing and in the wrong place—misdirection, they call it, I believe."

"Well," I remarked, "so far everybody seems to have looked in the wrong place for our lunatic at large."

"I should be inclined, myself," said Miss Marple, "to look for somebody very sane."

"Yes," I said thoughtfully, "that's what Nash said. I remember he stressed respectability, too."

"Yes," agreed Miss Marple. "That's very important."

Well, we all seemed agreed.

I addressed Mrs. Calthrop. "Nash thinks," I said, "that there will be more anonymous letters. What do you think?"

"There may be," she said slowly, "I suppose."

"If the police think that, there will have to be, no doubt," said Miss Marple.

I went on doggedly to Mrs. Dane Calthrop: "Are you still sorry for the writer?"

She flushed. "Why not?"

"I don't think I agree with you, dear," said Miss Marple. "Not in this case."

I said hotly, "They've driven one woman to suicide, and caused untold misery and heartburnings!"

"Have you had one, Miss Burton?" asked Miss Marple of Joanna.

Joanna gurgled: "Oh, yes! It said the most frightful things."

"I'm afraid," said Miss Marple, "that the people who are young and pretty are apt to be singled out by the writer."

"That's why I certainly think it's odd that Elsie Holland hasn't had any," I said.

"Let me see," said Miss Marple. "Is that the Symmingtons' nursery governess—the one you dreamed about, Mr. Burton?"

"Yes."

"She's probably had one and won't say so," said Joanna.

"No," I said, "I believe her. So does Nash."

"Dear me," said Miss Marple. "Now that's very interesting. That's the most interesting thing I've heard yet."

As we were going home Joanna told me that I ought not to have repeated what Nash said about more letters coming.

"Why not?"

"Because Mrs. Dane Calthrop might be It."

"You don't really believe that!"

"I'm not sure. She's a queer woman."

We began our discussion of probables all over again.

It was two nights later that I was coming back in the car from Exhampton. I had had dinner there and then started back and it was already dark before I got into Lymstock.

Something was wrong with the car lights, and after slowing up and switching on and off, I finally got out to see what I could do. I was some time fiddling, but I managed to fix them up finally.

The road was quite deserted. Nobody in Lymstock is about after dark. The first few houses were just ahead, among them the ugly gabled building of the Women's Institute. It loomed up in the dim starlight and something impelled me to go and have a look at it. I don't know whether I had caught a faint glimpse of a stealthy figure flitting through the gate—if so, it must have been so indeterminate that it did not register in my conscious mind, but I did suddenly feel a kind of overweening curiosity about the place.

The gate was slightly ajar, and I pushed it open and walked in. A short path and four steps led up to the door.

I stood there a moment hesitating. What was I really doing there? I didn't know, and then, suddenly, just near at hand, I caught the sound of a rustle. It sounded like a woman's dress.

I took a sharp turn and went around the corner of the building toward where the sound had come from.

I couldn't see anybody. I went on and again turned a corner. I was at the back of the house now and suddenly I saw, only two feet away from me, an open window.

I crept up to it and listened. I could hear nothing, but somehow or other I felt convinced that there was someone inside.

My back wasn't too good for acrobatics as yet, but I managed to hoist myself up and drop over the sill inside. I made rather a noise unfortunately.

I stood just inside the window listening. Then I walked forward, my hands outstretched. I heard then the faintest sound ahead of me to my right.

I had a torch in my pocket and I switched it on.

Immediately a low, sharp voice said, "Put that out."

I obeyed instantly, for in that brief second I had recognized Superintendent Nash.

I felt him take my arm and propel me through a door and into a passage. Here, where there was no window to betray our presence to anyone outside, he switched on a lamp and looked at me more in sorrow than in anger.

"You would have to butt in just that minute, Mr. Burton."

"Sorry," I apologized. "But I got a hunch that I was on to something."

"And so you were probably. Did you see anyone?"

I hesitated.

"I'm not sure," I said slowly. "I've got a vague feeling I saw someone sneak in through the front gate but I didn't really see anyone. Then I heard a rustle around the side of the house."

Nash nodded. "That's right. Somebody came around the house before you. He—or she—hesitated by the window, then went on quickly—heard you, I expect."

I apologized again. "What's the big idea?" I asked.

Nash said:

"I'm banking on the fact that an anonymous letter writer can't stop writing letters. She may know it's dangerous, but she'll have to do it. It's like a craving for drink or drugs."

I nodded.

"Now you see, Mr. Burton, I fancy whoever it is will want to keep the letters looking the same as much as possible. She's got the cutout pages of that book, and can go on using letters and words cut out of them. But the envelopes present a difficulty. She'll want to type them on the same machine. She can't risk using another typewriter or her own handwriting."

"Do you really think she'll go on with the game?" I asked incredulously.

"Yes, I do. And I'll bet you anything you like she's full of confidence. They're always vain as hell, these people! Well, then, I figured out that whoever it was would come to the Institute after dark so as to get at the typewriter."

"Miss Ginch," I said.

"Maybe."

"You don't know yet?"

"I don't know."

"But you suspect?"

"Yes. But somebody's very cunning, Mr. Burton. Somebody knows all the tricks of the game."

I could imagine some of the network that Nash had spread abroad. I had no doubt that every letter written by a suspect and posted or left by hand was immediately inspected. Sooner or later the criminal would slip up, would grow careless.

For the third time I apologized for my zealous and unwanted presence.

"Oh, well," said Nash philosophically, "it can't be helped. Better luck next time."

I went out into the night. A dim figure was standing beside my car. To my astonishment I recognized Megan.

"Hullo!" she said. "I thought this was your car. What have you been doing?"

"What are you doing is much more to the point?" I said.

"I'm out for a walk. I like walking at night. Nobody stops you and says silly things, and I like the stars, and things smell better, and everyday things look all mysterious."

"All of that I grant you freely," I said. "But only cats and witches walk in the dark. They'll wonder about you at home."

"No, they won't. They never wonder where I am or what I'm doing."

"How are you getting on?" I asked.

"All right, I suppose."

"Miss Holland look after you and all that?"

"Elsie's all right. She can't help being a perfect fool."

"Unkind—but probably true," I said. "Hop in and I'll drive you home."

It was not quite true that Megan was never missed.

Symmington was standing on the doorstep as we drove up.

He peered toward us.

"Hullo, is Megan there?"

"Yes," I said. "I've brought her home."

Symmington said sharply, "You mustn't go off like this without telling us, Megan. Miss Holland has been quite worried about you."

Megan muttered something and went past him into the house.

Symmington sighed. "A grown-up girl is a great responsibility with no mother to look after her. She's too old for school, I suppose."

He looked toward me rather suspiciously.

"I suppose you took her for a drive?" I thought it best to leave it like that.

VII

ON THE FOLLOWING day I went mad. Looking back on it, that is really the only explanation I can find.

I was due for my monthly visit to Marcus Kent. . . . I went up by train. To my intense surprise Joanna elected to stay behind. As a rule she was eager to come and we usually stayed up for a couple of days.

This time, however, I proposed to return the same day by the evening train, but even so I was astonished at Joanna. She merely said enigmatically that she'd got plenty to do, and why spend hours in a nasty stuffy train when it was a lovely day in the country?

That, of course, was undeniable, but sounded very unlike Joanna.

She said she didn't want the car, so I was to drive it to the station and leave it parked there against my return.

The station of Lymstock is situated, for some obscure reason known to railway companies only, quite half a mile from Lymstock itself. Halfway along the road I overtook Megan shuffling along in an aimless manner. I pulled up.

"Hullo, what are you doing?"

"Just out for a walk."

"But not what is called a good brisk walk, I gather. You were crawling along like a dispirited crab."

"Well, I wasn't going anywhere particular."

"Then you'd better come and see me off at the station." I opened the door of the car and Megan jumped in.

"Where are you going?" she asked.

"London. To see my doctor."

"Your back's not worse, is it?"

"No, it's practically all right again. I'm expecting him to be very pleased about it."

Megan nodded.

We drew up at the station. I parked the car and went in and bought my ticket at the booking office. There were very few people on the platform and nobody I knew.

"You wouldn't like to lend me a penny, would you?" said Megan. "Then I'd get a bit of chocolate out of the slot machine."

"Here you are, baby," I said, handing her the coin in question. "Sure you wouldn't like some clear gums or some throat pastilles as well?"

"I like chocolate best," said Megan without suspecting sarcasm.

She went off to the chocolate machine, and I looked after her with a feeling of mounting irritation.

She was wearing trodden-over shoes, and coarse unattractive stockings and a particularly shapeless jumper and skirt. I don't know why all this should have infuriated me, but it did.

I said angrily as she came back, "Why do you wear those disgusting stockings?"

Megan looked down at them, surprised. "What's the matter with them?"

"Everything's the matter with them. They're loathsome. And why wear a pullover like a decayed cabbage?"

"It's all right, isn't it? I've had it for years."

"So I should imagine. And why do you—"

At this minute the train came in and interrupted my angry lecture.

I got into an empty first-class carriage, let down the window and leaned out to continue the conversation.

Megan stood below me, her face upturned. She asked me why I was so cross.

"I'm not cross," I said untruly. "It just infuriates me to see you so slack, and not caring how you look."

"I couldn't look nice, anyway, so what does it matter?"

"Cut it!" I said. "I'd like to see you turned out properly. I'd like to take you to London and outfit you from tip to toe."

"I wish you could," said Megan.

The train began to move. I looked down into Megan's upturned, wistful face.

And then as I have said, madness came upon me.

I opened the door, grabbed Megan with one arm and fairly hauled her into the carriage.

There was an outraged shout from a porter, but all he could do was dexterously to bang shut the door again. I pulled Megan up from the floor where my impetuous action had landed her.

"What on earth did you do that for?" she demanded, rubbing one knee.

"Shut up," I said. "You're coming to London with me and when I've done with you you won't know yourself. I'll show you what you can look like if you try. I'm tired of seeing you mouch about down at heel and all anyhow."

"Oh!" said Megan in an ecstatic whisper.

The ticket collector came along and I bought Megan a return ticket. She sat in her corner looking at me in a kind of awed respect.

"I say," she said when the man had gone. "You are sudden, aren't you?"

"Very," I said. "It runs in our family."

How explain to Megan the impulse that had come over me?—She had looked like a wistful dog being left behind. She now had on her face the incredulous pleasure of the dog who has been taken on the walk after all.

"I suppose you don't know London very well?" I said to Megan.

"Yes, I do," said Megan. "I always went through it to school. And I've been to the dentist there and to a pantomime."

"This," I said darkly, "will be a different London."

We arrived with half an hour to spare before my appointment in Harley Street.

I took a taxi and we drove straight to Mirotin, Joanna's dressmaker. Mirotin is, in the flesh, an unconventional and breezy woman of forty-five, Mary Grey. She is a clever woman and very good company. I have always liked her.

I said to Megan, "You're my cousin."

"Why?"

"Don't argue," I said.

Mary Grey was being firm with a stout woman who was enamored of a skin-tight powder-blue evening dress. I detached her and took her aside.

"Listen," I said. "I've brought a little cousin of mine along. Joanna was coming up but was prevented. But she said I could leave it all to you. You see what the girl looks like now?"

"I most certainly do!" said Mary Grey with feeling.

"Well, I want her turned out right in every particular from head to foot. Carte blanche. Stockings, shoes, undies, everything! By the way, the man who does Joanna's hair is close around here, isn't he?"

"Antoine? Around the corner. I'll see to that too."

"You're a woman in a thousand."

"Oh, I shall enjoy it—apart from the money—and that's not to be sneezed at in these days—half my damned brutes of women never pay their bills. But as I say, I shall enjoy it." She shot a quick professional glance at Megan standing a little way off. "She's got a lovely figure."

"You must have X-ray eyes," I said. "She looks completely shapeless to me."

Mary Grey laughed.

"It's these schools," she said. "They seem to take a pride in turning out girls who preen themselves on looking like nothing on earth. They call it being sweet and unsophisticated. Sometimes it takes a whole season before a girl can pull herself together and look human. Don't worry, leave it all to me."

"Right," I said. "I'll come back and fetch her about six."

Marcus Kent was pleased with me. He told me that I surpassed his wildest expectations.

"You must have the constitution of an elephant," he said, "to make a comeback like this. Oh, well, wonderful what country air and no late hours or excitement will do for a man if he can only stick it."

"I grant you your first two," I said. "But don't think that the country is free from excitement. We've had a good deal in my part."

"What sort of excitement?"

"Murder," I said.

Marcus Kent pursed up his mouth and whistled. "Some bucolic love tragedy? Farm lad kills his lass?"

"Not at all. A crafty, determined lunatic killer."

"I haven't read anything about it? When did they lay him by the heels?"

"They haven't, and it's a she!"

"Whew! I'm not sure that Lymstock's quite the right place for you, old boy."

I said firmly, "Yes, it is. And you're not going to get me out of it."

Marcus Kent has a low mind. He said at once, "So that's it! Found a blonde?"

"Not at all," I said, with a guilty thought of Elsie Holland. "It's merely that the psychology of crime interests me a good deal."

"Oh, all right. It certainly hasn't done you any harm so far, but just make sure that your lunatic killer doesn't obliterate you."

"No fear of that," I said.

"What about dining with me this evening? You can tell me all about your revolting murder."

"Sorry. I'm booked."

"Date with a lady—eh? Yes, you're definitely on the mend."

"I suppose you could call it that," I said, rather tickled at the idea of Megan in the role.

I was at Mirotin's at six o'clock when the establishment was officially closing. Mary Grey came to meet me at the top of the stairs outside the showroom. She had a finger to her lips.

"You're going to have a shock! If I say it myself, I've put in a good bit of work."

I went on into the big showroom. Megan was standing looking at herself in a long mirror. I give you my word I hardly recognized her! For the minute it took my breath away. Tall and slim as a willow with delicate ankles and feet shown off by sheer silk stockings and well-cut shoes. Yes, lovely feet and hands, small bones—quality and distinction in every line of her. Her hair had been trimmed and shaped to her head and it was glowing like a glossy chestnut. They'd had the sense to leave her face alone. She was not made up, or if she was it was so slight and delicate that it did not show. Her mouth needed no lipstick.

Moreover there was about her something that I had never seen before, a new innocent pride in the arch of her neck. She looked at me gravely with a small, shy smile.

"I do look—rather nice, don't I?" said Megan.

"Nice?" I said. "Nice isn't the word! Come on out to dinner and if every second man doesn't turn round to look at you I'll be surprised. You'll knock all the other girls into a cocked hat."

Megan was not beautiful, but she was unusual and striking-looking. She had personality. She walked into the restaurant ahead of me and as the head waiter hurried toward us, I felt the thrill of idiotic pride that a man feels when he has got something out of the ordinary with him.

We had cocktails first and lingered over them. Then we dined. And later we danced. Megan was keen to dance and I didn't want to disappoint her, but for some reason or other I hadn't thought she would dance well. But she did. She was light as a feather in my arms, and her body and feet followed the rhythm perfectly.

"Gosh!" I said. "You can dance!"

She seemed a little surprised.

"Well, of course I can. We had dancing class every week at school."

"It takes more than dancing class to make a dancer," I said.

We went back to our table.

"Isn't this food lovely?" said Megan. "And everything!"

She heaved a delighted sigh.

"Exactly my sentiments," I said.

It was a delirious evening. I was still mad. Megan brought me down to earth when she said doubtfully, "Oughtn't we to be going home?"

My jaw dropped. Yes, definitely I was mad. I had forgotten everything! I was in a world divorced from reality, existing in it with the creature I had created.

"Good Lord!" I said.

I realized that the last train had gone.

"Stay there," I said. "I'm going to telephone."

I rang up the Llewellyn Hire people and ordered their biggest and fastest car to come around as soon as possible.

I came back to Megan.

"The last train has gone," I said. "So we're going home by car."

"Are we? What fun!"

What a nice child she was, I thought. So pleased with everything, so unquestioning, accepting all my suggestions without fuss or bother.

The car came, and it was large and fast, but all the same it was very very late when we came into Lymstock.

Suddenly conscience-stricken, I said, "They'll have been sending out search parties for you!"

But Megan seemed in an equable mood. "Oh, I don't think so," she said vaguely. "I often go out and don't come home for lunch."

"Yes, my dear child, but you've been out for tea and dinner too."

However, Megan's lucky star was in the ascendant. The house was dark and silent. On Megan's advice, we went around to the back and threw stones at Rose's window.

In due course Rose looked out and with many suppressed exclamations and palpitations came down to let us in.

"Well now, and I saying you were asleep in your bed. The master and Miss Holland—" (slight sniff after Miss Holland's name) "had early supper and went for a drive. I said I'd keep an eye to the boys. I thought I heard you come in when I was up in the nursery trying to quiet Colin, who was playing up, but you weren't about when I came down so I thought you'd gone up to bed. And that's what I said when the master came in and asked for you."

I cut short the conversation by remarking that that was where Megan had better go now.

"Good night," said Megan, "and thank you awfully. It's been the loveliest day I've ever had."

I drove home slightly lightheaded still, and tipped the chauffeur handsomely, offering him a bed if he liked. But he preferred to drive back through the night.

The hall door had opened during our colloquy and as he drove away it was flung wide open and Joanna said, "So it's you at last, is it?"

"Were you worried about me?" I asked, coming in and shutting the door.

Joanna went into the drawing room and I followed her. There was a coffee-pot on the trivet and Joanna made herself coffee while I helped myself to a whisky-and-soda.

"Worried about you? No, of course not. I thought you'd decided to stay in town and have a binge."

"I've had a binge—of a kind."

I grinned and then began to laugh.

Joanna asked what I was laughing at and I told her.

"But, Jerry, you must have been mad—quite mad!"

"I suppose I was."

"But, my dear boy, you can't do things like that—not in a place like this. It will be all around Lymstock tomorrow."

"I suppose it will. But, after all, Megan's only a child."

"She isn't. She's twenty. You can't take a girl of twenty to London and buy her clothes without a most frightful scandal. Good gracious, Jerry, you'll probably have to marry the girl."

Joanna was half serious, half laughing.

It was at that moment that I made a very important discovery.

"Damn it all," I said. "I don't mind if I do. In fact—I should like it."

A very funny expression came over Joanna's face. She got up and said drily, as she went toward the door, "Yes, I've known that for some time . . ."

She left me standing, glass in hand, aghast at my new discovery.

I don't know what the usual reactions are of a man who goes to propose marriage.

In fiction his throat is dry and his collar feels too tight and he is in a pitiable state of nervousness.

I didn't feel at all like that. Having thought of a good idea I just wanted to get it all settled as soon as possible. I didn't see any particular need for embarrassment.

I went along to the Symmingtons' house about eleven o'clock. I rang the bell and when Rose came, I asked for Miss Megan.

It was the knowing look that Rose gave me that first made me feel slightly shy.

She put me in the little morning room and while waiting there I hoped uneasily that they hadn't been upsetting Megan.

When the door opened and I wheeled around, I was instantly relieved. Megan was not looking shy or upset at all. Her head was still like a glossy chestnut, and she wore that air of pride and self-respect that she had acquired yesterday. She was in her old clothes again but she had managed to make them look different. It's wonderful what knowledge of her own attractiveness will do for a girl. Megan, I realized suddenly, had grown up.

I suppose I must really have been rather nervous, otherwise I should not have opened the conversation by saying affectionately: "Hullo, catfish!" It was hardly, in the circumstances, a loverlike greeting.

It seemed to suit Megan. She grinned and said, "Hullo!"

"Look here," I said. "You didn't get into a row about yesterday, I hope?"

Megan said with assurance, "Oh, no," and then blinked, and said vaguely, "Yes, I believe I did. I mean, they said a lot of things and seemed to think it had been very odd—but then you know what people are and what fusses they make all about nothing."

I was relieved to see that shocked disapproval had slipped off Megan like water off a duck's back.

"I came around this morning," I said, "because I've a suggestion to make. You see I like you a lot, and I think you like me—"

"Frightfully," said Megan with rather disquieting enthusiasm.

"And we get on awfully well together, so I think it would be a good idea if we got married."

"Oh," said Megan.

She looked surprised. Just that. Not startled. Not shocked. Just mildly surprised.

"You mean you really want to marry me?" she asked with the air of one getting a thing perfectly clear.

"More than anything in the world," I said—and I meant it.

"You mean, you're in love with me?"

"I'm in love with you."

Her eyes were steady and grave. She said, "I think you're the nicest person in the world—but I'm not in love with you."

"I'll make you love me."

"That wouldn't do. I don't want to be made." She paused and then said gravely, "I'm not the sort of wife for you. I'm better at hating than at loving."

She said it with a queer intensity.

I said, "Hate doesn't last. Love does."

"Is that true?"

"It's what I believe."

Again there was a silence. Then I said, "So it's 'no,' is it?"

"Yes, it's 'no.' "

"And you don't encourage me to hope?"

"What would be the good of that?"

"None whatever," I agreed. "Quite redundant in fact—because I'm going to hope whether you tell me to or not."

Well, that was that.

I walked away from the house feeling slightly dazed but irritatingly conscious of Rose's passionately interested gaze following me.

Rose had had a good deal to say before I could escape.

That she'd never felt the same since that awful day! That she wouldn't have stayed except for the children and being sorry for poor Mr. Symmington. That she wasn't going to stay unless they got another maid quick—and they wouldn't be likely to do that when there had been a murder in the house! That it was all very well for that Miss Holland to say she'd do the housework in the meantime.

Very sweet and obliging she was—oh, yes, but it was mistress of the house that she was fancying herself going to be one fine day! Mr. Symmington, poor man, never saw anything—but one knew what a widower was, a poor helpless creature made to be the prey of a designing woman. And that it wouldn't be for want of trying if Miss Holland didn't step into the dead mistress's shoes!

I assented mechanically to everything, yearning to get away and unable to do so because Rose was holding firmly on to my hat while she indulged in her flood of spite.

I wondered if there was any truth in what she said. Had Elsie Holland envisaged the possibility of becoming the second Mrs. Symmington? Or was she just a decent kindhearted girl doing her best to look after a bereaved household?

The result would quite likely be the same in either case. And why not? Symmington's young children needed a mother—Elsie was a decent soul—besides being quite indecently beautiful—a point which a man might appreciate—even such a stuffed fish as Symmington!

I thought all this, I know, because I was trying to put off thinking about Megan.

You may say that I had gone to ask Megan to marry me in an absurdly complacent frame of mind and that I deserved what I got—but it was not really like that. It was because I felt so assured, so certain, that Megan belonged to me—that she was my business, that to look after her and make her happy and keep her from harm was the only natural right way of life for me, that I had expected her to feel, too—that she and I—belonged to each other.

But I was not giving up. Oh, no! Megan was my woman and I was going to have her.

After a moment's thought, I went to Symmington's office. Megan might pay no attention to strictures on her conduct, but I would like to get things straight.

Mr. Symmington was disengaged, I was told, and I was shown into the room.

By a pinching of the lips, and an additional stiffness of manner, I gathered that I was not exactly popular at the moment.

"Good morning," I said. "I'm afraid this isn't a professional call, but a personal one. I'll put it plainly. I dare say you'll have realized that I'm in love with Megan. I've asked her to marry me and she has refused. But I'm not taking that as final."

I saw Symmington's expression change, and I read his mind with ludicrous ease. Megan was a disharmonious element in his house. He was, I felt sure, a just and kindly man, and he would never have dreamed of not providing a home for his dead wife's daughter. But her marriage to me would certainly be a relief. The frozen halibut thawed. He gave me a pale, cautious smile.

"Frankly, do you know, Burton, I had no idea of such a thing. I know you've taken a lot of notice of her, but we've always regarded her as such a child."

"She's not a child," I said shortly.

"No, no, not in years."

"She can be her age any time she's allowed to be," I said, still slightly angry. "She's not of age, I know, but she will be in a month or two. I'll let you have all the information about myself you want. I'm well off and have led quite a decent life. I'll look after her and do all I can to make her happy."

"Quite—quite. Still, it's up to Megan herself."

"She'll come round in time," I said. "But I just thought I'd like to get straight with you about it."

He said he appreciated that, and we parted amicably.

I ran into Miss Emily Barton outside. She had a shopping basket on her arm.

"Good morning, Mr. Burton, I hear you went to London yesterday."

Yes, she had heard all right. Her eyes were, I thought, kindly, but full of curiosity, too.

"I went to see my doctor," I said.

Miss Emily smiled.

That smile made little of Marcus Kent. She murmured, "I hear Megan nearly missed the train. She jumped in when it was going."

"Helped by me," I said. "I hauled her in."

"How very lucky you were there. Otherwise there might have been an accident."

It is extraordinary how much of a fool one gentle, inquisitive, old maiden lady can make a man feel!

I was saved further suffering by the onslaught of Mrs. Dane Calthrop. She had her own tame elderly maiden lady in tow, but she herself was full of direct speech.

"Good morning," she said. "I hear you've made Megan buy herself some decent clothes? Very sensible of you. It takes a man to think of something really practical like that. I've been worried about that girl for a long time. Girls with brains are so liable to turn into morons, aren't they?"

With which remarkable statement, she shot into the fish shop.

Miss Marple, left standing by me, twinkled a little and said, "Mrs. Dane Calthrop is a very remarkable woman, you know. She's nearly always right."

"It makes her rather alarming," I said.

"Sincerity has that effect," said Miss Marple.

Mrs. Dane Calthrop shot out of the fish shop again and rejoined us. She was holding a large red lobster.

"Have you ever seen anything so unlike Mr. Pye?" she said. "Very virile and handsome, isn't it?"

I was a little nervous of meeting Joanna but I found when I got home that I needn't have worried. She was out and she did not return for lunch. This aggrieved Partridge a good deal, who said sourly as she proffered two loin chops in an entrée dish:

"Miss Burton said specially as she was going to be in."

I ate both chops in an attempt to atone for Joanna's lapse. All the same, I wondered where my sister was. She had taken to being very mysterious about her doings of late.

It was half past three when Joanna burst into the drawing room. I had heard a car stop outside and I half expected to see Griffith, but the car drove on and Joanna came in alone.

Her face was very red and she seemed upset. I perceived that something had happened.

"What's the matter?" I asked.

Joanna opened her mouth, closed it again, sighed, plumped herself down in a chair and stared in front of her.

She said, "I've had the most awful day."

"What's happened?"

"I've done the most incredible things. It was awful—"

"But what—"

"I just started out for a walk, an ordinary walk—I went up over the hill and on to the moor. I walked miles—I felt like it. Then I dropped down into a hollow. There's a farm there—a God-forsaken lonely sort of spot. I was thirsty and I wondered if they had any milk or something. So I wandered into the farmyard and then the door opened and Owen came out."

"Yes?"

"He thought it might be the district nurse. There was a woman in there having a baby. He was expecting the nurse and he'd sent word to her to get hold of another doctor. It—things were going wrong."

"Yes?"

"So he said—to me, 'Come on, you'll do—better than nobody.' I said I couldn't, and he said what did I mean? I said I'd never done anything like that, that I didn't know anything—

"He asked me what the hell that mattered. And then he was awful. He turned on me. He said, 'You're a woman, aren't you? I suppose you can do your durnedest to help another woman?' And he went on at me—said I'd talked as though I was interested in doctoring and had said I wished I was a nurse. 'All pretty talk, I suppose! You didn't mean anything real by it, but this is real and you're going to behave like a decent human being and not a useless ornamental nitwit!'

"I've done the most indiscernible things, Jerry. Held instruments and boiled them and handed things. I'm so tired I can hardly stand up. It was dreadful. But he saved her—and the baby. It was born alive. He didn't think at one time he could save it. Oh, dear!"

Joanna covered her face with her hands.

I contemplated her with a certain amount of pleasure and mentally took my hat off to Owen Griffith. He'd brought Joanna slap up against reality for once.

I said, "There's a letter for you in the hall. From Paul, I think."

"Eh?" She paused for a minute and then said, "I'd no idea, Jerry, what doctors had to do. The nerve they've got to have!"

I went out into the hall and brought Joanna her letter. She opened it, glanced vaguely at its contents, and let it drop.

"He was—really—rather wonderful. The way he fought—the way he wouldn't be beaten! He was rude and horrible to me—but he was wonderful."

I observed Paul's disregarded letter with some pleasure. Plainly, Joanna was cured of Paul.

Things never come when they are expected.

I was full of Joanna's and my personal affairs and was quite taken aback the next morning when Nash's voice said over the telephone:

"We've got her, Mr. Burton!"

I was so startled I nearly dropped the receiver.

"You mean the—"

He interrupted: "Can you be overheard where you are?"

"No, I don't think so—well, perhaps—"

It seemed to me that the baize door to the kitchen had swung open a trifle.

"Perhaps you'd care to come down to the station?"

"I will. Right away."

I was at the police station in next to no time. In an inner room Nash and Sergeant Parkins were together. Nash was wreathed in smiles.

"It's been a long chase," he said. "But we're there at last."

He flicked a letter across the table. This time it was all typewritten. It was, of its kind, fairly mild:

"It's no use thinking you're going to step into a dead woman's shoes. The whole town is laughing at you. Get out now. Soon it will be too late. This is a warning. Remember what happened to that other girl. Get out and stay out."

It finished with some mildly obscene language.

"That reached Miss Holland this morning," said Nash.

"Thought it was funny she hadn't had one before," said Sergeant Parkins.

"Who wrote it?" I asked.

Some of the exultation faded out of Nash's face.

He looked tired and concerned. He said soberly:

"I'm sorry about it, because it will hit a decent man hard, but there it is. Perhaps he's had his suspicions already."

"Who wrote it?" I reiterated.

"Miss Aimée Griffith."

Nash and Parkins went to the Griffiths' house that afternoon with a warrant.

By Nash's invitation I went with them.

"The doctor," he said, "is very fond of you. He hasn't many friends in this place. I think if it is not too painful to you, Mr. Burton, that you might help him to bear up under the shock."

I said I would come. I didn't relish the job, but I thought I might be some good.

We rang the bell and asked for Miss Griffith and we were shown into the drawing room. Elsie Holland, Megan and Symmington were there having tea.

Nash behaved very circumspectly.

He asked Aimée if he might have a few words with her privately.

She got up and came toward us. I thought I saw just a faint hunted look in her eye. If so, it went again. She was perfectly normal and hearty.

"Want me? Not in trouble over my car lights again, I hope?"

She led the way out of the drawing room and across the hall into a small study.

As I closed the drawing-room door, I saw Symmington's head jerk up sharply. I supposed his legal training had brought him in contact with police cases, and he had recognized something in Nash's manner. He half rose.

That is all I saw before I shut the door and followed the others.

Nash was saying his piece. He was very quiet and correct. He cautioned her and then told her that he must ask her to accompany him. He had a warrant for her arrest and he read out the charge.

I forget now the exact legal term. It was the letters, not murder yet.

Aimée Griffith flung up her head and bayed with laughter. She boomed out:

"What ridiculous nonsense! As though I'd write a packet of indecent stuff like that. You must be mad. I've never written a word of the kind."

Nash had produced the letter to Elsie Holland. He said, "Do you deny having written this, Miss Griffith?"

If she hesitated it was only for a split second.

"Of course I do. I've never seen it before."

Nash said quietly:

"I must tell you, Miss Griffith, that you were observed to type that letter on the machine at the Women's Institute between eleven and eleven-thirty P.M. on the night before last. Yesterday you entered the post office with a bunch of letters in your hand—"

"I never posted this."

"No, you did not. While waiting for stamps, you dropped it inconspicuously on the floor, so that somebody should come along unsuspectingly and pick it up and post it."

"I never—"

The door opened and Symmington came in. He said sharply, "What's going on? Aimée, if there is anything wrong, you ought to be legally represented. If you wish me—"

She broke then. Covered her face with her hands and staggered to a chair. She said, "Go away, Dick, go away. Not you! Not you!"

"You need a solicitor, my dear girl."

"Not you. I—I—couldn't bear it. I don't want you to know—all this."

He understood then, perhaps. He said quietly, "I'll get hold of Mildmay, of Exhampton. Will that do?"

She nodded. She was sobbing now.

Symmington went out of the room. In the doorway he collided with Owen Griffith.

"What's this?" said Owen violently. "My sister—"

"I'm sorry, Dr. Griffith. Very sorry. But we have no alternative."

"You think she—was responsible for those letters?"

"I'm afraid there is no doubt of it, sir," said Nash—he turned to Aimée: "You must come with us now, please, Miss Griffith—you shall have every facility for seeing a solicitor, you know."

Owen cried, "Aimée?"

She brushed past him without looking at him.

She said, "Don't talk to me. Don't say anything. And for heaven's sake don't look at me!"

They went out. Owen stood like a man in a dream.

I waited a bit, then I came up to him.

"If there's anything I can do, Griffith, tell me."

He said like a man in a dream, "Aimée? I don't believe it."

"It may be a mistake," I suggested feebly.

He said slowly, "She wouldn't take it like that if it were. But I would never have believed it. I can't believe it."

He sank down on a chair. I made myself useful by finding a stiff drink and bringing it to him. He swallowed it down and it seemed to do him good.

He said, "I couldn't take it in at first. I'm all right now. Thanks, Burton, but there's nothing you can do. Nothing anyone can do."

The door opened and Joanna came in. She was very white.

She came over to Owen and looked at me.

She said, "Get out, Jerry. This is my business."

As I went out of the door, I saw her kneel down by his chair.

VIII

I CAN'T TELL you coherently the events of the next twenty-four hours. Various incidents stand out, unrelated to other incidents.

I remember Joanna coming home, very white and drawn and of how I tried to cheer her up, saying:

"Now who's being a ministering angel?"

And of how she smiled in a pitiful twisted way and said, "He says he won't have me, Jerry. He's very very proud and stiff!"

And I said, "My girl won't have me either. . . ."

We sat there for a while, Joanna saying at last, "The Burton family isn't exactly in demand at the moment!"

I said, "Never mind, my sweet, we still have each other," and Joanna said, "Somehow or other, Jerry, that doesn't comfort me much just now. . . ."

Owen came the next day and rhapsodized in the most fulsome way about Joanna. She was wonderful, marvelous! The way she'd come to him, the way she was willing to marry him—at once if he liked. But he wasn't going to let her do that. No, she was too good, too fine to be associated with the kind of muck that would start as soon as the papers got hold of the news.

I was fond of Joanna, and knew she was the kind who's all right when standing by in trouble, but I got rather bored with all this highfalutin' stuff. I told Owen rather irritably not to be so damned noble.

I went down to the High Street and found everybody's tongue wagging nineteen to the dozen. Emily Barton was saying that she had never really trusted Aimée Griffith. The grocer's wife was saying with gusto that she'd always thought Miss Griffith had a queer look in her eye—

They had completed the case against Aimée, so I learned from Nash. A search of the house had brought to light the cut pages of Emily Barton's book—in the cupboard under the stairs, of all places, wrapped up in an old roll of wallpaper.

"And a jolly good place too," said Nash appreciatively. "You never know when a prying servant won't tamper with a desk or a locked drawer —but those junk cupboards full of last year's tennis balls and old wallpaper are never opened except to shove something more in."

"The lady would seem to have had a penchant for that particular hiding place," I said.

"Yes. The criminal mind seldom has much variety. By the way, talking of the dead girl, we've got one fact to go upon: There's a large heavy pestle missing from the doctor's dispensary. I'll bet anything you like that's what she was stunned with."

"Rather an awkward thing to carry about," I objected.

"Not for Miss Griffith. She was going to the Guides that afternoon, but she was going to leave flowers and vegetables at the Red Cross stall on the way, so she'd got a whopping great basket with her."

"You haven't found the skewer?"

"No, and I shan't. The poor devil may be mad, but she wasn't mad enough to keep a bloodstained skewer just to make it easy for us, when all she'd got to do was to wash it and return it to a kitchen drawer."

"I suppose," I conceded, "that you can't have everything."

The vicarage had been one of the last places to hear the news. Old Miss Marple was very much distressed by it. She spoke to me very earnestly on the subject:

"It isn't true, Mr. Burton. I'm sure it isn't true."

"It's true enough, I'm afraid. They were lying in wait, you know. They actually saw her type that letter."

"Yes, yes—perhaps they did. Yes, I can understand that."

"And the printed pages from which the letters were cut were found where she'd hidden them in her house."

Miss Marple stared at me. Then she said, in a very low voice, "But that is horrible—really wicked."

Mrs. Dane Calthrop came up with a rush and joined us and said, "What's the matter, Jane?"

Miss Marple was murmuring helplessly, "Oh, dear, oh, dear, what can one do?"

"What's upset you, Jane?"

Miss Marple said, "There must be something. But I am so old and so ignorant and, I am afraid, so foolish."

I felt rather embarrassed and was glad when Mrs. Dane Calthrop took her friend away.

I was to see Miss Marple again that afternoon, however. Much later when I was on my way home.

She was standing near the little bridge at the end of the village, near Mrs. Cleat's cottage, and talking to Megan, of all people.

I wanted to see Megan. I had been wanting to see her all day. I quickened my pace. But as I came up to them, Megan turned on her heel and went off in the other direction.

It made me angry and I would have followed her, but Miss Marple blocked my way.

"I wanted to speak to you," she said. "No, don't go after Megan now. It wouldn't be wise."

I was just going to make a sharp rejoinder when she disarmed me by saying, "That girl has great courage—a very high order of courage."

I still wanted to go after Megan, but Miss Marple said, "Don't try and see her now. I do know what I am talking about. She must keep her courage intact."

There was something about the old lady's assertion that chilled me. It was as though she knew something that I didn't.

I was afraid and didn't know why I was afraid.

I didn't go home. I went back into the High Street and walked up and down aimlessly. I don't know what I was waiting for, nor what I was thinking about. . . .

I got caught by that awful old bore Colonel Appleby. He asked after my pretty sister as usual and then went on:

"What's all this about Griffith's sister being mad as a hatter? They say she's been at the bottom of this anonymous letter business that's been such a confounded nuisance to everybody? Couldn't believe it at first, but they say it's quite true."

I said it was true enough.

"Well, well—I must say our police force is pretty good on the whole. Give 'em time, that's all, give 'em time. Funny business this anonymous letter stunt—these desiccated old women are always the ones who go in for it—though the Griffith woman wasn't bad-looking even if she was a bit long in the tooth. But there aren't any decent-looking girls in this part of the world—except that governess girl of the Symmingtons. She's worth looking at. Pleasant girl, too. Grateful if one does any little thing for her.

"Came across her having a picnic or something with those kids not long ago. They were romping about in the heather and she was knitting—ever so vexed she'd run out of wool. 'Well,' I said, 'like me to run you into Lymstock? I've got to call for a rod of mine there. I shan't be more than ten minutes getting it, then I'll run you back again.' She was a bit doubtful about leaving the boys. 'They'll be all right,' I said. 'Who's to harm them?' Wasn't going to have the boys along, no fear! So I ran her in, dropped her at the wool shop, picked her up again later and that was that. Thanked me very prettily. Grateful and all that. Nice girl."

I managed to get away from him.

It was after that, that I caught sight of Miss Marple for the third time. She was coming out of the police station.

Where do one's fears come from? Where do they shape themselves? Where do they hide before coming out into the open?

Just one short phrase. Heard and noted and never quite put aside:

"Take me away— It's so awful being here—feeling so wicked . . ."

Why had Megan said that? What had she to feel wicked about?

There could be nothing in Mrs. Symmington's death to make Megan feel wicked.

Why had the child felt wicked? Why? Why?

Could it be because she felt responsible in any way?

Megan? Impossible! Megan couldn't have had anything to do with those letters—those foul obscene letters.

Owen Griffith had known a case up north—a schoolgirl . . .

What had Inspector Graves said?

Something about an adolescent mind . . .

Innocent middle-aged ladies on operating tables babbled words they hardly knew. Little boys chalking up things on walls.

No, no, not Megan.

Heredity? Bad blood? An unconscious inheritance of something abnormal? Her misfortune, not her fault, a curse laid upon her by a past generation?

"I'm not the wife for you. I'm better at hating than loving."

Oh, my Megan, my little child. Not that! Anything but that. And that old Tabby is after you, she suspects. She says you have courage. Courage to do what?

It was only a brainstorm. It passed. But I wanted to see Megan—I wanted to see her badly.

At half past nine that night I left the house and went down to the town and along to the Symmingtons'.

It was then that an entirely new idea came into my mind. The idea of a woman whom nobody had considered for a moment.

(Or had Nash considered her?)

Wildly unlikely, wildly improbable, and I would have said up to today impossible, too. But that was not so. No, not impossible.

I redoubled my pace. Because it was now even more imperative that I should see Megan straightaway.

I passed through the Symmingtons' gate and up to the house. It was a dark overcast night. A little rain was beginning to fall. The visibility was bad.

I saw a line of light from one of the windows. The little morning room?

I hesitated a moment or two, then instead of going up to the front door, I swerved and crept very quietly up to the window, skirting a big bush and keeping low.

The light came from a chink in the curtains, which were not quite drawn. It was easy to look through and see.

It was a strangely peaceful and domestic scene. Symmington in a big armchair, and Elsie Holland, her head bent, busily patching a boy's torn shirt.

I could hear as well as see, for the window was open at the top.

Elsie Holland was speaking:

"But I do think, really, Mr. Symmington, that the boys are quite old enough to go to boarding school. Not that I shan't hate leaving them because I shall. I'm ever so fond of them both."

Symmington said, "I think perhaps you're right about Brian, Miss Holland. I've decided that he shall start next term at Winhays—my old prep school. But Colin is a little young yet. I'd prefer him to wait another year."

"Well, of course I see what you mean. And Colin is perhaps a little young for his age—"

Quiet domestic talk—quiet domestic scene—and a golden head bent over needlework.

Then the door opened and Megan came in.

She stood very straight in the doorway, and I was aware at once of something tense and strung up about her. The skin of her face was tight and drawn and her eyes bright and resolute. There was no diffidence about her tonight and no childishness.

She said, addressing Symmington, but giving him no title (and I suddenly reflected that I never had heard her call him anything. Did she address him as father or as Dick or what?):

"I would like to speak to you, please. Alone."

Symmington looked surprised and, I fancied, not best pleased. He frowned, but Megan carried her point with a determination unusual in her.

She turned to Elsie Holland and said, "Do you mind, Elsie?"

"Oh, of course." Elsie Holland jumped up. She looked startled and a little flurried.

She went to the door and Megan came farther in so that Elsie passed her.

Just for a minute Elsie stood motionless in the doorway looking over her shoulder.

Her lips were closed, she stood quite still, one hand stretched out, the other clasping her needlework to her.

I caught my breath, overwhelmed suddenly by her beauty.

When I think of her now, I always think of her like that—in arrested motion, with that matchless deathless perfection that belonged to ancient Greece.

Then she went out shutting the door.

Symmington said rather fretfully, "Well, Megan, what is it? What do you want?"

Megan had come right up to the table. She stood there looking down at Symmington. I was struck anew by the resolute determination of her face and by something else—a hardness new to me.

Then she opened her lips and said something that startled me to the core.

"I want some money," she said.

The request didn't improve Symmington's temper. He said sharply, "Couldn't you have waited until tomorrow morning? What's the matter, do you think your allowance is inadequate?"

A fair man, I thought even then, open to reason, though not to emotional appeal.

Megan said, "I want a good deal of money."

Symmington sat up straight in his chair. He said coldly:

"You will come of age in a few months' time. Then the money left you by your grandmother will be turned over to you by the Public Trustee."

Megan said:

"You don't understand. I want money from you." She went on, speaking faster: "Nobody's ever talked much to me about my father. They've not wanted me to know about him. But I do know that he went to prison and I know why. It was for blackmail!"

She paused.

"Well, I'm his daughter. And perhaps I take after him. Anyway, I'm asking you to give me money because—if you don't—" She stopped and then went on very slowly and evenly—"if you don't—I shall say what I saw you doing to the cachet that day in my mother's room."

There was a pause. Then Symmington said in a completely emotionless voice, "I don't know what you mean."

Megan said, "I think you do."

And she smiled. It was not a nice smile.

Symmington got up. He went over to the writing desk. He took a checkbook from his pocket and wrote out a check. He blotted it carefully and then came back. He held it out to Megan.

"You're grown up now," he said. "I can understand that you may feel you want to buy something rather special in the way of clothes and all that. I don't know what you're talking about. I didn't pay attention. But here's a check."

Megan looked at it, then she said, "Thank you. That will do to go on with."

She turned and went out of the room. Symmington stared after her and at the closed door, then he turned around and as I saw his face I made a quick uncontrolled movement forward.

It was checked in the most extraordinary fashion. The big bush that I had noticed by the wall stopped being a bush. Superintendent Nash's arms went around me and Superintendent Nash's voice just breathed in my ear:

"Quiet, Burton. For God's sake."

Then, with infinite caution he beat a retreat, his arm impelling me to accompany him.

Around the side of the house he straightened himself and wiped his forehead.

"Of course," he said. "You would have to butt in!"

"That girl isn't safe," I said urgently. "You saw his face? We've got to get her out of here."

Nash took a firm grip of my arm.

"Now, look here, Mr. Burton, you've got to listen."

Well, I listened.

I didn't like it—but I gave in.

But I insisted on being on the spot and I swore to obey orders implicitly.

So that is how I came with Nash and Parkins into the house by the back door, which was already unlocked.

And I waited with Nash on the upstairs landing behind the velvet curtain masking the window alcove until the clocks in the house struck two, and Symmington's door opened and he went across the landing and into Megan's room.

I did not stir or make a move for I knew that Sergeant Parkins was inside masked by the opening door, and I knew that Parkins was a good man and knew his job, and I knew that I couldn't have trusted myself to keep quiet and not break out.

And waiting there, with my heart thudding, I saw Symmington come out with Megan in his arms and carry her downstairs, with Nash and myself a discreet distance behind him.

He carried her through to the kitchen and he had just arranged her comfortably with her head in the gas oven and had turned on the gas when Nash and I came through the kitchen door and switched on the light.

And that was the end of Richard Symmington. He collapsed. Even while I was hauling Megan out and turning off the gas I saw the collapse. He didn't even try to fight. He knew he'd played and lost.

Upstairs I sat by Megan's bed waiting for her to come around and occasionally cursing Nash.

"How do you know she's all right? It was too big a risk."

Nash was very soothing.

"Just a soporific in the milk she always had by her bed. Nothing more. It stands to reason, he couldn't risk her being poisoned. As far as he's concerned the whole business is closed with Miss Griffith's arrest. He can't afford to have any mysterious death. No violence, no poison. But if a rather unhappy type of girl broods over her mother's suicide, and finally goes and puts her head in the gas oven—well, people just say that she was never quite normal and the shock of her mother's death finished her."

I said, watching Megan, "She's a long time coming around."

"You heard what Dr. Griffith said? Heart and pulse quite all right—she'll just sleep and wake naturally. Stuff he gives a lot of his patients, he says."

Megan stirred. She murmured something.

Superintendent Nash unobtrusively left the room.

Presently Megan opened her eyes.

"Jerry."

"Hullo, sweet."

"Did I do it well?"

"You might have been blackmailing ever since your cradle!"

Megan closed her eyes again. Then she murmured:

"Last night—I was writing to you—in case anything went—went wrong. But I was too sleepy to finish. It's over there."

I went across to the writing table. In a shabby little blotter I found Megan's unfinished letter.

"My dear Jerry," it began primly:

"I was reading my school Shakespeare and the sonnet that begins:

" '*So are you to my thoughts as food to life*
Or as sweet-season'd showers are to the ground'

and I see that I am in love with you after all, because that is what I feel." . . .

"So you see," said Mrs. Dane Calthrop, "I was quite right to call in an expert."

I stared at her. We were all at the vicarage. The rain was pouring down outside and there was a pleasant log fire, and Mrs. Dane Calthrop had just wandered around, beat up a sofa cushion and put it for some reason of her own on the top of the grand piano.

"But did you?" I said, surprised. "Who was it? What did he do?"

"It wasn't a he," said Mrs. Dane Calthrop.

With a sweeping gesture she indicated Miss Marple. Miss Marple had finished the fleecy knitting and was now engaged with a crochet hook and a ball of cotton.

"That's my expert," said Mrs. Dane Calthrop. "Jane Marple. Look at her well. I tell you, that woman knows more about the different kinds of human wickedness than anyone I've ever known."

"I don't think you should put it quite like that, dear," murmured Miss Marple.

"But you do."

"One sees a good deal of human nature living in a village all the year around," said Miss Marple placidly.

Then, seeming to feel it was expected of her, she laid down her crochet, and delivered a gentle old-maidish dissertation on murder.

"The great thing in these cases is to keep an absolutely open mind. Most crimes, you see, are so absurdly simple. This one was. Quite sane and straightforward—and quite understandable—in an unpleasant way, of course."

"Very unpleasant!"

"The truth was really so very obvious. You saw it, you know, Mr. Burton."

"Indeed I did not."

"But you did. You indicated the whole thing to me. You saw perfectly the relationship of one thing to the other, but you just hadn't enough self-confidence to see what those feelings of yours meant. To begin with, that tiresome phrase 'No smoke without fire.' It irritated you, but you proceeded quite correctly to label it for what it was—a smoke screen. Misdirection, you see—everybody looking at the wrong thing—the anonymous letters, but the whole point was that there weren't any anonymous letters!"

"But, my dear Miss Marple, I can assure you that there were. I had one."

"Oh, yes, but they weren't real at all. Dear Maud here tumbled to that. Even in peaceful Lymstock there are plenty of scandals, and I can assure you any woman living in the place would have known about them and used them. But a man, you see, isn't interested in gossip in the same way—especially a detached logical man like Mr. Symmington. But a genuine woman writer of those letters would have made her letters much more to the point.

"So you see that if you disregard the smoke and come to the fire you know where you are. You just come down to the actual facts of what happened. And putting aside the letters, just one thing happened—Mrs. Symmington died.

"So then, naturally, one thinks of who might have wanted Mrs. Symmington to die, and of course the very first person one thinks of in such a case is, I am afraid, the husband. And one asks oneself is there any reason?—any motive?—for instance, any other woman?

"And the very first thing I hear is that there is a very attractive young governess in the house. So clear, isn't it? Mr. Symmington, a rather dry repressed unemotional man, tied to a querulous and neurotic wife and then suddenly this radiant young creature comes along.

"I'm afraid, you know, that gentlemen, when they fall in love at a certain age, get the disease very badly. It's quite a madness. And Mr. Symmington, as far as I can make out, was never actually a good man—he wasn't very kind or very affectionate or very sympathetic—his qualities were all negative—so he hadn't really the strength to fight his madness. And in a place like this, only his wife's death would solve his problem. He wanted to marry the girl, you see. She's very respectable and so is he. And besides, he's devoted to his children and didn't want to give them up. He wanted everything, his home, his children, his respectability and Elsie. And the price he would have to pay for that was murder.

"He chose, I do think, a very clever way. He knew so well from his experience of criminal cases how soon suspicion falls on the husband if a wife dies unexpectedly—and the possibility of exhumation in the case of poison. So he created a death which seemed only incidental to something else. He created a nonexistent anonymous letter writer. And the clever thing was that the police were certain to suspect a woman—and they were quite right in a way. All the letters were a woman's letters; he cribbed them very cleverly from the letters in the case last year and from a case Dr. Griffith told him about. I don't mean that he was so crude as to reproduce any letter verbatim, but he took phrases and expressions from them and mixed them up, and the net result was that the letters definitely represented a woman's mind—a half-crazy repressed personality.

"He knew all the tricks that the police use, handwriting, typewriting tests, etc. He's been preparing his crime for some time. He typed all the envelopes before he gave away the typewriter to the Women's Institute, and he cut the pages from the book at Little Furze probably quite a long time ago when he was waiting in the drawing room one day. People don't open books of sermons much!

"And finally, having got his false Poison Pen well established, he staged the real thing. A fine afternoon when the governess and the boys and his stepdaughter would be out, and the servants having their regular day out. He couldn't foresee that the little maid Agnes would quarrel with her boy friend and come back to the house."

Joanna asked, "But what did she see? Do you know that?"

"I don't know. I can only guess. My guess would be that she didn't see anything."

"That it was all a mare's nest?"

"No, no, my dear, I mean that she stood at the pantry window all the afternoon waiting for the young man to come and make it up and that—quite literally she saw nothing. That is, no one came to the house at all, not the postman, nor anybody else.

"It would take her some time, being slow, to realize that that was very odd—because apparently Mrs. Symmington had received an anonymous letter that afternoon."

"Didn't she receive one?" I asked, puzzled.

"But of course not! As I say, this crime is so simple. Her husband just put the cyanide in the top cachet of the ones she took in the afternoon when her sciatica came on after lunch. All Symmington had to do was to get home before, or at the same time as Elsie Holland, call his wife, get no answer, go up to her room, drop a spot of cyanide in the plain glass of water she had used to swallow the cachet, toss the crumpled-up anonymous letter into the grate, and put by her hand the scrap of paper with 'I can't go on' written on it."

Miss Marple turned to me.

"You were quite right about that, too, Mr. Burton. A 'scrap of paper' was all wrong. People don't leave suicide notes on small torn scraps of paper. They use a sheet of paper—and very often an envelope too. Yes, the scrap of paper was wrong and you knew it."

"You are rating me too high," I said. "I knew nothing."

"But you did, you really did, Mr. Burton. Otherwise why were you immediately impressed by the message your sister left scribbled on the telephone pad?"

I repeated slowly: "'Say that I can't go on Friday'—I see! 'I can't go on'?"

Miss Marple beamed on me.

"Exactly. Mr. Symmington came across such a message and saw its possibilities. He tore off the words he wanted for when the time came—a message genuinely in his wife's handwriting."

"Was there any further brilliance on my part?" I asked.

Miss Marple twinkled at me.

"You put me on the track, you know. You assembled those facts together for me—in sequence—and on top of it you told me the most important thing of all—that Elsie Holland had never received any anonymous letters."

"Do you know," I said, "last night I thought that she was the letter writer and that that was why there had been no letters written to her?"

"Oh, dear me, no. . . . The person who writes anonymous letters practically always sends them to herself as well. That's part of the—well, the excitement, I suppose. No, no, the fact interested me for quite another reason. It was really, you see, Mr. Symmington's one weakness. He couldn't bring himself to write a foul letter to the girl he loved. It's a very interesting sidelight on human nature—and a credit to him, in a way—but it's where he gave himself away."

Joanna said, "And he killed Agnes? But surely that was quite unnecessary?"

"Perhaps it was, but what you don't realize, my dear (not having killed anyone), is that your judgment is distorted afterward and everything seems exaggerated. No doubt he heard the girl telephoning to Partridge, saying she'd been worried ever since Mrs. Symmington's death, that there was something she didn't understand. He can't take any chances—this stupid foolish girl has seen something, knows something."

"Yet apparently he was at his office all that afternoon?"

"I should imagine he killed her before he went. Miss Holland was in the dining room and kitchen. He just went out into the hall, opened and shut the front door as though he was going out, then slipped into the little cloakroom.

"When only Agnes was left in the house, he probably rang the front-door bell, slipped back into the cloakroom, came out behind her and hit her on the head as she was opening the front door, and then after thrusting the body into the cupboard, he hurried along to his office, arriving just a little late if anyone had happened to notice it, but they probably didn't. You see, no one was suspecting a man."

"Abominable brute," said Mrs. Dane Calthrop.

"You're not sorry for him, Mrs. Dane Calthrop?" I inquired.

"Not in the least. Why?"

"I'm glad to hear it, that's all."

Joanna said:

"But why Aimée Griffith? I know that the police have found the pestle taken from Owen's dispensary—and the skewer too. I suppose it's not so easy for a man to return things to kitchen drawers. And guess where they were? Superintendent Nash only told me just now when I met him on my way here. In one of those musty old deed boxes in his office. Estate of Sir Jasper Harrington-West, deceased."

"Poor Jasper," said Mrs. Dane Calthrop. "He was a cousin of mine. Such a correct old boy. He would have had a fit!"

"Wasn't it madness to keep them?" I asked.

"Probably madder to throw them away," said Mrs. Dane Calthrop. "No one had any suspicions about Symmington."

"He didn't strike her with the pestle," said Joanna. "There was a clock weight there too, with hair and blood on it. He pinched the pestle, they think, on the day Aimée was arrested, and hid the book pages in her house.

And that brings me back to my original question. What about Aimée Griffith? The police actually saw her write that letter."

"Yes, of course," said Miss Marple. "She did write that letter."

"But why?"

"Oh, my dear, surely you have realized that Miss Griffith had been in love with Symmington all her life?"

"Poor thing!" said Mrs. Dane Calthrop mechanically.

"They'd always been good friends, and I daresay she thought, after Mrs. Symmington's death, that some day, perhaps—well—" Miss Marple coughed delicately. "And then the gossip began spreading about Elsie Holland and I expect that upset her badly. She thought of the girl as a designing minx worming her way into Symmington's affections and quite unworthy of him. And so, I think, she succumbed to temptation. Why not add one more anonymous letter, and frighten the girl out of the place? It must have seemed quite safe to her and she took, as she thought, every precaution."

"Well?" said Joanna. "Finish the story."

"I should imagine," said Miss Marple slowly, "that when Miss Holland showed that letter to Symmington he realized at once who had written it, and he saw a chance to finish the case once and for all, and make himself safe. Not very nice—no, not very nice, but he was frightened, you see. The police wouldn't be satisfied until they'd got the anonymous letter writer. When he took the letter down to the police and he found they'd actually seen Aimée writing it, he felt he'd got a chance in a thousand of finishing the whole thing.

"He took the family to tea there that afternoon and as he came from the office with his attaché case, he could easily bring the torn-out book pages to hide under the stairs and clinch the case. Hiding them under the stairs was a neat touch. It recalled the disposal of Agnes' body, and, from the practical point of view, it was very easy for him. When he followed Aimée and the police, just a minute or two in the hall passing through would be enough."

"All the same," I said, "there's one thing I can't forgive you for, Miss Marple—roping in Megan."

Miss Marple put down her crochet which she had resumed. She looked at me over her spectacles and her eyes were stern.

"My dear young man, something had to be done. There was no evidence against this very clever and unscrupulous man. I needed someone to help me, someone of high courage and good brains. I found the person I needed."

"It was very dangerous for her."

"Yes, it was dangerous, but we are not put into this world, Mr. Burton, to avoid danger when an innocent fellow creature's life is at stake. You understand me?"

I understood.

It was morning in the High Street.

Miss Emily Barton came out of the grocer's with her shopping bag. Her cheeks were pink and her eyes were excited.

"Oh, dear, Mr. Burton, I really am in such a flutter. To think I really am going on a cruise at last!"

"I hope you'll enjoy it."

"Oh, I'm sure I shall. I should never have dared to go by myself. It does seem so providential the way everything has turned out. For a long time I've felt that I ought to part with Little Furze, that my means were really too straitened, but I couldn't bear the idea of strangers there.

"But now that you have bought it and are going to live there with Megan—it is quite different. And then dear Aimée, after her terrible ordeal, not quite knowing what to do with herself, and her brother getting married (how nice to think you have both settled down with us!), and agreeing to come with me. We mean to be away quite a long time. We might even"—Miss Emily dropped her voice—"go around the world! And Aimée is so splendid and so practical. I really do think—don't you?—that everything turns out for the best."

Just for a fleeting moment I thought of Mrs. Symmington and Agnes Woddell in their graves in the churchyard and wondered if they would agree, and then I remembered that Agnes' boy friend hadn't been very fond of her and that Mrs. Symmington hadn't been very nice to Megan and, what the hell? We've all got to die some time! And I agreed with happy Miss Emily that everything was for the best in the best of possible worlds.

I went along the High Street and in at the Symmingtons' gate and Megan came out to meet me.

It was not a romantic meeting because an out-size old English sheep dog came out with Megan and nearly knocked me over with his ill-timed exuberance.

"Isn't he adorable?" said Megan.

"A little overwhelming. Is he ours?"

"Yes, he's a wedding present from Joanna. We have had nice wedding presents, haven't we? That fluffy woolly thing that we don't know what it's for from Miss Marple, and the lovely Crown Derby tea set from Mr. Pye, and Elsie has sent me a toast rack—"

"How typical!" I interjected.

"And she's got a post with a dentist and is very happy. And—where was I?"

"Enumerating wedding presents. Don't forget if you change your mind you'll have to send them all back."

"I shan't change my mind. What else have we got? Oh, yes, Mrs. Dane Calthrop has sent an Egyptian scarab."

"Original woman," I said.

"Oh! Oh! But you don't know the best. Partridge has actually sent me a present. It's the most hideous tea cloth you've ever seen. But I think she must like me now because she says she embroidered it all with her own hands."

"In a design of sour grapes and thistles, I suppose?"

"No; true lover's knots."

"Dear, dear," I said, "Partridge is coming on."

Megan had dragged me into the house.

She said:

"There's just one thing I can't make out. Besides the dog's own collar and lead, Joanna has sent an extra collar and lead. What do you think that's for?"

"That," I said, "is Joanna's little joke."